"How are you, Eva?"

He went through the motions, giving her a casual hug and a peck on the cheek.

Ridiculously, her skin flamed at the contact, and she lost her breath as his big hands touched her shoulders, as his arms brushed, warm and solid, against her bare skin. Then his lips delivered a devastating split-second flash of fire.

She took a moment to recover. "I'm very well, thanks, Griff." Thank heavens she was able to speak calmly, but she hadn't told him the truth. She wasn't feeling well at all. She felt sick. And her hip was in agony. She prayed that she didn't blush as Griff's glittering gray gaze remained concentrated on her.

"And how are you?" she remembered to ask.

"Fighting fit, thank you."

With the conventions over, an awkward silence fell. She wondered if he was about to say something conciliatory. It would be helpful to at least share a few pleasantries to bridge the wide chasm of years. Of silence.

And guilty secrets.

D0928341

REUNITED BY A
BABY BOMBSHELL

BY
BARBARA HANNAY

MILLS &
BOON

All rights reserved including the right of reproduction in whole or in part in any form. This edition is published by arrangement with Harlequin Books S.A.

This is a work of fiction. Names, characters, places, locations and incidents are purely fictional and bear no relationship to any real life individuals, living or dead, or to any actual places, business establishments, locations, events or incidents. Any resemblance is entirely coincidental.

This book is sold subject to the condition that it shall not, by way of trade or otherwise, be lent, resold, hired out or otherwise circulated without the prior consent of the publisher in any form of binding or cover other than that in which it is published and without a similar condition including this condition being imposed on the subsequent purchaser.

® and ™ are trademarks owned and used by the trademark owner and/or its licensee. Trademarks marked with ® are registered with the United Kingdom Patent Office and/or the Office for Harmonisation in the Internal Market and in other countries.

First Published in Great Britain 2017
By Mills & Boon, an imprint of HarperCollins*Publishers*
1 London Bridge Street, London, SE1 9GF

© 2017 Barbara Hannay

ISBN: 978-0-263-92287-5

23-0417

Our policy is to use papers that are natural, renewable and recyclable products and made from wood grown in sustainable forests. The logging and manufacturing processes conform to the legal environmental regulations of the country of origin.

Printed and bound in Spain
by CPI, Barcelona

Barbara Hannay has written over forty romance novels and has won a RITA® Award, an RT Reviewers' Choice award, as well as Australia's Romantic Book of the Year.

A city-bred girl with a yen for country life, Barbara lives with her husband on a misty hillside in beautiful Far North Queensland, where they raise pigs and chickens and enjoy an untidy but productive garden.

CHAPTER ONE

WHEN THE INVITATION arrived Eva Hennessey was away in Prague, dancing the role of Odette in *Swan Lake*. On her return to Paris a week later, she found her mailbox crammed, mostly with an assortment of bills and dance magazines. She was riding the rickety old lift to her apartment on the fifth floor when the bright sunny Australian stamp caught her eye. Then she read the postmark. Emerald Bay.

The sharp pang in her chest made her gasp. It wasn't homesickness. Eva's feelings about the beach town where she'd grown up were far more complicated. These days, she rarely allowed herself to unpack the mixed bag of emotions that accompanied memories from her youth.

She always ended up thinking about Griffin Fletcher...and the other harrowing memory that would never leave her.

She'd worked hard to put that life behind her. She'd *had* to. Long ago.

Today, as the hum of Parisian traffic reached Eva from the street below, she let herself into the apartment that had been her home for the past ten years. Nanette, the concierge, had already turned on the heating and the apartment was welcoming and warm. Eva had loved this place from the day she'd first found it.

Decorated simply in quiet creamy tones with occasional touches of blue, the main living area was dominated by a far wall of windows that looked out over tiled rooftops, chimneys and church spires to the top of the Eiffel Tower. At night, on the hour, the Tower glittered with beautiful lights. It was a view Eva never tired of.

Stopping for a moment, she smiled to herself as she looked about the space she'd carefully assembled over the years—the beautiful cushion covers she'd picked up on various tours, the collection of blue and white pottery from all over Europe, the wide-brimmed bowl full of shells and stones she'd collected from beaches in Greece and Italy, in Spain and the UK. So many happy memories to counteract the sad ones from her past.

She set down her luggage and dumped the envelope from Australia on the coffee table along with the rest of her mail. Then she went through to the bathroom and had a long hot shower, massaging the nagging pain in her hip under the steady stream of water.

She washed her hair, dried it roughly with a towel, letting the damp dark tresses hang loose past her shoulders as she changed into a comfy pair of stretch slacks and an oversized T-shirt.

Soon she would make her supper. A simple herb omelette would suffice. But first a glass of wine, an indulgence she could allow herself now that the performance tour was behind her.

Curled on the sofa, with the wine within reach and a cushion positioned to support her painful hip, Eva

retrieved the envelope from Australia and slit it open.
A card depicting an iconic Queensland beach fell out.

Beneath the picture, a message—an invitation to
a reunion of her classmates to celebrate twenty years
since their last year of high school.

Eva felt sick as she read the details.

Where: Emerald Bay Golf Club
When: Saturday October 20th

The simple wording hit her like a punch to the chest.
A thousand long-suppressed images crashed in. The
beach in summer and the thrill of riding the rolling
green surf. The smooth trunk of a palm tree at her
back as she sat at the edge of the sand, eating salty fish
and chips wrapped in paper. The smell of sunscreen
and citronella.

Her thoughts flashed to hot summer days in class-
rooms with windows opened wide to catch a sea breeze.
And then, despite her best efforts to block them, there
were memories of Griffin Fletcher.

Griff, sitting at the desk just behind her in class,
all shaggy-haired and wide-shouldered, catching her
eye when she turned and sending her a cheeky grin.

Griff on the football field. The flash of his solid
thighs as he sped past to score a try.

Griff holding her close in the dark. The surprising
gentleness of his lips.

And, flashing between those sweeter memories, the
fear and the crushing weight of her terrible secret. The
overwhelming heartbreak and pain.

Enough.

Stop it.

Eva knew at once what her response would be. What it *must* be. Of course she couldn't possibly go. With deep regret, she would be unable to accept the kind invitation. She was very grateful to be remembered by her old school friends, but her schedule was far too tight.

It wasn't untrue. She had a new set of rehearsals for *The Nutcracker* lined up and she couldn't really afford the time away. And why would she want to go back to the Bay anyway? Her mother no longer lived there. It was many years now since her mum had married and settled in Cairns in the far north of the state. As for Eva's classmates and the rest of her memories—of necessity, she'd very deliberately left all that behind.

Instead, she'd worked as hard as possible for those twenty years, putting in endless, punishing hours to build the career of her dreams. These days, posters of Eva Hennessey, dancing as Giselle, as Cinderella or as Romeo's Juliet, were on display in almost every theatre or train station in Europe.

After long years of hard work, this was Eva's reward. Rave reviews claimed her as 'technically poised and polished and lyrically perfect'. Wherever she went, audiences cheered *Bravo!* and gave her standing ovations. Her dressing rooms were crammed with beautiful flowers.

Eva's world was now different in every way imaginable from the life she'd known in the sleepy seaside town of her youth. She might as well be living on a different planet. If she ever returned to Emerald Bay, she would not only awaken past hurts, she would feel like an alien.

Just the same, she felt sick to the stomach as she

tucked the card back into the envelope. She told herself she was simply overtired after the gruelling weeks on tour.

In the morning she would post an 'inability to accept' and she would delete all thoughts of Emerald Bay.

Bees buzzed in the bottlebrush hedge. Small children laughed and squealed as they splashed at the shallow end of the elegant swimming pool, while their mothers watched, dangling their bare legs in the water as they sipped Pimm's from long glasses. The smell of frying onions floated on the balmiest of breezes. It was a typical Sunday afternoon in suburban Brisbane.

Griff Fletcher was the host on this particular Sunday and his guests were a couple of long-time mates and their families. Griff was repaying their hospitality while his girlfriend, Amanda, was away in Sydney on business. It made sense. Amanda hadn't known these guys for decades as he had. They weren't really part of her scene—she was so much younger than their wives—and she didn't 'do' little kids.

As Griff added steaks to the sizzling barbecue plate, the men helped themselves to fresh beers and kept him company.

'So what do you reckon about the school reunion?' asked Tim, who, like Griff, had moved from Emerald Bay to live and work in Queensland's capital city. 'Are you planning to check it out, Griff?'

Griff shrugged. He'd known that Tim and Barney were bound to talk about the reunion today, but he really wasn't that interested. 'I think I might give it a miss,' he said.

Tim pulled a face, clearly disappointed. 'But surely

you must be curious about your old mates? Wouldn't you like to catch up with the gang?'

The best Griff could manage was a crooked grin. 'I see you two often enough.'

Barney gave an awkward smile and Tim scowled and took a long drink of his beer. Griff scowled too, as he began to flip steaks. He knew it wouldn't be long before one of the guys had another dig at him.

Tim shook his head. 'I know you're a hotshot barrister, Griff, but I didn't take you for a snob.'

Griff gave another shrug as he turned the sausages for the children. 'I just don't see the point in revisiting the past. You know what these reunions are like. The only people who turn up are the ones who've been successful, or the ones who've bred a swag of offspring. Then they swan around feeling smug, gossiping about the ones who stayed away.'

'That's a bit harsh,' Tim said stiffly.

'I wasn't talking about you of course, mate.'

His mate wasn't mollified. 'Have you ever been to a school reunion?'

'No, but it's easy to—'

'I have,' cut in Barney. 'My folks still live in the Bay, so I'm up there pretty regularly and I went to the ten-year reunion.' He looked a tad defensive. 'I enjoyed meeting up with everyone again, even after just ten years. There were some who'd really changed and others who looked exactly the same. Not that any of that mattered. We all had plenty of laughs and swapped war stories. It was interesting to hear what everyone's doing.'

'See!' crowed Tim with a triumphant grin.

Griff shrugged again and used the egg flip to shift

the browned onions away from the heat. Then he turned to call to the women. 'Steaks won't be long.'

'Right,' Tim's wife, Kylie, called back. 'We'd better get these kids dry then.'

Tim, meanwhile, moved closer to Griff. Out of the corner of his mouth, he said, 'Eva Hennessey's not likely to be there.'

Griff stiffened, and was immediately annoyed that the mere mention of Eva could still raise a reaction. It really shouldn't matter if he ran into a girl he'd known a million years ago.

The reaction didn't make sense. Sure, Eva had been his first girlfriend, but he'd eventually got over the shock of her leaving town so abruptly. It wasn't as if he'd been planning to marry her straight out of high school and settle down in the Bay. He'd had big plans for his future.

He'd carried on with his life, with university and his subsequent career. And in the past two decades he'd had more than his fair share of relationships with glamorous, beautiful, passionate women.

He supposed it didn't really make sense that he wanted to avoid Eva, but he'd moved on, so why ask for trouble?

'Of course she won't be there,' he said, pleased that he managed to sound offhand. He added another non-chalant shrug for good measure, but he bit back the other comment that had sprung to mind—that Eva Hennessey was far too busy and world-famous to come back for such a piddling, unimportant event.

'Well, Barney's already put his name down, haven't you, Barnes?' Tim called to their mate, who was retrieving an inflatable ball that had bounced out of the pool.

Barney sent them a thumbs up.

'And I reckon it'd be a blast for the three of us to go back to the Bay,' Tim persisted. 'You know, just the Three Amigos, without the women and billy-lids. Like the good old days.'

Griff was about to respond in the negative, but Tim stopped him with a raised hand.

'Just think about it, Griff. We could stay at a pub on the beachfront, catch a few waves, even do a little snorkelling and diving on the reef.'

Well, yeah.

Griff couldn't deny the great times he and these mates had enjoyed as teenagers, lapping up the free and easy outdoor lifestyle of a bayside country town.

Griff's family had moved back to the city as soon as he'd finished school, and he could barely remember the last time he'd donned goggles and flippers to dive into the secret underwater world of coral and fish.

But there'd been a time when he'd lived and breathed diving…and surfing. Throughout his teenage years, he'd spent a part of every single day at the beach, in the sea. And every night, in bed, he'd listened to the sound of the surf pounding on the sand. The rhythm of the sea had been as familiar and essential to him as the beating of his heart.

By contrast, these days, the only water he saw was when he was rowing on the Brisbane River, which was usually flat and brown and still.

But the sea was different. And the Bay was special.

More to the point, these two mates were important to Griff. Amanda wasn't especially fond of them, but she did have a tendency to be slightly snooty. She preferred mixing with Griff's barrister colleagues and their partners, whereas Griff knew that these guys kept him grounded. Tim worked in a bank and Barney was an electrician and, between them, they provided a good balance to the eminent judges and silks who filled Griff's working life.

He'd be crazy to let the haunting memory of one slim, dark-haired girl with astonishing aqua eyes spoil the chance to go back and recapture a little of the camaraderie and magic he'd enjoyed in his youth.

'I'll think about it,' he said cautiously.

He was rewarded with a hearty and enthusiastic back-slap.

Eva stared at the doctor in dismay as two words echoed in her head like a tolling funeral bell… Hip replacement…hip replacement…

It was the worst possible news. She couldn't take it in. She didn't want to believe it.

A few days earlier, during a rehearsal of *The Nutcracker*, she'd landed awkwardly after performing a *grand jeté*, a demanding movement that involved propelling herself gracefully into the air and doing the splits while above the ground. Eva had performed the move thousands of times, of course, but this time, when she'd landed, the pain in her hip had been agonising.

Since then, the hip hadn't improved. She'd stayed away from rehearsals, claiming a heavy cold, which was something she'd never done before. Normally, Eva danced through every painful mishap. She'd danced on broken toes, through colds and flu, had even performed for weeks with a torn ligament in her shoulder.

Such stoicism wasn't unusual in ballet circles. A culture of secrecy about injury was a given. Every dancer was terrified of being branded as *fragile*. They all understood it was a euphemism for *on the way out*—the end of a career.

This time, however, Eva found it too difficult to keep hiding her pain. Even if she faked her way through class and rehearsals, by the time she got home she could barely walk. So she'd seen an osteopath. But now, to her horror, the doctor had shown her disturbing results from her MRI scan.

She'd never dreamed the damage could be so bad.

'You've torn the labrum,' the doctor told her solemnly as he pointed to the scan. 'That's the ring of cartilage around your left hip joint. Normally, the labrum helps with shock absorption and lubrication of the joint, but now—' He shook his head. 'The tear on its own wouldn't be such a great problem, but there are other degenerative changes as well.' He waved his hand over the scan. 'Extensive arthritic inflammation of the whole joint.'

Arthritis? A chill washed over Eva. Wasn't that something that happened to elderly people?

'I strongly recommend a complete hip replacement. Otherwise—' the doctor sighed expressively '—I don't really see how you can avoid it.'

No, please no.

On a page from his writing pad, he wrote the names of two consultant orthopaedic and trauma surgeons. He handed the paper to Eva.

Sweat broke out on her skin and she swayed a little dizzily in her chair. A hip replacement was a death knell, the end of her career. The prospect filled her with such desolation that it didn't bear imagining.

It would be the end of my life.

'Aren't there other things I can try?' she asked in desperation. 'Besides surgery?'

The doctor gave a shrug. 'We can talk about physiotherapy and painkillers and diet. And rest,' he added, giving her a dark look. 'But I think you'll find that the pain will still be too severe, certainly if you want to continue dancing. Ballet requires movements that are very unnatural.'

Eva knew this all too well, of course. She'd spent a lifetime perfecting the demanding movements most people never even tried. Pirouettes and adagios and grand allegros *en pointe* all made exacting demands on her limbs and joints, and she knew she was only human. She was at the wrong end of her thirties and there was a limit to what she could expect from her body. But she couldn't give up dancing.

Not yet! She'd worked too hard, had sacrificed too much. Sure, she'd known that her career couldn't last for ever, but she'd hoped for at least five more years.

Dancing was her life. Without it, she would drown, would completely lose her identity.

She was in no way ready for this.

The osteopath was staring at her a little impatiently now. He had no more advice to offer.

In a daze, Eva rose from her chair, thanked him and bade him goodbye. As the door to his office closed behind her, she walked through reception without seeing anyone, trying not to limp, to prove to herself that the doctor must have been wrong, but even walking was painful.

Glass doors led to a long empty corridor. What could she do now?

She tried to think clearly, but her mind kept spinning. If she gave in and had the surgery, she was sure the company wouldn't want her back—certainly not as their prima ballerina—and she couldn't conscience the idea of going back into the corps de ballet.

The worst of it was, this wasn't a problem she dared discuss with her colleagues. She didn't want anyone in the dancing world to know. The news would spread like wildfire. It would be in the press by lunchtime. By supper time, her career would be over.

As she made her way carefully down a short flight of stairs and onto the Parisian pavement outside, Eva, who had always been strong and independent, valuing her privacy, had never felt more vulnerable and alone. On the wrong side of the world.

'Hello, this is Jane. How can I help you?'

Griff grimaced. He couldn't believe he was tense about speaking to Jane Simpson. In their school days, Jane had been the Emerald Bay baker's daughter. Since then she'd married a cane farmer and was now convening the class reunion.

'Hi, there, Jane.' He cleared his throat nervously and was immediately annoyed with himself. 'Griff Fletcher, here. I'm ringing about the school reunion weekend.'

'Oh, yes.' Jane sounded excited. 'It's great to hear from you after all this time, Griff. I hope you'll be able to come.'

'Well, I'm still trying to see if I can…er…fit it into my schedule. But I was curious—how are the…er… numbers shaping up?'

'They're great, actually. We have about thirty-five

coming so far—and that's not counting partners. It's really exciting,' Jane enthused. 'I do hope you can make it.'

'Yeah, thanks.'

Since the barbecue with Tim and Barney, Griff had been warming to the idea of going back to the Bay. But he wanted to ask about Eva. The thought of running into her in front of everyone from their school days completely ruined the picture. There was too much unfinished business between them. There was bound to be tension. And friction. It would be unavoidable.

If Eva was going to be there—which Griff very much doubted—he would stay well clear of the place.

The simple question should have been easy to put to Jane. Griff couldn't believe he was uptight.

It wasn't as if he'd spent the past twenty years pining for his high school sweetheart. Many of the relationships he'd enjoyed since then had been fabulously passionate and borderline serious.

Admittedly, Griff's relationships did have a habit of petering out. While almost all of his friends and colleagues had tied the knot and were starting families, Griff didn't seem to have the staying power. He either tired of his girlfriends, or they got tired of waiting for him to commit to something more permanent.

At least he and Amanda were still hanging together. So far.

Now, he braced himself to get to the point of this phone call. Every day in court he faced criminals, judges and juries, and he prided himself on posing the most searching and intimate of questions. It should be a cinch to ask Jane Simpson a quick, straightforward question about Eva.

'I don't suppose…' Griff began and stopped, as

memories of Eva's smile flashed before him. The view of her pale neck as she'd leaned over her books in class. The fresh taste of her kisses. Her slim, lithe body pressing temptingly close.

'Have you heard from Eva?' Jane asked, mercifully cutting into his thoughts.

Jane had been one of Eva's closest friends at school, so she knew that he and Eva had once been an item.

Griff grabbed the opening now offered. 'No, I haven't heard from her in ages. We're…not in contact these days. Has she been in touch with you?'

'Yes, and I'm afraid she's not coming,' Jane said. 'It's such a pity she can't make it.'

OK. So now he knew without having to ask. Relief and disappointment slugged Griff in equal parts.

'I'm not at all surprised,' he said.

'No, I'm sure Eva's incredibly busy with her dancing. It's wonderful how amazingly well she's done, though, isn't it?'

'Yes—amazing.'

'Anyway, Griff, let me know if you do decide you can come. It should be a fun get-together. Do you have my email address?'

Jane dictated the address while Griff jotted it down. He would leave it a few days before he emailed her. In the meantime, he would swing by Tim's favourite lunching hangout and let him know he was free to join him and Barney on a nostalgic trip back to their schoolboy haunts. And if he did happen to see Eva again, of course he wouldn't lose his cool.

Eva sat beneath the red awning of a pavement café, clutching a cup of blissfully decadent hot chocolate as she watched the rainy Paris streetscape. Beyond the awning's protection, raindrops danced in little splashes in the gutter. Across the street, the lights of another café glowed, yellow beacons of warmth in the bleak grey day.

Even in the rain Paris looked beautiful but, for the first time in ages, Eva felt like a tourist rather than a resident. She could no longer dance here and everything had changed.

She'd come to Paris to work, to further her career. Until now she'd been a professional with a full and busy life. Her days had a rhythm—limbering and stretching, promotions and interviews, rehearsals and performances.

If she lost all that, what would she do?

She hadn't felt this low since she'd broken up with Vasily, her Russian boyfriend, who had left her for a lovely blonde dancer from the Netherlands.

Such a dreadful blow that had been.

For eight years, Eva had loved good-looking Vasily Stepanov and his sinfully magnificent body. They had danced together and lived and loved together, and she had looked on him as her partner in every sense. Her dancing had never been more assured, more sensitive. Her life had never been happier.

She'd learned to cook Vasily's favourite Russian dishes—borsch and blini and potato salad with crunchy pickles, and she'd put up with his outbursts of temper. She'd even taken classes to learn his language, and she'd hoped they would marry, have a baby or two.

Getting over him had been the second hardest lesson of her life—after that other terrible lesson in her distant past. But now the devastating news about her hip was an even worse blow for Eva.

Sipping her rich, thick *chocolat chaud*, watching car tyres swish past on the shiny wet street, she found herself longing for sunshine and she remembered how easily the sun was taken for granted in Australia. A beat later, she was remembering the beach at Emerald Bay, the smooth curve of sand and the frothy blue and white surf.

And, out of nowhere, came the sudden suggestion that it made perfect sense to go back home to Australia for her surgery.

She could ask for leave from the company. Pierre was already rehearsing a new Clara for *The Nutcracker*, and the understudy was shaping up well. Eva was, to all intents and purposes, free. She found herself smiling at the prospect of going home.

She would make up some excuse about needing to see her mother. It wasn't a total lie. It was years since she'd taken extended leave and it was at least two years since she'd been home, and her mum wasn't getting any younger. If she had the surgery in an Australian city hospital, she'd have a much better chance of flying under the radar than she would here in ballet-mad Paris.

There might even be a chance—just a minuscule chance—that she could come back here to Paris as good as new. She'd been researching on the Internet and had read about a leading dancer in America who was performing again after a hip replacement. The girl was younger than Eva, but still, the story had given her hope.

And, Eva thought, as she drained the last of the

creamy rich chocolate, if she was returning to Australia, she might as well go to that school reunion. She'd had an email from Jane Simpson telling her that Griff was undecided so, if she went, she was unlikely to have the ordeal of facing him.

She would love to catch up with everyone else. It felt suddenly important to her to chat with people who lived 'normal' lives.

Yes, she decided. She would go.

As soon as this thought was born, Eva was hit by a burst of exhilaration. This was swiftly followed by a shiver of fear when she thought about Griff, but she shook it off.

It was time to be positive and brave about her future. Perhaps it was also time to lay to rest the ghosts of her past.

CHAPTER TWO

THE BAY HAD changed a great deal. Griff and Tim were surprised and impressed by the new suburbs and shopping centres that had sprung up in their home town. The school was almost unrecognisable, with a host of extra buildings, including a big new gymnasium and performing arts centre.

At least the fish and chip shop looked much the same, painted white with a blue trim and with big blue pots spilling with red geraniums. And the natural features of sea, sky and beach were as alluring as ever. Now, though, smart cafés graced the prime spots along the seafront, and there were neatly mown parks with landscaped gardens.

The guys remembered paddocks of prickly bindi-eye weeds that they'd had to run across to get to the beach, but now there were very civilised paved walking paths, and carefully planted vines crawled over the sand dunes to hold them in place.

Nevertheless, the three friends had a great afternoon trying to recapture the fun of their youth, falling off surfboards, getting sunburnt, donning snorkels, goggles and flippers to explore the striped and colourful fish and coral on the inshore reefs that rimmed the headland.

Griff was certainly glad that he'd come. It was refreshing to spend some quality time with friends whose links stretched way back. Despite his high-powered job, or perhaps because of it, he'd lately found himself going to too many dinner parties and concerts with the same snooty circle, rehashing the same old conversations, the same narrow views of politics, the same tired jokes.

Now, as the sun slid towards the west, washing the sky with a bright pink blush that lent gold tints to the sea, the trio returned to their hotel to shower and change for the reunion.

Griff, changed into pale chinos and a white open-necked shirt with long sleeves rolled back to the elbows, checked his phone, half expecting a message from Amanda, even though they'd broken up. He was sure she would be still keeping tabs on him. She'd had plenty to say about his 'boys' weekend'.

They'd had another row, of course. He'd accused her of not trusting him. She'd claimed she would trust him if he put a ring on her finger.

In the end, she'd walked out and the next day she'd sent a taxi to collect her belongings.

Unfortunately, she wasn't the first girlfriend to leave in this manner, but his love life was a hassle Griff didn't want to think about now. After an afternoon of sun, sea and mateship, he was feeling more relaxed than he had in ages. He wanted to keep it that way.

The trio were crossing the wide stretch of mown lawn in front the Emerald Bay Golf Club when Griff came to a sudden halt, as if he'd slammed into an invisible glass wall.

He'd caught just the merest glimpse of a slim, dark-haired woman on the side balcony overlooking the golf course and he'd known immediately that it was Eva.

Hell, she wasn't supposed to be here.

But here she was—wearing a sleeveless white dress, and laughing and chatting with a group. Even at a distance, Griff recognised her. No other woman was so slim and toned and poised. No one else had such perfect deportment, was so naturally elegant.

Hell. Now Griff knew he'd been fooling himself. His confidence that he could see Eva again and remain indifferent was shattered.

He was back in the past, remembering it all—helping her to adjust a pair of goggles and then teaching her to skin dive, helping her with her maths homework, dancing with her at the school formal. She'd worn a long silky dress in an aqua colour that exactly matched her eyes, and she'd made him feel like a prince.

He'd been saving for a surfboard, but he'd spent all his carefully hoarded pocket money on Eva's birthday, buying her an aquamarine pendant on a silver chain.

'What's the matter, Griff?' Barney's voice intruded his thoughts.

Both Tim and Barney were staring at him.

'Nothing,' Griff responded quickly.

The guys frowned at him, then shrugged and walked on. Griff, grim-faced, kept pace with them.

Hell. He gave himself a mental shakedown. Of course he could do this. He was used to hiding his feelings. He did it every day in court. Sure, he could play the role of an old friend, who'd barely given his high school sweetheart a second thought during the past twenty years. Sure, he could grit his teeth and sweat this scene out. For an entire weekend.

Jane had only warned Eva at the very last minute that Griff was coming. Actually, Jane hadn't couched the news as a warning. She had passed it on in high excitement, certain that Eva would be totally delighted.

By then, Eva had already arrived in the Bay and was settled into a pleasant motel room with ocean views, so it had been too late to change her mind. Just the same, when Jane shared this news, Eva found it devilish hard to grin and pretend to be pleased.

'He's not bringing his girlfriend, though,' Jane had added.

The existence of a girlfriend was good news at least. The possibility that Griff was still single and at a loose end had bothered Eva for all sorts of ridiculous reasons. Instead, he was safely in a relationship, which meant there were no loose ends.

Great. Their past was a closed door and that was how it would remain.

Eva had told herself she was stupid to fret. After all these years, Griff would have forgotten all about her. There was absolutely no reason he'd still be interested. After she'd left town, he'd studied for years at university and since then he'd been fighting the good fight in the justice system. Griffin Fletcher was a top drawer barrister these days, totally brilliant. Such a lofty and noble pursuit.

No doubt he would look down on a ballerina who spent her days pirouetting and leaping about, and see her as someone fluffy and inconsequential.

At least Eva was used to keeping her emotions under wraps and remaining composed in public, and now, with the reunion well underway, she tried to ignore any stirrings of tension as she chatted with old school friends. Everyone was eager to hear all about her dancing career and her life in Europe, but she tried to keep her story low-key.

She was keen to hear about their lives as accountants and teachers, as nurses and farmers, and she was more than happy to look at their photographs of their adorable kids.

She was exclaiming over a photo of Rose Gardner's six-month-old identical twins when she heard Jane's voice lift with excitement.

'Oh, hi, Barney and Tim. Hi, Griff.'

Griff.

Despite her calming self-talk, Eva's heart took off like a runaway thief. Unhelpfully, she turned Griff's way, which wasn't wise, but the instinct was too powerful to resist.

She thought she was well prepared for her first sight of him, but in a moment she knew that was nonsense. She was trembling like the last leaf on an autumn branch.

There he was. A man who would stand out in any crowd. Probably no taller than before, but certainly broader across the shoulders and chest. Still with the same shaggy brown hair, the same rugged cheekbones, the slightly crooked nose and square, shadowed jaw. The same intelligent grey eyes that missed nothing.

Not quite handsome, Griff Fletcher was undeniably masculine. There were perpendicular grooves down his cheeks that hadn't been there at eighteen, and he'd lost his easy, boyish smile. Now he had the air of a gladiator about to do battle, and Eva felt as if she might burst into flames.

'Griff,' Jane was gushing, 'how lovely to see you again.' A beat later, too soon, 'Isn't it wonderful that Eva was able to join us after all?'

With a beaming smile, Jane turned to Eva and beckoned. 'I told Griff that you weren't coming.' She giggled, as if this were an enormous joke.

Eva saw the fierce blaze in Griff's eyes. It wasn't a glare, exactly, but she got the distinct impression that he would definitely have stayed away if he'd known she would be here.

Thud.

She desperately wanted to flee, but she forced herself to stand her ground and to dredge up a smile. This became easier when she shifted her gaze from Griff to his old schoolmates, Tim and Barney.

Barney had grown round and was losing his hair, but his blue eyes twinkled and his smile was genuine and welcoming. 'Hey, Eva,' he said. 'Great to see you again.' He clasped her hand and gave her a friendly kiss on her cheek. 'I'm going to have to get your autograph for my daughter, Sophie. She's just started to learn ballet.'

'How lovely. Good for Sophie.' Eva gave Barney her smiling, super-focused attention. 'How many children do you have now?'

'Two and a half. A boy and a girl, with another on the way.'

'Barney's working on having enough kids to field a football team,' commented Tim as he shot his mate a cheeky grin.

Eva laughed. 'I hope your wife's in on that plan, Barney.'

Tim gave her a kiss, too. He told her that he worked in a bank and that he and his wife had just one child at this point, a little boy of two called Sam.

All too soon, it was Griff's turn to greet Eva and the light-hearted atmosphere noticeably chilled, as if someone had flicked a switch. The sudden tension was palpable—in everyone—in Tim and Barney and herself. Eva's heart was beating so loudly she feared they must hear it.

Griff smiled at her. It was a tilted, lopsided effort, but to the bystanders it probably passed as affable and casual. Eva, however, saw the expression in his eyes. Cold. Unfathomable. Cutting.

'How are you, Eva?' He went through the motions, giving her a casual hug and a peck on the cheek.

Ridiculously, her skin flamed at the contact, and she lost her breath as his big hands touched her shoulders, as his arms brushed, warm and solid, against her bare skin. Then his lips delivered a devastating, split-second flash of fire.

She took a moment to recover, to remember that she was supposed to answer his simple question. *How are you, Eva?*

'I'm very well, thanks, Griff.' Thank heavens she was able to speak calmly, but she hadn't told him the truth. She wasn't feeling well at all. She felt sick and scared—scared about the secrets she'd never shared with this man, that she'd hoped she would never have to share.

And her hip was agony. She'd foolishly, in a fit of vanity, worn high heels, and now she was paying the price. She prayed that she didn't blush as Griff's glittering grey gaze remained concentrated on her.

'And how are you?' she remembered to ask.

'Fighting fit, thank you.'

With the conventions over, an awkward silence fell. Tim and Barney looked at their shoes, and then at each other.

'We should grab a drink,' Tim said.

'Sure,' Barney agreed with obvious enthusiasm. They both turned to head for the bar, seeming keen to get away. 'Catch you two later.'

Griff remained still, watching Eva in stony silence and making her feel like one of his guilty criminals in the dock. This time her face flamed and she knew he could see it.

'You haven't changed,' he said quietly.

She shook her head. Of course she'd changed. They'd all changed in so many ways, both on the outside and, undoubtedly, within. But she played the game. 'Neither have you, Griff. Not really.'

At this, his smile almost reached his eyes.

She wondered if he was about to say something conciliatory. It would be helpful to at least share a few pleasantries to bridge the wide chasm of years. Of silence.

And guilty secrets.

'I hear you've been very successful,' he said. 'You're world-famous now. Congratulations.'

Receiving this praise from Griff, delivered in such a chilling tone, she wanted to cry.

But she swallowed the burning lump in her throat, squared her shoulders and lifted her chin. 'You've been very successful, too.'

He responded with the merest nod and only the very faintest trace of a smile. 'I imagine we've both worked hard.'

'Yes.'

People all around them were chatting and laughing, waving and calling greetings, sharing hugs, enjoying themselves immensely, but Eva couldn't think of anything else to say.

Griff said, 'If you'll excuse me, Eva, I'll head over to the bar and grab a drink, too.'

'Of course.'

'I'm sure we'll run into each other again during the weekend.'

'I… I…yes, I'm sure.'

With another nod, he dismissed her. As he moved away, she felt horribly deserted, as if she'd been left alone on a stage with a spotlight shining on her so everyone could see her. She could almost hear the music that accompanied *The Dying Swan*, the sad notes of a lone cello.

Oh, for heaven's sake.

Eva blinked and looked around her. The reunion was gathering steam. The balcony and the large dining room inside the clubhouse were almost full now with chattering, happy people and no one was staring at her.

She drifted, clutching her warming glass of champagne. She looked at the corkboard covered with old photographs. There were class photos, sporting teams, the senior formal, the school camp on Fraser Island. She saw a photo of herself in the netball team, Griff and his mates in striped football jerseys and shorts. Another photo showed her in a ballet tutu and pointe shoes, performing a solo for the school concert.

The old photographs conjured memories—the school disco when she and Griff danced together for the very first time, the dates when he'd taken her to the movies and they'd snogged each other senseless in the popcorn-scented dark, the barbecue for his eighteenth, the bonfire on the beach. And afterwards…

The memories were beyond painful and the urge to cry wouldn't go away.

'Would you like something to eat?'

Eva turned. A young girl was offering her a tray laden with canapés.

'Prosciutto crostini with dried cherries and goats' cheese,' the girl said. 'Or potato cakes with smoked salmon.'

Eva wasn't hungry, but she took a potato cake. Anything was better than staring miserably at those photos. She even managed to smile at the girl, who was rather interesting-looking, with dark hair cut into a trendy asymmetrical style. She had a silver nose stud as well, and there were purple streaks in the long fringe of hair that hung low, framing one side of her pretty heart-shaped face.

The girl returned Eva's smile. 'You might like a napkin.' She nodded to the small pile on one side of her tray.

'Thanks,' Eva said.

The girl was staring at Eva and there was something intriguing, almost familiar, about her clear grey eyes. 'You're Eva Hennessey,' the girl said. 'The ballet dancer.'

'Yes, that's right.'

The girl's eyes widened. 'Wow,' she said. 'You live in Paris, don't you? How amazing to meet you.'

Eva smiled, feeling calmer. This was familiar ground. 'It's great to be back in Australia,' she said. 'Are you from the Bay?'

The girl gave a small laugh that might have been nervous. 'Kinda. But I'm studying at university in Brisbane now.' Then she must have realised she was spending too long in one place. 'Better get going,' she said, and she hurried away to offer the platter to a nearby group.

Before long, Eva was absorbed into another group of schoolmates and was once again fielding friendly questions or listening to their stories about their old teachers, about their jobs, their kids or their holidays in New Zealand or Bali.

It was easy enough to avoid Griff and she was beginning to relax a little and to enjoy herself once more. If she and Griff kept apart by mutual agreement, the evening might be manageable after all.

Griff was feeling calmer as he stood in a group by the bar. Half his old rugby league team were gathered there and the guys were having a great old time sharing memories—the game when Tony King broke his leg while scoring a try, or the year they won the regional premiership by a whisker, when Jonno Briggs kicked a freakish field goal.

The whole time, though, Griff was all too aware of Eva's presence, even though she was at the far end of the room with her back to him. He did his damnedest to stop looking her way, but it was as if he had special radar beaming back sensory messages about her every move.

'Would you like something to eat, sir?'

A girl arrived, offering canapés.

'Thanks.' The savouries looked appetising. Griff smiled. 'I might take two.'

The girl laughed and there was a flash in her eyes, a tilt to her smile—something that felt uncannily familiar. For a moment longer than was necessary, the girl's gaze stayed on Griff, almost as if she were studying him. Fine hairs lifted on the back of his neck.

The feeling was unsettling and he might have said something, but then she turned and began serving the others. She didn't look Griff's way again and he decided he must have been more on edge about the whole Eva business than he'd realised.

He would be glad when this night was over.

Dinner was about to be served and everyone settled at long tables. Eva sat with some old girlfriends and their husbands. Griff was two tables away, almost out of sight, and she did her best to stop her gaze from stealing in his direction. She was relatively successful, but twice he caught her sending a furtive glance his way. Both times he looked angry and she felt her cheeks heat brightly.

'Are you all right, Eva?' asked Jane, who was sitting opposite her.

'Yes, of course.' Eva knew she must look flushed and she reached for her water glass. 'Just feeling the heat.'

Jane nodded sympathetically. 'It must be hard for you, coming back from a lovely cool autumn in Europe to the start of a sweltering summer in Queensland.'

'Yes,' Eva said. 'You tend to forget about the heat and just remember the lovely sunshine.'

Others around her nodded in agreement or laughed politely.

As they finished their main course, speeches were made. Jonno Briggs, who'd gone on after school to become a professional footballer, told a funny story about running into Barney in a pub in Glasgow. Jane gave a touching speech about one of their classmates who had died.

There were tributes to a couple of their old teachers who had also returned for the reunion. Then someone decided to point out their most successful classmates and Eva, among others, was asked to stand. As she did so, somewhat reluctantly, there was a burst of loud applause.

'Give us a pirouette, Eva!' called Barney.

She winced inwardly, remembering the way she'd liked to show off when she was still at school. So many times she'd performed arabesques and grand jetés on the beach.

'I couldn't possibly,' she told them now.

'Oh, come on!' called a jocular fellow at the back.

'Sorry. My dress is too tight.'

This was accepted with good-natured laughter.

At least she didn't have to mention the flaring pain in her hip. She would prefer no one knew about that.

The desserts arrived. Eva was served by the girl with the purple-streaked hair who had chatted to her earlier. She gave Eva an especially bright smile and a sly wink, as if they were great mates.

Eva usually avoided desserts and she only ate half of her *crème brulée*. With the speeches over, people were rising from their seats and starting to mingle again.

There was self-serve coffee at one end of the bar and Eva crossed the room to collect a cup.

'We should talk,' a deep voice said at her elbow.

Griff's voice. Eva almost spilled her coffee.

His expression was serious. Determined. Eva supposed he was going to grill her, ply her with questions. She was rather afraid of that clever lawyer's mind of his. Would he try to uncover her secret?

A flood of terror made her tremble. When she turned his way, she did so slowly, hoping to appear unruffled. 'What would you like to talk about?'

Griff's cool smile warned her not to play games. 'I suspect we'd both benefit from laying a few ghosts.'

She couldn't think how to respond to this. 'I… guess.'

'Let's go outside. You can bring your coffee with you.'

Eva was struggling with her hip and the high heels and she didn't trust herself to carry a cup of hot liquid. 'I'd prefer to drink it here.'

His expression remained unruffled. 'As you wish. There's no rush.'

'Well, no, I guess not.' In an attempt to banish her nervousness, she tried for lightness. 'Not after twenty years.'

But with Griff standing there, waiting for their 'talk', she was suddenly so tense the coffee curdled in her stomach. After three sips she set the cup down.

He frowned. 'You're finished?'

'Yes, thanks. Where would you like to go?'

He nodded towards a pair of glass doors that led to another, smaller, balcony. 'We should have more privacy out there.'

Privacy with this man. *Great*. Just what she didn't need, but she knew she shouldn't refuse him. From the moment she'd decided to come back to the Bay, she'd been aware that this encounter was a possibility.

Perhaps it was time.

If only she felt ready.

As Griff opened the door for her to precede him, the only light on the balcony came from an almost full moon. They were facing the sea now and a breeze brought a flurry of salty spray. The moon shone over the surf, highlighting the silvery curl of the waves and the white froth of foam as it crashed on the pale sand.

Eva gripped the balcony railing, grateful for its support. Now, in the moonlit darkness, Griff seemed to loom larger than ever.

'So,' she said, turning bravely to face him. 'What would you like to discuss?'

'I'm sure you must know, Eva. Perhaps you're hoping that after twenty years I'd simply overlook the way we broke up, but I'm afraid I'd like to know why you took off like that.'

She nodded, drew a deep breath. Of course she'd guessed this would be Griff's question and she knew she must tell him the truth. If only it wasn't so difficult, after all this time. When they were young they'd been able to talk endlessly, with an easy, trusting intimacy that would be impossible now. They'd shared everything.

Well, *almost* everything.

Now, they were virtually strangers.

She was tempted to use her mother as her excuse, but that would be cowardly. Although it *had* been her mum's idea to take off, leaving no word.

'I know you, Eva,' her mother had said on that fateful night before they'd left Emerald Bay under cover of darkness, as Eva had wept and begged to go to Griff. 'Be sensible, darling. If you try to explain what we're doing, you'll end up telling him everything. He might make demands and it will become way too complicated.'

Eva had tried to protest, but her mother had insisted. 'You need to make a clean break now. You have to think of your dancing career. You have so much promise, darling. Everybody says so—your teacher, the examiners, the Eisteddfod judges. You can't throw that away. I won't let you.'

There had been tears in her mother's eyes. Eva's potential career was incredibly important to her. She'd started dressing Eva in ballet tutus when she was three years old. By the time she was eighteen, Eva's ballet career had probably been more important to Lizzie Hennessey than it had been to Eva.

It was only much later, with the benefit of distance and maturity, that Eva had understood that her struggling single mother had been desperate to ensure that her daughter wasn't trapped and held back, as she had been.

Eva hadn't allowed herself to question whether she'd been wrong to listen to her mother. Of necessity, she'd clung to the belief that she had done the right thing. And her career had repaid her a thousandfold.

The wind swept her hair over her face. With shaking fingers, she brushed it away. 'I know it was bad of us to take off like that,' she told Griff. 'I've always felt guilty about it.'

'You were my first girlfriend,' he said. 'But you were also the first girl to dump me.' He sounded less aggressive, closer to the friendly Griff of old. 'I admit my ego took a blow.'

He stepped up to the railing, standing beside her now, with his hands deep in his trouser pockets as he looked out to sea. Eva could see his profile: his broad, intelligent forehead, his strong nose, his lips that she'd once explored with such excitement and daring.

'I thought I must have upset you,' he said quietly. 'We were both virgins. At the time, you seemed keen. I know you were keen, but I've often wondered if… I don't know…if I'd scared you.'

Oh, Griff, never. Tears stung Eva's eyes. 'That wasn't the problem, honestly. It was—'

'Excuse me.'

A voice brought them both swinging round. It was a girl—the waitress with the purple streaks in her hair.

Had she been sent to summon them inside? Eva wasn't sure if she was annoyed or relieved by the interruption.

'What is it?' Griff snapped, making his own reaction quite clear.

'I was hoping to speak to you both,' the girl said, but she seemed less confident now. She was wearing a white shirt and black skirt and she fiddled with the buckle at her waist.

Eva glanced Griff's way and saw his eyes narrow as he frowned at the girl. 'Well?' he demanded impatiently.

'I wanted to introduce myself.' Her grey eyes were huge with an emotion that might have been overwhelming excitement or fear. 'You see,' she added, lifting her hands from her sides, palms facing up in a gesture that was both nervous and helpless, 'I'm your daughter.'

CHAPTER THREE

GRIFF FELT AS if he'd been king-hit, knocked to the ground, left in a gutter, bruised and battered. He stared at the girl in appalled disbelief. Surely he hadn't heard her correctly.

Their daughter?

Impossible.

And yet, as he slowly gathered his wits, he had to ask himself if this wasn't also entirely possible. He'd used precautions back then, but heaven knew he'd been inexperienced and overexcited at the time. *Hell.* There was evidence enough in what had followed—Eva's rapid departure and silence.

And now, twenty years later, this creature, this attractive young woman, tall and dark-haired, with clear pale skin and shiny grey eyes and an air of familiarity that had nagged at Griff from the moment he'd seen her.

Their daughter?

Emotions tumbled through him like the pounding surf. Shock. Anger. Sadness. Regret. And then another thumping wave of anger.

All this time, all these years—Eva had kept their child a secret? His first impulse now was to round on her, to demand a full explanation.

A quick glance Eva's way, however, showed her sagged against the railing, white and trembling, possibly even more shocked than he was. Unfortunately, she wasn't denying the girl's claim.

'I'm sorry,' the girl said. 'I know this must be a huge surprise. A shock, I expect. But I was so anxious to meet you both. That's why I took this waitressing job as soon as I heard about the reunion. I was so excited when I saw the list of names and realised that you were both going to be here.'

Dazed, Griff rubbed at his temple. Could this girl, this unique, vibrant being, really be an amalgam of his and Eva's genes? A life they'd created?

He still couldn't quite believe he was a father. He didn't want to believe he'd been a father all this time. *Bloody hell.*

A thousand questions demanded answers, but he wasn't prepared to expose his total ignorance in front of the girl. At this point, there was no way of verifying her outrageous claim.

'What's your name?' Eva asked in a whisper, while she kept a white-knuckled grip on the railing, as if it were the only thing keeping her upright.

'Laine,' the girl said. 'That's the name you gave me, isn't it? Laine Elizabeth?'

Tears shone in Eva's eyes as she gave a sad, slow nod. 'Yes,' she said and, with a single syllable, she answered Griff's biggest question.

'I'm Laine Templeton now,' the girl said. 'Or sometimes Lettie to my closest friends, because my initials are L.E.T. The people who adopted me—the Templetons—live in Brisbane.'

'And they told you about me?' Eva sent a frightened glance Griff's way. 'About…us?'

Laine shook her head. 'No, I didn't want to upset them, so I went straight to the adoption agency. I'm over eighteen, so I was perfectly entitled to find out the names of my birth parents.' Her gaze met Griff's. 'I'm studying law at UQ. I was intrigued to look you up on the Internet and discover you're a barrister.'

Griff felt as if he'd swallowed glass. He supposed he should feel some kind of fatherly connection to this girl. He wanted to feel sympathy for Eva, but he was too busy dealing with his own roiling emotions.

Eva shouldn't have kept this from him. She shouldn't have carried this burden alone. Damn it, she should have shared the news of her pregnancy.

Sure, they'd been young at the time, only just out of school, and both of them with big career dreams with absolutely no plans to start a family. He hadn't been anywhere near ready for parenthood, but it cut deep to realise he'd been denied the chance to face up to this challenge, to at least be part of the decision-making.

'Look, I know this is a bolt out of the blue,' Laine said, and she was already taking a step backwards as she looked carefully from Griff to Eva. 'I just wanted to introduce myself initially, but I guess you need time to…adjust.'

'Yes, we do,' Griff told her more sternly than he'd meant to.

She smiled shyly, awkwardly.

'I'm sorry,' Eva said through trembling lips: 'I…
I…'

Clearly, Eva was struggling to say anything coherent. Laine lifted her hand then and gave a shy, shining-eyed smile and a stiff wave. 'OK,' she said. 'I dare say my timing hasn't been great.'

Griff felt torn. This was his daughter, after all. It felt totally inadequate to just greet her with *Hi and 'bye*. But he was too shocked to think straight. 'Look, this really is a shock,' he said. Maybe—'

Eva spoke up. 'Maybe tomorrow.'

'Yes, sure,' said Laine. 'I'm sorry if I've upset you. I... I...'

'We can at least exchange contact details tomorrow,' Griff suggested. That would be a start, and about all they could manage under the circumstances. Eva looked as if she was about to collapse.

'Thanks,' said Laine. 'I'll see you then.'

She backed away quickly and as she left via the glass doors Eva opened her mouth as if she wanted to say goodbye, but no sound emerged and she looked as if she was about to collapse.

Griff stepped towards Eva again, torn between wanting to tear strips off her and feeling desperately sorry for her. What must it be like for a mother to be reunited with her baby after nineteen long years?

'Are you OK?' he asked.

Eva shook her head. 'Not really.'

She was still clinging to the railing as if it were a life raft. Clearly, she needed to sit down and Griff was wondering where he could take her so that they could be private.

'Would you mind walking me back to my motel?' Eva asked, as if her mind had been on a similar track.

It was the perfect option. 'No, of course not.'

Griff slipped his arm around Eva's shoulders. He felt the softness of her bare skin, sensed the supple strength of her slender frame, toned by years of dancing. But now he knew that her magnificent career had come with a huge price tag. He wasn't sure he could forgive her.

It was a relief to lean into Griff's massive shoulder and to have his strong arm firmly around her as they walked the short distance across the lawn to the beachfront motel where Eva was staying.

She should have been terribly self-conscious about this sudden proximity to the man she'd avoided for so many years, but now her thoughts were filled to the brim with Laine. For so long, that beautiful girl had lived in Eva's head and heart as a tiny newborn.

Such a shock to see her baby now. Out of the blue. So astonishingly alive and grown-up and beautiful, and wanting to get to know her and Griff.

And Griff. She still hadn't come to terms with seeing him again. In one night, the love of her life and the daughter she had given up were both suddenly back in her life. It was too much. Too unreal. Too overwhelming.

Eva couldn't quite take it all in. She'd never felt such see-sawing emotions, teetering between joy and sorrow and guilt. Huge guilt.

'There hasn't been a day when I haven't thought about her, haven't wondered.' She only realised she'd spoken this out loud when she felt Griff's arm tighten around her.

He didn't say anything, however, and Eva couldn't imagine what he must be thinking. He would be terribly angry with her of course.

Keeping secrets was dangerous. They were usually exposed sooner or later, and the longer the secret was kept in the dark, the more likely it was that people would be hurt. Deeply hurt.

Would Griff ever forgive her?

It wasn't long before they reached the motel. Griff dropped his arm from Eva's shoulders and she fished in her bag for the room key.

'Would you like to come in?' she asked him, knowing she couldn't reasonably send him away like this, with so many unasked and unanswered questions.

'Yes, of course. We need to talk.'

Eva nodded, pushed the door open and slipped the key-card into the slot that turned on the lights. The motel room was large and comfortable, with a small sitting area comprising a couple of armchairs, a coffee table and a shaded table lamp.

She quickly switched off the lamps by the king-sized bed. A silly reaction, no doubt, but she didn't want to draw attention to the seductive banks of pillows, the soft throw rug arranged artistically across the grey silk quilt. She kicked off her shoes. Her hip was screaming and for a moment she had no choice but to stand there with her eyes closed, massaging the inflamed joint with her thumb.

Ah, that was better.

When she opened her eyes, she saw Griff watching her, his gaze narrowed, his expression concerned.

She smiled weakly. 'I think I'm getting too old for high heels.'

He shook his head in obvious disbelief and Eva quickly changed the subject. 'I'm sure you could do with a drink, Griff.' She crossed the room and checked out the minibar. 'What would you like? I seem to have it all here—Scotch, gin, rum, beer, red or white wine, champagne.'

'I'm sure I need a Scotch.'

'With water? Ice?'

'A little ice.'

He didn't say please, which probably meant he was angry, and he remained silent, seeming to fill the motel room with his dark and brooding presence as Eva poured the contents of the small bottle into a glass, found the ice cubes in the fridge's tiny freezer and twisted them free to tumble with a soft clink.

She emptied a packet of nuts into a small green dish and set them on the glass coffee table in front of him.

'Thanks,' he said as she handed him the drink. 'You'll join me, won't you?'

Eva doubted that anything could soothe her shaken nerves tonight, but she opted for white wine. With her glass filled, she took the seat opposite Griff, surreptitiously arranging a cushion to support her hip.

Griff, by contrast, looked surprisingly at ease, lounging in his pale chinos with an ankle propped on a knee. Distractingly attractive too, with his white shirt open at the throat, the sleeves rolled back to reveal muscular forearms, and his thick, longish hair curling boyishly at the ends.

Lifting his glass in a salute, he smiled, but his smile was a complicated mix of sadness and caution. 'Cheers. I guess I should say: Here's to our daughter.'

Our daughter.

The words were like splinters pressing into Eva's heart. She thought again of Laine as a tiny baby, thought of the years of gut-wrenching loss and longing, of not knowing, and her mouth pulled out of shape. She had to press a fist to her lips to hold back the threat of tears.

Not now. He will hate it if I cry.

To her relief, she managed, with a supreme effort, to compose herself.

'Laine's beautiful, isn't she?' she couldn't help saying.

'She is, yes.' Griff took a deep swallow of his Scotch and regarded Eva sternly. 'And you owe me one hell of an explanation.'

'I know.' She set her glass down without even bothering to taste the wine. Her hand was shaking and a little of the wine spilled, but she didn't get up to find something to wipe it. Neither of them needed another delay. 'I guess you realise now why I left the Bay in such a hurry.'

'I put two and two together, yes, but I have no idea why you chose to leave me in the dark.' Griff's eyes were fierce as he glared at her. 'I had a right to know that I'd fathered a child.'

'Yes, Griff. I know. I'm sorry.' It was hard to think clearly under his vigilant scrutiny. Eva dropped her gaze to the serviceable grey carpet. 'I do feel bad about it.'

'So why did you lock me out?'

Eva swallowed nervously, knowing that her excuse didn't sound nearly as valid now as it had seemed at the time. 'Do you remember the debate in our English class, when you argued in favour of abortion?'

A kind of strangled gasp broke from Griff. 'Not especially—there were so many debates. But don't tell me—' He stopped, clearly shocked.

'You were so clever and persuasive, Griff. Putting your case so strongly, slashing every argument the opposition tried to put up. Even at school you already sounded like a brilliant lawyer. And you made abortion sound so logical and sensible.'

'But it was a debate, for God's sake.' Griff was staring at her now in total disbelief. 'Eva, I was handed the topic. I didn't choose which side to take. You know how those school debates worked.'

'Yes, but at the time I had just found out I was pregnant and I couldn't help feeling that you were speaking to me, telling me that abortion was the right choice, the only sensible choice.'

He gave an angry shake of his head. 'I can't even remember the damned debate, but the argument would have been purely theoretical. I might have been persuasive. I'd have wanted our team to win. But you must know that's not necessarily how I would have reacted in a real life situation.'

'Well, yes, I know that now.' Eva sighed, recognising how frustrating this must be for him. 'And I suppose I sort of guessed it at the time, but you were so convincing, Griff. And I wanted to keep the baby— or at least I wanted it to be born, to have a life. I was scared that if I told you I was pregnant, you might want me to get rid of it and I wouldn't be clever enough to argue my case.'

She expected Griff to protest, but his eyes were so round with concern that she found it hard to breathe.

When he didn't say anything, she pushed on, needing him to understand. 'I was already under a lot of pressure from my mother. She was very keen for me to have a termination. She'd been a single mum and she knew how hard it could be. She wanted everything to be so much better for me. And she was so worried I would ruin my chances of ever becoming a dancer.'

'Well, I'm sure that was a distinct possibility,' Griff said. 'Weren't you auditioning for the Australian Ballet at the time?'

Eva nodded. 'For the Aussie Ballet *School*. I'd been through the regional auditions and I'd been selected for the finals in Melbourne. It was a huge deal for me—and for Mum. Oh, my God, Mum was beside herself with excitement.'

'Did you go to Melbourne?'

She shook her head. 'There was no point. I was going to have a baby.'

Griff swallowed, looked distressed. Then he frowned and stared pensively at the distant wall, as if he needed to take a good long time before he spoke. Watching him, Eva thought this might be how a judge might look in court, as he weighed up the evidence before he announced his sentence.

'So now your choice has been vindicated,' he said at last. 'You've had a brilliant career and you've been able to see that your baby has grown into a healthy and bright young woman.'

'Yes.' Eva swallowed the horrible lump in her throat. The results weren't as perfect as Griff made them sound. She had made these decisions with the best of intentions but, by keeping Laine a secret from him and then handing her over for adoption, three lives had been scarred for ever.

'I do apologise for not telling you,' she said. It was on the tip of her tongue to add that giving him up had been as hard for her as giving up her baby. Her heart had been broken twice over. But it was rather too late to mention romantic feelings from twenty years ago. She could imagine Griff's disbelieving laugh. 'I've always felt guilty about keeping the pregnancy a secret,' she said instead.

He sighed, looked at his glass again, then took another hefty swig of Scotch. As he set it down, he met her gaze directly.

'What happened after you left here? If you didn't go to Melbourne, where did you go instead?'

'To Bowen.'

'Bowen?' He looked shocked. Bowen was a small town a thousand kilometres away in north Queensland.

'It was quiet up there,' she said. 'No one knew us. The locals weren't likely to gossip or spread rumours, so Mum and I could stay under the radar. Mum got a job in a fish and chip shop. I spent a few months helping at the local ballet school, until I got too huge.'

'So Laine was born in Bowen?'

'No, we came down to Brisbane for the last month of the pregnancy. She was born in the Royal Brisbane and Women's Hospital. The adoption was already arranged.'

Eva said this as quickly and matter-of-factly as she could, and then looked away, staring hard at the opposite wall, willing herself not to cry. She didn't add that she'd almost tried to find Griff in Brisbane when the baby was about to be born. There was no point in telling him now that she'd come so close to seeking him out at university, hoping for one last, desperate chance.

At the time, she'd still been weaving foolish fantasies about the two of them raising the baby together, with Griff at university during the day and her working in ballet schools in the evenings. She'd imagined that, between them, they might have sorted something out. But, in the end, despite the allure of these dreams, she hadn't gone to Griff.

After so many months, she hadn't been brave enough to land such a last-minute bombshell at his feet. After all, he hadn't come after her when she'd left. He could have followed her, found her. He would have done if he'd really cared. Never mind that she'd handed him a terrible rejection, given him no reason to believe such an approach would be successful. He still could have followed her. Hollow as the thought was, she'd tried to cling onto it. It was all she'd had.

He frowned. 'You must have had to work incredibly hard to get yourself fit again after the baby. The ballet scene is so competitive. Were you still able to go to Melbourne?'

'No, I'd missed that chance. Mum and I moved to Sydney and I signed up with a suburban ballet school, just to get back into shape. But, while I was there, I went to workshops with the professional companies whenever I could and I met a visiting choreographer from the Netherlands. He encouraged me to head for Europe. He told me to audition with companies everywhere. He was sure I would find a home.'

Griff pulled a face. 'I suppose that must have been good advice. It's certainly worked well for you, but didn't you feel terribly young to just head off like that?'

'I was almost twenty and I'd had a baby. I felt very grown-up.'

He acknowledged this with a rueful quarter-smile.

'I've been with four or five different companies in Europe,' Eva said, keen to finish her story. 'But I've stayed with the one company in Paris for the last ten years.'

'As their star, their prima ballerina.'

'Not at first, but yes, eventually.'

With her story now off her chest, Eva felt calmer. She drank a little of her wine, while Griff remained silent as if he was digesting everything that she'd told him. She wondered if he would grill her further about her decision to keep the baby a secret. Or would he leave now? He had the bare essentials and there was little point in chatting away into the night like old friends.

'You never married,' he said suddenly.

It was almost an accusation and Eva felt the impact like a slap.

Defensively, she sat a little straighter, tucked a wing of dark hair behind her ear. 'No, I haven't.'

'It can't have been for lack of offers.'

She felt her cheeks grow warm, but she was too proud to tell Griff about her eight years with Vasily, and the subsequent painful dumping, so she held her tongue.

'I suppose you haven't had time for marriage,' Griff suggested drily. 'You've been too busy touring.'

'Well, yes, it's a gypsy life, being on stage.'

His eyes glimmered with the merest hint of amusement. 'A gypsy? What kind of caravan do you have?'

'An apartment in Paris. I love it, actually. In the seventh *arrondissement*.'

Griff looked impressed, gave a nod of approval.

'Have you been there?' she asked.

'In the Eiffel Tower district? Yes, of course.'

This was another small shock to add to the many Eva had received this evening. She wondered when

Griff had been in Paris. He must have been within a mere block or two, possibly metres from her home. Could they have passed in the street? Missed each other by moments? The possibilities made her eyes sting.

She blinked hard. So many years…they'd drifted so far apart, and yet she could still remember everything about their youth. The fun of swimming and diving with Griff, the long walks over the headland, the secret trysts behind the dunes.

Was Griff remembering all of this, too?

In the silence, Eva grabbed the chance to ask him a careful question of her own. 'You have a partner, I believe?'

One of Griff's dark eyebrows hiked high. 'Who told you that?'

'Jane Simpson.'

'Ah, yes, Jane. She's an unreliable source, you know.'

'Why do you say that? Because she told you I wasn't coming to the reunion?'

Griff downed the last of his drink. 'That and also the fact that Amanda and I have split up.'

Eva gulped as she stared at him. For a moment there, she'd almost been pleased about the split, before she remembered there was nothing to be pleased about. There was absolutely no chance that she and Griff would ever get together again.

But she couldn't help wondering what had gone wrong. She couldn't imagine why any girl would willingly leave Griff. 'I suppose you must have broken up recently then?'

'Yes.' He looked for a moment as if he was going to add more, but he must have changed his mind.

'That doesn't seem—' She stopped, confused, not quite sure what she was trying to say.

'Don't get yourself in a stew,' Griff told her. 'Amanda and I were already heading for the rocks and I think this reunion was the last straw.'

His candour surprised Eva and the realisation that Griff was no longer in a relationship had a strangely inappropriate effect on her breathing. 'I'm sorry.'

'Don't be,' he said calmly. 'I'm an old hand when it comes to ending relationships.'

This latest revelation sent a jolt through her. It made absolutely no sense. The Griff she knew was gorgeous, clever, easy to get on with. A perfect catch any woman would be lucky to snare.

She was remembering the powerful, fierce love that she'd once felt for him—the schoolgirl crush that had blossomed over their last summer into something huge.

Griff Fletcher had been an all-round star in the classroom and on the sporting field and yet he'd chosen her, Eva Hennessey, as his girlfriend, even though the only thing she'd been really good at was dancing.

She remembered the way Griff used to look at her, the way his intelligent grey eyes used to shimmer with unexpected emotion, letting her see straight into his heart. Perhaps it was the rawness of youth, but no one else, not even her mother or Vasily, had ever looked at her with such transparent and touchingly honest emotion.

Surely other women must have experienced the thrill of that passionate look? Surely they had been similarly smitten? Over the years, Eva had imagined a host of women throwing themselves at Griff's feet.

She'd made herself quite sick at times, just thinking about Griff and everything she'd missed.

'I'm sure you must be tired.'

She jumped as his deep voice intruded into her thoughts. 'Yes, I suppose I must be. It's been a big day.'

'Huge,' Griff agreed. His face was tight, unhappy.

Eva felt as if they'd made little headway. 'What are we going to do about Laine?'

Griff frowned. 'Right now I don't feel in a fit state to make any kind of decision. I need to get my head around…everything.'

'Yes, of course.'

Griff rose from his chair. Eva stood too. In her bare feet, he seemed to tower over her, but she resisted the temptation to stand on tiptoe.

And now, as he looked at her, an emotion that might have been sorrow or tenderness, or a mixture of both, showed in his handsome face. 'I meant it when I said you hadn't changed, Eva.'

She looked at him, noticed the grooves beside his mouth, the crow's feet, the beginnings of grey in his thick, shaggy hair. But in every way that mattered he was still the handsome guy she'd once loved.

'I was honest too, when I said the same about you.'

He smiled, a silent *as if.*

Then he stepped closer, put his hands on her shoulders, clasping her gently.

Eva's heart juddered in her chest. Surely he wasn't going to kiss her? She held her breath as Griff remained mere inches from her, holding her in his silvery gaze, while the memories from their past circled around them like prowling ghosts.

Her throat felt so dry she swallowed and she knew

that she wouldn't stop him if he did try to kiss her. He was Griff, after all.

He lifted a hand and touched her cheek, a soft brush of fingertips that reached deep inside her.

'Just for the record,' he said. 'I do understand how very much you loved your dancing, how important it was to you, and I think you made a very brave choice.'

Ohhh.

Eva was so relieved and grateful she could have hugged him, but before she could do anything Griff pressed a kiss to her forehead, then stepped quickly away and turned for the door.

'Sleep well,' he said over his shoulder, but there was a sarcastic edge to his voice now, an acknowledgement that neither of them was likely to sleep easily tonight. Then he left, letting the door click softly closed behind him.

CHAPTER FOUR

GRIFF'S EMOTIONS WERE rioting as he strode away from the motel. Until this evening he'd always considered himself to be pretty calm and clear-headed, but tonight that belief had been shattered. Tonight his brain had been well and truly fried. Hell, he'd actually come within a whisker of kissing Eva.

What the deuce had he been thinking?

As he reached the edge of the grassy parkland beside the beach, he stopped, hands sunk deep in his pockets, looking out to the breakers and, beyond them, to the smoother moonlit sea. He needed to collect his thoughts before he reached the hotel and encountered Tim and Barney. His mates knew he'd been with Eva and, while he was reasonably confident that they wouldn't grill him about it, he needed to have a story ready that did not include Laine.

He wasn't prepared to share the startling news about his daughter. He was still coming to terms with her existence, let alone everything else Eva had told him tonight.

He'd been on an emotional roller coaster, that was for sure, swinging from disbelief and anger to guilt and regret. And yet the whole time he'd been listening to

Eva's story, he'd found himself watching her, drinking in the delicious remembered details. The lustrous sheen of her dark hair, the slender grace of her neck, her expressive hands, her gorgeous legs, her astonishingly beautiful eyes.

She was even lovelier now. There was an extra layer, a depth he found himself longing to get to know. But that didn't mean he had to say out loud that she was as lovely now as she'd ever been. He was actually annoyed to think that Eva still had some kind of hold over him. Anyone would think he was still eighteen.

I should have followed my damn instincts and stayed away from this place...

A gust of wind blew in from the sea, bringing with it the fresh tang of salt and seaweed. Griff watched the moon riding high in the night sky, trailing delicate clouds like scarves. It was right here, under this moon, on this beach, that he'd kissed Eva for the very first time.

He could still remember the feel of her in his arms, so soft and sexy, despite her toned and slender frame, and he could remember the way she'd laughed with surprise when he'd drawn her in close. The laughter had died when she realised his intentions.

He'd been scared she would refuse him. They were only friends at that point, part of the gang of kids who spent as much of their spare time as possible at the beach. They'd never even been on an actual date. But, miraculously, Eva had been as eager for a kiss as he was, letting her soft lips part to meet his and winding her arms around him, wriggling her hips against him, teasing him mercilessly.

'You make me feel all glittery,' she'd told him later that night.

'Glittery?'

'Yes, sparkling and tinkling. It's kind of a look and a sound and a feeling, all wrapped into one.'

If he hadn't already been in love with her, he'd become a complete and helpless goner in that moment.

And he and Eva had become such experts at kissing. Of course it wasn't long before they'd wanted more than kisses. A few more months had passed, though, before the fateful night Griff invited Eva back to his place, while his parents and sister were away in Brisbane.

Griff had prepared dinner—baked fish and potatoes with an avocado salad—with wine and half a dozen candles. It was such a big deal. He'd been desperate to impress.

Eva had grinned when she'd seen how much trouble he'd gone to. 'Gosh, Griff, you wouldn't be trying to seduce me, would you?'

Her light-hearted comment had brought his high hopes crashing about his feet. Clearly he'd gone overboard. He was an idiot. A total loser. Seduction was supposed to be subtle.

But then Eva had turned the tables on him by leaping into his arms. 'You didn't have to go to all this trouble, you know,' she said, nibbling at his ear. 'We've been seducing each other for weeks now and I can't wait a minute longer. Let's have dinner later.'

So it was much later by the time they had their meal. By then the food in the oven had all dried out and the salad was limp, but neither of them had minded.

Damn.

Griff gritted his teeth, angry that he was feeling so choked up over ancient history. What was the point of remembering such juvenile nonsense? There was nothing about their past that either he or Eva could change.

He wasn't even sure that they would want to.

What he needed to concentrate on now were the consequences presented to him this evening. A baby. A daughter, given up for adoption. The stark pain in Eva's face when she'd seen their child. His own huge feelings of isolation and loss.

If only he'd known. If only Eva had told him. He'd deserved to know.

And what would you have done? his conscience whispered.

It was a fair enough question.

Realistically, what would he have done at the age of eighteen? He and Eva had both been so young, scarcely out of school, both ambitious, with all their lives ahead of them. He hadn't been remotely ready to think about settling down, or facing parenthood, let alone lasting love or matrimony.

And yet he'd been hopelessly crazy about Eva, so chances were…

Dragging in a deep breath of sea air, Griff shook his head. It was way too late to trawl through what might have been. There was no point in harbouring regrets.

But what about now?

How was he going to handle this new situation? Laine, a lovely daughter, living in his city, studying law. The thought that she'd been living there all this time, without his knowledge, did his head in.

And Eva, as lovely and hauntingly bewitching as

ever, sent his head spinning too, sent his heart taking flight.

He'd never felt so side-swiped. So torn. One minute he wanted to turn on his heel and head straight back to Eva's motel room, to pull her into his arms and taste those enticing lips of hers. To trace the shape of her lithe, tempting body with his hands. To unleash the longing that was raging inside him, driving him crazy.

Next minute he came to his senses and knew that he should just keep on walking. Now. Walk out of the Bay. All the way back to Brisbane.

And then, heaven help him, he was wanting Eva again. Wanting her desperately.

Damn it. He was in for a very long night.

Eva tossed and turned restlessly for most of the night. At three a.m. she got up to make a mug of camomile tea and to pace the motel room.

Haunted by Griff.

Seeing him again had rocked her to the core, lifting the lid on all her carefully bottled feelings and longings, reminding her of everything wonderful that she'd lost when she left him.

She'd been shocked by the storm that seeing Griff had wrought. It didn't make sense that she should feel this way. Anyone would think she'd travelled back in time, that she was eighteen again. Inexperienced. Unworldly. Swept away by one man.

And then, of all things, she'd seen Laine again on the very same night...

Such a shock. At first, Eva hadn't been sure she could survive it.

Every day of the past nineteen years, she had relived

the moment when her baby was placed in her arms, warm and squirming within the tightly wrapped blanket. She'd remember Laine's damp, dark hair, her shiny little eyes and her intoxicating newborn smell, the little birthmark shaped like a butterfly on her left ankle.

Laine had been a strong little thing and had fought free of the blanket, kicking to expose one little foot and to wave a tiny, tiny pink hand at Eva. A baby hello.

A deep, painful love had welled in Eva's chest, had burst into her throat in a noisy, heartbroken sob. Within moments, an officious nursing sister had taken her baby away.

'We can't have her upsetting you, dear.'

Eva's mum had been there and she'd hugged Eva hard and had assured her over and over that the adoption was for the best, but Eva couldn't be consoled. She'd cried so hard and so long that eventually they had made her take a pill. And then she'd slept.

She only saw Laine briefly, one more time, on the day she'd signed the papers.

They'd given her a photograph, but that was all she had. Over the years she'd tried to imagine Laine growing into a toddler, a cute little girl, a teenager. She'd longed to know details. What did she look like? Was she happy? Was she sporty and brainy like Griff, or was she more like herself, dreamy and artistic?

The anniversaries had been especially hard— Laine's birthday, Christmas, Mother's Day. Eva had coped the only way she could, by dancing from dawn until dark.

She'd consoled herself that all the advice had been right. She had done the right thing. Laine had gone to a good home, to parents who desperately wanted her and would give her a happy childhood. But Laine had been denied ever knowing her real parents. No matter how well she was cared for, at some deep level she must have known she'd been abandoned by her mother, the one person in the world who should have loved her most.

Eva wished she'd known at the age of eighteen that keeping a big secret like that from the man she loved would leave a painful crack in her soul. She'd been told the sense of loss would be temporary, but it wasn't. It stayed there.

Eva finally got to sleep again just after dawn, and she slept late. When she woke, she still felt lonely and scared. Useless.

It was so upsetting to feel this way, after working so hard to put it all behind her. In Paris, the ballet company she worked with adored her. Her life was predictable and orderly. Her work was satisfying and safe.

Now, she'd been back in Emerald Bay for less than twenty-four hours and already the mirage of her life as a dancing star had been stripped away to reveal her as a fraud. In every way that truly mattered Eva felt like a failure. The huge decisions she'd made for all the best reasons—leaving Griff and giving up Laine—no longer made sense.

And no amount of floor-pacing could ease her turmoil.

She was just stepping out of the shower when she heard the knock on her door.

Her first thought was that it must be Griff, and her heart was racing as she dried herself and pulled on the towelling robe that the motel supplied. She hurried to the door in bare feet.

And, indeed, Griff was standing on her doorstep.

He looked as tired as Eva felt and he hadn't shaved, but the dark stubble suited him, to a sinful degree. It went with his shaggy hair. And he was dressed in faded denim jeans and a loose white T-shirt that made him look like the Griff of old. Her high school surfie boyfriend.

Eva drew a deep breath. *Calm down. Just deal with whatever he has to say. Think of this as another performance.*

'I probably should have warned you I was coming over,' he said, obviously sensing her tension, and yet making no attempt to hide his curiosity as he took in her robe and damp, towel-dried hair.

Self-consciously, Eva tightened the knot on her robe's sash. 'How…how can I help you?'

'I don't know about you, but I've had a pretty grim night. There seems to be so much unfinished business. Can we talk?'

'Well, yes—'

'My head's all over the place. I need to talk about Laine and—' Griff didn't fill in the rest of his sentence.

'Yes, of course.' Eva pressed a hand to the sudden aching pulse in her throat. 'Come in.' She opened the door wider and took a step back.

Griff only hesitated for half a second before entering her motel room yet again. Of course, he couldn't miss the rumpled sheets of the unmade bed, but he politely looked away. Not, however, before several hot flashes streaked through Eva. She felt ridiculously naked beneath the towelling robe.

'Take a seat,' she said nervously. 'Can you give me a moment to get dressed?'

'Of course.'

She would have to dress in the bathroom and she felt stupidly self-conscious as she collected her underwear from a drawer and snatched the most convenient item of clothing from the nearest hanger in the wardrobe.

'I'll fill the kettle from the bathroom tap and you might like to make us both a cup of coffee,' she said.

'Sure.'

Eva handed Griff the filled kettle and disappeared into the bathroom, without looking back to catch his expression.

She did, however, see the appreciative look in his eyes as she emerged scant minutes later in a halter-neck aqua sundress. It was silly the way warmth spread from her chest to her face. She hoped it didn't show.

At least, judging by the aroma filling the room, Griff had made a pot of good strong coffee.

'Thanks,' she said as he handed her a steaming mug, and she took a grateful sip. 'Mmm, I needed this.'

'Haven't you had breakfast?'

'No, I slept in, but this is good. Coffee's fine.' It wasn't all that long now till the reunion's farewell lunch and that was bound to be huge, Eva was sure.

She and Griff sat in chairs opposite each other, just as they had on the previous night. Unfortunately, Eva didn't feel any calmer now than she had then. She took another, deeper sip of coffee. 'So,' she said. 'We need to talk about Laine.'

'Yes.' Griff shifted in his chair as if he wasn't quite comfortable either. 'I imagine she might have had a bad a night too. It's not every day you front up to your long-lost parents.'

Eva nodded sadly. 'We should be talking to her. I spent half the night wishing I hadn't sent her away. The poor girl must be wondering what we think of her, how we're going to react going forward.'

Griff's face was stern. 'A public venue like a high school reunion isn't exactly the best setting for a highly charged personal revelation.'

'No.'

'The last thing any of us needs is to give the old school gossips something extra juicy to gab about.'

Eva felt compelled to defend her daughter. 'At least Laine had the sense to find us when we were on our own last night.'

'That's true.'

'It was just such a shock, though. I couldn't think straight.' Eva clutched her coffee mug more tightly. Their gazes met. This morning, Griff gave no sign that he harboured anger or resentment about her secrecy, but it was she who looked away first. It wasn't just her guilt that bothered her. The silvery-grey shimmer in Griff's eyes had haunted her for twenty years, and now it made her feel hot in the cheeks, as if she was once again a shy schoolgirl with an enormous crush.

'Are you angry, Griff?' She forced herself to look his way.

'Yes,' he said, meeting her gaze squarely. 'Actually, I swing between anger and—' he shrugged '—and feeling sorry for you, I guess. It's doing my head in, to be honest.'

'I'm sorry.'

'Yeah, I know you're sorry. You don't have to keep saying it.'

Eva accepted this small reprimand with a rueful smile. 'Well, I'm worried about how Laine feels too. I… I hope she's not too angry with me—'

'I certainly didn't get that impression.' Griff shrugged. 'It might be just normal, healthy curiosity on her part.'

'Perhaps.' But Eva was again swamped with the too familiar memories of the tiny baby she'd given away. The strong little body wriggling inside the tight blanket. The tiny foot kicking, the hand waving.

She shivered.

'Are you all right?' Griff asked.

She shook her head. She was scared. Her arms were cold, despite the warmth of the day, and she rubbed at them. 'I don't want Laine to think she was the worst thing that ever happened to me.'

'Was she?' Griff asked sharply and Eva saw her own worry and pain mirrored in his eyes.

She couldn't tell him the truth, couldn't expose him to the depth of her pain. The adoption had been her decision and hers alone.

And if she allowed herself to relive those memories now, she would break down completely. The last thing Griff needed was a blubbering ex-girlfriend.

'I suppose we already made the most sensible suggestion last night and that is to give Laine our contact details,' she said, determined to be more positive and practical. 'Our phone numbers at least.' In truth, she longed to spend ages with her daughter, getting to know everything about her, but she would need to feel stronger. More composed.

'I'd certainly like to have more contact with Laine,' Griff agreed. 'I don't want my daughter to think that I don't care about her.'

My daughter.

Goosebumps broke out on Eva's arms as he said these two simple but oh, so significant words.

'No, I'd hate that too,' she said quickly, and then she took another deeper sip of her coffee, hoping for extra courage. It was important to remain practical. To give Griff space. 'I don't suppose there's any real need for us to see Laine together,' she said next. 'I mean—after today, we'll be going our separate ways again, won't we?'

'I dare say.' Griff's tone was dry and hard to read. Even so, it sent inappropriate tingles all over Eva's skin.

It was so unhelpful that she kept remembering him as her boyfriend. Dancing on the beach with him. His kisses. That perfect night so long ago. The meal he'd gone to so much trouble to prepare. The candles…

Stop it.

'So,' she pushed on bravely, 'I guess it's probably best if we make contact with Laine separately, in our own time.'

Griff nodded. Drained his coffee mug.

She supposed he would leave now.

'How are your parents?' she asked, suddenly desperate to keep him there for just a little longer.

Griff looked surprised by her question, but then he shrugged. 'They're fine. In the peak of condition, retired to Mount Tamborine in the Gold Coast hinterland.'

'That must be very nice. And your sister?' Eva remembered Griff's sister, Julia, as rather intimidatingly clever. Julia had been school captain when they'd been mere eighth graders and she'd scooped up all the awards on speech night.

'Julia's married with five kids at last count, and she's also a high court judge, would you believe?'

'Truly? As well as five children? How does she do it?'

'I have no idea. I don't think anyone knows, but there's been a procession of nannies and household help.' Griff smiled crookedly. 'She's the jewel in my father's crown.'

Eva could well imagine this. Griff's parents had always had high expectations for their children and, while Griff had done very well for himself, he'd lived in his sister's shadow.

Back in their school days, Griff's parents had never met Eva, the daughter of a hippie single mum. They certainly wouldn't have approved of her, which was possibly why Griff had escaped to the beach whenever he could.

'I've been thinking about how lucky we were to grow up here,' he said, looking out of the window to a view through palm trees of the golden stretch of beach. 'So much sunshine and fresh air and open space.'

'I know.' Eva had spent far too much time during the night lost in unhelpful memories of her life here at the Bay. 'No one ever worried about whether we were getting enough exercise.'

'The hard part was dragging us inside to study.'

They shared smiles but, to Eva's dismay, a smile from Griff was almost as dangerous now as it had been in her teens. She dropped her gaze to the coffee table between them and spotted the piece of weathered coral that she'd found on the beach yesterday.

She reached for it now. It was bleached snow-white by the sea and the sun, and she could run her thumb over the smooth ends that had once been sharp, pointy branches.

Griff noticed and raised a curious eyebrow. 'A souvenir?' he asked.

'Perhaps. I have a collection of stones and shells I've found on various beaches around the world.'

'And you keep them in Paris?'

'Yes.'

He nodded thoughtfully. 'I'm sure you must love living in such a beautiful city.'

'Well, yes, I do. It's wonderful.' It was easy to wax lyrical about Paris and she was suddenly keen to justify her choice of living abroad. 'There's so much to love. The beautiful architecture, the gardens and parks, the food.'

'Oh, my God, the French food.' Griff rubbed his stomach and gave an exaggerated groan. 'And it's not just the food in the restaurants. There are all those amazing markets as well.'

'Yes, mountains of mushrooms in autumn. Amazing berries in spring and summer, lavender honey.'

'Not to mention *foie gras*.'

She laughed at his enthusiasm, remembering him as a teenager with a constant interest in food. 'And in Paris there's the bonus that you don't need a car,' she said. 'And I adore the flower stands. I can buy a beautiful bouquet for three euros!'

'Sounds like you've totally adapted to the city life then.'

'Well, yes, I have. You can never feel lonely in a city like Paris—even if you're sitting on your own in a bar.'

Griff shot her a sharp, questioning glance. 'Do you spend a lot of time on your own?'

Thud.

Eva winced as she realised she'd steered herself straight into that trap. But the sad truth was that since Vasily had left her she'd spent more time on her own than she would have liked, but she wasn't about to admit that now to this man.

'Not a *lot* of time,' she hedged. 'But I do like the fact that I can be comfortably on my own if I choose to.'

'And that's fair enough,' Griff said easily.

'What about your life in Brisbane?' She was keen to shift the focus. 'Are you glad you made the move to the city?'

'Well, yes, I can't complain. I live in a suburb in the foothills of Mount Coot-tha. It's close to the city, so it's a quick commute, but there are plenty of bush walking tracks nearby. I have the best of both worlds really.'

This did sound rather attractive. Despite her love of Paris, Eva had missed the Australian bush. There'd been many times when she'd longed to smell the eucalyptus trees, or to see wattles flowering in winter, bright yellow against a clear blue sky. She'd missed hearing the ridiculous laughter of kookaburras, or catching the occasional sight of loping kangaroos. Tasting the first juicy mango at the very beginning of summer.

They fell silent, but Eva no longer felt quite as awkward as she had earlier. She knew it was foolish to dream, but she almost felt now as if she could spend the entire weekend talking to Griff, getting to know him again.

Not that he would want that, of course.

After a bit, she said, 'It's good that you love where you live. It's important.'

'Yes.' Griff looked at his watch. 'I guess I should make tracks.'

There was almost an hour until the lunch, but Eva supposed he didn't want to hang around chatting with her any longer than was strictly necessary. They'd skipped over the important things, like how they still felt about each other after all this time and why they were both still single. But what could she expect? Her secret had hurt Griff terribly and she was lucky he'd been so tolerant.

Just the same, she couldn't help feeling disappointed that he was so eager to leave.

They rose from their chairs and she showed Griff to the door, where he kissed her on the cheek, a brush of his lips as light as a moth's wings. Such a simple kiss, really, the kind a brother might give, but as Eva felt Griff's touch she caught the scent of his skin and she knew she was as susceptible to this man now as she'd been at eighteen.

She'd felt so adrift this weekend. Torn free from her moorings. And now, without warning, she was longing for the impossible.

She wanted to have Griff's lips on her lips, warm and seeking. She wanted to kiss him properly, deep and daring, wanted his arms around her as she pressed into his big, powerful body, letting the tight knot of longing inside her unravel and run free.

Griff was so close she was aware of the same tension

in him. He made no move to leave and she sensed, in that moment, that they were a hair's breadth from giving in to crazy, nostalgic longing. It would only take one move from Griff and she would be helplessly lost.

Their passion would be stormy, Eva had no doubt, fuelled by years of longing and wondering, of regrets that needed to be assuaged.

A kind of wildness hummed in her veins.

Then she saw it—the warning in Griff's eyes. He wasn't going to make any mistakes this time.

He took a step back.

Not again.

Griff couldn't believe he'd been on the brink of kissing Eva again. Worse. This time, she had been all too aware of how close he'd come.

He could see the knowledge blazing in her eyes. Even more dismaying, he could see that she wanted him too, was almost willing him to kiss her. But that was crazy.

The list of reasons why they shouldn't give in to a kiss was almost as long as from here to Paris. Problem was, Griff couldn't recall a single one of those reasons now. His entire focus was riveted to the woman before him. Eva, the girl who had haunted him for ever. So lovely still.

Pale-skinned, slim as a reed, she was the sweetest temptation he'd ever known. Instead of backing away, he stepped closer.

So close that there could be no turning back.

His hands reached towards hers, just a brush of their fingertips that sent a hot jolt of desire shooting through him. Eva made a soft sound, a catch of her breath, lifted her lovely face to his, let him read the raw want in her eyes, and he was lost.

Their lips met and they kissed hungrily as he backed her into the room, toeing the door closed behind him. This was a storm that had been brewing since they'd first set eyes on each other yesterday and now they kissed with all the fierceness of a passion too long suppressed.

By the time they reached the bed, Griff's shirt had come off, tossed to the floor, and Eva's halter-neck ties were undone.

'We shouldn't,' she said once in a voice urgent with desire.

'I know,' he whispered back. 'This is crazy.'

But, instead of being sensible, they helped each other out of the rest of their clothing, all the while sharing frantic, eager, desperate kisses…

'Is this safe?' he remembered to ask.

Eva nodded, whispered against his lips, 'Yes, I promise.'

He kissed a path from her lovely bare shoulder to the sweet curve of her neck, to her chin. In turn, she nibble-kissed the grainy skin of his jaw while she explored his chest with her hands, possessively sliding her palms over his skin, tracing each dip and plane.

She was breathtakingly beautiful. Her dark silky hair skimmed past her pale shoulders and her slim dancer's body was lithe and supple, her breasts as small and soft and tantalising as ever. As he dipped his head to each needy pink peak, she gave herself up to him with the same wanton eagerness that he remembered from so long ago, and with an emotional honesty that he'd never known since.

* * *

It was only afterwards that the guilt came, as they lay together. Eva was on her side, with her back against Griff's broad chest, his arm draped intimately over her hip.

Being with him again had been so exquisitely beautiful she'd come close to the brink of tears again, but she'd been too excited, too stirred to give in to them.

Now, they lay very still, not talking, while their heartbeats slowed, while her mind raced, marvelling at what had just happened.

She'd never dreamed that making love with Griff could be even better than she remembered—so beautiful, so passionate, so breathtakingly intense that it felt as if a spell had been cast over them.

Another blissful memory to hold close.

Sadly, Eva knew that a memory was all this could be—a treasured memory to take with her when she returned to Paris after her surgery. When Griff returned to his busy and important work as a barrister. While they both, separately, tried to forge a new tentative relationship with their daughter. Laine.

Good heavens.

The guilt came with a slam. Why hadn't she been thinking about Laine in the lust-crazed, breathless seconds before they'd finally started kissing each other senseless? Why hadn't Griff remembered her?

A cold shiver shook Eva. How foolish they were, no wiser now than when they'd been eighteen.

And what a cliché—teenage lovers meeting up again years later at a school reunion, unable to resist the temptation of one more fling, for old times' sake.

No doubt they would look back on this as yet another foolish mistake.

Such a pity when, scant moments earlier, she'd felt more joyful than she had in a long, long time. Now she felt almost fearful as she rolled to face Griff.

The intensity in his eyes sent a tremble through her, but he simply stared at her and didn't speak. Time seemed to stretch for ever and they watched each other in silence, almost as if they were afraid to give voice to their individual thoughts, as if they both knew that anything they said now might spoil this perfect moment, might undo the magic. Bring them back to reality, to the admission that this amazing, perfect experience should, almost certainly, not have happened.

But then a faint smile appeared in Griff's eyes and tilted the corners of his mouth. 'Well, that's answered a lot of questions,' he said quietly.

Eva nodded—all the years of wondering were behind them. Now they shared the knowledge that their chemistry was as potent as ever, possibly more so.

He traced the dip of her waist and the rise of her hip with his hand. 'Is this hip painful?'

She grimaced. She'd tried so hard to hide the few moments of pain. 'It catches me sometimes.' Then she couldn't help adding, 'It's one of the problems of an ageing dancer.'

Griff shrugged. 'I guess all dancers have a shelf life, like athletes.'

'I'm afraid so.' Eva almost told him about her planned surgery, but her habit of silence regarding such matters was too deeply ingrained.

Griff stopped stroking her hip and she was intensely conscious of the precise moment he withdrew his hand, leaving her skin suddenly cool where it had been wonderfully warm. He was still watching her closely. 'Do you have a retirement plan, Eva?'

Her heart gave a scared little thump and she sat up quickly. Where was this conversation heading?

'There's no need to panic,' he said. 'I was simply curious.'

Yes, of course. She was overreacting, jumping ahead. His casual question about her career plan was not a signal that he was about to ask her to change her future and to spend it with him.

They'd had sex, nothing more than a nostalgic fling. Eva suspected they were now in a precarious post-coital situation that could be completely ruined by too much talking. And while she and Griff had shared sensational, unforgettable passion, they couldn't really guess at each other's emotions now that it was over. They were still strangers. Really.

They knew each other superficially, but true understanding was impossible after twenty years of living completely separate lives. And now, in this fragile aftermath of lovemaking, it would be so easy to say something stupid.

The wisest move was to allow this day to remain for ever in their memories as an exciting, very moving reunion. A one-off chance to say hello and goodbye before they went back to where they belonged. Apart.

This was closure. Nothing more. Certainly not the start of something new.

Eva just wished she felt happier about letting this go. Why was being sensible always so hard, especially when Griff Fletcher was involved?

Conscious of the growing awkwardness between

them, she inched towards the edge of the bed. 'We're going to be late for this lunch.'

'Yeah,' said Griff with a sigh. 'Guess I'd better get going.'

Almost shy now, she wrapped herself again in the towelling dressing gown and she sat on the edge of the bed, keeping her back to Griff as he dressed. She couldn't bear to watch him as he pulled on his clothes. She didn't want to see that powerful masculine body disappear beneath fabric.

Now, she could finally admit to herself that she'd missed this man so much. Too much. And being with him again had confirmed her worst fears—no other man, not even Vasily, could measure up to this—her first love.

After she and Griff parted today, she would miss him all over again. No doubt she would spend the rest of her life missing him. It was such a depressing prospect.

In no time Griff was dressed and standing in the middle of the room, ready to leave. 'I assume I'll see you shortly over at the Golf Club,' he said.

'Yes.' Eva rose from the bed too, and her hip complained. She felt stiff, like an old lady, though she was not yet forty.

She squeezed her facial muscles, forcing her mouth into a grimacing smile. She was sure she should say something about what had happened. But what? 'I suppose I should say thank you,' she suggested.

'Don't you dare. Not that.' Griff looked fierce and it was hard to tell if he was mad at her.

'Anything else feels trite,' she said. 'Or over the top.'

A glimmer of amusement shone in his eyes and his

expression was gentler. For a moment they were kindred spirits.

But I wouldn't dare tell you how I really feel about you, Griff.

He said, 'I should go.'

Eva nodded.

But, instead of leaving, he came around the end of the bed. Cupping her chin, he tilted her face towards him and kissed her again without haste. 'You're the beautiful mother of my child,' he murmured.

Oh, Griff.

Before she could think of an appropriate response, he turned and once again headed for the door.

'See you at the Golf Club,' he said over his shoulder, and this time Eva felt as if she was watching something vital leave her, like her own lifeblood.

CHAPTER FIVE

T IM AND B ARNEY had given up waiting for Griff at their prearranged meeting place in the hotel lobby. He showered and changed super-quickly and found them in the bar at the Golf Club. They eyed him suspiciously when he turned up.

'Hello, stranger.' Tim had never been one to beat around the bush.

Griff responded as smoothly as he could and asked them about the reunion golf tournament which they'd both played in that morning. Apparently, his mates had ended up with very ordinary scores and Tim was very keen to change the subject.

'So what's with you and Eva?' he asked in a voice dripping with innuendo.

Griff was used to flipping glib answers in response to almost any sticky question, but he found himself floundering. Truth to tell, he was still coming to terms with everything that had happened between him and Eva.

'We've had a lot to catch up on,' he said, knowing it sounded lame.

Tim rolled his eyes. 'No kidding?'

'Something's come up,' Griff added, because he

couldn't fob his mates off indefinitely. 'Something big, actually, and Eva and I needed to discuss it.'

'Hmm.' Tim looked unconvinced.

Barney, who was more sensitive, offered a sympathetic nod. 'Did Eva need legal advice?' he asked.

Griff ignored Tim's scoffing reaction to this innocent question. 'I should be able to fill you guys in soon,' he told them. 'In the car on the way home, perhaps.'

His mates looked intrigued, but at least they stopped needling him, and it wasn't long before they moved on to chat with others. Griff, however, remained, staring into his beer and pondering the crazy turn of events that his life had taken over the past twenty-four hours.

He'd known from the outset that he should have stayed well away from this school reunion. It was supposed to have been a bit of harmless fun with a few mates. *Ha!* The fun had turned serious from the moment he'd set eyes on Eva.

Being with her again had proved even more devastating than he'd feared. She'd thrown him into a total tailspin, which even now didn't really make sense.

What was it about the woman?

Why was his behaviour so out of control?

Sure, Eva had been his first love. So what? Every guy had a first love. Running into her again at a school reunion wasn't supposed to be a big deal. It made no sense that he'd behaved like a lost and lovesick soul responding to some mythical siren's call.

The result? Naturally, he'd crashed headlong into dangerous rocks.

With a heavy sigh, Griff picked up his beer glass and stared at it, and then set it down again without tasting it. Beer was a drink he enjoyed when he was relaxed, but today his thoughts and his stomach were churning.

As a lawyer, he'd had plenty of experience in analysing the behaviour and motives of others, both the innocent and the guilty. Now it totally bugged him that he couldn't understand his own behaviour.

He could hardly plead that he and Eva had been in a motel room, and the whole time the damn bed had been there—just *there*, mere feet away from them— the hugest temptation known to man.

At least Griff was certain of one thing. He knew that he wanted to be a part of Laine's future. And he was damned if he'd keep her a secret. She'd been a secret for far too long.

Strangely, his feelings about Laine were surprisingly clear-cut and straightforward. While his feelings for Eva—

Griff let out another heavy sigh. His feelings for Eva were a different matter entirely, defying reason and logic. Eva was like a drug for him, like pollen to a bee. Irresistible.

More than that, he now realised with a shock, his first girlfriend had remained the yardstick by which he'd measured every woman he'd met since. With the grand result that his love life was a stuffed-up mess.

'Oh, there you are!' Jane Simpson almost pounced on Eva as she arrived at the lunch. 'I was worried that you'd had to leave early and we'd missed saying goodbye.'

'No, still here. Sorry I'm late.' Eva reached into her shoulder bag. 'I found some *Swan Lake* programmes in my suitcase and I've signed them for your daughter and her friends. And Barney's daughter, Sophie, as well. I gather they're all ballet-mad.'

'Oh, Eva!' Jane's eyes were huge with excitement. 'How wonderful. The girls will be ecstatic.'

She studied the programmes Eva offered, looking with particular interest at the photo on the front cover of Eva dressed as Odette in a white tutu and the famous white feathered headdress.

Jane touched the signature scrawled in black ink. 'We'll have this framed. Our little Molly can hang it on her bedroom wall. She'll be so thrilled. All the girls will be. Eva, that's *so* thoughtful. Thank you.'

'Not at all. It's my pleasure.' Eva could see Griff at the far end of the room near the bar and, despite the magnetic pull of his tall, dark-haired, broad-shouldered physique, she was happy to linger with Jane and her circle. After the intensity of her weekend, it was a relief to listen to other people's holiday plans, or to answer their questions about her life overseas, or about her mother, whom many of her school friends remembered fondly.

Which was no surprise. Eva's mum had always come across as relaxed and easy-going, with a great sense of humour. The only subject Lizzie Hennessey had been serious and strict about was Eva's dancing and that hadn't happened until Eva was into her teens, when people in the know started to comment on her daughter's rather special talent.

To everyone else in Emerald Bay, Eva's mum, in her tie-dyed hippie sarongs and silver ankle bracelets, had always seemed laid-back, almost to the point of carelessness. Only Eva and her ballet teacher had seen Lizzie Hennessey's super-focused, competitive edge.

Eva was about to take her place at one of the long tables set for lunch when she noticed Laine moving among the guests with a drinks tray. It was hard to keep her eyes away from her daughter. Eva wanted to watch her every move, every smile. Was it her imagination, or did the girl look pale and tired?

Excusing herself, she made her way over to her. She took a deep breath. 'Hi, Laine.'

Laine turned to her and her smile brightened at once. 'Eva, hi.'

'I just wanted to catch you, in case you got too busy later. I'm sorry we haven't had more time to talk. It was such a shock to meet you last night.'

'Yes, I know.' The girl smiled, but her eyes were a little too shiny.

'I wanted to make sure I thanked you for coming here to the Bay, for finding me—finding both of us.' Eva took a quick calming breath. She was in danger of becoming too emotional again.

She handed Laine a piece of paper with her carefully written contact details. 'I'll be in Brisbane in a week or so.'

The girl's eyes widened. 'So we can meet up again? That'd be awesome. Griff and I are planning to catch up for coffee.'

'Oh?' So Griff had already spoken to their daughter. This was wonderful news, of course, a perfect outcome from an imperfect situation.

After Eva returned to Paris, Griff and Laine might continue to see each other regularly. Eva was dismayed by the ripple of envy this possibility caused.

'That's lovely,' she said. 'I really hope you can stay in contact with Griff.'

'Yes, he's rather cool, isn't he?'

The girl didn't know the half of it.

'Where's Laine?' a bossy woman's voice called sternly.

'I've got to get back to work.' Laine made a throat-cutting gesture with her finger.

The contact was far too brief.

'Please call me,' Eva called after her as she hurried away.

'Yes, of course,' Laine called back.

Eva's eyes were so misty she could barely see.

It wasn't till the end of the lunch that Eva spoke to Griff. The final speeches had been made and plans for an Emerald Bay High School Facebook page were launched, along with mention of another reunion in ten years' time.

Eva supposed everyone was wondering, as she was, where they might be or what they might be doing in another ten years. She certainly had no idea about her own future, although she was pretty sure she wouldn't still be dancing.

She wondered about Griff's plans. Would he become a judge like his older sister? And what about Laine? What would she be doing in another decade? This question brought an unexpected wave of desolation.

'Eva.'

She jumped when she heard Griff's voice close behind her. She turned quickly and wished her heart wouldn't leap at the mere sight of him.

'The boys and I will be heading off soon,' he said.

'Yes.' She rose from her chair. 'You're driving?'

'Yes, with Tim and Barney. What about you?'

'I'm flying back to Brisbane, then I have another flight up to Cairns first thing in the morning.'

He nodded. 'To spend time with your mother.'

'And her husband, yes.' Eva hated that their conversation was so stiff and careful, so different from their earlier steamy passion.

She had to forget that passion now. She had no rights to Griff. She'd given those away many years ago.

'And then I guess you'll be heading back to Paris?' he asked.

'More or less.' Again, Eva chose not to tell him about her surgery. The operation and the weeks of physiotherapy that would follow were ordeals she planned to endure in private.

It wasn't merely a matter of pride. The fewer people who knew about her condition, the fewer chances there were of word getting out and filtering back to her ballet company, damaging her career prospects.

Griff drew a deep breath that expanded his chest and made his shoulders seem wider than ever. 'It's been good to see you again, Eva.'

'You too.' She tried for a smile, but couldn't quite manage one. It didn't help that Griff looked as tense as she felt, and it certainly didn't help that her mind kept flashing to memories of him touching her, teasing her, bringing her to ecstasy.

'I'll try to keep an eye on Laine,' he said.

'Yes, she told me you were going to meet for coffee. That's great. I… I'm really pleased.'

Griff nodded and the muscles in his throat rippled as he swallowed.

It was tempting to believe, in this moment, that he cared, that he might even be keen to be a part of her future, but Eva knew this wasn't realistic. She shouldn't allow herself to be distracted by foolish whims. She had to remember the clear goals she'd set herself before she'd set out for this reunion.

A quick catch-up with her old school friends was to be followed by her surgery, and then her return to Paris.

She was going back to her lovely apartment, to her home. To the city she adored, to the career she cherished.

Her only focus now was to beat this hip problem, to remain dancing for as long as she could.

'I guess it's goodbye, then,' Griff said.

Goodbye. It shouldn't matter that it sounded so final but, for Eva, leaving Emerald Bay today suddenly felt as difficult as it had been twenty years ago, when she'd driven off with her mother and had wept all the way to Bowen.

Griff kissed her cheek and she suppressed a choked gasp, which could so easily have turned into a sob.

Be strong, Eva. Don't you dare make a scene.

'Goodbye, Griff,' she said, returning his kiss, and somehow she dredged up the semblance of a smile.

He gripped her hand hard and she saw the look in his eyes that she remembered from all those years ago, the look that told of a deep and powerful emotion. Just as it had in the past, the look reached deep inside her, wrenching at her heartstrings.

Now, as he stepped away, she had to open her eyes very wide to hold back the welling tears. Then he began to walk towards the door where his friends were, no doubt, waiting.

'Griff!' she called, his name springing from her lips instinctively.

When he turned to her, his eyes were once again cautious. 'Yes?'

'Can I just ask one question?'

'What is it?'

Eva took two steps closer. 'You never ever came to watch me dance, did you? Not to any of the concerts?'

A muscle twitched in his jaw. 'No, I'm afraid I didn't.'

Of course it shouldn't have still bothered her after all this time, but she couldn't help pushing for an answer. It was like picking at the scab of an itchy sore. 'Can you tell me why?'

At first he didn't respond, but then he gave a sad, off-kilter smile. 'It was never my world. But I knew you'd light up that stage. I didn't have to see you to know that. You were born to dance. Born to win.'

With that, he continued on his way. His back was straight and his shoulders squared, his head high, and this time he didn't turn back.

'Guess who turned up at the school reunion.'

Eva and her mum were drinking tea on the balcony of the new house in Cairns, which had been built by Lizzie's husband, who had his own building firm. It was a beautiful modern place, constructed of timber and with masses of glass, and set on a rainforest-covered hill with spectacular views of the Coral Sea. So different from the humble two-bedroom cottage that had been Lizzie and Eva's home in Emerald Bay.

Lizzie shrugged. 'How can I guess? I don't suppose your old boyfriend would have gone to a school reunion. He's such a bigwig these days. What's his name again?'

'Oh, Mum, don't pretend you've forgotten. You know it's Griff. Griffin Fletcher.' Even the simple act of saying his name aloud sent a jolt through Eva. 'And Griff *was* there, as a matter of fact, although I don't think it was voluntary on his part. I suspect his mates, Tim and Barney, dragged him there, virtually kicking and screaming. But someone else was there too.'

Her mother frowned. These days she had replaced her hand-dyed sarongs with much more elegant clothes, like the white linen trousers and green silk shirt she was wearing now. Her frizzy and greying ginger hair had been professionally straightened and bleached to a sleek and sophisticated ash-blonde bob, and her toe-nails and fingernails were carefully painted. But, despite the new glamour, Lizzie looked uncomfortable now, as if she sensed that Eva might be trying to catch her out.

'Well, I can only assume it has to be one of your classmates, Eva. I'm sure Jane Simpson would have been there. But heavens, I can't be expected to remember all their names.'

'Laine was there too,' Eva said quietly.

A fearful light crept into Lizzie's eyes. 'Laine? Not…not your…' She stopped, as if she couldn't bring herself to finish the sentence.

Eva nodded. 'My baby. Your granddaughter.'

Lizzie swore softly, an echo from her rougher past. 'How on earth—?' She swallowed, looked distressed.

'Laine was working there as a waitress, Mum. She'd found out that both Griff and I were going to be there and she managed to score a casual job, just for the weekend.'

Lizzie paled, gave a dazed shake of her head. 'For

heaven's sake.' She reached for her teacup but her hand was shaking and she set it down quickly, clattering against the saucer. Eventually, she asked, 'What's she like?'

Eva could well imagine her mum's shock and she gave her as many details as efficiently as she could, explaining about Laine's appearance, her adoptive parents, her law studies.

'How amazing,' Lizzie said when Eva had finished, and she looked much calmer now. 'Well, I guess that's all turned out lovely, hasn't it?'

'In some ways,' Eva agreed.

'In every way, Eva. You were able to have your brilliant career. And I'm sure Laine made the Templetons very happy, and it seems they've looked after her beautifully and sent her to uni and everything. I can't see any downsides.'

'Except for the fact that I've missed her,' Eva said in a voice tightly choked by emotion. 'I've missed my daughter dreadfully, Mum, every day for the past nineteen years.' As she said this, the pain welled inside her again, bringing with it a rising tide of misery. Eva closed her eyes and pressed a hand to her mouth to hold back the threatening sobs.

'Oh, Eva.' There was sympathy in her mother's voice, but exasperation too. 'You can't mean that, darling. Don't exaggerate. You've been so busy with your dancing. It's been such a wonderful and fulfilling career for you.'

'Oh, yes,' Eva said tightly. 'Of course, I've had my dancing.'

And she heard Griff's voice.

You were born to dance. Born to win.

The struggle with her tears was huge, but she was determined not to give in. Not now, in front of her mother. She'd shed enough tears in the past couple of days to last her a lifetime. But, given the pain she felt now, Eva had to wonder why on earth she'd thought it was a good idea to come back to Australia.

If she'd stayed in Paris, she could have kept herself cocooned, safe from the truth. Her loss would have been there like a stone in her heart, but Laine wouldn't have been a visible fact, living and breathing and real. The pain wouldn't have been nearly as intense and unbearable as it was now.

Now, having seen Laine and Griff again, Eva knew exactly what she'd lost and it was hard to believe that she had ever thought that dancing was more important than those two very special human beings.

Even the knowledge that Laine had been well cared for wasn't nearly as comforting as it should have been. It could never undo the fact that Eva had given away her precious baby, and had denied herself the chance to be with Griff, as his lover, as his life partner, as the mother of his child.

'You're not blaming me for this, are you?' Lizzie asked in a soft, almost frightened voice. 'Do you think I forced you to…to give Laine away?'

It would have been so easy to lay the blame at her mum's feet, but Eva couldn't be so cruel. Besides, she knew it wouldn't relieve her pain. Seeing her mother's distress would only make everything worse.

'No,' she said firmly. 'I'm not blaming you, Mum. Ultimately, it was my decision.'

'But I do feel guilty,' Lizzie said.

Eva managed a small smile. 'I'm beginning to suspect that most mothers manage to find reasons to feel guilty, no matter how hard they try to do the right thing.'

Lizzie watched her for a moment with sorrowful eyes, then she smiled sadly and rose from her seat, arms outstretched. 'Come here,' she said. 'I'm sure a hug always helps.'

As her mum's arms closed around her, Lizzie wished she and Laine had hugged like this. It was true. A hug always helped.

Then she spoilt the moment by wishing she'd received a healing hug of forgiveness from Griff. Their passion had been something else entirely.

CHAPTER SIX

ON THE SECOND day after her surgery, Eva could walk with the help of crutches, and she was returning from the bathroom when she saw a tall masculine figure standing at the end of her bed. Not a white-coated doctor, but Griff in a dark suit and tie. She was so surprised she almost stumbled.

Griff quickly stepped to her aid, cupping her elbow with a steadying hand. 'I didn't mean to startle you,' he said. 'Are you OK?'

'Yes, of course,' she responded a little too abruptly. 'What are you doing here?'

It was only then that she saw how worried he looked.

'I came to ask you the same question. What happened, Eva?'

'It's just my hip,' she reassured him, adding a shrug to show that it was no big deal.

Griff's relief was obvious and Eva wondered what he'd imagined might be wrong with her. The fact that he'd been worried bothered her. He wasn't supposed to care. They were going their separate ways now.

'Can I help you back into bed?' he asked.

Eva had been managing this by herself, but that was without the weak knees that Griff's presence caused.

'Thank you.' Despite the shock of his sudden arrival, combined with the embarrassment of being caught in her nightgown and without any make-up, she was truly grateful for his strong arm around her as she eased onto the bed and then carefully negotiated the new hip into position, bolstered by a pillow.

Nevertheless, she felt compelled to quiz Griff as soon as she was settled with more pillows plumped behind her. 'How on earth did you know I was here?'

'Laine told me.'

'Laine?' This didn't make sense. 'But how did she know? I certainly didn't tell her.' So far, Eva had only exchanged a few brief text messages with their daughter. She'd been determined to lie low until her hip was properly healed. Now, she couldn't decide whether she was pleased or dismayed to have been caught out. By Griff, of all people.

To make matters more complicated, instead of sitting in the available chair like any normal, polite visitor, Griff had taken off his jacket and tossed it onto the visitor's chair, then loosened his collar and tie and perched on the edge of Eva's bed.

He looked far too sexy. Eva found herself taking far too keen an interest in the way he looked. She couldn't help admiring the strong lines of his clean-shaven jaw, the expensive cloth of his trousers, the crispness of his white shirt and the way his shoulders filled it, almost straining the seams. She supposed he'd come straight to the hospital from court.

'Laine tried to ring you,' he explained. 'But you were just coming out of the anaesthetic. Apparently, the nurse who was with you tried to hand you the phone, but you were too groggy. The nurse was very apologetic, and Laine couldn't get any more out of her after that.'

Griff gave a shrugging smile. 'So then she rang me. We realised you must be in a hospital and we were worried, of course, but I managed to track you down. I happen to know one or two doctors who work at this hospital.'

'You and Laine are becoming quite a team,' she said, hoping she didn't sound too crushed.

'Well, it's early days. But she seems open to having a relationship. And I want that chance, Eva.'

'Yes. Of course.' Eva felt hope bloom. Until now, she hadn't dared to hope that she and Laine might be able to bridge the chasm of years and secrecy. Was it possible? For her and for Griff?

In a few weeks she would return to Paris, but Griff and Laine would continue to see each other. Over the coming months, they could become closer and closer.

She quickly stifled the niggle of jealousy that this scenario kindled, and she realised that Griff was frowning, eyeing her sternly now.

'So what's the story, Eva?' he asked. 'What's your situation? I assume you've had some kind of surgery?'

'A hip replacement,' she said with an accompanying eye-roll. 'It makes me sound like a granny, doesn't it?'

He gave an awkward smile and shrugged. 'I'm sure that must be painful. How are you feeling?'

Old, stiff and sore. 'Wonderful,' she lied. 'I'm making fabulous progress, so I'm told.'

'That's great. And you're super fit from your dancing, so I'm sure you'll break records when it comes to healing and rehabilitation.'

Well, yes, she needed to break *world* records if she

was to return to dancing as a prima ballerina. The thought of the weeks of hard work ahead of her was a daunting one, but she'd been tough in the past and she supposed she could be tough again.

'So how long will you be in hospital?' Griff asked.

'Probably only another day.'

'And what then?'

'I'm moving into an apartment nearby and a nurse and physiotherapist will visit.'

Griff was frowning again. 'It won't be much fun, stuck in an apartment on your own.'

'This isn't about having fun, Griff. It's about recovery. Anyway, I live in an apartment on my own in Paris.'

'That's different.'

Eva dropped her gaze. She was very aware of how gruelling the next couple of weeks would be. And yes, it was true that her life in Paris was very different. In Paris, she spent most of her time at the dance studios or rehearsing or performing. In her spare time she visited her friends, or hung out with them at a variety of fascinating venues. Even when she was on her own, there were galleries, theatres, cafés and gardens all within an easy walking distance.

'I'll be fine, Griff. I plan to get plenty of reading done.' She tilted her chin to a determined angle.

Griff didn't look impressed.

Eva was putting on a brave front, Griff decided.

He watched her grim little smile, the wariness in her eyes and he was sure she was trying very hard to hide how vulnerable and scared she felt.

After all, she'd put everything she had into her career. She'd given up her child for it, and now she faced the very real danger of losing everything she'd worked so hard to attain.

And now she was going to vanish from his life again, hiding away in some grim apartment until she was well enough to hurry back to Paris, leaving him with a raft of unanswered questions.

Who was Eva Hennessey now? Really? How did she truly feel about Laine? Who were the men in her life? For that matter, how did she feel about him?

At the Bay, their bubbling chemistry had been out of control and it had got in the way of sensible, useful conversation. After they'd made love, they'd both been so careful, so worried about saying the wrong thing.

Griff, however, was a man who liked to have answers. In his work, he applied himself diligently to understanding his clients, to getting to the truth.

And yet Eva, his first love and the mother of his child, was still an enigma.

'You're very welcome to stay at my house,' he said.

Eva knew she must look shocked. She was. Totally. Shocked. Not only was Griff's proposal a bolt from the blue, it was unwise from every angle.

'I couldn't possibly stay at your place,' she said in a breathless whisper.

To her annoyance, Griff merely smiled. 'Ah, but that's where you're wrong. It would be *very* possible for you to stay there. My house is quite roomy. It's all on one level, so it's easy to get around. It's also fairly central, so it's not too far for a nurse or physiotherapist to travel. And I have an exercise bike and a swimming pool, which I'm sure would be quite useful for your rehabilitation.'

This did sound wonderfully convenient, but Eva was sure spending more time with Griff would be totally unwise. They'd said their goodbyes at Emerald Bay and she'd spent most of her time in Cairns carefully filing her memories of Griff Fletcher back where they belonged. Well and truly behind her. In the past. Yet again.

Or at least she'd been *trying* to file them away, with disappointingly poor success.

'Look,' he said, watching her carefully. 'I know this is awkward, after what happened at the Bay.'

What happened at the Bay...

Such a causal summing up of their lovemaking, which had been for Eva the most passionate and beautiful encounter of her adult life.

Griff's expression was guarded now, and he swallowed as if he might be more nervous than she'd first imagined. Even so, the flash in his eyes set sparks inside her.

'I know jumping into bed wasn't our smartest move,' he said. 'But perhaps it was something that had to happen.'

'I suppose you're talking about closure,' Eva said quietly.

'Something like that, yes.'

An awkward silence fell. Eva made a show of smoothing the bed sheet over her legs.

'The point is,' Griff went on, 'I'm not trying to entice you to my place now for any other reason than friendship.' Without waiting for her response, he rose from the edge of her bed and walked to the window, staring intently out.

She knew there was nothing to interest him out there—nothing more than the other hospital buildings.

'I don't like to think of you holed up in some apartment when my place is available,' he said quietly, still facing the window.

After a bit, he turned back to her and his eyes betrayed the merest hint of a smile. 'I've done my best to reassure you, Eva. You don't need to look so worried.'

It might be simple for him to make this offer but, obviously, he had no idea how susceptible she was. How vulnerable. He didn't understand that being with him again brought everything back. All the old longing and pain and hope and despair.

'It's very kind of you,' she began.

He was waiting for her to continue, to accept or reject his offer, and Eva knew it was time to make her own position crystal-clear.

'I'll be leaving Australia as soon as I can, Griff. I'm going back to Paris. I've set myself a huge goal, you see.'

'That's commendable.'

She shook her head to make her point. 'You asked me if I had a retirement plan, but I don't have one at the moment. I don't want to think about retirement. My goal is to keep dancing for as long as I can.'

'I certainly don't want to stand in your way,' he said firmly. A beat later, he shot her a searching glance. 'But can you really dance at the same professional level that you're used to, after a hip replacement?'

'It's been done.' Eva shoved her chin even more stubbornly forward. 'It's not common, I must admit, but I plan to give it a jolly good try. I certainly won't give up easily.'

'Of course you won't.' This time there was no hint of amusement in Griff's smile. 'And I wouldn't expect anything less from you.' With his back to the window now, he folded his arms over his chest. 'It doesn't change my invitation, Eva. You're welcome to use my house as a staging post.'

'But—'

'Relax, woman. How many times do I have to tell you this isn't a devious plot to try to win you back?'

'No, I know.' Just the same, it was useful to have this point clarified yet again, and Eva hoped Griff couldn't guess the many stupid scenarios her stupid brain had already imagined.

'At my place, you'll almost certainly have more opportunities to see Laine,' he added.

Yes, Eva had already thought of that tempting prospect and, despite her fears, she could feel herself weakening.

Now Griff stepped away from the window and scooped up his jacket from the chair. Hooking it with two fingers, he slung it casually over one shoulder, a simple gesture that should not have made him look hotter than ever.

'You don't have to give me an answer now,' he said. 'Think about it. I'll give you a call tomorrow.'

'All right.' Eva swallowed. 'And thanks,' she remembered to add quickly, when he was almost out of the door.

'No worries.'

As Griff steered his car back into the heavy lanes of city traffic that streamed past the hospital, he told himself he'd done the right thing by inviting Eva into his home, back into his life.

She was recovering from surgery, after all, so of course they weren't going to be tempted into further indiscretions of the bedroom variety. His invitation truly was, as he'd told her, no more than an offer from an old friend. A friend who needed to lay to rest a few ghosts.

It helped that Eva was as determined as ever to return to her dancing career. It made their ground rules clearer.

Of course they could both handle the proximity without another juvenile meltdown. For God's sake, they were middle-aged people with an adult daughter. It made sense that they should develop a friendly basis for further communication.

The plan was sensible. His motives were rock-solid.

The fact that he'd been scared witless when he'd heard that Eva was in hospital was no longer relevant. She was obviously fine now. He had calmed down and he wouldn't worry like that again.

In fact, a couple of weeks of closer proximity with Eva Hennessey might very well cure him of any lingering lovelorn emotions from his youth. Getting to know her on a purely friendly basis might even clear the way for him to move forward with his personal life. Finally.

A guy could always hope.

Eva caved in. The decision wasn't easy and she spent a sleepless night. The temptation to spend more time with Griff was both exciting and scary, but the added allure of the chance to get to know Laine was, in the end, too strong. For the past ten days, Eva had thought about her daughter constantly, remembering how she'd looked in her black and white waitress uniform and asking herself so many questions. She was curious about even the tiniest details—even how her daughter might look in clothes of her own choosing.

Did Laine prefer jeans and T-shirts to dresses? Did she like florals or stripes? Was she a fan of solid colours, or didn't she really care? Eva's curiosity about her daughter was voracious, and the next morning, when Griff rang, she accepted his kind invitation.

He picked her up from the hospital that evening in a sleek silver Mercedes with luxuriously soft leather upholstery. He drove expertly through the peak hour traffic, and they arrived at his place, as he'd promised, inside fifteen minutes.

Griff's house was set back from the street behind a tall brick wall painted grey. The house was very modern, with large windows framed in natural timber and concrete walls painted in a slate tone that blended subtly with the garden of native Australian plants. Remote-controlled garage doors slid quietly open, but Griff stopped the car on the driveway and helped Eva out of her seat.

She willed herself not to react every time he touched her. He was only giving her the assistance she needed, after all, but so far her willpower wasn't as effective as she'd hoped. His hand at her elbow or at the small of her back caused ridiculous flashes of heat.

At the front door, she was greeted by a smiling woman with her hair in a tight bun, wearing an old-fashioned apron over her simple blue dress.

'This is Malina,' Griff said. 'She runs my house like a dream and she has everything ready for you.'

Malina was delightfully round, with rosy cheeks and

a strong accent that was possibly Polish. While Griff garaged the car, Malina showed Eva to a beautiful spacious bedroom decorated in contemporary tones and with a soft grey fitted carpet. A huge white bed had a rose-pink mohair throw rug folded over the foot and a mountain of pillows in grey and deep pink at its head. A television was positioned for viewing from the bed.

A door led to an en suite bathroom where soaps and lotions and thick fluffy towels were neatly stowed on glass shelving. On the bedroom's opposite wall, a huge picture window looked out onto a hillside covered in bush.

'Ohh…'

Eva stood very still, entranced by the beautiful view of the hillside covered in gum trees with spotted trunks and softly drooping leaves. Every so often, there was the golden glow of wattle flowers and tufts of pale grass stalks sprouted between granite boulders. It was all so distinctly Australian, and so wonderfully quiet and peaceful.

She found it hard to believe that there was a busy road filled with heavy traffic only a block away. Goodness, she could even see a brush turkey, black-feathered with a red and gold frill around its scrawny neck, pecking its way down the hillside on spindly legs.

A wave of nostalgia swept through her and she knew Griff had been right. This was a perfect place for her to rest and to recuperate. And to heal.

'I'll show you the kitchen,' Malina said. 'So you can find the kettle and make yourself a cup of tea or coffee whenever you fancy.'

'Thank you.' Eva followed, walking carefully with the aid of her crutches.

* * *

Malina, having left their dinner in the oven, went home and Eva and Griff ate roast lamb and a warm mushroom and spinach salad at one end of the dining table. From here, subtle outdoor lighting showed them a view of the long timber deck that surrounded an elegant swimming pool.

'You have a beautiful home,' Eva told Griff. 'I can see why you love living here.'

He looked pleased. 'I'm glad you like it.'

'I especially love the view of the bushy hillside from my room. I even saw a brush turkey.'

'You'll see plenty of them here. And rock wallabies too.'

'Wallabies!' She smiled. 'Then I'll really know I'm home.'

'Home?' Griff raised a questioning eyebrow.

'In Australia,' Eva quickly clarified.

'So you still think of Australia as home?'

'Well…yes. I… I guess.' It was unsettling to realise that right at this moment her lovely apartment and the glittering Eiffel Tower felt light years away. It was almost as if they were part of another world, a make-believe world, like the props and scenery on the stages where she'd danced.

It was a timely reminder that she had to be super-careful while she was here. She mustn't be seduced by this gorgeous man's kindness, by his lovely home, or by the history they shared. They'd made a pact and it was important to honour it. She had to remember the goals she'd set herself—to return to Paris as strong and supple as ever.

Surely it shouldn't be too hard to remember everything she'd worked so hard to achieve over the past twenty years?

* * *

All went well over the next few days. The nurse and the physiotherapist seemed quite happy to visit Eva in Griff's house, and Eva continued to make good, steady progress.

Eva rarely saw Griff in the mornings before he left for work. During the day, Malina was there to provide her with light nourishing meals, and Eva conscientiously went through the gentle exercises she'd been given. Between eating and exercising, she enjoyed reading books from Griff's extensive library.

In the evenings she and Griff had dinner together, and these times became incredibly precious to Eva. She knew she shouldn't look forward so eagerly to their conversations, but she found it fascinating to mesh images of the old Griff she knew from Emerald Bay with the man he'd become.

Primed with a glass of very fine wine, they talked—carefully at first, like old friends who'd been out of touch for twenty years—about the places they'd visited, about music and movies. Griff told Eva about a few of the more fascinating cases he'd been involved with, and she talked about her life in the ballet world. They'd both come across fascinating, eccentric characters and the conversations were often lively and fun.

Eventually they became bolder, even stepping into more dangerous ground by talking about religion and politics and they were surprised to discover how often their views converged.

For many nights they avoided talking about their relationships, but eventually Griff prodded Eva.

'I can't believe you haven't had hordes of men throwing themselves at your feet.'

And so Eva told him about Vasily.

'Eight years?' Griff said, eyeing her with obvious sympathy. 'That's a long time to invest in a relationship that doesn't work out.'

'It is,' she agreed but, remarkably, the pain of losing Vasily seemed to have lost its sting since she'd returned to Australia. Not that she would admit such a thing to this man and he made no further comment.

Their partings each evening were super-careful. No touching, not even a kiss on the cheek. They were sticking to the rules they'd set, but Eva couldn't help noticing that this seemed to be much easier for Griff than it was for her.

Each night when she retired to her room, she spent ridiculous ages thinking about him, replaying in her head everything that he'd said, every gesture, every look. She knew she was falling for him again, even though it was dangerous and stupid.

The days were easier. Each day she felt stronger and could move more easily and she was growing more confident that she really could achieve her goal of returning to the stage.

She just wished she felt happier about that.

CHAPTER SEVEN

IT WAS A few nights later that Griff received a phone call from Laine.

'Can I come round to talk to you and Eva?' she asked. 'It's rather important.'

Excitement and worry duelled inside Griff. He wondered if he should consult with Eva about this, but he was sure she would want this meeting with their daughter. Lately her conversations had often drifted towards Laine. And they were both over the shock now and more than ready to get to know Laine.

'Of course you can come,' he told her. 'But try to make it soon if you can. Eva shouldn't stay up too late.'

'That's nice that you're fussing over her,' Laine said.

'I'm not fussing.' He was being sensible.

Laine actually laughed. ''Course you are.'

Griff suppressed a sigh. 'Just try and keep an eye on the time, that's all I'm saying.'

'I'm on my way.'

He was frowning as he disconnected. He hoped his instincts were right and that he and Eva were more than ready to take this next step.

He found Eva in the lounge room, sitting in an armchair in a pool of lamplight that made her soft, pale skin glow and her dark hair shine like a river of silk. The urge to scoop her up out of that chair and into his arms was as strong as ever.

Damn. He'd thought it would be easier than this.

At least he'd *hoped* it would be easier to have Eva in his home. He'd hoped that after a few days, when he got to know the real, grown-up Eva rather than his romanticised boyhood memory, he would see her imperfections and become a little disenchanted.

Sadly, this wasn't the case.

'That was Laine on the phone,' he told her. 'She wants to come over to talk to us.'

'What did you tell her?' Eva asked quickly. 'You said yes, didn't you?'

'I did.'

'But you're worried? You look upset.'

'Do I?' Hastily, Griff feigned surprise. He was only upset because he still fancied Eva. That wasn't supposed to have happened. 'I'm fine,' he said. 'I think Laine sounded quite excited, actually.'

Eva looked excited now. Her eyes were bright, her cheeks flushed and she got to her feet perhaps a little more eagerly than she should have. 'I've been so hoping for this. Should we offer her some supper?'

'I guess.' Griff held up a hand to slow her down. 'But stay there while I get your crutches.'

'No, I'm OK. I've been walking without them. What would Laine like, do you think?'

Griff watched Eva for a moment, unable to stop himself from staring at her rosy cheeks and shiny blue eyes.

'What?' she said.

Had she any idea how lovely she looked when she was excited?

Her flush deepened under his gaze, but then she looked away, her mouth twisting anxiously. Had she guessed the crazy direction of his thoughts?

'Why don't we check out the freezer?' he replied without answering her question.

'Good idea.' Eva set off purposefully towards the kitchen. 'That Malina of yours is such a gem. She's bound to have just the right thing tucked away in there.'

Eva's heart took off like a rocket when she heard the doorbell ring. Griff went ahead to answer it, and Eva followed as quickly as she could.

Laine was dressed in jeans and a simple paisley print top in shades of lavender and aqua blue. It was the kind of top Eva might have bought for herself if she'd seen it in a shop and she felt a happy-sad pang as she recognised another point of connection to the girl.

Her daughter.

She wondered how she should greet her. A kiss on the cheek? A hug?

No, not yet. She didn't want to rush the poor girl.

'I'm so pleased that you're staying at Griff's place,' Laine said after they'd exchanged polite cheek kisses.

'Yes, it's very kind of him.'

'Kind?' Laine laughed.

Of course Eva was anxious to set the girl straight. 'Laine, you mustn't read anything into this. I'm just staying here while I get over the surgery.'

'Yeah, I know, I know. Griff went to great lengths to explain that you haven't been in touch and have a lot to catch up on.'

But the amusement in the girl's eyes suggested that she still thought there was something deeper going on.

'Yes, well—' Slightly rattled, Eva managed to keep her smile firmly in place as she gestured down the hallway. 'Come in, Laine. Will you have a cuppa?'

They all opted for tea and Griff insisted on looking after this as he didn't want Eva struggling to carry a tea tray, so she found herself in the lounge room with Laine.

Laine seemed quite relaxed, at least on the outside, Eva was pleased to see. While Griff disappeared into the kitchen, Laine asked Eva about her healing hip, and Eva asked her about her studies.

She felt surprisingly calmer when Griff reappeared, handing around mugs and offering the tiny cherry lattice tarts that Eva had instructed him to reheat in the microwave.

Seeing father and daughter together now, Eva noticed similarities between them. The shape of Laine's forehead, the same shade of grey in her darkly lashed eyes, the way she squinted ever so slightly when she smiled.

The girl was sitting with her long legs comfortably crossed. The hem of her jeans rode up a little and Eva could see her shapely ankle and the small butterfly-shaped birthmark she remembered so well.

Stay calm. Remember to breathe.

'These are delicious,' Laine said as she munched on a cherry tart. 'Did you make them, Eva?'

'Um, no.' Eva felt a bit of a fraud, recalling how happy she'd been when she'd found these tarts, as if somehow she'd created them with her own fair hands. In truth, she had very few domestic skills, and she was especially lacking when it came to baking. She'd always been so careful about her diet. 'Griff's house-keeper made them. I just chose them to go with our tea.'

'Well, they're divine.' Laine licked crumbs from her fingers.

'I imagine you have all sorts of questions,' Griff said to Laine.

'Hundreds,' the girl admitted. 'For starters, I was intrigued that you both kept quite separate at that re-union. It was really hard to find the two of you to-gether.'

'That's easy to explain,' said Griff. 'Neither of us knew the other was going to be there.'

'Really?' Laine's eyes widened with obvious sur-prise. 'So you didn't communicate beforehand?'

Eva and Griff both shook their heads.

'You mean…you two really haven't been in touch?'

'Not for—' Eva swallowed. 'No, we haven't.'

Laine gave a puzzled shake of her head. 'How long had it been since you'd seen each other?'

Eva avoided making eye contact with Griff, but there was no point in skirting the truth. 'Not since I left the Bay. Twenty years ago.'

'Oh, my God.' Laine's eyes were huge as she took this information in. 'You mean…you only met again at this reunion?'

'Yes.'

Laine turned to Griff. 'So am I right in guessing that you didn't even know about me?'

Eva, sitting in an opposite chair, tensed, clutching her mug of tea.

'No, I didn't,' Griff told her calmly.

Laine swore softly and she no longer looked quite

so cheerful. 'So you only found out about me when I burst in on you at the reunion?'

Griff nodded, and Eva realised she was holding her breath.

Laine looked pale as she stared at her father. 'What was it like to find out now, after all this time?'

'A shock, of course.' Griff seemed to be searching for the right things to say, and Eva could imagine him discarding words that were too close to the gut-wrenching devastation that he must have felt on that fateful evening. 'The main thing is,' he said at last, and he even managed to smile, 'I'm very, very happy to know you now.'

Laine nodded, momentarily silenced, but eventually she turned to Eva with clear grey eyes so like Griff's. 'Can I ask why you didn't tell him?'

Whack. It was the question Eva had known must come, but she still wasn't prepared. Where should she start?

In the past she'd excused herself by loading a good share of the blame onto her mother and Griff. This evening she didn't want to lay blame at anyone else's feet. She knew it was time to accept that the final decision had been hers. But how could she justify her choice of a career over mothering her very own baby?

'There were several very good reasons,' Griff said, gallantly intervening on Eva's behalf.

'Well, I really need to hear them,' said Laine. 'I want to know why you made the decisions you made and how you feel about them now. It's very important to me.' Laine looked from one parent to the other, her expression super-serious and intense. 'You see, I'm pregnant.'

* * *

Eva wasn't sure whose jaw dropped faster—hers or Griff's. For a moment she could only stare at Laine in shock but, as the truth sank in, she was out of her chair, opening her arms to her daughter. For an awkward moment, she was poised like a bird about to take flight, but then Laine rose too, shyly at first, but at last, with a sob, she launched forward.

'Oh!' she cried as Eva's arms closed around her.

And then they were hugging. Mother and daughter, weeping and clinging tight. Eva could feel Laine's shoulders shaking, could feel her daughter's warm arms wrapped around her, feel her own love, pouring like a flood.

Twenty years of longing. And now, here was her precious daughter, facing the same potential pain and loss that had caused her so much heartbreak.

They were like this for some time before she remembered Griff. Poor man, standing there beside them, watching on helplessly.

With an effort, Eva released Laine and swiped at her eyes with her hands. 'Gosh, look at us. I think there's a box of tissues here somewhere.'

'I'll get them,' Griff offered, clearly relieved to at last have something to do.

Promptly, he returned from the kitchen with a full box of tissues and Laine and Eva took handfuls and mopped at their faces.

'What a pair we are,' Eva said, managing a small smile.

Laine smiled wanly back at her. They sat down again and picked up their cooling mugs of tea, and Eva wondered if they had woven the first delicate threads in a new but fragile bond. She only wished that the circumstances could have been happier.

Griff retrieved his mug but he remained standing, almost as if he needed to distance himself from their overt feminine displays of emotion. Eva sent him a rueful smile of gratitude and wondered if he was plotting for a quick retreat.

His response was to raise his eyebrows, as if to ask—*where do we go from here?*

It was Laine who spoke first. 'I know it's crazy that I'm pregnant too. Like history repeating itself.'

'For the third time,' said Eva.

Laine frowned at her. 'The third time?'

'My mother was a single mum too. She had me when she was only nineteen.'

Now it was Laine whose jaw dropped. 'Wow.'

Eva offered Laine another shaky smile. 'I'm sorry. I really am sorry for you, Laine. It's a hard place to find yourself, especially hard when you've just started your university studies.'

'Yes,' said Laine. 'Life can be messy, can't it?' She looked at Eva over the rim of her tea mug. 'So, were you adopted too?'

Eva had to take a deep breath before she could answer. 'No,' she said quietly. 'No—my mother raised me on her own—as a single mum.'

Unlike me. Tears threatened again and Eva closed her eyes, drew another deep breath and willed herself not to give in to the urge to weep.

To her surprise, she felt a hand on her shoulder. Griff was standing behind her now and he gave her shoulder a reassuring squeeze. She felt a warm surge of gratitude, but it wasn't helpful to realise after all this time that she might have underestimated this man's capacity for compassion.

'Eva was under a lot of pressure back then,' he said.

'Because of the dancing?' Laine asked.

'Yes,' Griff and Eva answered together. Eva looked up at him and felt a zap of electricity shooting over her skin. It was there again in his eyes—the shimmering look she had never forgotten.

Laine was watching them closely. 'You have an amazing talent, Eva, so I can imagine the pressure.' She set her mug down, folded her arms and crossed her legs. 'I'm not especially talented. I did pretty well at school, but nothing amazing, but I still feel the pressure to just…get rid of this problem.'

Restless, she uncrossed her legs again, sat straighter. 'I haven't told my parents yet—not my adoptive parents at least—or my boyfriend. I'm really struggling with trying to work out what to do. But I'm running out of time. I'm going to have to decide soon. I'd be grateful for any advice. Any words of wisdom.'

Nervously, Eva ran her tongue over her dry lips and she wished she felt wiser. Surely she should have learned some important lessons from her own experiences?

'If you're wondering whether I have regrets about giving you away,' she said, 'I have to tell you that I do.'

Laine nodded, and then she pressed her lips together, as if she was also trying not to cry again. 'But you've had a wonderful career,' she said.

'Yes, I have,' Eva agreed and, until now, she had clung to that career almost as if it were a life raft. But this evening, so far away from Europe, here in Australia with this man and their daughter, she found it hard to remember exactly why her dancing had ever been so all-consuming.

'My parents—the Templetons—are good, ordinary, hard-working people,' said Laine. 'My dad's a teacher and my mum works as an aid in a kindergarten. They've been saving like mad and they're about to go on their first overseas trip. An extended holiday. They're so happy and excited and I'd hate to ruin it by giving them something like this to worry about.'

She sighed. 'As for my boyfriend—he's a med student.' She gave a small uncertain shrug. 'I'm sure he'd be horrified if he had to admit to his circle of very clever friends that he'd slipped up and made his girlfriend pregnant.'

'But you can't be sure that's how he'd react,' said Griff, speaking up for the first time.

Laine frowned up at him. 'I guess—'

'Aren't you planning to tell this fellow?' Griff challenged.

The girl gave a helpless shrug. 'I… I don't know. I'm sure he has no plans to settle down. I'm not sure I want to either. At…at the time, I thought we were madly in love, but we're certainly not…we weren't planning to tie the knot.'

A small silence fell and Eva was aware of the three of them mentally tiptoeing carefully as they negotiated this difficult conversation.

Laine said, 'I was thinking of doing what you did, Eva—having the baby adopted. I mean, I really want to finish my degree, and I can't imagine trying to study and look after a baby on my own, and I don't want to burden my parents just when they're trying to wind down and—'

She looked up, looked directly at Eva, her lovely eyes pleading. 'Was it worth it? Giving me up so you could have your career?'

Eva's heart thumped hard. She'd been terrified of something happening at the reunion, but she'd never dreamed it would end up like this. Now, not only were the secrets from her past exposed but they were being taken out and examined, prodded and questioned. And she had no choice but to face up to the painful truth she'd avoided for so long.

This was no time for cowardice. She had to dig deep, to find the courage to be honest with Laine.

'I can't tell you what to do,' she said, carefully feeling her way forward. 'I have the benefit of hindsight, but you're young and you're facing a very difficult decision.' She swallowed and pushed on. 'It seems to me that difficult choices are hard because there are reasonable arguments on every side. But I think the thing to remember is that giving up a child is not a one-time event. I was told the pain would be temporary, but—'

Eva's mouth pulled out of shape and she had to wait and take a breath before she could go on. 'But it wasn't. The pain's stayed there. And I've relived that day over and over.'

Tears shone in Laine's eyes.

'And,' Eva added without looking Griff's way, 'I feel bad, *really* bad, that I denied a man the right to have a relationship with his own child.'

'I… I see.' Laine looked towards Griff. Her chin trembled and the emotion shining in her eyes spoke volumes.

Eventually, she turned back to Eva. 'But I guess the upside for you is that you're world-famous now.'

Eva shivered. 'That makes me sound so selfish.'

'But it would have been hard to give that up. You must have known when you were young that you had a huge talent. Not many people get to be a prima ballerina.'

'No,' Eva said, but she had to look away, unable to meet the direct grey gaze that reminded her so much of Griff's.

It was difficult to believe that leaving Paris and coming back to Australia could so completely shift her perspective but, right now, none of her choices made the same clear and perfect sense that they always had in the past. Nevertheless, she didn't want to burden Laine with her own crazy confusion.

'I suppose my best advice,' she said carefully, 'is to follow your own heart. Make the choice that's right for you, but also don't jump to conclusions about what other people might be thinking. Griff's right—you should talk to your boyfriend.'

'Right. OK, thanks.' Laine looked at her wristwatch. 'I guess I'd better get going. I promised I wouldn't keep you up too late.'

'I'm fine,' Eva protested, but Laine was already on her feet. 'Thanks for this chance to chat,' she said. 'It's been pretty mind-blowing to meet you guys and I know you can't solve my problems, but it's been really helpful to talk. And…and to get to know you a bit.'

'Well, you know where we are and we're both very keen to stay in touch,' Eva said, also getting to her feet. She tried to smile, but this evening had been so precious. If she wasn't careful, she'd become too emotional again.

Laine must have felt the same way. Having told them

that she was leaving, she was backing away fast, but she gave them a teary smile and blew them a kiss as she hurried to the door.

Eva didn't follow as Griff accompanied her. She heard the soft murmur of their voices as they bade each other goodnight and she thought how incredibly fortunate she was that neither Griff nor Laine had been bitter or resentful.

This scene could have been so much uglier.

Letting out a deep breath, she sank into her chair, exhausted. But she was exhilarated too.

She'd met Laine at last. Properly. She now knew exactly what her daughter looked like, how her voice sounded, how she liked her tea.

She looked towards Griff as he returned and lowered himself into a chair opposite her.

'We didn't think to take a photo,' she said.

He rolled his eyes, gave a crooked smile. 'Possibly because there were higher priorities?'

'Yes, of course.'

'And you would have hated the photo, anyway. Your face is all puffy from crying.'

'Yes, I suppose I must look a fright.' Thank heavens she wasn't wearing stage make-up.

They sat for a moment in silence, a surprisingly comfortable silence.

'You did well, Eva,' Griff said gently.

'You think so? Was my advice useful, do you think?'

He nodded. 'It was a tough call.'

'The poor girl. I can't believe it's happening again.' After a bit, she sent him a shy smile. 'Thanks for sticking up for me. You didn't have to. Under the circumstances, it was very good of you.'

'That girl has enough on her plate without having to deal with parents at war with each other.'

'That's very true.' Eva wondered if he had always been this wise. She set down her empty mug. 'I wonder what Laine will decide?'

'I certainly hope she tells her boyfriend.'

'I think she probably will, especially now that she's met you. She was upset to realise how long you—' Eva stopped, and compressed her lips as the weight of her deception brought a fresh wave of despair.

Griff made no comment. After a bit, he said, 'It's getting late.'

'Yes.' There was probably no point in continuing the conversation. Eva knew she would almost certainly get weepy again and Griff had suffered more than his fair share of feminine tears.

But she didn't feel as relaxed as she would have liked. The realities of their past seemed to suck the available air from the room. She was remembering her secrecy, and the way she'd excluded Griff, and then, months later, her painful decision to give Laine away.

As the memories crowded in, she pushed herself out of the chair. She needed to leave before she made a scene. A crushing weight pressed on her chest. Tears stung her throat and eyes.

She couldn't look at Griff, but she felt compelled to speak. 'I'm sorry,' she said tearfully. 'I'm so sorry I didn't give you a chance to be her father.' Then the tears began to fall in earnest.

'Eva.' Griff's voice was rough with emotion.

She felt his hand on her arm, but she shook it away.

'No!' she cried. The very worst thing she could do now would be to fall, weeping into his arms. She was terrified that her willpower would break completely and she'd give in to her overwhelming despair and longing.

She couldn't let this happen. Not after their careful agreement. Blindly, she hurried across the lounge room towards the door to her room, keeping one hand out to steady and guide her past the furniture.

Griff didn't try to follow.

CHAPTER EIGHT

EVA TOOK AGES to get to sleep and, when she did, she dreamed she was back in Emerald Bay…

It was a rainy morning and she was lying in her bed in the little rented cottage where she lived with her mother near the base of the rocky headland. Outside, the waves were crashing on the shore and rainwater was trickling through holes in the guttering. She felt nauseous again. It was the third morning in a row that she'd experienced this queasiness in her stomach. And her period was three weeks late.

Eva knew what these symptoms almost certainly meant.

Her next thought was Griff and then, in the miraculous way that only happens in dreams, she was instantly down on the beach with her surfer boyfriend. The rain had disappeared and it was sunny and his arms were around her. Her cheek was pressed against his lovely tanned and muscly chest. She could feel the warmth of the sun on his skin, could smell the salt of the sea in his rough, dark hair.

His arms tightened around her, holding her closer, and she felt safe and happy and madly in love. Happiness was rising through her like a bright tide of bubbles.

'Don't worry,' Griff whispered close to her ear. 'Don't worry about anything, Damsel.'

Damsel was his nickname for Eva. He'd chosen it after their first dive together on the reef when she'd been so thrilled by the discovery of the pretty little blue and yellow damsel fish.

'But what are we going to do about the baby?' she asked him now.

'We'll become parents,' Griff said, making it sound incredibly simple and OK. 'We'll have a beautiful little damsel of our own and the three of us will live happily and make our lives together.'

'But you have to go to university,' Eva protested.

'Shh.' He pressed a warm finger to her lips. 'Don't worry about that. Don't stress, Eva. I'll find a way to make this work for us.'

Griff was smiling and he looked so certain and confident that she wanted to believe him. But surely it couldn't be that easy? Griff's parents would be furious when they found out about her pregnancy. They might even try to claim that she'd trapped their son.

And yet… Eva could already sense deep inside her that none of this really mattered. A kind of sixth sense told her that Griff would dismiss every one of the problems she raised. No matter what happened, he was going to protect her and look after her and make everything right.

I'll find a way to make this work for us.

'Aren't you even a little bit scared?' she asked.

'No, not at all.'

'Why not?'

He smiled and kissed the tip of her nose. 'Only one reason.' His grey eyes glowed with a deeply stirring emotion. 'You're my Damsel and I love you. I'm crazy about you. And now I get to keep you.'

Eva woke wrapped in a warm cloud of happiness. A peaceful, bone-deep happiness, better than anything she could ever remember.

For a blissful few moments, she lingered in that happy space between dreaming and waking. Then a kookaburra laughed in a tree outside her window. She opened her eyes, saw that she was in the back bedroom in Griff's house in Brisbane and reality came crashing back in all its cruel and harsh bleakness.

Griff had never made such beautiful promises to her. She'd never given him the chance. Instead, she'd kept the pregnancy a dark secret and had taken the long and lonely road on her own to fame and glory.

Now, cold misery swept in to replace the happy warmth. Eva lay stiffly in her bed, listening not to the sea but to the sounds of Griff moving about in the kitchen, making coffee for himself. Soon she would hear his departing footsteps in the hall and then the front door closing behind him, the car backing out of the garage. Then there would be silence until Malina arrived in about half an hour's time.

This was the pattern of their mornings. It was part of the deal Eva and Griff had settled on when she'd arrived as his house guest. His *temporary* house guest.

Unhappily, Eva threw off the bed covers and started the morning exercises she'd been assigned by the physiotherapist. First, while she was lying down, there were ankle pumps and rotations, knee bends, buttock contractions and leg raises. Then, standing, she did more knee raises, hip abductions and hip extensions. Later she would use Griff's exercise bike.

She was being very conscientious about this regime. Of course she was. Looking after her body was second nature to her.

If only she could shake off the lingering sense of loss. This morning a blanket of sadness enveloped her like a heavy fog that wouldn't lift. She kept thinking about her dream and the words that might have been said but were never voiced, the choices she'd never made.

And now she could only hope that her daughter might have learned an important lesson from her mother's mistakes. She prayed that Laine would make the right decisions and reap the happy rewards.

Two days later, on Malina's afternoon off, Eva was using the exercise bike on the back deck when she heard the doorbell ring.

Her hip was healing well but she still couldn't hurry, so it took some time for her to make her way through the house to the front door.

'Oh!' The caller was a young woman, a very pretty and curvy blonde, dressed to kill in a scoop-necked, tight-fitting black and white polka dot dress and heels higher than anything Eva had ever worn.

The young woman was clearly very surprised to see Eva. Her brightly painted mouth seemed frozen in an O shape as round as her baby blue eyes.

'Can I help you?' Eva asked.

'Is…is Griff home?'

'No. Were you expecting him to be home now?'

'Well, yes, I thought we had an…an arrangement.' The girl pouted.

'I'm sorry, Griff didn't mention that he was expecting you.' Eva was frantically trying *not* to imagine what this arrangement might be. 'I'm pretty sure he's at work.'

'Hmm.' The girl looked Eva up and down rather deliberately.

Dressed in her exercise gear, which amounted to knee-length black tights and a strapless pink and aqua tube top, Eva supposed she must look exceptionally at home in Griff's private domain.

'Who are you?' the girl asked.

'I'm Eva Hennessey.' Eva smiled and offered her hand. 'I'm an old friend of Griff's, a very old friend from way back.'

'Oh, really?' The girl's expression was cautious, her handshake limp.

'And you are?' Eva kept her bright smile carefully in place.

'Josie.'

'Hello, Josie, nice to meet you.'

Josie chose not to respond and she gave no answering smile. She was still pouting and obviously quite put out.

Eva did her best to placate her. 'I'm only staying here because I've had an operation,' she said. 'I had to have a hip replacement, and Griff kindly invited me to stay at his place while I was recovering.'

A doubtful eyebrow lifted.

'It was very kind of him,' Eva hurried on, needing to fill in the gaps in this one-sided conversation. 'But

I'm only here for a little while, of course. As soon as I'm fit enough, I'll be flying back to France.'

'France?' Josie brightened at this prospect. Emboldened, she lifted her chin. 'Did Griff tell you about our plans for the weekend?'

'I don't think so.' Eva hoped she hid her surprise, not to mention the ridiculous jealousy that this news aroused.

'He didn't say anything?' Now Josie looked crushed.

'Well, maybe he did mention it and I've forgotten,' Eva quickly amended.

'We're going to Stradbroke Island.'

'How…lovely.'

To Eva's dismay, she found herself noticing all the attractions this woman had to offer—attractions that she lacked. Josie was younger, probably not yet thirty, and meticulously made-up, whereas Eva hardly ever bothered with make-up at home. After so many years of wearing heavy stage make-up, she loved cleansing her skin and using nothing more than a little light moisturiser, but she supposed she must look exceptionally plain by comparison with this pretty creature. And Josie's curving bust line and high heels were attributes Eva could never hope to achieve.

Not that any of this should matter. They didn't matter. Of course they didn't. Eva wasn't trying to win Griff's affection, and his private affairs were none of her business.

Just the same, she couldn't help feeling a teensy bit hurt that he hadn't thought to mention his plans for spending the weekend away.

Josie still looked unhappy and Eva wished she could feel more pity for the girl. She did her best to reassure her. 'As I said, I knew Griff years and years ago when he was still at school. We're just friends. I live in Paris and I'll be gone from here just as soon as I'm strong enough.'

Afterwards, when Josie had driven off in her little red sedan, Eva wondered if she'd overdone the reassurances. Then she wondered if she'd needed the message that she and Griff were not an item even more than Josie had.

It was almost seven in the evening when Griff rang. 'I'm running overtime tonight,' he said. 'There's a complicated case on the go and I need to do more research. You should eat without me.'

Eva knew this was a perfectly reasonable request. 'All right,' she said and she hoped she didn't sound disappointed.

'Or you could meet me in the city for dinner,' Griff amended quickly. 'If you can wait another hour or so, I'll take you to dinner somewhere nice.' He sounded rather pleased by this new idea.

'Malina's made a lasagne,' Eva told him.

'That's OK. We can have it tomorrow, or Malina can stow it in the freezer.'

'I guess.'

'Come on, Eva. You've been stuck in that house night and day. You need a little brightening up.'

Eva couldn't deny she loved the idea of an outing and dinner somewhere *nice*, with Griff as her companion, had very definite appeal. Already, her mind was running through her wardrobe. Would she wear the grey silk dress with the deep V back? Or something more casual?

Then a chill ran through her. 'Will Josie mind if I'm dining out with you?'

'Josie?' Griff repeated sharply.

'The pretty blonde who seems to have a special arrangement with you? And an important weekend planned? On Stradbroke Island?'

'Oh, hell.' He swore softly.

'Surely you can't have forgotten Josie?'

'There was nothing to remember,' he said quickly. 'But don't worry, I'll call her. What about tonight? Will you come to dinner?'

Eva hesitated. Now that she'd had time for second thoughts, dinner in the city felt like a date, and she and Griff weren't supposed to be dating.

'I'll send a car for you,' Griff said.

'But—'

'Damsel, you're not getting into a stew over this, are you?'

She couldn't believe he'd called her Damsel. After all this time. Echoes of her dream whispered through her, bringing ripples of warmth.

'I gave you my word before you moved in,' Griff said. 'You've got to trust me. There won't be any pressure.'

'I know that. I do trust you, Griff.'

'Good. Then you'll come? Don't worry about getting dressed up. We can go somewhere casual. There's an Italian place near our chambers. You'll love it. They do amazing pasta.'

'All right. I'd love to come. Thank you.'

'Good. I'll send the car. Expect it shortly after eight.'

Griff consulted with his secretary about a missing file and held a phone conversation with one of the key detectives working on the tricky case he was wrestling with, before he turned to the task of ringing Josie.

'Who's Eva Hennessey?' the girl demanded almost as soon as he got through to her.

Griff clenched his teeth. He wasn't in the mood for an argument. He had enough on his plate. Besides, he'd never made any promises to Josie. She was one of those girls who latched onto a casual throwaway line at a party and then made a nuisance of herself. He didn't have time for extra complications right now.

'Eva's an old friend,' he told her. 'From way back.'

'That's what she reckoned too.' Josie sounded petulant.

'Because it's the truth.'

'Yeah? So is that why she gets around your house in tights and a tube top?'

She does? Griff wished he'd been around to witness this. Eva was always very modestly dressed whenever he was home.

'Well, she's a dancer,' he offered as explanation.

'What kind of a dancer?'

A pole dancer, he was tempted to say, but he restrained himself. 'Classical ballet,' he said. Not that it was any of Josie's business. 'Look, Josie, I think you got the wrong end of the stick. I don't think we actually had any plans in place for this weekend.'

'We did. You promised.' She sounded like a little girl.

'No, there was never a promise.' At best it had been a vague suggestion.

'I bought a new bikini.'

Griff pressed two fingers to the knotted frown between his eyebrows. 'Sorry. I'm extremely busy. I simply don't have time. We'll have to cancel. I've got to go now.'

After he hung up, there was another phone call from Detective Sweeney and Josie was swiftly forgotten.

The Italian restaurant was busy and humming with the voices of happy diners. The place had a rustic feel, with brick archways and stone floors and plain timber tables and chairs, softened by candles in amber glass holders. Tempting aromas of sizzling tomatoes, garlic and herbs hung in the air.

Griff, minus his jacket and tie and with his collar loosened and sleeves rolled back, looked tired but relaxed. And way too sexy for Eva's comfort.

He was waiting at a table and rose to kiss her cheek when she arrived. Eva was wearing white jeans and a simple boat-necked aqua silk top and he smiled his approval, letting his gaze linger on her.

She tried to ignore the flush of pleasure this caused. 'Were you able to get your problems sorted?' she asked.

'Some of them, thanks. The evidence is finally becoming clearer.'

He explained that he'd been working with a detective and a forensic psychologist on a particularly complicated case. Eva had heard on the news that a local woman had been accused of killing her own children, and she wondered if this was the same case but she didn't ask Griff about it. The details were sure to be unbearably sad and tonight he needed to relax.

They ordered red wine and, when it came, it was rich and aromatic, perfect for sipping while they read through the menu at their leisure, mulling over choices and chatting about favourite dishes and memorable meals from their separate pasts.

Eventually, Eva ordered sweet potato ravioli and Griff chose a seafood linguine dish. When the food came, everything was so delicious they ended up sharing. For Eva, the relaxed intimacy was dangerously beguiling.

As they ate, she mentioned a book she'd found in Griff's library—an inspiring autobiography all about being adventurous and not staying stuck in a safe, secure life.

'I guess it's a bit late for me to be reading that message,' she said.

Griff smiled, but there was a watchful light in his eyes. 'It's never too late to encounter new ideas.'

'Well, yes, that's true.'

'And many people would think you already live a very adventurous life, jet-setting about Europe.'

'Not exactly jet-setting. To be honest, I have a pretty gruelling regime.'

'But more exciting than the life of someone like Jane Simpson, who has spent her entire life in the Bay.'

Eva laughed.

'What's so funny?'

'It's just that I was thinking at the reunion how nice Jane's life must be, living in a quiet place like the Bay, with her little family and the beach close by, almost like being on a permanent holiday.'

Griff's eyes narrowed, taking on a shrewd air, and it was hard to tell what he was thinking. 'You do realise Jane's very envious of everything you've achieved?'

'Maybe it's a case of the grass always being greener somewhere else.'

'Maybe.' He set down his fork and lifted his wine glass. For a moment he studied the ruby liquid, then he raised his gaze to meet Eva's. 'Jane told me you've been very generous with donations to help Katie Jones.'

'Did she?' The sudden change of subject surprised Eva. Katie was a classmate who'd had a terrible surfing accident in her early twenties.

'Well, actually, Jane told me that you'd been helping Katie too,' she said. 'But, honestly, Griff, it was the least I could do for an old school friend, as I'm sure you'd agree. I felt so devastated when I heard about Katie's accident. She was always such an athletic girl, and she was a promising dancer too. It was just awful to hear she'd been paralysed.'

'Did you know she's trying out for the Gliders, the Australian women's wheelchair basketball team?'

'Wow, that's fantastic. I hope she makes it.' After a bit, Eva said, 'Now *that* takes courage.'

Griff nodded. His gaze met hers and held. 'I suppose we all need courage to make the most of our lives.'

At this, Eva's heart gave a strangely dull thud. Had she made the most of her life? Since she'd come back to Australia she'd felt less and less certain about the choices she'd made. And she was still uncertain about the direction her life should take now.

In terms of her career, she'd been very successful but her inner life, her sense of personal satisfaction had been deeply shaken. She no longer felt grounded and certain.

'Do you think it's courage that we need or wisdom, Griff?'

He watched her for the longest time before he answered. 'I guess courage isn't much good on its own.'

'No,' said Eva and of course she was thinking about giving up Laine. At the time, the sacrifice had felt hugely courageous but, since then, she'd questioned the decision over and over.

'I guess courage without wisdom could lead to people making the wrong choices.'

Griff smiled. 'I assume you're referring to people like Napoleon or Hitler.'

Eva couldn't help smiling back at him. Of course she hadn't been thinking of Napoleon or Hitler at all. She'd been obsessing again about her own mistakes.

Perhaps Griff had guessed this and was wisely leading their conversation away from anything too personal. This evening was supposed to be about relaxing, after all.

'Hello, there. Fancy seeing you two!'

The booming voice brought them both turning to see Griff's mate Tim grinning at them like a fool.

Eva heard Griff's soft groan and immediately sensed the tension in him.

'Well, well, well,' said Tim and, if possible, his grin widened.

Eva decided it was her responsibility to set Griff's old friend straight quickly, before any teasing began. It should have been a simple matter to explain about her surgery and recovery but, no matter how carefully she outlined the properness of their situation, Tim kept up his knowing grin.

'It's just great to see how well you guys are getting on,' Tim said with a smirk and he was still grinning as he left them.

Griff and Eva both rolled their eyes as he headed off. They'd done their best. It was annoying that people like Laine and Tim were so smug while jumping to wrong conclusions. Even Malina had started making comments about how pleased she was to see Mr Fletcher looking so happy these days.

'You're good medicine for each other,' Malina had told Eva only this morning.

Considering their particular circumstances, these weren't helpful thoughts to be having at the end of a very pleasant evening out. A careful silence fell as she and Griff left the restaurant. He took her arm, tucking it firmly and safely under his as he guided her towards his parked car. Eva knew there was nothing romantic about the gesture but, unfortunately, that knowledge didn't stop her from enjoying every sweet moment of close contact.

Their careful silence continued as Griff drove home through the busy city streets. Eva supposed he was thinking about the case he was dealing with, which was a pity. For a while there tonight, he seemed to have put it aside, until Tim's smirk spoiled their happy and relaxed mood.

'Thanks for a lovely evening,' she said, hoping to distract him.

'Yeah, it was great,' Griff said.

In the glow of traffic lights she saw the smile he flashed her way. 'You're good company.'

Zap. The small compliment thrilled Eva way more than it should have.

'I must admit,' Griff said as he steered the car up the steep hill towards his street, 'I thought you would have driven me nuts by now.'

This comment certainly brought Eva swiftly back to earth. 'Why? What did you expect?'

His big shoulders lifted in a shrug. 'There was every chance after twenty years that we'd have nothing in common. We could have found ourselves miles apart in taste, interests. Everything.'

They were at the top of the hill now and, as he steered the car around the corner, Griff let out his breath in a small huff. 'OK, maybe what I should have said was I'd been *hoping* that you'd drive me nuts.'

'Really?' Eva asked, now completely confused.

'Not liking you would have made life a hell of a lot easier,' Griff said.

Was this his indirect way of telling her that he still cared about her?

'Did you know you called me Damsel tonight? On the phone?' she couldn't help asking.

'Of course I know.'

He spoke quietly, giving the words significance. When he turned Eva's way, she saw a fierce, impassioned light in his eyes and she felt as if she'd suddenly caught fire. Until this moment, she'd been sure Griff's use of Damsel was a slip that he hadn't even noticed.

Now, as he turned the car into his driveway, she could scarcely breathe. But, before she could get her thoughts properly sorted, Griff was out of the car and opening her door for her. Once again, his hand was at her elbow as he helped her out.

Apart from her murmured thanks, they didn't speak as he steered her to the front door, but her heart kept up a frantic beating and her skin burned with awareness of his touch.

At the door, Griff waited for Eva to go ahead of him and she felt as tense as she had in her teens, wondering if he might act on the chemistry arcing between them. Would he kiss her?

Oh, help! She was hoping that he would. Hoping desperately, in spite of a thousand inner warnings.

The light came on in the hall, spilling over them. She saw Griff, standing perfectly still, watching her. She could sense the tension in him and she was gripped by the deepest kind of longing. She stayed where she was, not wanting to move, hardly daring to breathe.

Griff didn't move either.

Despite their stillness, they were drawing closer, as if pulled by an invisible string, and Eva knew then that it was going to happen.

All it took was a little courage.

Griff whispered, 'Eva,' and he reached for her.

At the same moment a bell-like noise erupted.

Griff cursed. It was his phone. 'I should take this,' he said with grim reluctance, and already he was reaching into his pocket.

Weak-kneed, heart racing, Eva sagged against the wall. In a daze, she heard Griff's end of the phone conversation. Mostly, it involved him trying to calm someone down.

His face was grave as he disconnected. 'My client's in a bad way,' he said. 'She's in danger of harming herself. I have to go.'

Eva nodded. 'Of course.'

She was shaken and Griff looked as upset as she felt. They'd come so close, within a hair's breadth, of breaking their careful rules. Wisdom had flown out of the window.

Now, common sense and necessity prevailed.

Griff sighed, however. 'I'll say goodnight. I don't know when I'll be back.'

Eva nodded. 'I'll see you whenever. Good luck—with everything.'

'Thanks.' He managed a quarter smile before he turned and left.

Watching the door close behind him, Eva hoped all would be well with his client, but she couldn't help feeling sorry for Griff too. He'd already put in a long day and heaven knew how much sleep he would get tonight before he faced another busy day in the morning.

She also felt sorry for herself. An important and precious moment had been lost, perhaps for ever. A fragile bridge was still broken.

CHAPTER NINE

GRIFF WAS BUSIER than ever in the weeks that followed. On several nights he didn't make it home till very late, but there were no more occasions when he asked Eva to join him in the city for dinner.

She supposed he'd realised his mistake and, after a great deal of self-talk, she'd accepted that this was for the best. She should be grateful that his work got in the way.

After their indiscretion at Emerald Bay, they knew it would have been beyond foolish to break the careful protocols they'd both agreed on. Grown adults in their late thirties knew better than to give in to the same lusty longings that had led them into trouble in their youth.

On the evenings that Griff was home, they continued with sensible, pleasant conversation over dinner. At times they laughed over funny memories they shared, at others their conversations went deeper, touching on philosophy and politics and current events. But they scrupulously avoided another lapse. Any kind of intimacy was strictly off the agenda.

In the meantime, Eva continued diligently with her exercise regime, and she was becoming so strong and supple that she'd started to believe she might actually return to the demanding dancing roles that had made her famous. Undoubtedly, there were more months of practice ahead of her, but she was used to working hard towards a challenging goal.

Goals always made her life clearer and more straightforward. And, as far as she could tell, Griff seemed to have the same outlook, his own goals being centred around the people he defended in court.

Their clear goals had led them down very different paths, however, and the only true bond between them now was their daughter. Eva supposed she should be grateful that the lines of communication with Griff and Laine were open and amicable for her. Really, that was all she could hope for after twenty years of silence.

Her role in both Griff's and Laine's futures would be minimal. She just wished she didn't have to remind herself of this over and over.

It was during the final days before Eva was due to head back to Paris that Malina called her to the phone.

'Hi, it's Laine,' said an excited voice.

'Hello!' Eva was equally excited to hear from her. 'How are you?'

'Very relieved and happy. I've told my boyfriend, Dylan, about the baby.'

'Well done. And how did he take the news?'

'He was adorable.' Laine sounded over-the-top excited now and her story came tumbling out… Dylan had told Laine that he was madly in love with her and, no matter what, he was determined to find a way to support her. Or, rather, Laine amended, they would find a way to support each other and the baby while they finished their university studies.

They weren't announcing a formal engagement and they certainly weren't wasting precious money on a ring at this point. That could come later, down the track.

'For us it's the baby first and then Dylan's exams, and the wedding much later.'

Eva realised that by that time she planned to be back on the stage in Paris, resuming her career, but she didn't mention this now, while Laine explained her hope to take a semester off, or even a whole year if she needed to, before resuming her studies. Dylan would find a part-time job and he would apply for scholarships, or get an extension on his student loan. He was confident they'd work something out.

'That's—' Eva had to swallow the painful lump that had suddenly ballooned in her throat. Just thinking about her daughter's wedding made her feel tearful and emotional. 'That's wonderful, Laine. I'm so happy for you. Thanks for letting me know. I'll pass the good news on to Griff.'

Later on the same day she was called to the phone again. This time the call was from a board member of Ballet Pacifique, a prestigious company based in Brisbane.

'Our artistic director is leaving for a job in the Czech Republic in six months' time,' the caller told Eva. 'We're going to need a replacement and our first thought was you, Eva, so we wanted to get in early. I know you have a wealth of wonderful experience in both contemporary and classical dance and we heard you were back in Queensland. I don't suppose we could entice you to stay?'

Eva was stunned. 'How did you find me?' she blurted.

'Oh, the gossip chain in ballet circles is still as effective as ever.'

Eva supposed this rep from Ballet Pacifique also knew about her surgery. The woman probably assumed Eva would never dance again.

'Eva, would you consider an artistic directorship?' she asked. 'We'd love to show you what we do.'

'I've seen your dancers.' Eva had taken herself to see several shows on the nights when Griff was extra busy. She'd been to the symphony orchestra, the Queensland Ballet, as well as the Ballet Pacifique. 'Your dancers are wonderful. I loved their work.'

'Thank you.' The woman sounded delighted. 'That's high praise coming from you. Our company is going from strength to strength and we could offer you quite a generous package.'

Standing there, gripping the phone, Eva was, for a giddy moment, very tempted. An artistic directorship was an obvious progression for a dancer facing the potential end of her stage career. Finding such a position right here in Brisbane was a very alluring prospect, especially as it meant that she would also be able to see Laine and her baby. And she would be only a short plane flight away from her mother. In time, she could introduce Laine to her grandmother.

But—

Of course there were buts.

First, there was Eva's important goal to prove that she could get back to full dancing strength. For weeks now, she'd been working really hard, all the while focusing on her triumphant return to the Parisian theatres.

Then there was the Griff factor.

If she remained in Brisbane, she would stay within Griff Fletcher's radius, but forever keeping at a carefully polite distance.

This shouldn't have been a problem, of course, but, unfortunately, for Eva, it felt like a huge problem. Despite her best efforts to resist the man, she'd fallen hard. Again.

The daily contact with Griff had proved every bit as dangerous as she'd feared it would be. She knew now that she loved him, loved everything about him—the way he looked, the way he thought, the lovely home he'd chosen, the way he balanced his work with his home life. She adored just *being* with Griff.

Problem was—since the night they'd gone out to dinner and had come so close to making another mistake, Griff had backed right away. It was clear that he wasn't prepared to risk starting a relationship with Eva. And she understood that.

She'd hurt him terribly when they were young and she didn't deserve another chance at love with this man. But, given the strength of her feelings, she also knew it would break her heart to live in the same city as Griff when they had no future.

It would be torture to see him at Laine's place while keeping up the pretence of distanced, polite friendship.

Behaving as if she didn't care about him was too hard. Eva knew she couldn't keep up the pretence indefinitely. Her only chance for personal happiness was to escape, to flee once again to the other side of the world.

She was pleased Ballet Pacifique's board member couldn't see her face as she declined the wonderful offer. 'I'm sorry,' she said. 'I'm planning to go back to Paris very soon.'

'Oh, well, that's— I guess—' The woman sounded truly surprised and disappointed. 'That's wonderful for you, Eva, but it's jolly bad luck for us.'

After Eva hung up, she went for a long walk and forced herself to think about Paris and her lovely apartment and all the people and places she was looking forward to seeing again. Nanette, the concierge of her apartment block. Celeste, who had the flower stall on the corner. Louis, the waiter at her favourite café, all her dancer friends.

Eva recalled her favourite sights. The view of roofs and chimney pots from her apartment, the beautiful gardens nearby, the market stalls, the cathedrals and her own personal landmark, the Eiffel Tower. Surely, if she told herself often enough that Paris was where she belonged, she would eventually remember that it was true.

When Griff came home, Eva gave him Laine's news and of course he was delighted.

'Dylan's from a big family and family is very important to him,' she recounted, delivering Laine's message as accurately as she could.

She added that Dylan wanted their baby to be part of that 'big happy mob' as he called it. Better still, in his family there were oodles of arms willing to help with minding the baby, so Laine and Dylan wouldn't have to pay too much for childcare.

As far as Dylan was concerned, the most important things were that Laine and the baby remained well and that the three of them were able to be together.

As she shared this with Griff, there was something in his expression—a sadness that made her feel a zap of connection with him. Or was it the sting of her own guilt?

Eva was sure that he was remembering, as she was, that he'd never been given the chance to step up to the role of heroic boyfriend and provider in the same commendable way that Laine's Dylan was doing now.

Laine had gone on and on, adding more and more details to the happy scenario, but Eva didn't pass all of this on to Griff. She was thrilled for her daughter, of course she was. It was fabulous to know that Laine would not be a third generation single mother, and that she would keep her baby and have the backup of a supportive family network.

And it meant that Eva would have no reason to worry about Laine or the little one when she returned to the other side of the world and pushed on with her career dreams. She just wished—

No, she mustn't wish.

She'd made her decision and it would be foolish to change her plans now, especially when it seemed that she wouldn't really be needed even if she stayed here in Brisbane.

To Eva's surprise, Griff took her out to dinner again on the night before she left for France.

This time they went to a seafood restaurant with

a wall of glass that housed an astonishing floor-to-ceiling aquarium filled with gorgeous tropical fish. There were striped fish, spotted fish, pink and purple and green fish and, of course, the cute blue damsels with their bright yellow fins.

'I thought you might enjoy them,' Griff said.

'For old times' sake?' Eva asked in a choked voice.

His eyes shimmered in the candlelight. 'At least we have happy memories of the sea.'

'Yes, we do,' she whispered, and she hated that most of their other memories were unhappy.

Even these recent weeks of recuperation, which had been lovely, had been overshadowed by the knowledge that she and Griff could never act on their ever-present sizzling tension. There'd been several times when Eva had wished with all her heart that she hadn't set herself the goal of returning to the stage.

Perhaps, if Griff had asked her to stay, she would have happily changed her mind, but he'd stuck to his word. He'd remained the perfect host and a wonderfully interesting conversationalist and friend, a gorgeous temptation who remained just out of reach.

It was painfully clear that he'd made one huge mistake in that motel in Emerald Bay and he wasn't going to repeat it.

The hardest ordeal came the next morning when Eva flew back to France.

Griff insisted on driving her to the airport. 'I've kept my diary free,' he said curtly when she tried to protest.

At the airport, he also insisted on helping Eva with her luggage and escorting her through Security, continuing all the way to the queue at the Customs gates, where he could go no further.

During all of this, Eva wondered—or, rather, she *hoped*—that Griff was accompanying her because he had something significant to say to her before she left Australia.

She didn't really think there was a last chance possibility for them, but she wondered if he would express regret that she had to leave.

She wasn't sure what she might say or do if Griff gave the slightest hint that he still held deeper feelings for her. There was a very good chance she would hurl herself into his arms and tell him this was where she belonged, where she wanted to stay. For ever.

Eva's heart fluttered dangerously and her legs felt hollow as she stopped near Customs, a mere metre from the end of the queue. Nervously, she rearranged the straps of her bag over her shoulder. She looked down at her boarding pass and passport, then lifted her gaze to meet Griff's and a painful jolt shuddered through her.

Oh, Griff. The look in his eyes almost felled her. Such sadness, as if he hated saying goodbye even more than she hated to leave.

'So this is it,' he said, giving a sadly crooked smile.

Eva swallowed. 'Yes. Thanks so much for everything, Griff.' Her lips were trembling, but she forced herself to continue. 'You've been very generous—not only with your wonderful hospitality, but in the way you've accepted Laine and…and you haven't tried to lay blame. You were entitled to be terribly angry, but you've been perfect.'

'You make me sound like a saint.' Griff gave a smiling shake of his head. 'Haloes don't suit me.'

A dangerous light entered his eyes, hinting at extremely unsaintly thoughts, and reminding Eva of his kisses, of his touch, of his gloriously sexy lovemaking. She felt a tug of longing deep inside and she almost launched forward, hurling herself against him.

'All the best with the hip,' he said. 'I'm sure you'll make a brilliant comeback.'

Eva choked back a foolish whimper. It was stupid to be upset. Of course Griff couldn't read her mind, and he was behaving exactly as he'd promised. He would do nothing to interfere with her plans of returning to the stage and it was too late for her to suddenly change her goals at the very last minute.

Only the lowest kind of former girlfriend would try to wriggle back into a man's life at the last gasp, when she'd spent weeks being adamant that it wasn't what she wanted.

'Thank you,' she said.

The queue was moving through Customs. Another group of travellers arrived, all happy and excited.

Griff smiled at Eva. 'Give my regards to Paris.'

She nodded. 'Yes, I'll do that.' Despite her breaking heart, she pinned on a bright smile of her own. 'Don't forget to send photos of the baby when it arrives. Laine will probably be too busy.'

'Of course.'

'And I hope you'll see Laine from time to time.'

'I will, certainly. We're going to meet for coffee on Saturday mornings. Actually,' he added with a smile, 'Laine will have peppermint tea.'

'So you'll meet *every* Saturday morning?' Eva couldn't help asking.

'Yes, Laine has a favourite café in Paddington, not very far from my place.'

'How lovely. That's wonderful.' Eva was proud that she said this without giving way to tears, but she'd never felt more isolated and left out.

This was right, though, she had to accept sadly. Griff wasn't burdened by a history of mistakes in the same way that she was and he had slipped very naturally and calmly into his role as a father. For Eva, however, having failed Laine as a baby, she feared she would never feel truly confident about offering her daughter ongoing advice.

Bravely now, she straightened her shoulders. There was no point in prolonging the dreadful agony. She should let the poor man go. 'OK,' she said more definitely. 'I guess—'

'You should go,' Griff supplied.

'Yes.'

She was trembling all over now, wondering if Griff would hug her and kiss her properly in an emotional and passionate airport farewell. He stepped forward, lightly touched her shoulder as he leaned closer.

He kissed her cheek.

'Take care, Eva.'

'You too,' she said, but suddenly she couldn't see him. Her eyes were too filled with tears.

Blinking hard, she cleared the tears and saw his look of agonised despair. The pain was only there in his face for a heartbeat and then it was gone. A beat later he turned and began to walk away from her.

Every cell in Eva screamed for her to chase after

him, to tell him they were making a terrible mistake. They belonged together, not hemispheres apart.

But she had no right. She'd given up that right twenty years ago.

Now she had no choice but to join the queue of happy travellers bound for Paris. Within no time, her passport and boarding pass were verified and she was entering the departure lounge. Meanwhile, Griff would be finding his car in the enormous car park and driving back into the city, to his work, to his life, to girls like Josie.

Eva found a seat in a café and ordered a coffee, which sat in front of her untouched, growing cold. She was remembering Griff's words from their farewell at the school reunion.

You were born to dance.

So…it was over. Done. Eva was gone.

As Griff steered his vehicle into the busy stream of morning traffic, he told himself he was OK. Of course he was OK. He was an old hand at farewelling the women in his life. He'd made an art form out of breaking up with them. And he'd been planning this particular break-up for weeks.

Now, his prime reaction was relief. It was the only sensible reaction.

Griff planned to put the experience of having Eva Hennessey as his house guest well and truly behind him. He'd been crazy to offer his home to her in the first place and the self-control that living with her required had damn near killed him.

He'd got through it unscathed, however. There had been no more mistakes in the bedroom and Eva was safely winging her way back to France, where she planned to stage a magnificent comeback.

Now Griff could look forward to arriving home at the end of a long day, knowing that she wouldn't be there to tempt him with her lithe, supple elegance. Never again would he be driven crazy by the flash of her slim, shapely legs as she curled comfortably in an armchair. He wouldn't be trapped by her bewitching smile, by her surprisingly engaging conversation.

Now he would be able to breathe again, without catching the fresh berry scent of her perfume.

Eva was gone and Griff was relieved. Or at least he tried to tell himself that he was pleased and relieved to wave her goodbye. But, as he steered his car into its customary space in an underground car park, he caught his reflection in the rear-vision mirror.

He saw the bleakness in his eyes, the deep creases bracketing his downturned mouth. He saw an expression of gut-churning hopelessness and he knew the ruse wasn't working.

He missed Eva. Already. *Damn it, he missed her like crazy.*

After all this time, he still wanted her. He was as madly in love with her now as he had been at eighteen. He wanted her in his bed. Hell, yeah. But, more than that, he wanted her in his life.

So many times over the past weeks he'd come close to declaring his feelings, to letting his emotions spill. The only thing that had stopped him was his damned pride.

Put simply, he wasn't prepared to cop another rejection.

He'd accepted Eva's reasons for her initial disappearance all those years ago, and he'd come to terms with her silence about his daughter. But a man could only take so many risks with his heart and Griff Fletcher had learned the hard way that with Eva he could never win. Dancing would always come first.

Now, sure enough, she was heading for Paris, and he had no choice but to bury the pain and move on.

CHAPTER TEN

ONCE AGAIN EVA HENNESSEY's photograph was displayed on posters all over Paris. The press had caught wind of her five-month break from dancing and rumours had been flying thick and fast about the cause. Now, with the announcement of a new performance, ballet circles were buzzing about Eva's return to the stage to dance the role that had made her famous in *Romeo and Juliet*.

Eva was excited too. Her painful hip was now a thing of the past and the doctors were really pleased with her recovery and rehabilitation. Within the dance company, the choreographer, the director and Eva's primary dance partner, Guillaume Belair, had all feared some sort of imbalance or caution in her movements, but now they declared that her dancing was as fluid and beautiful as ever.

At the end of the dress rehearsal of *Romeo and Juliet* the ballet company had applauded her.

'Dazzling!' the choreographer told Eva as he embraced her and kissed her on both cheeks.

A reviewer, who'd been allowed into the rehearsal, reported in the morning papers that Eva's return was a 'triumph of strength and perseverance' and that she now brought 'a new, more sorrowful edge' to the role of Juliet.

At home in her apartment, Eva felt calm as she went through her customary routine of pre-performance preparations. She had already prepared three pairs of pointe shoes, all of which were likely to be used on the opening night. She always measured and sewed the elastic and ribbons on the shoes herself, making sure they were in exactly the right places. Then she banged the points on a wooden floor to soften them, so that they didn't make a loud, distracting noise when she ran onto the stage.

Getting these details exactly right was vitally important. Shoes were the basis of everything a dancer did on stage and if her shoes didn't feel right it was like trying to dance with someone else's legs.

There had been a couple of tricky moments, as Eva worked on her shoes, when she'd thought of Laine and her baby that would soon be born, and remembered that tiny baby foot kicking free from the blanket all those years ago. As always, thoughts of Laine were accompanied by painful memories of Griff.

Griff at Emerald Bay, making love to her with heart-wrenching passion. Griff in his home in Brisbane, in the role of charming host. Griff at the Italian restaurant, and their conversation about wisdom and courage.

So many, many times since she'd left Emerald Bay, Eva had been overwhelmed with loneliness and longing. Often she'd come close to picking up the phone to enquire if Ballet Pacifique's directorship had been filled. But then, each time, she remembered Griff's careful withdrawal from her and the pointlessness of going back when all he was prepared to offer her was polite and distanced friendliness.

She was far better off here, pursuing her career.

So today, when her thoughts edged dangerously towards Griff, Eva quickly snatched her mind back from that distracting direction. Dance was an art form that required total concentration on the present. Every movement, every expression had to be sensitive and precise.

She couldn't possibly dance at her best if she was dwelling on the past. And now the day of her comeback had arrived and she had to stay completely focused.

After limbering and stretching, Eva ate a light, healthy breakfast and she refused to allow herself a single thought about Australia. She was Eva Hennessey, about to make a magnificent return, and tonight's performance had to be perfect.

Once this evening's presentation was behind her, she could look forward to many more years of dancing. She had overcome a huge obstacle and was set to continue with her dream.

When the plane touched down at Charles de Gaulle Airport, Griff was surprised by how composed he felt. He supposed it was the calmness that came after finally reaching a decision and then following it up with action.

He was here in Paris to watch Eva dance. For the first time ever, he would sit in the audience and watch her on stage, as she gave all of her heart and passion to the art form she'd chosen over him.

Griff hadn't told Eva he was doing this. They'd had minimal contact since she'd returned to Paris and most of his news about Eva had come via Laine. Griff had scoured the Internet, however, watching for news from Paris, and as soon as stories about Eva's return to the stage appeared he'd been gripped by a strangely forceful desire to see her perform. He now knew that he had to have Eva in his life. He needed her desperately. But he'd also realised that he had no right to her when he'd never bothered to truly understand her passion for dance. At the reunion she'd asked him an important question.

You never ever came to watch me dance, did you? Not to any of the concerts?

At the time, he'd brushed her off. It had taken weeks for the crazy truth to dawn on him, that he'd never been to watch her dance because he was jealous. Jealous of her dancing, as if it were a lover she'd chosen over him.

It was perhaps forgivable from a teenager, but these days Griff was supposed to be older and wiser. And yet he'd continued to cling stubbornly to his crazy prejudices.

Now, at last, Griff knew the time had come to finally face up to his stupidity. His plan was to watch Eva dance and, he hoped, to understand at last what he was up against.

So, yeah, here he was. In Paris, the city of lovers.

After tonight, Griff hoped to be armed with a sufficient depth of understanding to finally win Eva. This time she wouldn't have to choose. He'd make that crystal-clear.

At twelve there was a full warm-up class at the theatre. The dancers, dressed in tights, leg warmers and tops, began, as always, with the very basic positions and steps they'd first learned when they'd begun dancing classes as children.

Eva never tired of going through these simple routine moves that were as familiar to her as breathing and yet so critical to any dancer's technique. She found something very comforting about the sameness of the movements, and the eternal drive to perfect them, while Colette, their rehearsal director, called all the usual instructions.

'Keep the legs turned out.'

'Stretch back, back, back, and now extend to the front.'

Eva knew that these warm-ups were important, not only for preparing her body but also for releasing endorphins to help her feel happy and calm.

Happy and calm, she mentally chanted as she dipped in a *demi plié*. *Happy and calm,* she thought again, keeping in time with the beat from the piano as they moved on to *développés*.

Don't think about Griff. Stay happy and calm. This is it. Your big day. You can do it. Happy and calm.

Fortunately, the day was a full one. After the warmup class, there was another, final rehearsal where Oliver Damson, their artistic director, once again made certain that every element in the production was perfect.

Whenever Eva wasn't required on stage, she found a quiet place to remain alone while she visualised dancing her role perfectly. She pictured Juliet's first sighting of Romeo, and then the scenes with her nurse and the preparations for the ball. She imagined the balcony scene, and the Love Dance. Then the drama of the third act, with the beautiful scene with Romeo in Juliet's bedroom.

Eva did her best to remain deeply immersed in the pathos of the young lovers' dilemma, but suddenly Griff was there again, intruding into her thoughts.

And this time he wouldn't leave. Eva was seeing him again, as her own young lover, and then as a mature and gorgeous, sexy man. The father of her child, the stirrer of her senses, the keeper of her heart.

Griff Fletcher was the source of her deepest angst but also the cause of her greatest happiness, and she'd run away from him. Again.

And suddenly, in the middle of the final rehearsal, Eva realised the truth she'd been avoiding.

I'm an idiot. I'm a total and utter fool.

With sudden and blinding certainty, she knew what she must do.

At some point in the ninety minutes that were set aside for the dancers to get into their costumes and to have their hair and make-up done, Eva had to make a very important phone call, and she had to find Oliver Damson and tell him she'd reached an important and final decision.

Although Griff had been to Paris before, he'd avoided visiting the Opéra de Paris. This evening, as he ascended the steps leading to this magnificent edifice, he could totally understand why the building was regarded as one of the world's greatest opera and ballet houses.

The exterior was elaborately decorated with angels and gargoyles and magnificent archways, but the interior was even more breathtaking. Here there were grand marble staircases, dazzling chandeliers, beautiful paintings on the ceilings and all manner of balustrades and balconies. And then, of course, in the inner sanctum stood the few square metres that all this pomp and grandeur were designed to complement—the stage.

The famous stage where Eva Hennessey, the girl from the tiny Aussie town of Emerald Bay, would dance her socks off.

Griff, in a brand new black dinner suit and bow tie, had never felt as nervous as he did now when he took his seat. Somewhere backstage, behind those grand velvet curtains, Eva was waiting. *His* Eva.

As he took his seat, his composure evaporated.

He tried to concentrate on the programme, wondering why on earth Eva had chosen a story about youthful, star-crossed lovers for her comeback. All Griff could think about was their own ill-fated romance and his new understanding of the blame he shared.

He turned to Eva's bio. The photo of her was a black and white head shot that showed off the slender elegance of her lovely neck and shoulders and made the contrast between her pale skin and dark hair even more dramatic than usual.

So beautiful.

Soon she would be on that stage in front of him, dancing.

Sweat broke out on Griff's brow and his collar felt too tight.

He closed the programme and willed himself to relax by watching the people in the audience as they filed into the theatre and took their seats. Glamorous Parisians in their finery were a very impressive bunch. He wondered how many of them ever gave a thought to

Eva's background and her early life in a small beach-side town in rural Australia.

He considered the huge effort Eva had put in to reach this place. Natural ability and talent could only take a dancer so far. The rest only came with punishing hard work and perseverance.

Eva had achieved so much. And Griff was miserably aware, even before the curtain rose, that he was crazy to imagine that she might ever want to leave this life.

Needless to say, it was an evening of extraordinary revelation for Griff. *Romeo and Juliet* had it all—swordplay, bawdy humour, romance and tragedy, all unfolding within a stunningly rich set design. The combination of Prokofiev's heart-rending music with the dancers' exquisite beauty and astonishing athleticism was enthralling. He hadn't expected to be so utterly enchanted and moved.

There were so many surprises. For one, he'd been braced to see girls in tutus and pointe shoes, with their hair scraped into tight buns and accompanied by men in tights with ridiculous bulges.

Instead, these dancers were dressed in the richly brocaded costumes of the Italian Renaissance. For most of the ballet, Eva, as Juliet, wore a lovely calf-length dress in a soft, smoky pink fabric with a sleeveless bodice criss-crossed with bronze braid. And, instead of a bun, her hair was secured at the nape of her neck, then left to hang free in a silken river that reached halfway down her back.

She looked far more beautiful than Griff could have possibly imagined and, from his first sight of her, his gaze was riveted. He hardly dared to breathe.

She was so quick and graceful, so light on her feet, so utterly flawless and completely eye-catching in every sense of the word. And she was also deeply immersed in her role. Her look across the stage to Romeo had a completely new kind of bleakness that tore at Griff's soul.

No wonder she loved this work. No wonder the world adored her.

Eva was stunning, breathtaking. Griff wanted to kill her partner, with his male model looks, powerhouse physique and impeccable dancing technique. But Griff soon understood that it was the audience who were his main rivals.

When Eva took her bow at the end of the third act, the audience rose as one to applaud and cheer her and to throw bouquets onto the stage at her feet. The enthusiastic applause lasted for ages. Griff wasn't sure how long, but he feared he had his answer, and it wasn't the answer he'd hoped for.

There could be no doubt. This stage was where Eva belonged.

Eva was flushed and exhilarated as she returned to her dressing room, which was so crammed with flowers she could scarcely squeeze her way in.

She'd achieved what many had thought impossible. She'd danced as well tonight as she ever had, and she was satisfied.

Taking her seat before the mirror, she shoved some of the flowers aside and began to remove the false eyelashes that looked good on stage but were so unnatural close up. Then she began with the special cleansing lotion she routinely used to remove the rest of her make-up.

This ritual was almost complete when she saw the small bunch of white daisies with a note attached. The daisies grabbed her attention first, because they were so different from the rest of the fancy roses and carnations and lilies.

Eva had always loved the simplicity of daisies. Griff had known this and he'd given them to her at their school formal—

Her thoughts froze as she saw the handwriting on the attached card. Her heart seemed to stop beating altogether and then it took a huge, fearful bound as she snatched up the flowers and read the note.

Here I am in Paris at the ballet. Sorry it's taken me so long.
Any chance of seeing you after the show?
G xx

Griff was here?
Any chance?
Eva was already leaping to her feet, knocking the chair sideways in her rush to get to the dressing room door. Her thoughts were racing as fast as her actions. Where would Griff be waiting? In the Foyer de la Danse? Would he find his way backstage? Would he know who to ask? If only she'd known he was coming, she could have made arrangements.

She flung the door open.

And there he was, coming down the corridor, looking drop-dead divine in formal black evening clothes.

Eva's heart thumped hard. She was trembling. She couldn't believe it really was Griff. Here in Paris.

'Hi,' she whispered as he came to a halt.

'Hi,' was all he said too.

She had to grip the door for support while her heart kept up its reckless thumping. Griff had come all this way and he looked amazing. So tall and broad-shouldered and smooth in his dinner jacket, but still with that rough, untidy hair that she loved. So gorgeous, in fact, that she couldn't think of any of the appropriate things to say.

She didn't thank him for the flowers, or ask him why he was here, or whether he'd enjoyed the show. He had, after all, just witnessed his first ballet performance, but she didn't ask Griff any of these questions.

Instead, she acted on instincts that had been too long suppressed. She launched recklessly forward, flinging her arms around his neck.

'It's so good to see you.'

Griff's arms encircled her. 'Damsel, you were amazing tonight.'

She pressed closer, wanting to bury her nose where his sun-bronzed neck showed above his stiff collar. 'I've missed you so much.'

'Truly, you were magnificent.'

Griff smelled so good. And he felt good too. So strong beneath his sleek, expensive suit. 'Oh, Griff.'

'There were so many things I wanted to tell you, but that was before I saw you tonight.'

They were talking at cross purposes. Griff was in danger of being overawed by all the fuss, while Eva was simply desperate to have his arms around her, his lips locked with hers.

Grabbing his hand, she drew him with her as she backed towards the open doorway of her dressing room. 'Come in.'

He didn't need a second invitation.

But once he was inside and the door was safely closed and surreptitiously locked, he looked around at the huge piles of flowers.

'Wow!'

Eva gave an impatient shake of her head. She didn't want to talk about the performance, or the audience's wonderful, over-the-top reception. None of that mattered now.

All she wanted was for Griff to kiss her. He wouldn't back off now. Surely, not after coming all this way?

'It's so good to see you,' she said again.

'You too.' Griff's grey eyes were bright and shiny.

Now, in the well-lit dressing room, she could see that he seemed a little shaken.

Perhaps this wasn't quite the moment to jump his bones as she longed to do.

'So now you've had your first taste of the ballet,' she said instead, as she righted the chair she'd knocked in her haste to find him. 'What did you think of it?'

For the first time Griff smiled, although his smile was still a little shaky. 'You want my honest opinion?'

'Sure,' she said bravely, although she didn't know what she would do if he'd hated it.

'I think I'm hooked.'

'Hooked on the ballet?' She couldn't help grinning like an eager child. 'You liked *Romeo and Juliet*?'

'I loved it.' Griff's smile was warm now and his eyes held that special light that caused all kinds of melting sensations inside her. 'Especially you, Eva. You were sensational.'

She was blushing. His praise meant so much to her.

'But I have to apologise,' Griff said next.

The change in his tone made her suddenly nervous. 'Why?'

'For taking so damned long to get here. I was jealous of your dancing. I never thought you could love me as much as you loved to dance. It's stupid, I know. I'm wiser now, I promise.'

Eva drew a sharp breath. This was such a big admission. Huge. She had no idea where it might take them but, right at this moment, it didn't seem to matter.

'Well, you're here now,' she said, stepping boldly forward and slipping her arms around him again. 'And you're not going to reject me now, are you?'

A soft sound, half-laugh, half-groan, escaped Griff, but he didn't back away. Better still, his hands came up to frame Eva's face as he leaned in to kiss her.

CHAPTER ELEVEN

DON'T RUSH THIS, Griff warned himself as his lips met Eva's. He was sure there were serious matters they needed to discuss before they got carried away, but right now he couldn't remember a single one of them. Good intentions hardly counted when Eva was pressing close, pushing her heavenly slender body against him in ways guaranteed to blitz his self-control.

Within seconds Griff was lost. Lost in the deliciousness and the smell and the feel of her. As his hands glided over her lovely limbs and under her dress, he was lost to desire too strong for restraint.

If there were correct protocols for theatre dressing rooms, they flew out of the window now. He and Eva had been waiting too long. Their passions were running too high. They were lovers reunited. Tonight there were no holds barred.

Later, they spent a scant ten minutes at the party in the Foyer de la Danse, where Eva politely acknowledged the enthusiasm of the special audience members who'd been invited to the after show supper.

She hoped she didn't look too excited and inordinately happy as she introduced Griff to Oliver Damson.

In truth, she found it hard to concentrate on anything. She was too buzzy and elated. Too conscious of Griff's physical presence at her side. She kept wanting to touch him again.

Oliver looked Griff up and down and said, 'So you're the culprit, are you?'

Poor Griff was, of course, totally baffled.

'Griff has no idea what you're talking about,' Eva said, sending Oliver a warning frown.

'Hmm,' was Oliver's response, but then he offered them both a paternal smile. 'Off you go. Get home. Eva has another performance tomorrow night and she needs her beauty sleep.'

So he'd obviously guessed how madly in love she was. Eva wondered how many others had noticed.

'What was all that about?' Griff asked when they were outside on the pavement, hailing a taxi. 'Why am I a culprit?'

'I can explain,' Eva told him. 'You'll come back to my place, won't you?'

'Is that an invitation?' he asked with a smile.

'Of course,' she said as a taxi pulled into the kerb and she gave the driver her address.

It seemed Griff was happy to accept and, once they were inside, sitting together on the back seat, Eva took his hand, as she'd been dying to do. 'You probably won't believe this, but tonight, just before the show, I told Oliver that I want to retire.'

Griff stared at her. 'But you've just worked your butt off to get back on stage. You were fantastic tonight.'

'Well, yes, I've achieved my goal, but tonight I also realised that it wasn't enough.'

'What do you want to do?' Griff sounded worried now.

Eva couldn't help grinning as she told him. 'Apart from giving the younger dancers their chance at stardom by stepping out of the way, I'm taking a job in Brisbane with Ballet Pacifique.'

'As a dancer?'

'No, as their artistic director. I was incredibly lucky. They offered me the job last November and I turned them down. Today, when I called back, they'd got down to the shortlist and were about to start interviews.'

'But they still want you?'

'Yes. I managed to hang onto the job of my dreams by the skin of my teeth.'

'Well done.'

Now it was Eva's turn to be worried. 'Are you pleased, Griff?'

'Yes, of course,' he said. 'Congratulations.'

But he was quiet as the taxi turned into her street and pulled up outside her apartment. He insisted on paying the fare and Eva, somewhat subdued, introduced him to Balzac, the concierge's glamorous grey cat, while they waited for the lift to arrive.

The lift made its way creakily upwards and Eva started to feel nervous again, uneasy about the pause in their conversation at a crucial moment. She unlocked the door to her apartment and flicked a switch that turned on lamps.

'Oh, Eva,' Griff said. 'This is beautiful.' He walked into the lounge room, looking about him at her paintings, at her carefully chosen furnishings. He stepped closer to study her collection of shells, and the piece of coral she'd found in Emerald Bay. Then he turned his attention to the lovely view of city lights, including the Eiffel Tower.

At last, he turned to her. 'Can you really give this up?'

Eva nodded. 'Of course.' It was only bricks and mortar, after all.

Griff seemed to need a moment to take this in. His chest rose and fell as he inhaled deeply, then let his breath out again.

'Would you like a drink?' Eva remembered her hostess duties. 'Scotch? Wine? Coffee?'

'What are you having?'

She smiled. 'Hot chocolate.'

Griff smiled too. 'I'll go for the Scotch, thanks.' He followed her into her tiny kitchen and watched as she fixed his drink and set a pot of milk on the stove.

'Would you like ice with this?'

'Just a little, thanks.' Griff's gaze was serious as he took the glass she offered. 'What made you change your mind about the Brisbane job?' he asked. 'I suppose you wanted to be closer to Laine.'

Eva was about to reach for the tin of powdered chocolate, but now she stopped and turned to him. 'Well, yes, being able to see Laine is a bonus. How is she, by the way? I can't believe I didn't ask earlier, but I guess I was a little distracted.'

This brought another smile from Griff. 'She's fighting fit. Claims she's the size of a hippopotamus, but she looks perfect to me.'

For Eva, the fact that their daughter was due to give birth any day now truly highlighted the significance of Griff's journey here to the other side of the world.

His gaze was serious again. 'Are you sure about giving up dancing, Eva? It's a huge step.'

She nodded. It was vitally important that she explained this properly and she had to choose her words carefully. 'It came to me during the final rehearsal. I was remembering a conversation you and I had, about wisdom and courage. I realised that taking a job in Brisbane wasn't just wise and sensible; it was where I really wanted to be. Then I realised that I was only staying away because I lacked courage. I was scared.'

'Scared?'

'Yes, I was scared to live there if you didn't love me.' Eva couldn't believe she'd been brave enough to say this.

When Griff opened his mouth to protest, she held up her hand. 'Tonight, before the show, it dawned on me that I was going to miss you, Griff, wherever I was. Even living here in a lovely and exciting city like Paris, I've missed you terribly, so, at least, if I was in the same city, I could see you from time to time.' She swallowed nervously. 'Even if you were only ever on the fringes of my life.'

'The fringes? Why would I be on the fringes?'

'Well, I wasn't sure, you see.'

'Oh, Eva.' Setting aside his glass, Griff reached for her. 'I love you. I don't know why it's taken me so long to tell you. I need you. I want you in the *centre* of my life, not on the fringes. I love you so much.'

Such a wonderful rush of relief swamped Eva, she might have melted back into his arms at that moment, but a hissing noise behind her reminded her of the milk on the stove. Quickly, she turned, switched it off and shifted the pot to a cooler spot.

Shyly, she smiled at Griff. 'Is that why you're here? To tell me that you love me?'

'Yes, but, to be honest, I was scared too. I didn't want to take you away from your dancing. I was looking into the possibility of getting some kind of work visa and brushing up on my French.'

'Oh, Griff.' She was overawed by the thought of him giving up everything for her. Slipping her arms around him, she kissed his jaw, where a five o'clock shadow was starting to show.

'I love you,' she murmured as she kissed her way from his jaw to his lips.

He was already there to meet her, his lips parting, his arms tightening around her, and happiness swum in Eva's veins as they let their kiss deepen at a leisurely pace. Their drinks abandoned, Griff drew Eva closer and they kissed and kissed, like teenagers. Or, rather, like adults who at last had the luxury to enjoy the lack of haste, to savour a slow, seductive intimacy, secure and confident at last in the love that had been waiting for them for so long.

CHAPTER TWELVE

LAINE AND DYLAN were married at the very end of winter. By that time, Eva had returned to Brisbane and baby Leo was four months old. He was a gorgeous, roly-poly little fellow, full of smiles, who easily won everyone's hearts, especially Eva's and Griff's.

The day of the wedding dawned bright and sunny, perfect for an outdoor wedding, with blue skies, only a few fluffy white clouds and clear sunshine that brought the first hints of spring.

At Dylan's family home in Brookfield, a big white marquee had been erected on a pristine lawn. Seating for the ceremony was arranged under a huge spreading jacaranda tree and the path leading to this area was bordered by palm trees in pots decorated with white satin bows and white and silver balloons.

'Dylan's family have gone all out with the preparations,' Laine had told Eva and Griff, and now the stage was clearly set for a joyous occasion.

'Come a bit early,' Laine had also told Eva. 'I'll be getting dressed at Dylan's parents' house. It saves any worries about traffic and trying to get to the wedding on time, and it's a better venue for the photographer. I'd really love to see you before I walk down the aisle.'

Eva was touched by the invitation.

'I'll be in a little studio out the back of the house,' Laine added. 'And Dylan won't be allowed to get so much as a glimpse of me.'

Eva wore her grey silk dress, rather than buying anything new. She was very aware that this was Ruth Templeton's day to shine as mother of the bride, and she was prepared to stay very much in the background.

Eva's main task today, she'd decided, was to keep a check on her emotions. She was so very conscious that, in her family, Laine would be the first woman in three generations to marry her baby's father. The first to provide her child with the security of a complete family unit. Eva was immensely proud of Laine and so very happy for her and Dylan.

'Wow!' Griff said when he saw her dressed for the wedding.

Eva had chosen silver accessories to complement the grey silk and she'd pulled her hair into a low chignon with a pink rosebud tucked into it.

'You haven't brushed up too badly, yourself,' she told him, eyeing his beautifully cut charcoal suit and stylish grey and silver tie.

They shared happy smiles. It was almost as if they'd planned their outfits to match. As if they were meant to—

Don't, Eva warned herself. *Don't get too nostalgic today.*

She and Griff were blissfully happy and she had absolutely no doubt that her return to Brisbane had been the right decision. Annoyingly, the mistakes of her past still had the power to haunt her, but today her eyes were on the future and not on the past and the years that they'd lost.

Today she had to stay completely focused on Laine and Dylan. This was all about them.

When Eva and Griff arrived, they were greeted by Dylan's father, who was dressed rather grandly in a formal suit for the wedding, while happily sporting a towel over his shoulder to catch any dribbles from the grandson in his arms.

'Welcome, welcome,' he said, all beaming smiles, and he immediately offered Griff a calming snifter of Scotch.

'Would you like my help with the baby?' Eva offered, holding out her arms in readiness.

'Later, not now.' Her jovial host gave a wave of his hand towards the back of the house. 'I believe there's a bride out there who's expecting you.'

'Oh, lovely. Yes, of course.'

Eva found Laine, just as her daughter had promised, in a small garden studio at the back of the main house.

Although it was Ruth Templeton who met her at the door.

'Ruth,' Eva said. 'How lovely you look.'

Ruth was dressed in a crimson two piece suit and her normally limp grey hair had been curled and carefully styled. Her face was glowing with excitement. 'Thank you.' Her joyous smile broadened. 'I wanted to wear something bright and cheerful on such a happy day.'

'That colour's perfect on you,' Eva told her.

Eyes wide, Ruth nodded towards the studio's interior. 'Wait till you see our girl.'

Our girl. Eva hadn't expected to be so generously included and she felt the sting of tears.

No. Not now. She had to stay strong. Heaven knew she was used to putting on a performance face.

But then she saw Laine.

Oh, my goodness.

Her daughter was breathtakingly beautiful. Already Laine was almost back to her pre-pregnancy slimness and her wedding dress, made of exquisite filigree lace, was cleverly cut to flatter her slightly changed figure.

Laine's dark hair was gleaming with health. The purple streaks had grown out and a fresh, new wispy cut framed her face perfectly. Her complexion was flawless and glowing and her headdress was a simple, elegant arrangement of white flowers pinned into her hair. Laine smiled at Eva and her grey eyes were shining with happiness and excitement, and with irrepressible joy.

'Oh, Laine.'

It was all Eva could manage before her throat became painfully choked.

'She's going to blow Dylan away, isn't she?' Ruth said, still smiling broadly.

'Yes, absolutely,' Eva agreed, although she was also wondering how Griff would react when he saw his beautiful grown-up daughter.

'Thanks, both of you, darlings.' Laine hugged them carefully, so as not to smudge her make-up, before the photographer took photos of the three of them in different poses and combinations. Then Laine crossed the room to collect her bridal bouquet from a box on the table.

She was halfway across the room when it happened.

One minute she was fine, moving easily and confidently. Then she stumbled and let out a cry.

Eva's heart leapt high.

'Laine!' cried Ruth.

Both women rushed to her aid.

Luckily, Laine didn't fall, but she was reaching down to remove one of her glamorous silk-sheathed, high heeled shoes. With a look of dismay, she held it up. The slender heel had snapped.

'Oh!' cried a horrified Ruth. 'Oh, Laine, no! How can that have happened? What can we do?'

'I don't know.' The poor girl looked utterly forlorn as she stared at the sleek satin shoe with its snapped, dangling heel. In a blink she'd been transformed from an excited, hopeful and beautiful bride into a picture of utter dismay.

'Did you bring any spare shoes?' asked Ruth.

Laine gave a doleful shake of her head. 'I only have my blue sneakers. Not a great look for a bride.' She pushed the snapped heel back into place. 'I wonder if we can fix this… Maybe Dylan's parents have some superglue.'

'Oh, I don't think that's a good idea.' Ruth sounded frantic and she was madly looking about her, as if a miracle might materialise out of thin air. 'I know I'd spend the whole wedding on tenterhooks, waiting for your heel to snap again.'

Anxiously, Ruth looked down at her own feet. 'I'd lend you my shoes if I could, but my feet are too wide. You'd walk right out of them. And black's the wrong colour for you, anyway.'

'I'm afraid I'm no help.' The photographer pointed to his black leather lace-up boots with a rueful smile.

'Try mine,' said Eva, quickly slipping off a shoe.

Laine gave a huff of surprise. 'But—'

'Go on,' Eva said, holding out the silver shoe. 'You never know—it might fit.'

'But what about you? What will you wear?'

Eva gave a shrugging smile. 'I have ballet flats in my handbag. Ever since I had trouble with my hip, I've carried them as a safety precaution. So if these shoes fit you, you're very welcome to them. We can't send you off as a barefoot bride.'

'Wow, thanks,' said Laine.

'You should probably sit down to try them on.'

Laine did this, sitting carefully on the edge of a chair in her elegant lacy gown. The two mothers and the photographer all held their breath as she fitted her foot into the shoe.

'I think it fits,' Laine said in a cautious stage whisper, as if she didn't want to tempt fate.

'Oh, thank heavens,' breathed Ruth. 'Try the other one.'

Eva handed the second shoe over and Laine slipped it on. As she did so, Eva noticed again the butterfly birthmark on her daughter's ankle and her thoughts flashed straight back to the day of her baby's birth and her first sight of that tiny, memorable mark. For a dangerous moment, Eva felt tears threaten again.

She was saved by Ruth's intense command.

'Stand up now, Laine. See if you can walk in them.'

Obediently, Laine stood, then walked, gingerly at first and then more confidently. 'They do fit!' she cried excitedly. 'They're perfect.'

She shot Eva a look of joyful surprise. 'We must have exactly the same-sized feet.' Then, with a wondrous smile, she looked down at her feet, peeping from beneath the hem of her white silk gown. 'And the silver looks so pretty.'

'Then you're very welcome to them,' said Eva as she slipped on the black ballet flats.

Laine now looked at Eva's feet and frowned. 'Are you sure?'

'Absolutely. Of course I'm sure, darling.'

Eva had never been surer of anything. For the first time in twenty years, she had been able to perform one small motherly gesture for her daughter, and the tiny act filled her with intense satisfaction.

To her surprise, Ruth Templeton hugged her. 'Thank you, Eva,' the other woman said fervently. 'Thank you for the shoes, and thank you for giving us our beautiful daughter.'

Eva couldn't speak. Her heart was too full. She was glowing with over-the-top joy. For the first time, she could finally look at the adoption as a happy gift instead of a painful sacrifice. She saw the silver glitter of tears in Ruth's eyes and felt her own eyes well up.

'Hey, don't start bawling, you two!' ordered their daughter. 'I don't want two blubbering mothers.'

It was the warning the women needed, bringing them back from the brink. Instead of weeping, they shared wobbly smiles and then a shy laugh, just as Ruth's husband, Donald, appeared in the studio's doorway.

'I do believe there's a beautiful bride in here,' Donald said, grinning.

'There is, indeed,' Laine told him triumphantly. 'And she now has two shoes and she's waiting impatiently to be married.'

* * *

Griff frowned when he saw Eva in her ballet flats instead of the silver heels. 'Is your hip hurting?' he asked with concern.

'No,' Eva assured him and she explained about Laine's last-minute heel catastrophe. 'I lent her my silver shoes. They fitted her perfectly.'

She smiled at him. She was feeling so much better now. Calmer and happier, and relieved to throw off at least some of the guilt from her past, and to look forward instead to an ongoing loving relationship with Laine, Dylan and Leo. But she wondered how Griff would feel when he saw his daughter as a beautiful bride, and watched her walking down the aisle on another man's arm.

'I've been so worried about weeping all over the place today,' she told him. 'But I think I have a plan. Whenever I feel mopey, I'll just focus on those silver shoes and pray that the heels hold.'

Griff smiled and reached for her hand. 'Sounds like an excellent plan.' His warm fingers wrapped around hers and he squeezed her hand gently. 'I might adopt it too. Come, let's watch our kid get married.'

The wedding was an all-round happy occasion, as lovely as everyone had hoped it would be. Dylan's shiny-eyed smile as he watched Laine walking towards him had everyone melting, and the young couple's vows were beautifully sincere.

The reception in the marquee was relaxed and friendly. The other guests didn't know the significance of Eva and Griff's relationship to the happy couple, and if they were asked they merely said they were friends of the bride.

After the bridal waltz, Laine danced with Donald Templeton, and Eva and Griff were happy to watch on. But then, to their surprise, Laine crossed the dance floor and beckoned to Griff.

'Go on,' Eva whispered when he hesitated.

Laine was holding out her hand with a special smile just for Griff, and Eva's heart filled her throat as he rose and walked to their daughter. As Griff and Laine began to dance, Eva almost allowed the poignancy of the moment to touch her too deeply, but she focused on the shoes, her silver shoes.

She had spent decades as a professional ballerina and yet she knew this simple waltz on a temporary wooden floor would stay locked in her memory till the end of her days.

CHAPTER THIRTEEN

As a brilliant sun rose over the eastern rim of Emerald Bay, the household on the clifftop was stirring.

Twelve-month-old Leo woke first and crawled to the edge of his cot, where he grabbed at the bars and pulled himself up to stand on sturdy, chubby legs. When his first cry penetrated the morning stillness, Laine stirred in the next room.

'I'll get him,' Dylan said, slipping quickly out of their bed.

'Bless you.' Laine adored her beautiful baby boy but she'd also developed an enormous gratitude for the enthusiasm with which her husband viewed fatherhood. Now, she happily pulled the sheet over her head and snuggled down for a few extra minutes of precious peace.

Down the hallway in the main bedroom, Griff heard the baby's cry and woke. Almost immediately, Eva was stirring beside him. After an entire year, he still considered it a miracle to wake and find her beside him each morning. Now, he watched her eyes open slowly and saw the flash of aqua blue that had first bewitched him way back in high school.

'Morning,' she murmured sleepily, pressing her lips to his bare shoulder.

'Morning.' He kissed the tip of her nose. For a few minutes they lay, listening to the sounds of the sea and the gulls calling.

Eva yawned and stretched. 'I might go and get Leo.'

'I think Dylan's beaten you to it.'

'Oh.' She smiled. 'My turn tomorrow morning then.'

'Fancy an early morning swim?' Griff asked.

Her eyes flashed wide with interest, but then she pulled a face. 'I promised I'd do omelettes for breakfast.'

'We'd still have time for a quick dip.'

She grinned. 'Why not?' Already she was sitting up, throwing off the sheet and swinging her slim legs over the edge of the bed.

Suppressing the urge to roll her straight back onto the mattress, Griff went to fetch their bathers from the balcony where they'd been left to dry.

They'd bought this house at Emerald Bay six months ago and it had quickly proved to be a wonderful getaway—the perfect counterpoint to their busy city lives. At Christmas, with the addition of a couple of caravans parked in the yard, it would also be the perfect venue for a happy family gathering that would include Eva's mother and her husband, as well as the Templetons and Laine, Dylan and little Leo, who everyone agreed was a ripper of a kid.

Tomorrow Griff's parents would be arriving for one of their regular visits. To Griff's delight, they'd embraced Eva and their daughter and her family with reassuring warmth.

'It's so much more peaceful at your place than it is

at Julia's with her tribe,' his mother had confided. 'And Emerald Bay is so beautiful.'

True. This morning the view from their bedroom showed the autumn day was dawning fresh and clear, with a nice clean wave breaking onshore. Eva, looking incredibly youthful and slim, with a baggy old T-shirt over her bikini, grinned at Griff.

'Race you to the surf,' she dared, and then with a laugh, and without waiting while he gathered up their towels, was off, out of the door and over the lawn, down the stone steps that had been cut into the side of the cliff.

She had reached the bottom and was skirting the rocky headland at the end of the beach when she saw the bright flash of blue that stopped her.

'What is it?' Griff called as he caught up.

'Look!' She pointed to a small pool hollowed out of the rock. 'Look what's here.'

Coming closer, Griff saw, swimming in the clear basin of seawater, a small, perfect, bright blue fish with an even brighter yellow tail.

'A damsel,' he said softly.

'Yes. She must have washed in here with the tide. Isn't she beautiful?'

'Amazingly so.'

They stood together, watching the little fish circle the pond, slightly awed by their discovery.

'I'd hate to think she was going to be stuck here,' Eva said. 'But she'll leave again with the next high tide, won't she?'

'Yes.' Griff nodded and then he looked away, as if an unpleasant thought had struck him.

'What?' Eva asked. 'What's the matter?'

'Nothing.' He gave a careless shrug.

But Eva, with the new perceptiveness she'd gained from living side by side with this man, guessed the cause of his frown and she reached for his hand. 'I won't be leaving you again, Griff.'

'No, I know you won't.'

'You believe me, don't you?'

He was smiling now but, despite the smile, she saw that soul-deep look in his eyes that she remembered from so long ago.

'I promise, Griff.'

'That's good to know,' he said lightly. 'Because I was about to suggest that it's time we followed our daughter's good example and got married.'

Eva gasped, rendered suddenly breathless by shock and delight. Then a small, laughing huff escaped her. 'I thought you'd never ask.'

'I'm asking you now, Damsel.'

And indeed he was. Standing on the rocky headland where they'd once shared their first kiss, Griff took both of her hands in his. 'Will you do me the huge honour of becoming my wife?'

'Yes, please!'

The little blue fish completed yet another circuit of its tiny pond and Eva, with a shriek of unfettered joy, leapt into the arms of the one and only man who could make her world right.

* * * * *

Meet the Fortunes

Fortune of the Month: Kieran Fortune

Age: 31

Vital statistics: Oh. My. Hunk. Smart, sexy and rich.

Claim to Fame: Vice president of Robinson Tech, voted Most Likely to Break Hearts.

Romantic prospects: Excellent. Or at least they were until little Rosie came into his life. A three-year-old is not exactly an aphrodisiac.

"I'll admit it—I'm not the nurturing type. I should have said no when Zach asked me to be Rosabelle's guardian if anything should happen to him. But what were the odds?

Now I've got this crazy-cute toddler and no idea what to do with her. I'm lucky that Zach's old girlfriend, Dana, has offered to help. I wish I had half Dana's maternal instincts. To be honest, I wish I had Dana in my arms—no, in my bed. But even I have more scruples than that. Zach's barely cold in the ground, and Dana deserves more than I am able to give her. My fantasies of playing house with her need to remain exactly that…"

* * *

The Fortunes of Texas:
The Secret Fortunes—
A new generation of heroes and heartbreakers!

FROM FORTUNE
TO FAMILY MAN

BY
JUDY DUARTE

All rights reserved including the right of reproduction in whole or in part in any form. This edition is published by arrangement with Harlequin Books S.A.

This is a work of fiction. Names, characters, places, locations and incidents are purely fictional and bear no relationship to any real life individuals, living or dead, or to any actual places, business establishments, locations, events or incidents. Any resemblance is entirely coincidental.

This book is sold subject to the condition that it shall not, by way of trade or otherwise, be lent, resold, hired out or otherwise circulated without the prior consent of the publisher in any form of binding or cover other than that in which it is published and without a similar condition including this condition being imposed on the subsequent purchaser.

® and ™ are trademarks owned and used by the trademark owner and/or its licensee. Trademarks marked with ® are registered with the United Kingdom Patent Office and/or the Office for Harmonisation in the Internal Market and in other countries.

First Published in Great Britain 2017
By Mills & Boon, an imprint of HarperCollins*Publishers*
1 London Bridge Street, London, SE1 9GF

© 2017 Harlequin Books S.A.

Special thanks and acknowledgement are given to Judy Duarte for her contribution to the Fortunes of Texas: The Secret Fortunes continuity.

ISBN: 978-0-263-92287-5

23-0417

Our policy is to use papers that are natural, renewable and recyclable products and made from wood grown in sustainable forests. The logging and manufacturing processes conform to the legal environmental regulations of the country of origin.

Printed and bound in Spain
by CPI, Barcelona

Since 2002, *USA TODAY* bestselling author **Judy Duarte** has written over forty books for Mills & Boon Cherish, earned two RITA® Award nominations, won two Maggie Awards and received a National Readers' Choice Award. When she's not cooped up in her writing cave, she enjoys traveling with her husband and spending quality time with her grandchildren. You can learn more about Judy and her books at her website, www.judyduarte.com, or at Facebook.com/judyduartenovelist.

To Michelle Major, Stella Bagwell,
Karen Rose Smith, Marie Ferrarella,
Nancy Robards Thompson and Allison Leigh.
I can't think of a better team of authors
to work with on a continuity series.

Chapter One

As Kieran Fortune Robinson stood with the other mourners at the Oakdale Cemetery, the Texas sky was a stunning shade of blue, the sun was bright and a cluster of birds sang from their perch in the nearby magnolia tree. But the spring day was dismal, the mood somber.

Three weeks ago, Zach Lawson had been thrown from a horse and suffered a skull fracture. As soon as Kieran had gotten word of the tragic accident, he'd rushed to the hospital to visit his best friend and to offer his support to Zach's parents.

"Only family is allowed to visit patients in the ICU," a nurse had said.

Zach's father had slipped an arm around Kieran

and clutched him with a firm grip. "This is my second son."

In a way, that claim had been true. Sam and Sandra Lawson had treated Kieran as a family member ever since Zach had brought him home to visit during their first winter break at college. A born and bred city boy, Kieran had actually enjoyed the time he'd spent at the Leaning L, even though his busy schedule hadn't allowed for as many visits as he might have liked.

Oddly enough, he and Zach hadn't had much in common, other than a quick wit, a love of sports and a competitive spirit. They'd met on the football field their first semester at Texas A&M and had become fast friends. Other than that, they were as different as a cowboy and a techie could be.

Zach had been an only child, while Kieran had seven brothers and sisters, although that number seemed to be constantly growing, thanks to his dad's years of philandering and the illegitimate half siblings who'd increased their ranks.

And there lay their biggest difference of all—the men who'd fathered them. Sam Lawson was a rancher of modest means who owned a small spread outside Austin. On the other hand, Gerald Robinson, a quirky tech mogul who'd once been known as Jerome Fortune, had built a computer company into a billion-dollar corporation.

After graduation, Kieran had become a computer analyst and eventually the vice president of Robinson Tech. On the outside, it might appear that he'd done his family proud, and in a sense he probably had. But to this day, he felt a lot closer to Zach's parents than he did his own. And that was why Sam's announcement to the hospital staff that Kieran was his second son had touched his heart in a warm and unexpected way.

But nothing had prepared him for what he saw when he approached Zach's bedside, where his once vibrant buddy lay unconscious and hooked up to a beeping ventilator.

If there'd been a chance that Zach might pull through, that he'd be able to go home to Rosabelle, his three-year-old daughter, they all would have found their hospital vigil easier to handle. Still, Sam and Sandra clung to each other and held on to their faith, praying for a miracle that never came.

Zach had remained on life support for two long weeks before his parents finally accepted the fact that their only child, a son born to them late in life, was virtually dead. And now here they were, at the cemetery, saying their final goodbyes.

Kieran stood beside Zach's parents, trying to be the second son Sam had claimed he was and to offer his support. But he wasn't sure how much help he could be. Sandra and Sam, both in their seventies and not in the best of health, were overcome by grief.

What really tugged at Kieran's heart, though, was three-year-old Rosabelle, who held her grandma's hand, her little brow creased as if she was trying to understand all that was happening around her. But how could she, when even Kieran found it so unsettling, so unfair?

A monarch butterfly fluttered by, weaving through the mourners as if trying to lift the spirits of those who'd come to pay their last respects.

After the pastor of the community church finished the eulogy, little Rosie pulled her hand away from her grandma's and reached for Kieran, silently requesting that he pick her up.

He did so, holding her close, wishing what little comfort he had to give would help.

"My daddy went to heaven," Rosie whispered.

"I know, honey." Kieran rested his head against hers, catching the light fragrance of her baby shampoo.

"I'm gonna miss him," Rosie added.

"Me, too." Zach's death was a huge loss that would affect them all.

"Look!" Rosie pointed to the orange-and-black butterfly that now landed on a spray of yellow roses. "It's a flutterby."

"I see it," he whispered, not bothering to correct her pronunciation. What did it matter anyway? He was just glad that she had something to hold her interest, to keep her from thinking about her loss, about not ever seeing her daddy again.

Kieran glanced through the crowd and spotted Dana Trevino, the woman Zach had been dating at the time of the accident. Her long, red hair was swept up into a tidy topknot, reminding him of a librarian. In that plain black dress, she looked like one, too.

A grad student and a research librarian at the Austin History Center, Dana wasn't anything like the women Kieran dated. Not that she wasn't attractive. She had a pretty face and a warm smile. At five-foot-five, she also had a willowy build, although she tended to hide it behind loose-fitting skirts and conservative blouses.

Still, Kieran had thought the cowboy and the librarian an odd match, although he suspected that Dana had been drawn to Zach's country charm and his Will Rogers style, which had given him a combination of wisdom, common sense and humor.

To be honest, Kieran wasn't sure what it was about Dana that had appealed to Zach. They'd never talked about it, but there must have been something special about her.

Still, for some reason he'd never thought their relationship would last. But who was he to judge? He never dated anyone longer than a couple of months, so he had no idea how to even define words like *special* or *long-term.*

As the stoic rep from the mortuary thanked everyone for coming, Sandra Lawson turned to Kieran. "Will you come back to the house with us? Sam and I want to talk to you." Her eyes filled with tears, and her bottom lip wobbled.

"Of course," Kieran said, although he suddenly felt compelled to pass little Rosie to the couple, hurry to his Mercedes and get the hell out of Dodge. But like Sam had told the hospital staff, Kieran was their second son.

Thankfully, he seemed to have already shed most of his tears in the hospital. By the time Zach's organs had been donated to give others a chance at a new and better life, Kieran's grief had seemed to subside.

He stole a peek at Dana, who appeared as prim and proper as ever. She clutched a wadded up tissue in her hands, but no tears filled her eyes.

Had she, like Kieran, done most of her crying in the weeks and days before the funeral? Had she also begun to let go of Zach and move on?

"This concludes the service," the mortuary guy said. "The family would like to invite you all back to their house for refreshments."

Kieran wasn't the least bit hungry, but he could sure use a drink—a stiff one.

Sam slipped his arm around his wife. "You about ready to go, honey?"

Sandra merely nodded, then blotted her eyes with a lace handkerchief.

"Can I ride with Uncle Kieran?" Rosie asked.

"Your car seat is already in our car," Sandra said. "It'll be easier if you ride with us."

Sam placed a hand on Kieran's shoulder. "You're coming home with us, aren't you, son?"

"Yes, of course. I'll meet you there." Kieran brushed a kiss on the little girl's cheek then passed her to her grandparents.

As Sam, Sandra and Rosie walked away from the graveside, Kieran remained a little longer so he could say a final goodbye to his best friend.

The monarch butterfly was still fluttering about. When it landed on top of the spray of red and white carnations covering the casket, he glanced to his right, where Dana continued to stand.

"Are you going to the Lawsons' house?" he asked.

"Yes, I promised them I'd be there."

It wasn't a surprise that Sandra and Sam wanted—or needed—to hang on to everyone and everything that reminded them of Zach.

"How've you been?" Kieran asked. "Are you holding up okay?"

Dana turned and caught his eye, a slight smile chasing the grief from her face. "I'm doing all right. After the last two weeks...well, that was tough."

To say the least.

"I feel so bad for Rosie," she added.

"So do I."

"At least she and Zach had been living with Sam and Sandra. That should help her adjust to not having her daddy anymore."

Kieran sure hoped Dana was right. Again he studied the redhead, noting a simple, wholesome beauty he'd missed seeing before. She'd implied that she was adjusting to her own loss, but he wondered if that was really true or the kind of thing people said when they struggled for the right words.

"Sandra mentioned that you'd been at the ranch with them earlier today," he said.

"I went to help some of the ladies from her Bible study prepare food for after the service."

"Do you need a ride back?"

"No, I have my car." She nodded toward a white Honda Civic parked about ten feet from his black

Mercedes. It wasn't a fancy car or the latest model, but it was clean and recently polished, the wheel rims shiny.

Funny what things a guy noticed at times like these.

"Then I'll see you back at the house," Kieran said.

Dana smiled—not a smile that was joyful and happy, but one that was filled with compassion.

Was *that* what Zach had seen in her?

Actually, standing there with her now, the afternoon sun casting a glow on those auburn strands of hair, Kieran noted that she had a natural beauty that was almost alluring. But he shook off the inappropriate assessment as quickly as it awakened. Dana had been Zach's girlfriend, and even though he was gone now, Kieran wasn't about to overstep the bounds of male brotherhood.

As he got into his car, he made up his mind to do whatever he could to help the Lawsons move on with their lives.

Growing up in the Robinson family, Kieran had learned that money could fix just about anything. But all the gold in Fort Knox wasn't going to make things better or easier for him. Not when so many different feelings were in play and he'd always made it a point to avoid any touchy-feely stuff.

Still, while he might fall miserably short in his attempt to offer Zach's family his emotional support, he'd do his best.

He owed his best friend that much.

* * *

Dana had managed to hold back her tears during the funeral. But once she climbed into her car, her eyes welled.

She reached into the pocket of her skirt, pulled out the wadded tissue she'd stashed there earlier and blotted her tears.

Would she make it through the day without breaking down? She certainly hoped so. She wanted to stay strong for Sam and Sandra.

How are you holding up? Kieran had asked just minutes before. It seemed to be a regular question she'd been faced with…at school, at work and, most recently, at the Leaning L while she'd helped the church women prepare the food for today.

She really didn't blame people for assuming she'd been devastated by Zach's loss. She mourned him, of course, but she wasn't the grieving fiancée they thought her to be. They'd dated six months, but in fact, she wasn't sure she'd even been his girlfriend. She'd certainly found him attractive, and she'd adored his sense of humor. But it was his family life that had appealed to her the most. That was the reason she'd continued to date Zach after she realized he wasn't Mr. Right. She suspected Zach had known it, too.

His parents had created a warm, loving home on the Leaning L, and they'd always made her feel welcome. In addition, she adored Rosie, Zach's sweet, precocious daughter. Since her mother had signed over full custody to Zach right after birth, that pretty much made Rosie an orphan, just like Dana was.

When Dana was twelve, she'd lost her parents in an accident. Without anyone who was either willing or able to step up and take her in, she'd gone into foster care.

Fortunately, Rosie wouldn't have to worry about that. The Lawsons had always been a big part of her life, so it wasn't like she'd be completely uprooted and shipped off to another home to live with people she didn't know. Dana took great comfort in that.

When she arrived at the Leaning L, she parked next to Kieran's Mercedes. It was only natural that he'd be invited back to the Lawsons' house. He and Zach had been the best of friends, even though the two men had been so dissimilar—and not just when it came to the clothes they wore, the music they liked or the social circles in which they ran.

Still, they'd been very close.

Much closer than Dana and Zach had ever been.

Before Dana could climb the wooden porch steps and let herself in, Kieran swung open the front door as if he'd been waiting just for her. Then again, she'd been right behind him.

"Come on in." He stepped aside so she could enter the small, cozy house that had always reminded her of the kind of place a ranching family might have lived in during the 1950s, with its rough-hewn paneling, the overstuffed, floral furniture with crocheted doilies over the armrests and a rag rug on the floor. It was all very Norman Rockwell. The only thing missing was a big, boxy television with a small black-and-white screen.

Maybe that was another reason she liked this

house—well, the vintage feel as well as the warm welcome she'd always received.

As she crossed the threshold, she caught a whiff of Kieran's cologne, something musky and woodsy, reminding her of a lazy summer day in the mountains. Something undoubtedly expensive and sold at only the finest stores in Austin.

"Sandra took Rosie to her room for a nap," Kieran said. "The poor kid could hardly hold her eyes open."

Dana acknowledged the comment with a nod, then scanned the living room, where the pastor of the church and several close family friends had gathered. They were seated on the sofa as well as on some of the chairs that had been moved from around the linen-covered table in the adjoining dining room.

The women from Sandra's Bible study and Dana had arrived early this morning and prepared the food, which would be set out as a buffet. Before leaving for the service, they'd stacked blue paper plates, white napkins and plasticware at one edge of the rectangular table, and placed a bouquet of spring flowers in the center.

Sam greeted Dana with a hug. "I'm glad you're here. Sandra and I wanted to talk to you as well as to Kieran. As soon as Rosie is sound asleep, we can go into the kitchen, where it'll be more private."

"Of course." Dana had no idea what they intended to say, but she was glad to be included in what seemed like a family discussion. She shot a glance at Kieran. Their gazes locked, their sympathies clearly united.

Moments later, Sandra entered the living room,

her eyes dry, yet still red-rimmed. "Rosie's finally taking a nap."

Sam nodded, then lifted his right hand, directing them to the doorway that led to the kitchen. "Shall we?"

When they entered the small, cozy kitchen, the counters lined with cakes and platters of cookies, memories slammed into Dana, causing her to pause in the middle of the room. One mental snapshot after another struck, the first one reminding her of the cold, rainy night last winter when she'd joined Sam, Sandra and Zach to play cards. The memories of times spent in this very room clicked in her mind as if she were watching the scenes on an old nickelodeon— the morning she'd helped Sandra bake cakes for the church bazaar, the afternoon she'd washed a bushel of apples that had come from trees in the family orchard, then learned how to make and can applesauce.

This particular kitchen, with its light green walls, white Formica countertops and floral printed café curtains, was also where Dana had last seen Zach alive and well. Sandra had invited her to dinner just three days before the accident. They'd had pot roast, carrots, mashed potatoes and gravy...

Dana shook off the memories before she fell apart and cried for all she'd lost. She'd loved her visits to the Leaning L, but now that Zach was gone, she might never be invited back.

Sandra, always the hostess, asked, "Would anyone like coffee?"

"Let me serve it for you," Dana said.

Normally, Zach's mom would have declined the help, but this wasn't a normal day. She took a seat at the antique oak table, practically collapsing in her chair.

Dana placed cream and sugar on the table, then filled several mugs with hot coffee and passed them out to Sam, Sandra, Zach and the pastor of the Oakdale Community Church, who'd been asked to join them in the kitchen. Since Dana preferred tea, she passed on having anything at all to drink.

"Last night," Sam began, "we… That is, me and… my wife…" His voice wobbled and cracked. He cleared his throat, paused a beat, then looked to the minister.

Pastor Mark nodded, then pushed his mug aside. "Sam and Sandra read over Zach's will last night, and they have a concern as well as a heartfelt request."

Dana still had no clue where this conversation was heading, but it was obviously in a direction the older couple needed their minister's help expressing.

Pastor Mark Wilder, who'd served his congregation for the last thirty years, scooted back his chair and got to his feet as if he was preparing for a sermon. "Sam and Sandra believe that Zach's wishes should be followed, but they also know he hadn't expected to die so suddenly or so young. And their biggest concern is for little Rosabelle."

Dana had no doubt about that. The couple adored their precious granddaughter.

"As you know," the pastor continued, "Rosie and Zach have been living with Sam and Sandra for her entire life. So the Leaning L is the only home she's ever known."

Where was he going with this? Dana assumed Rosie would stay with her grandparents. After all, she'd just lost her father. Who else would take her? Where else would she live?

Oh, no. Surely her mother hadn't resurfaced. From what Zach had told Dana, her pregnancy had been unexpected and unwanted. She'd planned to give her baby up for adoption, but Zach had refused to sign the paperwork, insisting that he wanted sole custody of their child. The woman had agreed and then walked away without a backward glance the moment she'd been discharged from the hospital.

Dana stole a glance at Kieran. The expression of concern he'd been wearing moments earlier had morphed into one that almost appeared panicked.

It wasn't until Pastor Mark completed his speech that Dana realized why.

"Zach gave custody of his daughter to Kieran."

Chapter Two

Kieran hadn't been sure the Lawsons had even known about the existence of Zach's will, but he had. He'd also been well aware of Zach's wishes when it came to who would raise Rosabelle. He just hadn't planned to bring it up, especially now.

When Zach had first mentioned his visit to the attorney and had asked Kieran to be Rosie's guardian if the unthinkable should happen, Kieran had laughed. Sure, he'd been honored to be chosen, but he'd known there had to be someone much better qualified than him to finish raising Zach's daughter.

What did Kieran know about kids—or parenting?

He didn't have any insecurity about his competence to do anything else. As one of the legitimate offspring of Gerald Robinson, aka Jerome Fortune

Robinson, he was certainly capable of taking care of her financially. He was a millionaire many times over and a damn good computer analyst. He was also good at making and investing money. But he was a man who knew his strengths, and parenting was not one of them. Hell, he certainly hadn't had the perfect example of either a mother or father while he grew up. And he'd told Zach as much.

But Zach had disagreed. "If something ever happens to me," he'd said, "there's no one else I'd trust to take care of my daughter."

Kieran would have mentioned Rosie's biological mother, but the flighty brunette was completely out of the picture. She'd gladly signed over full custody of the newborn to Zach and had never looked back.

"It's just a formality," Zach had said. "We'll both be dancing at Rosie's wedding."

At the time, Kieran had believed that was probably true, so he'd reluctantly agreed. But obviously neither of them had foreseen the accident that would change everything.

Kieran, who actually liked having Rosie refer to him as her uncle and had no problem assuming that easy role, blew out a ragged sigh as he looked at the people around the room. "I knew about Zach's will, but neither of us expected him to die so soon."

"Sandra and Sam are hoping that you will hold off on exercising your right to custody," Pastor Mark said. "At least while Rosie is so young, and the loss of her father is so recent."

Kieran hadn't planned to assume custody, although the Lawsons probably didn't know that. And he wanted to put their minds at ease as well as his own. "If Zach could somehow talk to us right now, he'd agree that Rosie would be better off living with the two of you. Your bond with her is the strongest, now that he's gone. We can discuss the legalities later. But in the meantime, if there's anything she needs, anything at all, just say the word. I'll make sure she gets it."

Sandra's eyes overflowed with tears. "I'm so glad you feel that way, Kieran. We love that little girl with all our hearts, and she's…" The grieving mother and grandmother sniffled. "She's all we have left."

It might sound as if he'd made a huge concession, yet even though he adored the sweet little girl, he was actually relieved that she was going to continue living with Sam and Sandra on the Leaning L.

"We'd also like both of you to remain a part of her life," Sam added, looking first at Kieran, then at Dana. "Especially over the next few months, while her loss is so fresh."

"Of course," Dana said. "I'd hoped you'd allow me to continue visiting her—and you, too."

"Honey," Sandra said, gazing at her son's girlfriend, "over the past six months you've become the daughter I never had. I've enjoyed having you around, even if it wasn't as often as I'd have liked." Then she looked at Kieran. "I hope you'll come by regularly, too. I know your job keeps you busy, but…" A tear slipped down her cheek, and she paused to wipe it away.

But she didn't need to finish her words. Kieran

knew what she meant. He'd make it a point to come around more often than he had in the past. "I'll never be too busy for Rosie or the two of you."

"See?" The pastor placed a hand on Sam's shoulder. "I told you all we had to do was pray about it, and everything would work out."

Kieran wasn't very religious, but he appreciated them putting in a good word with the man upstairs. As far as he was concerned, this was working out for the best—for everyone involved.

"Why don't you go back into the living room?" he suggested to the grieving couple. "I'll help Dana get the food set out."

"That's so sweet of you," Sandra said as she got to her feet. "I feel funny not being the hostess, but…"

Dana slipped her arms around Zach's mom. "I know you do, Sandy, but let me take over your duties today. Besides, I have help." When she glanced at Kieran, he nodded his agreement.

"Come on," the minister said. "It's time for people to show you their love for a change, just as you've done for them in the past."

After the Lawsons and Pastor Mark returned to the living room, leaving Kieran and Dana alone, Dana said, "I hadn't realized Zach gave you custody."

"I'm not entirely sure why he did."

"He considered you his best friend."

Kieran had felt the same way about Zach, but still, what had he been thinking when he'd asked Kieran to step up and parent Rosie? He was a diehard bachelor and not the least bit family-oriented.

Sure, he loved and respected his siblings. But seriously? He would make a lousy parent.

"Just so you know," Dana said, "I agree that it's in Rosie's best interests to stay on the ranch with Sam and Sandra, but you need to consider something."

Kieran never made rash decisions. What did she think he'd failed to think about?

"Sam has heart trouble, and Sandra's health isn't very good. I'm not sure how long either of them will have the stamina to keep up with an active three-year-old."

She had a point, and while he had no idea what the future held, he was glad the couple wanted Rosie—and that they would be able to raise her, at least for the time being.

As Dana moved about the kitchen, pulling salads from the refrigerator and serving spoons from the drawer, Kieran watched her work. He was drawn to her hair, especially since the color reminded him of autumn. She usually wore those long red locks pulled into a topknot or woven into a twist held up with a clip. He'd seen her with it hanging down once, and it nearly reached the small of her back.

He'd always thought of redheads as being a little feisty, but Dana was more serious and a little old-fashioned. She was also bright and the studious type. At least, he'd always had that assumption because she was a graduate student and a researcher at the history center, so it was an easy jump to make. Either way, she wasn't the type of woman Kieran dated.

When Dana turned away from the kitchen counter with a bowl of macaroni salad in her hand, she caught Kieran studying her. For a moment, something stirred between them—a spark of some kind. Maybe a flash of chemistry. He'd dated enough to know when an attraction was mutual.

But if he was right about what he'd sensed, she seemed to get over it a lot faster than he did.

"Is something wrong?" she asked.

"No." *Hell, no.* He'd merely zoned out, caught up in a momentary fixation. He shook off his wild thought. "I... I just wasn't sure what to do next."

"Would you take this salad, along with the others on the counter, to the dining room and place them on the table?"

"Sure." Glad to have a job to do, one that would take him out of the kitchen and away from her, he took the bowl and did as instructed.

What was the matter with him? Even if he did find Dana attractive and interesting, she'd dated Zach. It wouldn't be right to think of her in a...well, in a romantic way.

So he'd better get his mind on either someone or something else. Quickly.

Dana reached into the drawer nearest the oven and pulled out a couple of pot holders. But she couldn't help glancing over her shoulder to see Kieran carry the first of the salads out to the dining room. The man might be well-dressed and gorgeous, but he was completely out of place in a kitchen, let alone one that was built in the 1950s.

Even when he wasn't dressed in a stylish gray Armani suit, the corporate vice president seemed to be cut from a different bolt of cloth than Zach. Kieran was made from expensive silk, like the fancy yellow tie he was wearing, while Zach had been made out of rugged and durable denim.

It was impossible not to compare the two men, to note their good qualities or admire their close friendship, although now that Zach was gone, there was no longer any reason to.

Dana returned to her work and pulled a ham from the oven, leaving two casseroles still baking inside.

When footsteps sounded in the open doorway, the kind made by Italian loafers and not cowboy boots, she turned to see Kieran return, his hands now empty.

"What next?" he asked.

She put the hot pan on the stove top, then set the pot holders on the counter. "Would you mind slicing this ham?"

"No, not at all."

"There's a serving platter in the small cupboard over the fridge. There might also be a couple of trivets in there. I'll need them to hold the casserole dishes."

His brow knit together. "What's a trivet?"

She couldn't help but smile. He'd probably been raised with a housekeeper, a cook and a nanny, so it was no wonder that he didn't know his way around a kitchen. But she had to give him credit for trying to help and to fit in. "A trivet is a small little rack that keeps a hot dish from resting directly on the table."

"Got it." He brushed past her, leaving a soft trail of that mountain fresh scent in his wake.

She couldn't help taking a second whiff, appreciating his unique fragrance. But that's the only arousing awareness she'd allow herself. She shook off her momentary attraction, took the pot holders in hand again, removed the two casseroles from the oven and placed them on the stovetop.

After Kieran set the platter on the counter, he removed the trivets from the cupboard. "Why don't I put these on the table so they'll be ready for those hot dishes?"

She thanked him. Then, in spite of her resolve to keep her mind off him and on her work, she watched him go. She'd never been interested in men like Kieran, although she had to admit he was more than attractive. At six feet tall, with light brown hair and blue eyes, he was a killer combination of bright and sexy. Most women wouldn't think twice about setting their sights on him, but Dana was more the down-home type. And she knew most men considered her to be a little too quirky to notice her in a romantic way.

In addition to the obvious, Kieran was also a member of the renowned Fortune family. And Dana had no family at all.

Of course, that didn't mean she'd been left destitute. Before their fatal accident, her parents had set up a trust fund for her, and last year, on her twenty-fifth birthday, the money had been released. She'd used most of it to purchase and to renovate a run-down house in Hyde Park that was built in the 1940s.

Still, even though she was a property owner and had a small nest egg, she wouldn't fit into the social circles in which Kieran and his family ran—nor would she even want to try. Not when her idea of a perfect afternoon was a trip to an antiques shop, where she scoured vintage photos, or a lazy walk through flea markets, where she searched for hidden treasures.

No, she'd feel completely uncomfortable hobnobbing with Kieran and his rich family and friends. Heck, she sometimes felt out of place in 2017 Austin, which was one reason she loved walking in her quaint, historical neighborhood.

So why complicate matters when she liked her life just the way it was?

"I'm finished," Kieran said, as he reentered the kitchen yet again.

Dana was finished, too. Not just getting the food ready, but comparing the different lives she and Kieran lived. Besides, even if she ever did consider going out with a man like him, it would never work out. From what she'd heard, Kieran dated a lot of gorgeous women, and Dana would never agree to be one of many.

She had a good life—and a busy one. She wasn't lacking anything other than a family of her own. And now that the Lawsons had invited her to come around more often, she'd be able to maintain and nurture the relationship she had with them.

It might not be the perfect setup for the holidays and other lonely days, but it was close enough to be a darn good substitute.

The call Kieran had been dreading came only a week after Zach's funeral, while he was in his office at Robinson Tech.

"Sam's in the hospital with angina," Sandra said. "It's pretty serious this time, and I'm not sure how long he'll need to stay. They're talking about surgery."

"Is there anything I can do?" Kieran asked.

"I have a babysitter at the house with Rosie. The granddaughter of a neighbor. The girl is good with kids and responsible, but she's only fourteen. She'll be able to handle things for a while, but I have no idea how long I'll need to be here with Sam."

"Don't worry about Rosie," Kieran told her, even though his own concern about the child's well-being, especially with him in charge of her, was mounting by the second. "I'll pick her up and relieve the sitter. But if you don't mind, since I'm not too far from the hospital, I'll stop by to see you and check on Sam first."

"Thanks, Kieran. He'd love to see you. He's on the third floor, in room 312."

"I'll be there in twenty minutes—maybe less."

Sandra paused a beat then asked, "What would we do without you, Kieran?"

He could ask her a similar question. *How in the world will Rosie be able to get by without you?*

"I'm happy to help out whenever and however I can," he responded.

"Bless you, honey. I'll see you soon."

After disconnecting the line, Kieran told his assistant to cancel an afternoon appointment and to reschedule tomorrow's board meeting. Then he left his high-rise office and drove to the hospital. The direct route he took reminded him of the times in weeks past that he'd traveled that same stretch of road on his way to see Zach in the ICU, hoping and praying that his friend would have made some improvement during the night, only to find that he hadn't.

Kieran felt that same cold and heavy weight of dread and fear now.

Sam has heart trouble, Dana had said last week, *and Sandra's health isn't very good. I'm not sure how long either of them will have the stamina to keep up with an active three-year-old.*

He'd known Dana was right, but he'd hoped the older couple would be able to keep Rosie for another few years—maybe even until she graduated from high school.

Was it already time for him to step in and take full custody of Rosie, as unready as he might be?

Maybe Zach's parents only needed him to provide temporary help and babysitting duties. Once Sam was feeling better and returned home, Sandra would want Rosie back again. Then Kieran's life would go back to normal. He convinced himself that was the case.

It would only be for a few days. He could handle child care duties for that long.

"I got this," he said out loud, hoping the sound of his voice would provide all the assurance he needed.

Yet those words, interlaced with the doubt that plagued him, were still ringing in his ears when he entered the hospital lobby. As he started toward the elevator, he spotted Dana coming out of the gift shop holding a yellow ceramic vase filled with brightly colored flowers.

She wore a simple black skirt and a white sleeveless blouse. Once again, her hair was pulled up in a topknot, with two turquoise chopsticks—or were they knitting needles?—poking out of it.

When she saw him, she broke into a smile that dimpled her cheeks. Again, he was struck by her simple beauty, something he'd failed to notice when she'd been with Zach.

"I take it Sandra called you," he said.

"Yes, she did."

"I guess this is what you meant when you told me you were concerned about Sam's health."

Dana blew out a soft sigh. "Yes, but I was hopeful that the doctors had his heart issues controlled by medication."

Kieran had hoped that was the case, too.

"I just stopped by for a quick visit," he said. "I told Sandra I'd relieve the babysitter and keep Rosie for a few days. Once Sam is released and ready to go home, I can take her back to the ranch."

"You may need to keep her longer than that. The doctor mentioned surgery, and those 'few days' could end up being more long-term."

"Yes, I know." Kieran was trying to prepare himself for that possibility. He glanced down at his leather loafers, then back into Dana's eyes. There was no need to lie or to pretend that he was ready to be a parent. "To tell you the truth, I'm a little nervous about being Rosie's guardian. As much as I adore her, I've never spent much time with kids."

"I can understand that, but you'll do fine. Zach wouldn't have chosen you to step up if he'd had any concern about that." Dana's eyes, a stunning shade of blue, filled with something akin to sympathy. "Not that I'm an expert on child rearing," she added.

"That's just it," Kieran said. "I'm great at giving piggyback rides and playing hide-and-seek for an hour or two. But being her legal guardian means choosing just the right preschool and knowing when she needs to see a pediatrician." Damn. Just the thought of doctor visits brought on a whole new worry that filled his gut with dread. "What do I do if she gets a fever or a tummy ache?"

And then there was the whole idea of shots, immunizations and making her take liquid medicine that tasted nasty.

Worry and fear must have altered his expression because Dana said, "You'll do just fine."

"Thanks for the vote of confidence."

She placed a soft and gentle hand on his shoulder, which sent a rush of warmth to his gut, chasing a bit of his fear away. "And remember, it's just a few days at this point. There's no need to borrow trouble."

"That's easy for you to say." He offered her a half-hearted grin, although he really did appreciate her support.

"If it'll make you feel better," she said, "I'd be happy to stop by your place so I can visit Rosie and give you a break at the same time."

Kieran would take all the help he could get, even if it was just an occasional visit. "I'd appreciate that, Dana. Before you leave I'll give my business card, along with my address."

The hand that had been resting on his shoulder slid down to his back, giving it a rub that suggested she wanted to provide him with comfort and understanding. But her touch, the trail of her fingers, triggered a spark of heat he hadn't expected. Nor did he have any idea what, if anything, to do about it.

"You'll do fine," she said.

God, he sure hoped she was right. But he couldn't very well remain in the hospital lobby, talking to a woman who'd sent his thoughts scampering in an entirely wrong direction. So he nodded toward the elevator. "Are you ready to visit Sam?"

"Yes, let's go." Dana fell into step beside him, but they didn't speak again until they reached the third floor.

As the doors opened up, Kieran said, "Here we are."

They started down the corridor together, their shoes clicking and tapping on the tile floor. Still, they didn't speak.

When they neared room 312, they spotted Sandra walking out the door and into the hall.

"How's Sam doing?" Kieran asked her.

"About the same. The doctor has ruled out by-pass surgery for the time being, and he's responding to treatment. But Sam has a few other health issues they'd like to get stabilized before they dishcharge him. So it looks like he'll be here for a while."

"What about you?" Kieran asked. "How are you holding up through all of this?"

Sandra took a deep breath, then slowly let it out. "I'm a little tired, but I'm doing all right. My blood pressure is higher than usual, which is a little concerning. My doctor would like me to get some rest and stop worrying about Sam. But that's not easy to do."

Under the circumstances, Kieran didn't suppose it would be. Not when Sandra had their granddaughter to worry about, too.

"I'll plan on having Rosie indefinitely," Kieran said. "Once Sam is feeling better, just say the word and I'll bring her home."

Sandra's eyes filled with tears. What she couldn't blink away, she dried with her index fingers. "As much as I hate to let Rosie go, especially when I fear it could end up being permanent, I really have my hands full with Sam right now."

"I'll take good care of her," Kieran said. "And if it makes you feel better, Dana promised to help me." He gave the attractive redhead a nudge.

Dana slipped her arm around Sandra and drew her close. "That's right, Sandy. I know how difficult this must be for you, but don't worry about anything or anyone except Sam—and yourself."

"We'll just be a phone call or a short drive away," Kieran added.

"Thank you." The older woman again swiped at her teary eyes. "That's probably for the best."

Kieran knew they'd made the right decision all the way around, although he still wasn't sure about his capabilities as a guardian, let alone as a paternal role model. But he'd do his best by Rosie.

"Don't worry about a thing," he told Sandra, although his gut twisted at the thought of being on his own with Rosie.

But, hey. He'd just take it one day at a time.

"Sandy," Dana said, "is there something I can do to help you? Do you want me to bring anything to you from the house? Or, if you give me a list, I can run errands or stop by the market and pick up groceries or whatever."

"Since I don't have to worry about being home with Rosie," Sandra said, "I'd like to camp out here at the hospital for a while. So, yes. If you don't mind, there are some things you can pick up from the house and a prescription that's ready at the pharmacy."

While the women continued to work out a game plan of sorts, Kieran looked up at the ceiling as if he could see through it and beyond, as if he could somehow connect with Zach and ask for his forgiveness. *I'm sorry I lied to your mom. I have no idea how to provide for Rosie's needs.*

But he made Zach—and himself—a promise right

then and there. He would do his best to provide everything Rosie needed—come hell or high water and damn the cost.

Chapter Three

Dana hadn't planned to visit Kieran and Rosie until
the weekend, but less than twenty-four hours after
running into him at the hospital, she changed her
mind.

He'd admitted to being nervous and uneasy about
his ability to fill Zach's shoes. In spite of the assurance he'd given Sandy, Dana suspected that he wasn't
feeling nearly as comfortable taking care of a three-
year-old as he might want everyone to believe.

So after putting in a full day at the history center,
she drove across town to the high-rise building in
which Kieran lived. She and Zach had once attended
a party here, where they'd hobnobbed with socialites,
techies and corporate types.

They'd moved about the well-dressed group, holding their drinks in hand and making small talk. Zach might have appeared to be a simple cowboy, but his wit, humor and charm had carried him through the evening, and he'd fit right in. Not so with Dana.

Sure, everyone had been kind and gracious to her, even when the only things she could think to say had to do with a new exhibit at the history center. She'd smiled and nodded, as if all was right in her world, but she'd felt lost, like a street urchin on the snowy lanes of eighteenth-century London.

Okay, so it really wasn't that bad. But she'd felt out of place among the rich and successful crowd.

And now, after parking across the street in the public lot next to a busy Starbucks, she began to have second thoughts about her surprise visit.

What had she been thinking? She shouldn't just drop in uninvited. Maybe she should head to the popular coffee spot instead. She could purchase a venti green tea and call it a day.

Then again, Kieran had said to come "anytime." She sat in her parked car, pondering her options.

What if he wasn't home?

Maybe she should give him a call. She reached into her purse, pulled out the business card he'd given her yesterday and read the personal contact information he'd written on the backside. Then she dialed his cell.

He answered on the third ring, although his voice sounded a little...tired. Or was he stressed?

"Are you up for a visitor?" she asked.

"If the visitor is *you*—and if you're talking about coming over *now*—I wouldn't mind a bit."

"Actually, I'm standing outside your building."

"Then come on up. I'm on the tenth floor, number 1014. My condo is on the east side, just to the left of the elevator doors."

"All right. I'll see you in a few minutes." She grabbed her purse and locked the car. Rather than jaywalk, she strode to the corner, waited for the green light and crossed the street to the impressive, curved building of glass and steel.

The doorman, a dapper, uniformed gentleman in his mid to late fifties, stood at the entrance. He must have been expecting her because he knew her name and greeted her with a smile. "Good afternoon, Ms. Trevino. Mr. Fortune said to send you right up."

She thanked him, then headed to the elevators. Once inside, a flutter started in her stomach and continued to build on the ride up to Kieran's luxury condominium, reaching a peak by the time she rang the bell.

The door swung open almost immediately, but when she caught a look at the handsome man, who appeared more than a little haggard, her momentary nervousness dissipated.

His mussed hair suggested that he'd just woken up from a long winter's nap, although she suspected he'd been raking his fingers through it more often than usual. He wore a black T-shirt and a pair of gray gym shorts, but she doubted he'd been working out. At least, not in the usual way. And even though his current appearance wasn't the least bit stylish, nor was he as impeccably put together as she was used to seeing him, it didn't make him any less attractive.

"I'm glad you're here." He stepped aside for her to enter. "Come on in."

She might have complied, but it looked as if an entire toy store had exploded in his living room. In fact, there was so much clutter on the floor she could hardly take a step for fear of tripping over something.

"What's all this?" she asked.

"Stuff I bought for Rosie."

Dana surveyed the results of his shopping spree— a blue-and-white doll house, a tiny pink kitchen setup along with plastic food items and a little red shopping cart. Puzzle pieces, crayons, books and a variety of stuffed animals littered the room.

Five different dolls of various hair color, skin tone and sizes were lined up on his dark leather sofa, each with a pink teacup in her lap.

"Where's Rosie?" Dana asked. "Or is she some-how lost in this mess?"

"She's been running on full throttle all day and finally went to sleep five minutes ago. But I have to tell you, I probably need a nap more than she does."

Dana furrowed her brow. It was after five o'clock. "Why'd you put her down for a nap this late in the day?"

"I didn't plan it that way. Every time I asked if she was sleepy, she told me no. Finally, she crashed on her own. I found her curled up on the floor in the guest room, next to her new toy box. I was afraid she'd wake up, so I covered her with a blanket and left her there."

Dana had no idea what to say. Kieran had admitted that he didn't know anything about kids, and she'd had no reason to doubt him. But she'd never expected anything like this, and she couldn't help but laugh at the absurdity.

"What's so funny?" he asked.

"Nothing." At least, not anything she wanted to actually say out loud. Poor Kieran looked as though he was ready to drop in his tracks, too. "Apparently, you've had a busy day."

He rolled his eyes. "You have *no* idea."

Dana continued to scan the room, just now noticing a pink motorized kiddie car parked in the dining area. Seriously? Kieran had purchased a big, outdoor plaything like that when he didn't even have a yard?

"This is mind-boggling," she said. "What'd you do? Take Rosie shopping and let her have free rein with your credit card?"

"No, I picked this out myself, along with some new clothes for her and a toddler bed. That's all in the guest room, which is where she'll sleep while she's here."

Apparently, Kieran had accepted the fact that Rosie's stay might not be temporary after all. "Did you purchase all of this today?"

"No, I bought it yesterday, before I picked her up from the sitter. I asked Karen, my assistant, to suggest a place I could find everything she might need, like toys, clothes and furniture. And Karen suggested Kids' World, which is supposed to be a popular place for parents to shop. I was able to get it all taken care of in less than an hour. The delivery guys brought it this morning."

"Talk about one-stop shopping."

"Yeah, that was the idea. I didn't have much time to get everything Rosie is going to need."

Children needed more than just toys and games. The most important thing was love, and that wasn't something Kieran could purchase.

Dana again scanned the clutter, unable to even guess how much all of this had cost him. For a woman who'd spent years in foster care, she couldn't fathom the extravagance.

"This must have cost you a year's salary," she said. Well, maybe not *his* salary, but certainly that of a grad student and research librarian.

"I'll admit, it wasn't cheap. But that doesn't matter. I just want Rosie to be happy while she's here."

Dana hated to criticize him for trying to do what he thought was best, but he needed to know that he'd wasted both his time and his money. "I hate to disappoint you, but Rosie probably would be just as happy with a picnic at the park, complete with peanut butter and jelly sandwiches. Or even a trip to the library for the preschool story hour, especially if she could also check out a few books and maybe a Disney DVD to bring home."

"For what it's worth," he said, "I did get a few of these things on sale. And they also delivered the whole kit and caboodle for free."

"And you think that means you got a bargain?"

Dana laughed again. "I'm surprised the happy owner didn't volunteer to carry it here on his back."

"Okay, so maybe I overdid it a little."

"You think?" Dana covered her mouth with her hand, hoping to stifle another laugh.

Kieran blew out a ragged sigh. "Okay, I probably blew it. But my heart was in the right place."

She had to agree with that. The man was not only wealthy and successful, but apparently generous, too.

"Don't just stand there," Kieran said. "Come on in." He moved aside the pink plastic shopping cart as well as the child-size kitchen, making a pathway for her. "Can I get you something to drink? I have every kind of fruit juice imaginable as well as Gatorade, punch and soda pop. Oh, there's also chocolate milk. But if you're up for something a little stronger, like I happen to be, you have your choice of beer and wine. I also have a full bar in the dining room."

"Actually, wine sounds good to me."

"You got it. What's your preference? Red or white?"

"Whatever's easiest."

"I have a sauvignon blanc in the fridge."

"Perfect."

"Have a seat." He directed her to the marble counter in the kitchen with a set of sleek black barstools. And she complied.

While Kieran uncorked the bottle, Dana scanned the interior of his home. She tried, in spite of the dolls and toys that littered the living room, to remember what his bachelor pad had looked like when she and Zach had attended his party.

The modern furnishings were both expensive and impressive. The artwork that adorned the walls and the sculptures that were displayed throughout also must have cost plenty, which made her suspect he'd hired a decorator.

What a contrast it was to her quaint little home, which she'd decorated herself, mostly with items she'd purchased at estate sales and antiques stores.

"There you go," Kieran said, as he placed a glass of chilled wine in front of her.

"Thank you." She took a long, appreciative sip and watched him move about the kitchen, with its state-of-the-art stainless-steel appliances that would please a master chef, and prepare a plate of crackers, cheese and grapes.

Did he usually fix dinner for a woman while they both enjoyed a glass of wine? Did he play soft, romantic music in the background?

Not that it mattered. But she had to admit she was curious about the women Kieran might bring home, the ones he found attractive. Did he prefer tall, leggy blondes? Maybe shapely and voluptuous brunettes?

Or how about quirky redheads?

She chased away that wacky thought as quickly as it crossed her mind. A man like Kieran Fortune wouldn't be the least bit interested in a woman like her. And while she found him more than a little appealing, he really wasn't her type, either. Still, she was intrigued by the handsome, dedicated bachelor who, according to Zach, claimed that he'd never settle down.

Yet here he was, apparently becoming a family man. How was that going to work out for him?

He removed a longneck bottle of Corona from the fridge, opened it and took a drink before sitting in the barstool next to hers.

"So tell me about you," he said, his gaze warm, his expression suggesting genuine interest.

She could understand that. Even though she'd dated his best friend for the past six months, Zach's priority in life was his daughter, which was fine with Dana. So when they'd dated, they'd stuck pretty close to the ranch or else they'd gone out for a hamburger and a movie. At that same time, Kieran had been working on a special project for Robinson Tech, so Dana had only run into him a couple of times.

Still, his comment and his curiosity took her aback. She wasn't here to make any kind of personal connection with him. Sure, she sympathized with him and wanted to offer her help with Rosie. But this visit wasn't about her.

"There's not much to tell," she said. "I'm in grad school, although I took a break from my classes this semester to focus on a special project for the Austin History Center. I work there as a researcher."

"I knew that much," he said. "What do you do on your days off?"

She didn't usually share that sort of thing with people her age, since her favorite things to do might be considered unusual. But she decided there wasn't any reason to worry about what Kieran might think. "I enjoy taking long walks in my neighborhood, shopping in my favorite antiques store and going to estate sales."

"Seriously?"

See? He was no different from anyone else.

"Yes," she admitted. "I bought a house in Hyde Park and like to find interesting things to decorate it the way it might have looked back in 1948, when it was built."

He studied her a moment, as if still trying to decide whether she was pulling his leg, then smiled. "I'd like to see your place someday."

Now she was the one to wonder if he was being sincere or just being polite and making small talk. But she shrugged it off and said, "I'd be happy to show it to you. I'm proud of the way it's all coming together."

"Do you own the house?" he asked. "Or are you renting?"

Was he wondering if she could afford to buy a place of her own?

She supposed he'd have no reason to ask, other than plain curiosity, so she leveled with him. "I purchased a two-bedroom fixer-upper about six months ago with the idea of flipping it, but the renovations took a while and were a lot of work. So now that it's done, I'd like to enjoy the fruits of my labor for a while."

"Are you going to keep it, then?"

"No, within the next six months, I'll sell it and buy another in the same neighborhood."

He took another drink of beer and eyed her carefully. "I'm impressed."

With *her*?

Or with the completed renovation project?

"Now I'd really like to see it," he added.

Okay, so it had been the work she'd done on the house that had surprised and intrigued him.

"You're more than welcome to stop by anytime," she said. "It's not as classy, modern or impressive as your place, but it's warm and appealing to me." And to be honest, even though she'd never admit it to anyone else, she was also proud of the house since she'd done most of the work herself.

"Why doesn't that surprise me?" he asked, a smile lighting his blue eyes.

She'd never been especially comfortable talking about herself or blowing her own horn, so she steered the conversation back to a topic that would suit them both better. "I hope you'll bring Rosie when you come."

"Of course."

"And speaking of Rosie, have you hired a nanny or housekeeper yet?"

"No, and I'd rather not—if I don't have to. She attends preschool three days a week, so I'll go to the office then. And on Tuesdays and Thursdays, I'll work from home."

"That sounds like a good plan."

"I hope so." He glanced past her, his gaze landing on the toys, dolls and games cluttering the living area. "But I'm probably going to need my cleaning lady to come more often than once a week. Who would have guessed a child could wreak so much havoc?"

As wild and wacky as she'd found Kieran's over-zealous attempt to provide for little Rosie, her heart went out to the poor man.

"You know," she said, "I was serious when I offered to help out whenever I can."

"Don't be surprised when I take you up on that offer." He flashed a dazzling smile that set off a flutter in her tummy again. But this time, the bevy of butterflies wasn't caused by nervousness. Instead, it was due to sheer anticipation.

Too bad she couldn't take back her offer to assist him with Rosie. Even the slightest thought of striking up a friendship—let alone a romance—with a man like Kieran Fortune was out of line.

And bound to end in disappointment.

Working from home two days a week wasn't the best situation, but as the vice president of Robinson Tech, Kieran could make his own schedule, so it was certainly doable. Besides, he'd promised Zach he would take care of his little girl, and he wasn't about to farm out the job.

Unfortunately, his work-from-home plan didn't last long. Being productive while having a preschooler underfoot was next to impossible. For some reason, he'd thought that Rosie would be able to play quietly and entertain herself, but he'd been wrong about that.

He'd also thought that, after practically buying out the toy section at Kids' World, she'd have enough to keep her busy until kindergarten. But that wasn't the case, either.

She might start out working on a puzzle or skimming the pictures in a book, but she got bored easily and wanted him to play with her. He'd put her off as often as he could, but before he knew it, he was the one doing the entertaining. The only time she sat still and let him work without interruption was when he put on a DVD for her, but he couldn't very well do that from morning until night.

Now, as he prepared a spreadsheet for tomorrow's board meeting, she again walked up to him and tugged on his sleeve. "Uncle Kieran?"

"Yes, honey?" He tore his gaze from the sales numbers and looked at the cute little imp, who held a toy medical bag in her hand.

Early this morning, he'd combed her hair and pulled her blond locks into an uneven and messy ponytail. But no matter how hard he'd tried, he hadn't been able to get the rubber band on evenly. And the red bow she'd insisted on wearing only served to point out how lopsided it was. Still, she was a cute kid, with big green eyes and thick dark lashes.

"Will you play with me?" she asked. "I'll be the doctor, and you can be sick."

"I'm pretty busy right now," he said. "Can't you find something else to do?"

Her lips curled into a pout, then she brightened. "I could make pizza and hamburgers for your dinner."

"That sounds great." Especially if her return to the

play kitchen in the living room would buy him another few minutes to finish his spreadsheet.

As she scampered off, he glanced at the time on his laptop. Weren't kids supposed to take afternoon naps? Dana said they did, but it looked as if Rosie hadn't gotten that memo.

As much as Kieran wanted to handle things on his own, he realized that wasn't going to work. His first thought was to ask one of his brothers or sisters to help out, but Rosie would probably be more comfortable with a woman.

The only problem was, Rachel lived in Horseback Hollow. Zoe was in charge of brand management for Robinson Computers, overseeing the company's presence on social media, plus organizing events to raise the company's profile. And if that wasn't enough to keep her occupied, she was happily married to Joaquin Mendoza, who took up any free time she might have.

Sophie worked as an assistant HR director at Robinson Tech, which kept her busy. She was also all starry-eyed these days, thanks to her recent engagement to Mason Montgomery. And Olivia, who was still single, was a computer programmer at the company. Clearly, his sisters all had lives of their own, so he couldn't ask any of them.

And even if they did have the time, they'd all been a little skeptical of his ability to be a father. So there was no way he'd reveal that he was struggling. Instead, he'd prove them wrong, even if it killed him.

At the sound of the battery-operated motor of the little car, Kieran swore under his breath. If Rosie ran it into the dining room table leg one more time…

Oh, hell. Why wait until then? As soon as she took a nap—if she ever did—he'd call the doorman and ask him to get rid of it, even if that meant putting it out on the curb with a sign saying: Free to a Good Home.

A loud thump sounded from the dining area, which meant Rosie had crashed into the table again. What in the world made him think he could handle child rearing on his own?

I'll help any way I can, Dana had said. And she'd seemed sincere.

Kieran whipped out his cell phone, ready to call her right now and take her up on that offer.

Of all the places Dana could have imagined having dinner on a Tuesday evening, Cowboy Fred's Funhouse and Pizza Emporium wasn't one of them. But when Kieran called to invite her to join him and Rosie for an early dinner, he'd sounded a little frazzled. And when he'd admitted that he wanted an adult to talk to, she'd agreed. Then she'd hurried home to shut off her Crock-Pot, in which she'd placed a small roast before leaving for work this morning. Once she'd placed the meat in the fridge, she'd changed her clothes.

She'd been a little flattered by Kieran's invitation until she realized there was no way he'd ever want to meet a date at one of the most popular kids' eateries in Austin. Still, she'd applied lipstick and hurried to meet him.

She found him standing out in front of Cowboy Fred's, holding Rosie's hand. He was dressed more casually than usual in a pair of black jeans and a maroon-and-white golf shirt bearing a Texas A&M logo.

When Rosie, who wore a pair of pink shorts and a white T-shirt with a princess graphic, spotted Dana, she burst into a happy grin and squealed, "Dannnnnnna!"

The girl's happy reaction was heartwarming, but it was Kieran's dazzling smile that set Dana's pulse soaring at a wacky rate.

"Thanks for joining us," he said, as he greeted Dana in front of the bright red door encircled with blinking theater lights. "I owe you."

She winked at him, then studied little Rosie's lop-sided ponytail, the red ribbon dangling unevenly and about to slide off.

"We've been cooped up all day," Kieran said, "so we both needed to get out. But next time, we'll invite you to have grilled steaks at my house."

Next time? So he'd be calling her again and asking her to join him, only next time at his place?

Now, that was an interesting thought.

He grabbed the brass handle and opened the red door for her and Rosie to enter. When the child dashed inside and waited for a greeter dressed in a cowboy costume to stamp her hand, Dana followed, dazed by the rows of mechanical ponies and cars, by the huge room filled with video games.

The flashing lights and the electronic bleeps made her think of a kiddie casino. Wow. This place was wild. And *loud*. Now she knew what Kieran meant about "owing her."

"Ma'am," the cowboy said, "I'll need to stamp your hand, too. Yours, too, sir. Each child's number needs to match the adults' who brought her."

"Uncle Kieran," Rosie asked, "can I please go play on the climb-y thing?"

"Sure, princess. You go ahead." He pointed to a blue bench that was stationed close to the structure. "As soon as we get our hands stamped, Dana and I will be sitting right there, waiting for you."

As the happy girl hurried off, Kieran turned to Dana and asked, "Can you believe this place?"

"I'd heard about it from a coworker who has a boy in kindergarten, but I'm a little surprised by the lights and noise. I'd think that would cause sensory overload for the kids. I wonder if any of them actually take time to sit down and eat."

Kieran laughed. "Maybe not, but I see a couple of dads ordering a beer near that sign that says Chuck Wagon. I think I'll follow their lead. Would you like something to drink, too?"

"I'll have a glass of wine—if they have it. Thanks."

While Kieran went to the counter, Dana made her way to the blue bench and took a seat. Moments later, he returned with his beer and her wine, both served in clear plastic glasses. "I'm afraid I'm going to owe you a better vintage when you come to my house."

So he hadn't been just blowing smoke about inviting her to his place for dinner. Not that she'd sensed anything romantic about it.

"How about Thursday?" he asked. "I'm not going into the office that day."

She rarely made evening plans during the week, so she didn't need to check her calendar. "Sure, that's fine." She studied the man seated beside her, the way he seemed comfortable in his skin, even at a place like Cowboy Fred's.

"You told me you were going to work from home a couple days a week," she said. "How's that going?"

"Not as well as I'd hoped. I haven't been able to get much done, so I end up staying at the office longer on the days Rosie's in preschool. Only trouble is, I have to pick her up before six o'clock, and when I finally arrived yesterday, she was the last kid there. She didn't seem unhappy about it, but I felt bad."

"I can understand that, but I'll bet things will begin to run smoothly soon. And then you'll fall into the perfect schedule."

He stretched his arm out along the back of the bench, his hand dangling close to her shoulder. Close enough to touch, actually.

"Thanks for your vote of confidence," he said, "but I have to admit I'm not so sure that'll ever happen."

She took a sip of the wine, something cheap and most likely out of a box. Not that she was a connoisseur by any means, but she didn't mind paying a little more for something decent.

"I have a favor to ask," he said. "Remember when you offered to help me out?"

"Yes, and I meant it." She adored Rosie and was

glad to play a role in her life. She also sympathized with Kieran, although she wondered if what she was feeling for him might be a little more than that. Still, she had no misconceptions about ever developing anything other than a friendship with the gorgeous and brilliant executive. But he clearly needed help, and he was asking for hers.

"I don't know anything about kids or child rearing," he said.

Neither did Dana, for that matter, but she planned to read some parenting books and articles so she'd have more to offer him than a respite now and then.

"What's on your mind?" she asked.

"That's just it. I'm not sure. My childhood wasn't typical, and I don't just mean because I grew up in a wealthy family. I was practically raised by nannies— and none of them stuck around very long."

"I'm afraid mine wasn't that much better," Dana said. "I lost both my parents in an accident, then I spent my teen years in foster care."

At that admission, Kieran turned in his seat, his knee pressing into hers and zapping her with a jolt of heat. His gaze latched on to hers, as if he'd felt it, too. But surely he hadn't.

"I'm sorry," he said. "I hope it didn't sound as if I was complaining about my lot in life, when yours…"

"I survived. And for the record, my time in foster care wasn't what you'd call a bad experience. I could have had it a lot worse."

When he didn't respond, she feared she'd put a

damper on things, so she smiled and said, "On the upside, my foster family lived next door to the public library, where I liked to hang out. I passed the time by reading all the books I could get my hands on, especially those in the history section. That's also where I did my homework, met my best friend, learned to do research and then created my career plan. So it all paid off in the long run."

"Now I understand why you work at the history center."

He probably found that incredibly boring, but she wasn't about to stretch the truth and make herself sound like someone he'd be more interested in. *Interested in for what?* she asked herself. Dating came to mind, but that wasn't going to happen, so she halted that line of thinking. She continued to tell him her life story as dull as he might find it.

"Once I turned eighteen," she said, "I was on my own. I was a good student, and a young librarian named Monica Flores convinced me that an education was the key to a successful life, so I went to college." She also graduated with honors, but decided not to mention it. She did, however add, "I'm not in school this semester, but I'm going to pick up a class this summer and two more in the fall. If all goes as planned, I'll have a master's degree in history by mid-December."

"You're a busy lady."

She offered him a shy but warm smile. "Not too busy for you and Rosie."

Again their gazes met and locked. That is, until Rosie yelled, "Dannnna!"

They both looked up to see the little girl in the yellow tunnel of the climbing structure. She waved at them through a plastic window.

Dana waved back. "We see you, sweetie."

"Are you hungry yet?" Kieran called out.

"No!" Rosie shrieked before crawling onto another section of the structure, one that housed a red slide.

"It might take a while for them to make the pizza," Kieran said. "I'd better order it now. I found out the hard way that Rosie goes from not being the least bit hungry to starving in the blink of an eye."

He'd no more than gotten to his feet when Rosie screamed. At least, it sounded like her cry and came from the direction she'd been heading.

They both jumped up and hurried to the far side of the structure where Rosie sat on a pad at the bottom of the slide. She was crying, the lower half of her face covered in blood.

"Oh, my God," Dana said, as she hurried to the injured child. "What happened, sweetie?"

"A bad boy punched my nose!" she shrieked.

Dana shot a glance at Kieran, who'd come up beside her. He'd paled at the sight of little Rosie, yet he scanned the structure as if looking for the boy.

"Come with me," Dana said, scooping up the bloodied child in her arms. "Let's get you cleaned up."

"Where's the kid who hurt you?" Kieran asked Rosie.

She pointed to the top of the slide. "He's the one. In the green shirt with a dragon."

Dana didn't see anyone there and assumed the boy had run away. But Kieran must have because he took off like a bolt, obviously in search of the boy who'd hurt his little princess.

Chapter Four

Kieran wasn't sure where the "bad boy" had gone, but he was determined to find him. What kind of hellion would bloody a little girl's nose?

Righteous indignation grew into flat-out anger with each step he took in his search. Not only would he confront the kid who'd hurt Rosie, but he was going to have a little talk with the mom and dad, too.

When he spotted the only boy wearing a green dragon shirt in the vicinity, he realized the bully was much smaller than he'd thought. In fact, he didn't appear to be any older than Rosie.

Before Kieran could take another step, the boy's mother swooped in and, from the crease in her forehead, the frown on her lips and the grip on his arm, she appeared to be well aware of what he'd done.

Kieran slowed to a stop. As he stood off to the side, close enough to hear the conversation, he observed the parent and child.

"What happened?" the mom asked the boy. "Did you *hit* that little girl?"

"Yes. But she punched me first!" He pointed to his eye, which appeared to be a little red. "Right here! And it *still* hurts."

The mother dropped to one knee and studied the alleged injury carefully. "Why did she do that?"

"I don't know." He grimaced. "I told her my dragon likes to eat princesses, and I told her she better get out of the way. Then she did this." He fisted his small hand and made a punching motion toward his eye.

"I'm sorry she hurt you, but that didn't mean you had the right to hit her back. You're going to have to tell her you're sorry."

The boy looked down at his scuffed sneakers then back at his mom with a frown. "Okay. But she has to say sorry, too."

"I'm not worried about her manners. I'm concerned about yours. You know better than to hurt someone, even if they hit you first."

His chin dropped to his chest, resting on the graphic, right about where a burst of fire came out of the dragon's mouth. "Okay. But will you come with me?"

"Yes, I will."

As the mother bent forward and placed a kiss on her son's cheek, Kieran realized he didn't need to get involved after all. The woman clearly loved the boy and was teaching him right from wrong, as well as showing him how to be kind and thoughtful. So he turned and walked away.

He wished he'd had a parent like that when he'd been growing up. Not that he hadn't been loved or disciplined, but more often than not, those lessons had come from nannies and au pairs—and minus the kiss on the cheek.

When he reached the big red slide, Dana still wasn't back from the restroom where she'd taken Rosie to wash off the blood. He hadn't liked seeing Rosie hurt, but she'd probably learned a hard and painful lesson.

Hopefully, she hadn't been seriously injured. When he'd been a boy, he'd gotten a couple of bloody noses, and he had never suffered any lasting damage.

But that didn't make this any easier. When he'd heard Rosie cry, when he'd seen the blood dribbling from her nose, his heart had dropped to the floor, and he'd almost lost it. All he could think about was chasing after that bully and making sure he didn't get away with hitting a little girl. But that was before he'd found out that the princess had struck the dragon first.

Now what? What would a real father do at a time like this?

Too bad he didn't have any memories to draw from so he could teach by example. His dad had been a workaholic, and by the time Kieran had come around, Gerald Robinson practically lived at the office or was flying off to who knew where.

And his mom hadn't been around much, either. She'd been too caught up in shopping trips to Manhattan, visits to spas and hair salons and whatever else it was some mothers did when they didn't have time for their kids.

Still, he was going to have to talk to Rosie, just as the boy's mom had done with him.

How would Zach have handled this?

Too bad Kieran couldn't just whip out his cell phone and ask.

No, he was on his own from now on, and his gut clenched at the thought.

That is, until Dana walked out of the bathroom, a reminder that he wasn't entirely alone. She still held Rosie in her arms. The new princess shirt he'd bought her was now bloodstained and probably ruined. So was Dana's lacy blouse.

On the upside, it appeared that the bleeding had stopped.

"How's she doing?" Kieran asked.

"She's all right. Just a little sore." Dana brushed a motherly kiss on Rosie's brow. It was a sweet move, a touching one.

Had Zach lived, Dana probably would have filled a maternal role in the child's life.

"Hey," Kieran said to Rosie. "You and I are going to have to go find that boy so you can apologize to him."

Dana didn't object, but she scrunched her brow, clearly confused by Kieran's comment.

"Apparently," he said, filling her in, "Rosie struck the first blow." Then he turned back to Rosie, "Of course, two wrongs don't make a right. And hitting hurts. That's why we don't punch people when we get mad."

"No." Rosie crossed her arms in an unexpected show of defiance. "I'm *not* gonna say sorry to him."

Kieran looked at Dana, hoping she'd help him figure out the proper approach.

She gave a slight shrug, then turned Rosie to face her. "When we hurt someone, we apologize. It's the right thing to do."

Rosie scrunched her little face. "Do I have to?"

"Yes, you do," Dana said.

"I'll go with you," Kieran offered, just as the boy's mom had done.

Rosie rolled her eyes. "Okay, but then I want to go home."

Now she was talking. Kieran had already spent more time at Cowboy Fred's than he wanted to. "I've got an even better idea, Rosie. I'll ask the guy at the counter to box up our pizza so we can take it with us. What do you say about that?"

"Okay," she said. "Can we eat it and watch a princess movie on TV?"

"Absolutely. Now come on, let's go face that dragon."

Moments later, they found the boy standing next to his mother, scanning the climbing structure and probably looking for Rosie. Dana placed the girl on the floor, and Kieran took her hand in his, but he had to give it a little tug to get her to move forward and face the boy and his mom.

"I'm sorry for punching you," she told the child.

The boy looked at Rosie. "I'm sorry, too. I didn't mean to make blood come out of your nose."

"Tell her your name," the boy's mother suggested. "That way, maybe you can be friends and play together."

The boy didn't say a word, and Rosie merely stared at him.

The mother placed her hand on her son's head. "This is Michael."

"Yeah," he said, directing his response to Rosie. "But sometimes people call me Indiana Jones, 'specially when I have my toy whip."

Rosie smiled. "Then you can call me Princess Rosabelle." She must have thought of something because her smile faded. "I'm not going to play with you when you have a whip."

Michael shrugged, then turned to his mother and wrapped his arms around her leg, clearly glad the apology was over.

Apparently so was Rosie because she hurried back to Dana and lifted her arms, making it known that she wanted to be picked up again.

When Dana complied, Rosie hugged her neck. "Let's go home now, Uncle Kieran."

"Maybe," Michael's mom said, "the next time you come to Cowboy Fred's, we'll be here, too. And then you and Michael can play together."

Kieran didn't know about that, but he offered the mom a smile. Then he went to the counter and told the teenage clerk to make their order to go.

"Perfect timing," the teen said. "Your pizza is just coming out of the oven."

Moments later, with the large pizza box in hand, Kieran found Dana and Rosie at the entrance, having the matching stamps on their hands verified.

"Why don't you follow us back to my place?" he suggested. "I promised you pizza for dinner, and I don't want you to think I'd ever renege on a deal like that."

Her pretty smile lit her eyes, reminding him of a field of bluebonnets.

"Sure, why not?"

When she shifted Rosie in her arms, he again spotted the blood splatter on her blouse. "Looks like I'm going to owe you a new top."

"Don't worry about it."

"I insist."

She shook her head. "Actually, you'd never be able to find another like this. I bought it at a vintage clothing shop downtown, so it's one of a kind."

If it was that rare, it was probably also expensive. "Now I really feel bad."

"Don't," she said, as she pushed open the door. "Believe it or not, I'm up on all the latest techniques for stain removal. I learned them because of the unique places I sometimes shop."

"You like to wear vintage clothing?"

"Yes. I actually prefer it."

At that, his steps slowed. Hers did, too. When their eyes met, he studied her for a moment. Dana was a novelty and one of a kind, just like her favorite articles of clothing.

With unabashed honesty, he said, "I've never met anyone like you."

He'd expected her to brighten, to take his flattering remark to heart, like most of the women he knew would have done. But her waifish smile made him wonder if she'd taken his comment differently than he'd actually meant it.

"I'm sure you haven't," she said, her voice soft and vulnerable—maybe even hurt.

"That was actually a compliment," he told her.

"Then thank you." She smiled again, and while it seemed a lot more genuine this time, her eyes weren't nearly as bright.

If she were another woman, one of those he usually dated, he'd apologize by surprising her with a piece of jewelry or by taking her someplace special.

But Dana didn't seem to be the kind of woman to get caught up in high-priced trappings. And, while that left him without a ready peace offering, it pleased him in an unexpected way.

Dana had to admit that an evening spent watching animated movies while eating pizza never had sounded appealing, at least not since she'd graduated from high school. But on the drive over to Kieran's condominium, she'd actually looked forward to having dinner with him and Rosie.

Now, as they sat on the floor, around a modern, glass-topped coffee table and watching a classic cartoon movie on television, she found herself having fun. Rosie was an absolute delight and said some of the cutest things. Her happy chatter had both adults smiling more often than not.

Dana's only complaint, if you could call it that, was the meal itself. Cowboy Fred's pizza was the worst she'd ever eaten. No, she'd have to take that back. When she was a teenager, her foster dad used to stop by a sports bar on his way home from work on Friday nights. He'd meet his wife there so they could have a couple of beers with their friends. After they'd "wound down" from a stressful workweek, they would bring home cold pizza for Dana and the other kids to eat. The topping was always greasy, the crust tough and hard to chew. Looking back, she suspected that, even if they'd brought it straight home still warm from the oven, it wouldn't have tasted any better.

Rosie reached for her glass and downed the last of her milk. "I'm all done." Then she pushed her plate aside and zeroed in on the movie.

Kieran, who sat next to Dana, turned to her and asked, "Do you think she had enough to eat? She ate the cheese off the top, but she only took a couple of bites of the crust."

Dana offered him a slight shrug. "Who knows? At least she drank her milk."

"Is that enough to hold her over until breakfast?" Kieran asked.

"It might be."

Dana had to force herself to finish her own single slice, but she didn't mention that to Kieran. She'd hate for him to think she was complaining about the meal he'd provided her.

"Actually," he said, "I've been known to eat almost an entire pizza by myself, but this one tastes like *C-R-A-P*."

At that, Dana broke into a grin. "That might be one reason she didn't finish. Should we offer her something else? If you have some fresh fruit or yogurt, we can tempt her with something more appealing."

"Good idea," he said. "You stay here, kick back and relax. I'll see what I can rustle up."

The children's movie wasn't all that bad. In fact, it was somewhat entertaining, but Dana got to her feet anyway. "Let me help."

"Are you sure you want to?"

She gave him a wink. "You bet."

Several minutes later, they'd prepared a fruit, cheese and cracker platter.

"Maybe I'd better spread some peanut butter on a few of these crackers," Kieran said. "Earlier today, during lunch, Rosie informed me that mouse cheese tastes yucky and that she only likes the square kind."

Dana tilted her head. "What did she mean by that?"

"I wondered the same thing, so I asked." Kieran laughed. "She said the cartoon mice eat cheese that has holes in it. So I came to an easy conclusion. She prefers American over Swiss."

"Well, what do you know? There's something new to learn every day."

"That's true, especially when there's a three-year-old around. But I catch on quickly. Now I have American cheese on my new grocery list, along with raisins and Oreos, although she informed me she only likes the 'white stuff inside' and not the cookie part."

"That's important to note," Dana said, as she finished slicing an apple to add to the platter, which was now filled with healthy munchies and adorned with both green and red grapes. "What do you think? Is this enough?"

Kieran made his way to where she stood, close enough for her to catch a taunting whiff of his woodsy aftershave. "That's perfect. We make a great team."

Did they? She liked the sound of that.

"And after the day we've had," he added, giving her a nudge with his elbow, "and the movie we're committed to finish, I'd like to have a glass of wine. How about you? I promise it'll come out of a bottle, rather than a box."

"That sounds good to me."

She watched as he opened the stainless-steel refrigerator door, pulled out a chilled chardonnay and placed it on the countertop. She again marveled at the way he moved through the kitchen, like a man comfortable being a host. Or, more accurately, like a bachelor who'd perfected the fine art of seduction.

And why wouldn't a rich, handsome single man like Kieran have those romantic moves down to a science?

Of course, giving Dana a glass of wine after an evening like this wasn't about romance or seduction. Still, if she were to ever be on the receiving end of Kieran Fortune's sexual attention, she'd be charmed to the core. And making love with him would be as natural as…falling into bed.

Now there was an amazing and completely un-likely image she wasn't going to dwell on.

After opening the bottle with a fancy corkscrew, Kieran removed two crystal goblets from the glass-door cupboard and filled them halfway.

He handed one to Dana, then lifted his in a toast. "To my trusty teammate, who happens to be a very good sport."

Her heart fluttered, as if they had actually become a team, but that's as far as it would go. She knew bet-ter than to let anything Kieran said go to her head. So she tamped down the little rush, determined to offer him a lighthearted toast of her own.

She clinked her glass against his, the resonating ring validating the glasses were crystal, and said, "To Cowboy Fred's search for a new chef."

At that, Kieran chuckled. "You've got that right. And to make matters worse, there's a great Italian restaurant close to my office that serves an awesome gourmet pizza—and for less than Fred charges for week-old marinara and stale cheese on top of baked cardboard."

Now it was Dana's turn to laugh. Then she reached for a grape, pulled it off the small cluster and popped it into her mouth.

"Come on," Kieran said. "Let's take this to Rosie and give her something healthier to eat for dinner."

They'd no more than returned to the living room

when they spotted Rosie stretched out on the floor, her eyes closed in slumber, her lips parted.

"Is she asleep?" Dana asked.

"It looks that way." Kieran set both his wineglass and the platter on the coffee table. "She should eat something, but…she's got to be exhausted. Maybe it would be best to let her sleep. If she wakes up hungry, I can give her something to eat then."

He stooped and picked up the child, then straightened, holding her close to his chest, gazing at her as if she was a fragile princess. She might be tiny and precious, but she'd battled a dragon today.

"I'll be right back," Kieran said. Then he carried Rosie out of the living room and down the hall.

Dana glanced at the platter of cheese and fruit as well as Kieran's glass of wine. Then she looked at her own. A nervous flutter erupted in her tummy.

With Rosie now out of the room, they would be alone. What in the world would they talk about?

That romantic spark she'd felt while bumping elbows with him in the kitchen flickered again, warming her cheeks and sending her heart in a tail-chasing circle. She tried her best to put the fire out, to tamp it down, just as she'd done before.

But this time, watching Kieran walk away, all tall, buff and handsome, his sexy swagger on, she just couldn't shake whatever he'd stirred inside her.

When Kieran returned to the living room, he found Dana seated on the sofa, rather than on the floor where they'd sat before. That made sense. There was no point in having a big, family-style evening when Rosie was sound asleep.

He looked at his new Bang & Olufsen television screen, where the animated movie continued to play, and reached for the remote, which rested on the lamp table. "I assume it's okay if I turn this off."

"That's fine by me." Dana offered him a shy smile, then studied the wine in her crystal goblet as if she'd never seen anything like it before.

He felt a little awkward, too. But he shook it off and took a seat on the sofa, one cushion away from her. Then he picked up his wineglass, which he'd left on the coffee table just moments ago. "It looks like we'll have the food to ourselves."

Dana bent forward and snatched a piece of cheese and a rice cracker from the platter. As she did, the lamplight splashed on her bent head in such a way that it lit up threads of gold in her auburn strands, causing her silky hair to shimmer and glisten like it was about to catch fire. He could only imagine what it would look like if she wore it hanging loose.

Kieran hadn't expected to notice something like that, let alone comment, but a question rolled off his tongue before he could give it a second thought. "Is there a reason you keep your hair pulled up most of the time?"

Dana gazed up at him, the cheese and cracker half raised to her mouth. Her lips parted as if the question had completely caught her off guard. But then, why wouldn't it take her aback? Kieran hadn't intended to ask her something so personal, even if he'd wondered about it more than once in the last few weeks.

"It's just a habit, I guess. I always put it up when I'm at work because it tends to get into my face whenever I'm bent over a book or a journal. But I…" She didn't finish what she was about to add.

The way she eyed him, carefully and cautiously, made him scamper to find an excuse or an explanation for asking such a question in the first place.

"It's a pretty color," he admitted, "and I'd think…" Oh, for cripe's sake. *Good job, man. Now you've made things worse.*

Where did he go from here? If she were a classy, beautiful woman seated alone in a swanky bar, sipping champagne and wearing a coquettish grin, he'd have no trouble knowing just what to do and say right now. And he wouldn't even consider changing the subject. But this was different.

Dana was different.

And in her own way, even with her hair pulled up and dressed in casual clothes, she seemed just as appealing as any woman he might meet in a bar. In fact, if she would consider letting her hair down and slipping into a slinky black dress…

Oh, hell. She didn't even need to go to that length. As it was, he found her pretty damn intriguing.

And there lay the crux of the problem. Under other circumstances, Kieran would have made a romantic move by now. But he couldn't very well do that when she'd been Zach's girlfriend. Guys didn't do things like that to each other.

"Is something wrong?" she asked.

Hell, yes. Even with her hair pulled up like a prim librarian and with a blood stain on her blouse, she'd caught his eye and his full attention. And he found her way more attractive than he should.

"No," he said, doing his damnedest to shake the sudden attraction and to pull himself together. "There's nothing wrong. My mind was just wandering back in time, back to when Zach was alive. The two of you came to a cocktail party here. And you wore your hair down that evening. It hung nearly to your waist and was so sleek and shiny. The color was even more striking. I didn't tell you then, but I commented about it later to Zach."

"He liked me to wear it long and loose, but…" She bit down on her bottom lip, as if trying to hold back whatever she'd been about to say.

But that was okay. In fact, it was almost a relief to know they'd both gotten caught up in a topic that needed to be redirected—and quickly. If he didn't get off this verbal merry-go-round, he could end up saying something really stupid, something that gave Dana the wrong idea.

"Unlike Zach," he said, grasping at straws, "I've always been attracted to blondes."

The second the words rolled off his tongue, heat flooded his face, and his breathing stopped.

How was that for failing miserably in his attempt to fix things?

Trying to recover, he added, "But I *do* like the color and think you should wear it down more often."

Oh, hell. Great recovery. That thoughtless attempt just threw him back into the quagmire he'd tried to escape.

"Thank you," she said. Then she reached for her glass and took another sip of wine.

So no harm, no foul?

Hopefully, they were back on the right track. He wasn't about to put the moves on his late friend's girlfriend, especially when he desperately needed her friendship.

He'd only screw things up by revealing his attraction to her. Besides, sexual partners were a dime a dozen as far as Kieran was concerned.

Yet for some reason, at least tonight, Dana appeared to be one in a million.

Chapter Five

Dana had no idea what Kieran meant by first complimenting her, then slamming her with the fact that he preferred blondes over redheads.

She'd been so dazed by his first comment that she'd caught her breath. She'd almost believed that he found her pretty, and she could have sworn that something sparked between them. She'd inadvertently lifted her hand and fingered the neatly woven strands.

Then, just when she'd thought he was going to say something romantic, he seemed to have realized his error. His smile faded, and his expression froze, making him look like a deer in the headlights. Or in this case, a bachelor in the headlights. He quickly recovered, although awkwardly, and changed the subject.

Apparently her initial instinct had been wrong. He

hadn't meant to lead her to believe he was actually interested in her, and she felt like a fool.

But what did she know about men like Kieran? Other than Zach, who'd felt more like a friend than a date, she'd only had one real boyfriend, and that relationship hadn't lasted very long.

It had taken a few years of college for her to shed her teenage insecurities, something she blamed on losing her parents so young and being a foster kid. But now she celebrated the fact that she was unique and valuable in her own right, something Monica Flores, the young librarian who'd befriended her, had helped her see. And she wasn't about to slip back into those old, bad habits again.

In an attempt to take control of her tender feelings, she reached for her wineglass, pretending to be completely unaffected by anything Kieran had said. But instead of taking a ladylike sip, she took a rather large gulp, choked and sputtered.

"Are you okay?" he asked.

Talk about uncomfortable moments. "Yes." She covered her mouth and coughed several times. "I'm… fine."

And she was. Kieran was probably afraid that Dana had taken his comment wrong. And maybe she had, but only for a moment. She knew better than to imagine he'd meant anything flirtatious.

Over the years, she'd gotten a lot of compliments on her hair. When she was a little girl, whether at the market or shopping in a department store with her mother, people would stop them all the time and comment about the color. Of course, most of them had been sweet, little old ladies. So her ego hadn't taken that big of a hit now. At least, not one that would be lasting.

Actually, she almost felt sorry for Kieran. He might be uneasy because of what he'd said and afraid of how she might have taken it. But she hadn't gotten the wrong idea. There was no way she'd ever assume that she could just waltz right into his world and easily fit in with the women who ran in his crowd.

"You know," she said, getting to her feet, "I've got to get going. I just realized I put something in my Crock-Pot early this morning."

It was the truth. Well, in a way, it was. He didn't have to know she'd already taken it out.

"I'm sorry if I made you uneasy," he said, rising quickly. "You really do have beautiful hair and probably should wear it down more often. But I don't want you to think I was hitting on you. I only mentioned my attraction to blondes because... Well, it was completely out of line. And it wasn't true."

She laughed, hoping her attempt to feign an unaffected, don't-give-it-a-second-thought attitude sounded real to him and not canned. "I knew you weren't being flirtatious."

At that, his expression softened, and his posture eased. "Good, because I'd really like your help with Rosie, and I'd hate to think you might feel uncomfortable around me."

So there you had it. He needed her to be a part of Team Rosie and nothing more. Dana was fine with that. Really. After all, Zach's little girl and her well-being were all that mattered. And Dana had never expected her and Kieran to be anything other than friends.

Still, as she gathered her purse and headed for the door, a wave of disappointment swept over her, threatening to flood every step she took.

Dana and Kieran hadn't talked since their last awkward evening, although there was more than one reason for that. She'd been especially busy at the history center for the past couple of days, working on a special project she didn't wrap up until Friday afternoon. Then she'd met Connie and Alisha, two of her coworkers, for happy hour, followed by dinner. She hadn't discussed Kieran with them because, while she considered them friends, she wouldn't call them confidantes.

Finally, on Saturday morning, she decided she'd bottled up her feelings for too long. So while having a cup of English breakfast tea and a toasted bagel with cream cheese, she called Monica, who still lived in Amarillo and worked at the library.

Monica was everything Dana wasn't—spunky, beautiful, stylish and petite. She also had a flawless olive complexion, expressive brown eyes and glossy, dark hair she often wore as a mass of riotous curls that bounced along her shoulders and onto her back.

At thirty-one, and six years older than Dana, Monica had easily slid into a mentor role. And before long, the two had grown incredibly close, best friends to be sure. But Monica had become the big sister Dana never had. She was also the only one in the world who understood the relationship Dana had shared with Zach, his daughter and his parents.

"Hey, girl!" Monica said. "How's it going? Are you holding up okay?"

"I'm doing well. How about you?"

"There've been a few changes since we last talked. Sergio and I decided to call it quits."

"I'm sorry to hear that."

"Me, too. But it was a mutual decision, and it's for the best. Most of our time was spent arguing, and I'm tired of it. I'd rather have a peaceful life."

"So what else is new?" Dana asked.

"My *abuelita* moved in with my parents. She's been doing the cooking, so I've been going home a lot, just to eat. And now I've put on about five pounds."

"I can understand why. Your grandmother is an awesome cook." Dana laughed and her spirits rose. She needed to talk to Monica more often than she did. "I really miss the time I used to spend at your parents' house. How are they?"

"Working their tails off. Business at their floral shop seems to have really taken off, so that's good."

Dana bit down on her bottom lip. She'd never held back when sharing her thoughts, fears or dreams with Monica, but how should she word her current dilemma when she didn't quite understand it herself?

She decided to start with the basics. "Zach's best friend, Kieran Fortune, has custody of Rosie. So I've been helping him when I can."

Silence stretched across the line for a couple of beats, then Monica, who'd apparently picked up on something in Dana's tone, prodded her for more details. "And…?"

"It's nothing, really. I just… Well, things are getting a little weird because, as much as I adore Rosie and want to help, Kieran is…well, he's handsome, successful and ultrawealthy. He's also so far out of my league that I'd never fit in with his family or friends if I tried. And on top of that, he'd never be interested in someone like me anyway."

"Awww…"

"What's that supposed to mean?"

"Don't doubt yourself, *chica*. You're brighter and far more beautiful than you've ever realized. And you have plenty to offer a man like that—particularly a loving and loyal heart."

Dana rolled her eyes. "Have you ever heard of Robinson Tech or the Fortune Foundation?"

There was another pause, then a long, drawn out whistle. "You mean he's *that* Kieran Fortune, as in Kieran Fortune Robinson? You mentioned the last name, but since he and Zach were friends, I didn't make the connection. I mean, Zach was a rancher."

"They met at college. Played football together, if I remember correctly and were in the same fraternity. Plus, believe it or not, Zach was pretty sharp. People didn't always recognize that since he tended to speak slowly and with a Texas twang."

"Still," Monica said, "I repeat—you're bright, beautiful and have a loving and loyal heart. You have a lot to offer any man, even one from a wealthy, renowned family."

"Intellectually I know that."

Monica clicked her tongue. "Don't let those old voices from your teen years make you deaf to the truth."

"You're right. I guess I just need to be reminded that some of the things my foster parents and the other kids used to say don't mean a darn thing."

"They certainly don't. And I'll be happy to remind you whenever I can. So will my *abuelita*, who adores you and wants to know if you'll be able to visit soon. She promised to make green chili and chicken mole, just for you."

Dana laughed. "How can I refuse an offer like that?"

"You can't. So check your calendar and let me know when you can take some time off. And speaking of time, I need to hang up. I'm going to meet the new elementary school principal for coffee."

"Ooh, that sounds interesting."

"He's gorgeous, but who knows? I'll definitely keep you posted."

When the call ended, Dana went for a walk in her neighborhood. She'd no more than returned to the house when her cell phone rang.

It was Sandra Lawson on the line.

"How's Sam doing?" Dana asked.

"He's weak and a little grumpy, but that's probably to be expected after spending more than a week in the hospital. I bought him home about ten minutes ago."

"That's great," Dana said. "I'm so glad to hear that. Is he up to having visitors? I'd love to come by and see you both."

"Yes, of course."

"Don't bother to cook," Dana added. "I'll bring dinner for you when I come. That is, unless someone else has already volunteered."

"No, you and Kieran are the first to know that Sam came home. I was just about to call Pastor Mark next."

"I'm glad I was at the top of your phone list," Dana said. "Give Sam my best and tell him I'll be there around four this afternoon."

As soon as they'd said goodbye and the call ended, Dana pulled out her favorite recipe books so she could start a grocery list. The first one she opened was a 1939 edition of *The Household Searchlight Recipe Book*, which was sure to have some great casseroles. Then she paused midsearch. She'd have to make something heart healthy for Sam, which meant she'd have to do some online research.

Several hours later, after preparing most of the meal, she arrived at the Leaning L. She'd placed the food in containers and packed them in a big cardboard box, which now rested on the front passenger seat. She'd also brought salad fixings, plus a variety of fruit for dessert, all of which she would assemble when she had the use of Sandra's kitchen.

As she steered her car into the yard, she spotted a familiar black Mercedes. Her heart did a series of somersaults that would make a gymnast proud. That is, until reality struck.

Kieran being here wasn't a surprise. Sandra had called him first. She and Sam had missed Rosie terribly and had to be eager to see her.

Dana parked and shut off the ignition, but she continued to sit behind the wheel a moment longer, gathering her thoughts and waiting for her pulse to return to a steady rate. Things had been so awkward when she'd left Kieran's house the other night that she wasn't quite sure what to expect now.

Maybe, since a few days had passed, they'd be able to forget about it and move on. She glanced at her reflection in the rearview mirror. After she'd showered and shampooed her hair, she'd blown it dry, then pulled it into a twist atop her head, using a big, brass clip to hold it in place.

It looked perfectly fine, but Kieran's comment came to mind. *You wore your hair down that evening. It hung nearly to your waist and was so sleek and shiny. The color was even more striking.*

For some silly reason, she reached behind her head, removed the clip and let the strands fall loose. Then, using her fingers, she combed through them.

As she studied her new reflection in the mirror, she was tempted to pull her locks back and clip them up again, just as she did before going into work each day. But she wasn't at the history center now. She was visiting friends, an older couple who treated her like family and a handsome man. What would it hurt to go into the house looking her best?

She blew off her self-doubt, climbed out of the car and circled around to the passenger side to get the cardboard box of food.

As she headed for the house, she berated herself—first for changing her hairstyle and then for stressing about her reason for doing it. The truth was, she found Kieran way too attractive for her own good, and she wasn't going to allow her imagination to run away with her.

Who cared what she looked like? She wouldn't give it another thought. Instead, she continued forward, putting one foot in front of the other and willing her heart to match the slower pace.

Once she'd climbed the steps and crossed the porch, she rang the bell. Moments later, Kieran answered the door.

"Hey," he said, as if he'd had no idea she was coming.

Her heart rate, which hadn't quite righted itself, stumbled for a moment. That is, until a small, happy voice cried out, "Dannnnna!"

At that sweet greeting, warmth filled Dana's chest, and the beats returned to normal. She smiled at the little girl, who wore two neat little pigtails, pale blue bows adorning each one. "Hi, sweetie. It's good to see you."

"Here," Kieran said, taking the cardboard box before Dana could decline. "Let me help you with that."

Releasing her burden was a good thing because, once her hands were free, Rosie practically jumped into her arms.

Dana held the little girl close, relishing the soft scent of baby shampoo and assuming her grandma had fixed her hair today.

Was there anything sweeter and more fulfilling than the love of a child?

"Did you come to see my grandpa?" Rosie asked Dana. "He told me he's all better because I came to see him. And you know what? He's going to get me a pony for my birthday." She held up a hand, her thumb bent to the palm, and showed off her fingers. "I'm gonna be four. And Grandpa said that's big enough to learn how to ride."

"That's awesome," Dana said, although Sam was far from being completely well. Still, seeing Rosie must have lifted his spirits and was sure to be the best medicine of all.

"Looks like we'll be spending a few weekends out here on the Leaning L," Kieran said.

"That's because I'm gonna live with my uncle at his house," Rosie added. "And we're gonna come to the ranch *all* the time so I can visit Grandma and Grandpa and my pony."

Apparently, the adults had already decided that Rosie's temporary living situation would become permanent.

Rosie tugged at the sleeve of Kieran's shirt. "You know what?"

There was no telling, Dana thought, as a smile crossed her lips. The precocious child always had something cute and original to say.

Kieran reached for one of Rosie's pigtails and gave it a gentle tug. "What's that, peanut?"

"Since I'm gonna live with you from now on, I'm gonna call you Uncle Daddy."

Dana had to hand it to the child. She'd not only come up with yet another clever thought, but also a new moniker for the handsome exec. She didn't dare comment. But she did look at Kieran, wondering what he was going to say to that.

Uncle Daddy?

Kieran had no idea how Rosie had come up with a nickname like that, nor did he know how to respond. Back when Rosie had first learned to talk, Zach had referred to Kieran as her uncle. While it had sounded a little odd to him at first, it had touched him in an unexpected way, and he'd soon gotten used to it.

But this was different. Was Rosie making an emotional segue from uncle to daddy? If so, it was more than a little unsettling, especially since he knew he'd never be able to fill Zach's shoes and feared he'd let her down someday.

Kieran glanced at Dana, hoping she'd help him out of this sticky wicket, but she was studying him just as closely as Rosie was. For that reason, the only thing he could think to say was, "Sure. I like that. Can I call you Princess Rosie?"

The little girl clapped her hands, causing Dana to sway with the unexpected movement. "Yes, you can! But call me Princess Rosabelle the Cowboy Girl."

"That's a long name," he said. "Would it be okay if I call you princess for short?"

Rosie nodded, then asked Dana to put her down. "I gotta tell Grandma and Grandpa so they'll know what to call me."

Once Dana bent to place her on the floor, Rosie

dashed off, leaving Dana and Kieran alone in the living room.

When Dana straightened and their gazes met, Kieran was again thrown back into a swirl of surprise and the rush of attraction he'd felt when he'd first answered the door and spotted her on the porch. He hadn't expected to see her at the ranch today, but what really threw him for a blood-rushing loop was the sight of her pretty red hair, glistening as it hung loose along her back and over her shoulders.

He'd nearly complimented her then and there, but before he could find the words to say, Rosie had interrupted them. Should he mention it now? He was tempted to, but he'd really fouled things up by speaking his mind the other night.

"I told Sandra that I'd bring dinner to them," Dana said. "I didn't realize you and Rosie would be here, although I should have. But it doesn't matter. There's plenty for all of us tonight with leftovers for tomorrow."

He couldn't blame her for maintaining ties with Sam and Sandra. She obviously missed Zach and felt his presence whenever she was here on the Leaning L with his parents. "I'll take the box into the kitchen for you."

"Thanks."

Again, he wanted to tell her that he'd noticed her hair, that he liked it. Had she worn it down because of what he'd told her the other night?

Hell, she hadn't expected him to be here today. Leaving it down was probably just a coincidence. It wasn't like she *never* wore it that way.

Shaking off the crazy speculation, he carried the box into the kitchen and placed it on the oak table. Dana, who'd followed him, removed a brown sack, a plastic container and two glass baking dishes.

"What's on the menu?" he asked.

"Baked skinless chicken breasts, brown rice with almonds, a garden salad and a fresh fruit cup for dessert."

Seriously? That sounded rather bland and dull. He'd almost prefer to eat Cowboy Fred's pizza, although he knew better than to say that. "It sounds..."

"Healthy?" She laughed, the lilt of her voice striking a chord deep inside, the vibrations threatening to shatter anything within its range. "Why do I get the feeling that tonight's meal doesn't sound all that tasty to you?"

He chuckled. "Because it...*doesn't*?"

"I wanted to make something that Sam's cardiologist would approve of, and so I did some research. Believe it or not, I'm actually a good cook, even when I'm cutting back on salt, sugar and fat."

"I've never been all that health conscious. But I won't complain."

"Oh, good! Now I won't have to punch you in the eye, like Rosie did to Michael when he annoyed her at Cowboy Fred's."

As much as Kieran wanted to cling tightly to the uneasiness he'd felt after being with Dana the other night, a smile tugged at his lips. "Just so you know, unlike Dragon Boy, I'm actually drawn to ladies in line for the throne."

In fact, he was growing a little too fond of this particular princess, who reminded him of Rapunzel. A man could get lost in hair like hers.

"So how's it going?" Dana asked. "Rosie seems happy, and you don't appear to be nearly as stressed as you did earlier in the week."

"It's getting easier, especially when I'm back at the Leaning L and know that Sandra can take over in a pinch." Actually, now that Dana was here, he felt even better. "So tonight's going to be a piece of cake— even if there isn't a gooey, sweet dessert in sight."

Dana laughed again. "Next time we have dinner together, I'll have to make something gooey and sweet and loaded with carbs and calories just for you."

So there was going to be a next time for them. That was good to know. Apparently, they'd both been able to put Awkward Tuesday behind them.

He supposed he could excuse himself now, but he found it pleasantly entertaining to watch her move about, washing fruits and vegetables, then removing a cutting board and a paring knife from one of the drawers. Obviously, she knew her way around Sandra's kitchen.

"I assume you're also getting used to working from home," she said.

"Not really. I hadn't wanted to hire someone to help me take care of Rosie, but I have a feeling I won't be getting a darn thing done on Tuesdays and Thursdays, so I might be forced to."

Dana began peeling two peaches as well as an

orange and an apple. "Finding a good nanny should solve that problem."

"I'm sure you're right. But for the record, I believe it's a parent's—or in my case, a guardian's—responsibility to raise their kids." He didn't go into detail about the nannies and au pairs he'd had while growing up. Nor did he mention that he'd often felt neglected by his parents.

He'd probably sound like a whiner to a woman who'd been orphaned and raised in foster care.

"I'm probably going to have to bite the bullet," he admitted. "And sooner rather than later. I have to make a business trip to Amarillo on Thursday, although I'll be back in town that same evening. I'm not sure what to do with Rosie while I'm gone. It's not a school day."

"I'd offer to take some vacation time and help you out," Dana said, "but I've got a meeting that day, and I can't reschedule it."

"I was just talking out loud. I wasn't asking for a volunteer." Although, it would have been nice to know Rosie was in Dana's care while he was gone.

Dana reached for the grapes, broke off a small cluster and handed it to Kieran. "Here, have a snack."

He thanked her and popped a couple of red seedless grapes in his mouth.

"I used to live in Amarillo," she said. "And my best friend still works there. Monica Flores. You remember I told you about her?"

He recalled the name. "The librarian, right?"

"Yes. We met at the library near the house where

I lived. She's just graduated from college and landed her first job as a librarian there. She's just a few years older than me, so I found myself talking to her about school, college and scholarships."

"That's great that you've remained friends. Other than Zach, I haven't stayed in contact with any of the other guys who went to school with me."

"Maybe you should look up a few of them."

He shrugged a single shoulder. "Maybe I will—someday. I'm pretty busy at the office, and now that I have Rosie…well, I really don't have any free time."

"I know what you mean. I haven't seen Monica in more than a year, mostly because I moved eight hours away to work at the history center. But we still keep in touch, on the phone and on Facebook." Dana grew pensive. "I really miss having her close."

"I'll be taking the corporate jet to Amarillo," he said, "so you can go with me. That is, if you can get the day off."

She studied him and he got the sneaking feeling he'd stepped over a line. And he probably had. She must think that he was making another move on her when he'd just offered to let her come because he'd wanted to be nice.

"Like I said before," she finally replied, "I've got an appointment. The people I'm meeting have a history foundation and will only be in town Thursday. But thanks for the offer."

"Maybe next time."

Again she studied him, her head tilted slightly to the side, her pretty red hair sluicing down her arm.

"Not that it's any of my business, but what's in Amarillo that can't be done over Skype or FaceTime?"

"Robinson Tech is considering a buyout, and I want to get a tour of their operation."

"That sounds important."

"We've had much bigger deals. I could probably ask someone else to go in my place, but everyone's busy. And I really want to see the outfit for myself. Only trouble is, I don't want to leave Rosie with Sandra while Sam is recovering. And there isn't time to hire a good nanny. Do you know any of the sitters Zach used in the past?"

"There's a teenager who attends Sandra's church. I think her name is Kelly. She's pretty young to have Rosie all day, especially with you so far away. But if you had her watch Rosie at the ranch, Sandra would be here and could oversee things."

"That sounds like a good plan."

"I can probably get time off in the afternoon, after my meeting. So I can come by to help."

It was sweet of her to offer, and he was tempted to take her up on it. Before he could decide, she spoke again.

"You didn't ask. I'm volunteering. Besides, I adore Rosie."

"I know how busy you are, and she isn't your responsibility, but the truth is, I can use all the help and advice I can get."

"I'd be happy to do whatever I can." She tucked a long strand of that gorgeous hair behind her ear. "I promise, if I can't step in or take care of her for whatever reason, I'll let you know. So don't feel bad about calling me if you need me—or if you need anything at all."

Oh, he had needs, all right. But those weren't the ones she was talking about easing. He'd be damned if he'd let her know where his thoughts had strayed, though.

Of course, why wouldn't they? Dana was a beautiful woman, one he was finding more and more attractive every day. Besides, it had been way too long since he'd had sex.

But he wasn't about to let his hormones run away with him.

Chapter Six

Sam might have told Rosie that he was well on the mend thanks to her visit, but he'd been too weak to get out of bed and join the family at the dinner table and remained in his room. When Rosie objected to his eating all by himself, Sandra suggested that she and the little girl have "a picnic" on Grandpa's bed.

That left Dana and Kieran seated alone in the kitchen, a dining experience that felt a little awkward, especially since the handsome man had a way of setting her heart on edge and her sexual awareness on high alert.

And why wouldn't his presence do that to her? All she had to do was take one look at him, with those gorgeous blue eyes and that light brown hair that was always well-groomed, and she was toast. Even now, dressed casually in a pair of designer jeans and a light blue button-down shirt, he commanded a woman's attention. And, he'd certainly captured hers tonight.

"This chicken is really good," he said. "You weren't kidding when you said you know how to cook."

Dana offered him a smile. "I'm glad you like it."

"Who would have guessed that you had a domestic streak?"

"Actually, I don't." For a beat, she wondered if she should be offended by his comment. After all, she had a busy life that wasn't centered at home, even if a man like Kieran wouldn't find it exciting. But after glancing across the scarred oak table and spotting the warmth in his expression and the glimmer in his eyes, she shrugged it off. "Believe it or not, I wasn't interested in cooking until I stumbled across a collection of old cookbooks at an estate sale last year. I began to research how earlier generations ate, so I tried out different recipes. And some of them were pretty tasty."

Kieran sat back in his seat, his grin morphing into a heart-strumming smile. "It sounds like you've picked up a few unique treasures during your shopping escapades."

"I really have. That's what makes shopping for antiques and going to estate sales fun." Again, she glanced at him. Had he found her quirky or odd, like some men did? If he did, his dazzling expression hid it well. "So then, just for the record, I'm not what you'd call a homebody."

"I never thought you were."

Good. But what *had* he thought of her? She certainly didn't frequent the fancy restaurants or attend stellar social events like he and his family and friends did. But then, not many people could afford to. Still, she found her life to be fulfilling. And she was happy with it. So what else mattered?

As they continued to eat, silence stretched between them, interrupted by the occasional sound of a fork clicking on a ceramic plate. Dana tried to focus on finishing her meal, but her hyped-up awareness of the man seated across from her didn't make it easy.

Get a grip, girl. This guy is way out of your league as well as your comfort zone.

And that was so true. Just mention the name *Fortune* and people's interest piqued for a variety of reasons, and not just because of all the charity work done by the Fortune Foundation. Gosh, there was even a royal branch of the family that garnered tabloid headlines!

"Oh," Kieran said, drawing her from her musing. "I nearly forgot. You mentioned a teenager who used to babysit for Zach."

"He called a couple of high school kids occasionally, but the one he used the most was Kelly Vandergrift."

"I'm going to need her phone number. Do you have it? I could ask Sandra, but she'll insist that she can handle watching Rosie for a day. And she really has her hands full with Sam right now."

"You're right." Dana pushed back her chair, the wooden legs scraping the worn, linoleum flooring, and got to her feet. Then she walked to the yellow, wall-mounted telephone and studied the small white-board hanging beside it, where Sandra had written important numbers. She scanned the list until she found Kelly's name. "Here it is. Let me write it down for you so you can take it with you."

Kieran whipped out his cell phone from the clip on his belt. "Just read it off to me. I'll call her now and then add her to my contacts. Even if I hire a full-time nanny, I'm sure I'll need a backup babysitter on occasion."

Moments later, Kelly must have answered, because after Kieran introduced himself and he explained his dilemma. "I realize you might be in school next week, but with Easter coming up, I thought there was a chance you'd be on spring break."

After a slight pause, his face brightened. "Oh, good. I'm glad to hear that. Are you available to watch her on Thursday at the Leaning L?" Again, he listened to Kelly's response, then added, "I'll need you around eight in the morning. Rosie's grandparents will be here, but I don't want them to have to worry about her or to feel as though they need to entertain her."

Kieran laughed. "You, too? In the past week, I've played more games of Candy Land and Go Fish than I can count. Anyway, I really appreciate this, Kelly. I'll have Rosie at the ranch before eight o'clock. I'm not sure how long I'll be gone, but I hope to be back before dark."

After ending the call, Kieran's gaze traveled to Dana. "That worked out great."

"Be sure to give her my phone number," Dana said.

"If she has a problem of any kind while you're in Amarillo, it'll only take me thirty minutes to get here."

"That makes me feel even better, although I hate bothering you, especially when you have a meeting that day, too."

"I really don't mind. I like being helpful."

He studied her a moment. "I didn't know you very well before, but I can now see that you're a special lady. I hadn't expected Zach to fall for a quiet librarian, but I guess there's a lot to be said for that old adage that opposites attract."

Dana wouldn't say that Zach had exactly "fallen" for her. They'd become good friends and gone out whenever he was free or needed a date, but things between them hadn't really clicked. They'd never had the kind of chemistry that made her tingle, or Zach, either, for that matter.

"Actually," she said, "when you get to know me, you'll find that I'm not all that quiet."

As his gaze zeroed in on hers, she tried to gauge his expression, which wasn't at all easy to read. She spotted something warm in his eyes, something soft and…

Darn it. She hoped it wasn't sympathy. She'd gotten so many pitying looks from friends and coworkers who assumed she'd been devastated by Zach's loss.

She'd been saddened, for sure, and disappointed that their relationship had never really gotten off the ground. But her real grief was for the motherless child who was now missing her daddy.

But did she dare admit that to the man who'd been Zach's best friend? She couldn't.

"I should probably know this," Kieran said, "but I never got around to asking Zach. How and when did you two meet?"

"I interviewed him last fall, when I was researching Austin's ranching history. He had a great sense of humor and had me in stitches. A few days later, he called and asked me out to lunch."

Their friendship had evolved into a dating relationship, but that's as far as things went. They'd gone out for six months but there hadn't been anything sexual between them. Something more serious might have developed between them in time, but Rosie's mother, who hadn't stuck around long enough to actually be a mom, had done a real number on his head. So he'd been gun-shy about making a commitment.

They'd talked about it, and while Zach had told Dana she was a "great gal," he said his focus had to be on his daughter. And Dana agreed. When her parents had been alive, they'd been totally committed to her.

Still, instead of pulling away from Zach, she'd been drawn to him, especially to his adorable daughter and his parents, who reminded her of her mom and dad. So her friendship with Zach had worked out nicely for everyone involved.

Then Zach died. Since he'd been her only tie to his family, it was like losing hers all over again.

But she'd never admit anything like that to Kieran. How could she? He'd probably think she was a clingy waif or a family crasher. And she'd walk away from him, Rosie and the Lawsons before she'd ever let that happen.

"I'm sorry for relying on you so much," Kieran said.

"Don't worry about that."

"I'm grateful for all you've done, and it's so easy to turn to you first. But I have a feeling that's making things more difficult for you."

"I'm glad to help. And to be honest, knowing that you, Rosie and the Lawsons need me makes me feel better."

And that was true. The part that complicated matters and made everything worse was her growing attraction to Zach's best friend, especially when Kieran was even more unsuited to her than Zach had been.

When Kieran had left the Leaning L with Rosie the other night, he'd been determined to back off and not rely on Dana too much. She might have said that she wanted to be helpful, but he didn't want to take advantage of her kindness.

Yet even as he came to that conclusion, a small, sarcastic voice piped up, jabbing at him.

How thoughtful—and noble—you are.

He had to admit that there was something else at play, something tempting him to call on her for just about anything. And it wasn't as a friend or as a babysitter who cared about Rosie's well-being. In fact, each time he was with her, he seemed to be more drawn to her, more intrigued by her.

Dana Trevino was a beautiful woman, with a willowy shape, expressive blue eyes and silky red hair a man could run his fingers through. She also had a warm and loving heart, especially with Rosie. And that's what had made her perfect for Zach. Kieran saw that clearly now. She would've been the kind of wife his best friend deserved.

Unlike Kieran, Zach had been both a rancher who loved the land and a man who adored his family. On the other hand, Kieran thrived in the city. And while he might care about his parents and siblings, he'd never been especially close to any of them. At least, he hadn't been in the past. Things were changing now that he'd gotten older and had proven himself to be worthy to step into an executive position at Robinson Tech.

No, it would be better if he left Dana alone so she could lead her own life before he made a complete mess of things. Besides, she still had ties to the Lawsons, and the last thing he wanted to do was to complicate things for the elderly couple who were already dealing with a tragic and painful loss.

Yet even after Kieran and Dana had eaten dinner at the Leaning L the other night and said their goodbyes, thoughts and images of the lovely, kindhearted research librarian continued to drift into his mind.

In fact, even at the office, while he was scheduling the corporate jet for his business trip to Amarillo, he'd thought of her once again and wished she'd been able to join him. And how crazy was that?

No, it was better that he go alone.

When Thursday morning finally rolled around,

Kieran arrived at the Leaning L at a quarter to eight with Rosie in tow, her backpack bulging with dolls, books, sketch pads and markers.

Sandra must have been watching for them, because she met them on the porch before he could knock at the door.

"There's my sweet pea," she said, as she stooped and wrapped Rosie in a warm embrace. "I'm so glad you're here. We're going to have fun today."

Kieran certainly hoped they had an enjoyable— and uneventful—day.

"How's Sam feeling?" he asked.

"A little better. He also seems to be getting stronger." Sandra straightened, then welcomed Kieran with a hug and a kiss on the cheek, an unexpected display of affection that caught him off guard, yet pleased him.

"How about you?" she asked. "Are you holding up all right?"

"Yep. Rosie and I are doing just fine."

"Good," Sandra said, as she led them into the house. "Kelly called a few minutes ago to tell me that she was on her way. That was nice of you to line her up, but you didn't have to. I could have watched Rosie for you."

"I had no doubt about that, but I'll feel better knowing there are two pairs of eyes on her."

And, of course, there was more to it than that. Sam might be responding well to his heart medication and getting stronger each day, but there was no guarantee that he wouldn't have a relapse. And knowing that Kelly would be there to help with Rosie meant Kieran could leave town with a certain confidence.

So once Kelly arrived and Rosie was settled, Kieran drove to the airport and met the company pilot. Then they flew to Amarillo for what he hoped would be a successful business trip.

He returned early that evening, tired and disappointed in the daily operations of the tech company he'd gone to check out.

Now here he was, back at the Leaning L and parked next to Dana's car. Apparently, just as she'd promised, she came by after work to make sure everything was going well while he was gone. He might have planned to back off and not rely on her too much, but he had to admit that he was glad she was here.

Apparently she hadn't felt the same way about cutting ties with him, which pleased him, too.

As he crossed the yard, heading for the house, the screen door swung open, and Dana stepped onto the porch. She wore a pair of black slacks and a white blouse, typical business attire and an attractive look. But what struck him was her hairstyle, which was pulled up into a soft, feminine style topknot like something a woman in the late 1800s might wear. He had no idea what to call it, but the term *Gibson Girl* came to mind.

He nearly complimented her, but the words jammed in his throat. How did a man go about telling a woman like Dana that she was beautiful and unpredictable without making her think he was interested in her?

Especially if he didn't want her or anyone else to suspect that he was.

Damn. Here he was, approaching Zach's house with an idea that was so inappropriate it was hard for him to admit, even to himself.

"How did things go today?" he asked her.

Dana lifted her index finger to her lips as if making a shushing sound. When he reached the porch and was within hearing distance, she lowered her voice to a whisper. "Everything went well, but Rosie's asleep."

Kieran glanced at his watch. "Isn't it a little late for a nap? Or is it early for bed?"

"She and Kelly had a big day, so she had a hard time winding down. She finally crashed about thirty minutes ago."

"It sounds like she had fun. But how did Sam and Sandra do?"

"They were delighted to have her, but Sam said he was tuckered out, too. I think he's asleep now. And Sandra is sitting in the living room with her feet up."

"In that case, I don't want to interrupt her quiet time." Kieran probably ought to take a seat on the porch and wind down from his own busy day, but he found himself asking Dana, "Are you up for a walk?"

"Sure." She carefully shut the screen door, then followed him down the steps and into the yard. "So how did your meeting in Amarillo go?"

"Not as well as I'd hoped. I wasn't impressed with the operation or their financials. So once I got back on the jet, I emailed the board of directors and advised against that buyout."

Then I'd say the trip went well. Your time wasn't wasted if you saved the company from making a bad investment."

"That's true." He glanced at the setting sun, which had streaked the western horizon in shades of pink, orange and gray.

"I hope you don't mind," Dana said, "but once I got here, I told Kelly she could go home. I also paid her."

"That's fine. Just let me know how much I owe you."

"Forty dollars," she said.

For some reason, he felt more indebted to Dana than that, which was a little disconcerting, although he wasn't sure why. When he'd mentioned that he hadn't wanted to make things difficult for her by asking too much of her, she'd insisted that helping him with Rosie made her feel better.

Why was that? The only answer he came up with was that being with Rosie, especially on the Leaning L, provided her with a connection to Zach. If that was the case, and Kieran suspected that it was, it just proved that she was clinging to his memory.

He stole a glance her way. She was studying the western horizon and what was turning out to be an amazing sunset. Yet it was Dana's beauty and the pretty copper color of her hair that struck him as gaze-worthy.

If things were different, if she'd never dated Zach, Kieran might suggest they take a bottle of wine and the Lawsons' all-terrain vehicle out to a quiet spot by the pond, where they could watch a waning sunset turn into a cozy, romantic evening.

As tempting as the thought might be, it was a bad idea. The last thing in the world he needed to do was make a move on Dana, who might never forget Zach.

Kieran had fought long and hard to stand out in his family and at Robinson Tech, and he'd succeeded. So he wasn't about to take a back seat to anyone, even if that guy had once been the best friend he'd ever had.

As Dana and Kieran passed a corral on their aimless walk to nowhere in particular, she didn't want it to end. The light breeze refreshed her after a day's work indoors, and so did the sights and sounds of the ranch preparing for nightfall. But it was the man beside her that commanded her full attention.

His swagger and his musky scent stirred a longing deep in her soul. When her shoulder inadvertently bumped his arm, his male presence slammed into her, creating thoughts that were way too romantic for her own good. And for one long beat, her heart stalled.

The weathervane creaked and a horse whinnied in the distance. Yet her thoughts centered on the man beside her who was so close that she could have easily reached out and taken his hand in hers, a move that seemed like the most natural thing in the world for her to do. But she'd never been that bold.

Instead she relied on her vivid imagination, which allowed her to live vicariously through the novels she read or the many historical figures who often came alive after she'd researched them at the center.

But Kieran Fortune was made of flesh and blood, a millennial man who wasn't the kind of hero a woman like her should even dream about. If she were to act on her silly romantic musings, she'd regret it for the rest of her life.

That might sound as if she thought she was unworthy of him, which wasn't true. She had a solid self-image. She just preferred not to hobnob with the rich and famous. And that's what he was.

People wrote magazine and newspaper articles about men like him all the time, which reminded her of the phone call she received earlier today.

"There's something I thought I'd better tell you," she said. "A journalist contacted me at the history center today and asked if she could set up an appointment to meet with me and to do some research for an article she's writing."

Kieran continued the pace they'd set, but he glanced at Dana with a quizzical expression. "And…?"

Apparently, he wasn't sure why she'd brought up something that was practically an everyday occurrence where she worked, but there was a good reason she wanted him to know.

"Her name is Ariana Lamonte, and she's profiling the 'new Fortunes' for her blog. Then she's going to merge the stories into an article for *Weird Life* magazine."

At that, Kieran's steps slowed to a near standstill. "I've heard about her. She interviewed my sister Sophie and my half brother, Keaton Whitfield."

Dana wasn't sure how to respond, since Kieran

probably had no idea how much she knew about his family. It wasn't all that much, but Zach had told her that several of Kieran's half siblings had turned up recently. Apparently, Gerald Robinson aka Jerome Fortune had been a real Romeo, although Zach had used the word *horndog* in relating the story.

"Ariana mentioned her interest in old newspapers and magazines," Dana said. "I can't deny her access to the archives, but under the circumstances, I thought you should know what she's planning to write."

Kieran took a deep breath, then slowly let it out. "It's no big secret that my dad cheated on my mom. Not just once, but time and again. And with our involvement in the Fortune Foundation as well as Peter's Place, a lot of people are probably curious about us."

They might wonder why, when Gerald Robinson had never admitted to having once been known as Jerome Fortune, although Kieran and his siblings had each added on the Fortune name. They also might want to know why he'd staged his own death when he left his family ties behind—another detail Zach had revealed—and why he'd changed his name before creating a billion-dollar tech company.

Dana might have asked Kieran for details since she counted herself as one of many people intrigued by the Fortune Robinson clan—particularly Kieran—but she kept her thoughts to herself. She'd simply have to be satisfied with what Zach had revealed and what little Kieran imparted.

"Besides," Kieran added, "Ms. Lamonte's article

might be good publicity for Robinson Tech as well as the Fortune Foundation."

"You're probably right. I'm glad you're not worried about it."

He shrugged. "I'm not proud of the things my father did, although I do admire his brilliance and his business acumen."

"Zach admired that, too."

Kieran merely nodded. "But I appreciate the heads-up, Dana. So thanks for letting me know, even though there isn't much I can do about stories like that getting out."

She smiled. "That's what friends are for."

But when their gazes locked, something more than a friendly look passed between them. Before she could convince herself that she might be reading him wrong, he lifted his hand and cupped her jaw. "You're amazing."

Her cheeks warmed, and when his thumb stroked her skin, she tingled from head to toe. For a moment, she thought he might kiss her.

But he didn't. In fact, he didn't move at all, and neither did she. Heck, she was afraid to even breathe for fear he'd remove his hand before she'd had a chance to savor his touch.

Should she ask him what his words and his gesture meant? Maybe, but her heart was fluttering so hard she thought it might fly away, and the words jammed in her throat. Unfortunately, about the time she nearly got her act together, his hand slid off her face. Then he tore his gaze away.

When he continued to walk, she fell into step beside him again. He didn't say another word as they circled the barn and headed back to the house. She wasn't ready to end the short time they'd spent together, and an ache settled deep in her chest.

She was, however, eager to read Ariana Lamonte's article when it came out. She was especially interested in the Fortune family now. And she found Kieran more intriguing than ever. So much so, that she'd be tempted to dip her toe into his world and try it on for size.

How was that for having a vivid imagination and creating a pipe dream that would never come true?

Chapter Seven

Kieran couldn't believe how close he'd come to kissing Dana last night. But when he'd gazed into her blue eyes, he'd nearly met a sweet death. His brains deserted him, and he'd reached out and touched her face.

That was bad enough, but then he'd brushed his thumb across her cheek, felt the softness of her skin, and his hormones had shot into overdrive. For a moment, he'd forgotten who she was.

And that was a big mistake. Thankfully, he'd finally wrapped his mind around what he'd almost done, and he'd come to a screeching halt and walked away. But the damage had already been done, and he had no idea how to correct it.

Dana must have been uncomfortable, too, because once they got back to the house, she'd quickly said her goodbyes, mentioning something about a neighbor who needed her to do a favor. But he'd wager that had only been an excuse to escape him—and one that was only slightly better than having to shampoo her hair.

Needless to say, he couldn't call her anymore to ask for her help. He couldn't risk the temptation. Because next time, he just might take her in his arms and kiss her senseless. And then he'd be in a real fix.

He needed to get contact numbers for other baby-sitters for when he was at the office and in meetings, but he couldn't ask Sandra. She'd insist upon watching Rosie herself, and she already had too much on her plate. Besides, her health wasn't the best.

Still, that meant he had to come up with something else—or rather, some*one* else. Someone permanent to look after Rosie for him.

For that reason, on Friday morning he'd spent an hour on the phone with an agency that provided experienced nannies for working families. Then he spent most of Saturday interviewing several potential care-givers.

He settled on Megan Baker, a reasonably attractive brunette in her late twenties, and asked her to show up bright and early on Tuesday morning. He would be going into the office, no longer working from home now that he'd hired a nanny who would solve his problem once and for all.

Megan was friendly and outgoing. She also seemed competent, so he'd left Rosie in her care. But after he returned from work Tuesday afternoon and Megan had left, Rosie met him in the kitchen with her arms crossed, her little face scrunched into a frown.

"What's wrong, princess?"

"I don't like her."

The new nanny had seemed nice enough to him. "You mean Megan? Why not?"

Rosie harrumphed, then unfolded her arms and slapped her hands on her hips. "Because she ate the pink ice cream *all gone*. And she made me eat the chocolate, even when I don't like it. Then she filled up her bowl again and wouldn't even share it with me. And she only wanted to watch TV. And even when I said please, she wouldn't play or color or read stories with me."

At that, Kieran decided he didn't like Megan, either.

"I'll tell you what, Rosie. We'll find a different nanny—one who *will* play with you and share the strawberry ice cream."

She made her way to where he stood, then lifted her arms to him, indicating she wanted him to pick her up. When he did, she rested her head against his and asked, "Why can't I just stay with you, Uncle Daddy? I'll be really, really good."

His heart swelled with myriad emotions, only one of which was remorse at having to leave her with a sitter. "Because I have to go into the office. And I also have to attend a lot of boring meetings."

In spite of the guilt, a flutter of pride rose in his chest. It was nice to know that she preferred to be with him.

So the next morning, after taking her to preschool, he told the agency that he wouldn't need Megan anymore and moved on to the next nanny candidate.

Darla Sue Williams, a maternal, heavyset woman in her midfifties, seemed to be the perfect choice. So when she arrived bright and early on Thursday morning, he again headed for the office. But when he returned just after five that evening, and after Darla Sue had waddled out the door, he turned to Rosie, who stood before him, frowning yet again.

But this time, he knew what was wrong. The little princess had found fault with nanny number two.

"I take it you didn't like Darla Sue, either," he said.

Rosie crossed her arms and shifted her weight to one hip. "She can't sit down on the floor and color with me 'cause she broke her knee one day and has Arthur Right Us in it. And when she was still eating lunch and I was going to play with my dolls, she let out a big toot and didn't say 'scuse me."

"She probably thought that you hadn't heard her."

Rosie rolled her eyes and sighed. "Then she has broken ears, too, because it was really loud and I think everyone in the world heard it."

Kieran bit back a laugh. There was no pleasing this kid, although he had to admit Darla Sue might not be the perfect fit, either. But now what?

"Uncle Daddy," Rosie said, "can't you work right here like you did before? I just want to be with *you*."

Damn. The blond-haired princess was too adorable for words, and it warmed his heart to know that she'd rather be with him—even if that wasn't possible.

The most obvious solution was to increase the number of days she spent at preschool, but he'd tried doing that the first week she'd moved in with him. Miss Peggy, the preschool director, said she was sorry, but they were full. She then offered to add Rosie to the waiting list, which had seemed fair enough. That is, until Kieran learned there were already more than a dozen names on it.

"I'm sure that's not what you wanted to hear," Miss Peggy had said. When he agreed, she'd added, "You may not know this, but we have one of the best preschools in Austin."

"Super," he'd said, although he'd wondered if it might help Rosie's chances of moving up to the top of the list if he made a donation of some kind. But the school wasn't a nonprofit organization. Besides, a move like that smacked of something his father might try to pull.

So that left only one thing for Kieran to do. He'd have to take Rosie to the office with him next Tuesday morning, because there was no way he'd call Dana— no matter how badly he wanted to.

At five minutes to one o'clock on Wednesday, right after Dana returned to work from lunch, a twenty-something brunette arrived at the history center.

Normally Dana didn't assess the visitors, but this one was attractive and had an interesting Bohemian style. Dressed in high-heeled boots, flared jeans and a paisley tunic top, the woman also carried a floppy, soft leather purse, a loose leaf notebook and a padded laptop case.

"I'm Ariana Lamonte," she said. "I spoke to someone on the telephone last week and made an appointment to do some research today."

"Actually, you talked to me." Dana reached out and shook Ariana's hand. "You're doing an article on the new Fortunes for your blog and for *Weird Life* magazine."

"That's right." Ariana smiled, as she wrapped Dana's hand in a strong, confident grip. "I came to check the archives for newspapers and magazines from about thirty years ago."

"No problem. But before I take you to the reading room, you'll need to sign in at the front desk."

Ariana did as instructed.

"You'll also have to place your bags in one of our lockers," Dana added.

At that, Ariana shot her a questioning look.

"We ask everyone to do that so we can ensure the security and preservation of our material."

"I understand," Ariana said. "But what about my laptop? I'd like to take notes, if that's all right."

"As long as you lock up the case, you can have the laptop."

"What about my cell phone?"

"If you take it out of your purse, you can have that, too."

"Perfect. Are there any other rules I should be aware of?"

"They're posted on the wall," Dana said. "But if

you want to take any handwritten notes, you can't use a pen. I can provide a pencil and notepaper. And once you're in the reading room, if you'd like a specific magazine or newspaper, you'll have to fill out a call slip. One of the staff will get it for you."

"I understand. And I guess it's safe to assume that I can't check out anything, and that all the material needs to stay on the premises."

"That's right."

After Ariana signed in, Dana took her first to the lockers. After she put away her bags, she took her to the reading room.

"Let me know if I can get anything for you," Dana said.

"Thank you." Ariana smiled. "I'll do that."

About an hour later, after requesting several different magazines and studying various microforms for news articles, Ariana began to close up her laptop.

"Did you find everything you were looking for?" Dana asked.

"Not really."

"What were you looking for?" Dana asked.

"At least a hint of why Jerome Fortune went to such extremes when he left home and changed his name to Gerald Robinson."

Dana wasn't about to say it, but from what she'd heard, Gerald's children all seemed to have accepted whatever reason he might have had. So who was she to question them?

"But that doesn't mean my research was a bust," Ariana said. "One of the interviews I read implied that Gerald Robinson came to Austin nursing a broken heart, and that Charlotte Prendergast helped him pick up the pieces."

That must be true. The couple had married and gone on to have eight children, one of whom was Kieran.

Dana had gotten most of her information from Zach, who hadn't told her a lot. But she knew that Gerald, or rather Jerome, had lost his father and had been rejected by his mother. Zach hadn't gone into detail, but she'd assumed that things had gotten so unbearable that Jerome Fortune had staged his own death, then changed his name.

"There's a lot to sort through," Ariana said.

"He was probably grief stricken by his father's death and hurt by his mother's rejection." Dana had no more than uttered the assumption out loud when she wished she could reel it back in. After all, she wasn't a family member and didn't know the facts.

"Maybe," Ariana said, "but I have reason to believe there was more to it than that."

Dana wasn't sure what the journalist meant, although she was curious and tempted to prod for more details. But she didn't want Ariana to think she had a personal interest in that article. And she really didn't.

She wasn't a Fortune and never would be.

Kieran's decision to take Rosie to the office with him the following Tuesday morning had seemed like a good idea at the time, but it hadn't worked out that way.

Sure, everyone at Robinson Tech had oohed and

aahed over the precocious little girl, who'd sat at the receptionist's desk for an hour that morning and chatted with each employee and guest. Then Karen, his administrative assistant, had taken her into the break room and given her something to drink and a granola bar for a snack. Things went well until Rosie dropped a full, adult-size glass of OJ, scattering broken glass and sticky juice all over the floor.

For lunch, Kieran took her to Gregorio's, a trendy Italian deli, for lunch. He ordered macaroni and cheese for her, but she pushed it aside after taking a single bite.

"What's the matter?" he asked.

"It's not the right kind. I like the mac and cheese that comes out of the box. This kind is yucky."

Kieran would have preferred Gregorio's variety, especially since they made the pasta on the premises and used three different types of cheese for the sauce. But what was he supposed to do if she wouldn't eat?

As a result, he ordered the chicken tenders to go.

By two o'clock, he realized she needed a nap. So he removed the cushions from the two chairs in front of his desk and made a small bed for her on the floor. She might have dozed off, but his phone rang several times, causing her to stir.

An hour later, he gave up and let her sit at his desk to color. But she must have left the cap off the orange marker for days, if not longer, because it was dry as a bone. Apparently, that was the only color she could possibly use to draw a butterfly, so she had a meltdown.

At that point, he gave up and took her home.

He hadn't thought that being a parent would be easy, but he hadn't had any idea how tough the job really was. Nor had he realized it would make it damn near impossible to get any work done.

And that wasn't the only thing that had suffered since he brought Rosie to live with him. His love life was at a complete standstill.

If he'd had a relationship with someone right now, he might actually have a love life. And that realization made him wonder why he'd been such a commitment phobe in the first place.

Not that he was sorry he had Rosie. He actually enjoyed being with her—when he didn't have any work or projects that needed to get done.

On Wednesday morning, while at the preschool, he asked the director if Rosie had moved up on the waitlist to attend full time. She had, but only by one child. "I'm not sure how helpful this will be," Miss Peggy added. "One of our families is on vacation this week, so we can let Rosie take her place this Thursday."

Kieran had thanked her, relieved that he had child care for the rest of the week. But then he received word on Friday afternoon that the board of directors had scheduled an important meeting on Saturday morning.

He'd called Kelly as soon as he'd heard the news, but she was on a camping trip with a friend's family. Even the nanny agency couldn't help since the office was closed for the weekend. So it was official: he'd run out of child care options once again.

That is, until Dana crossed his mind. Once he envisioned her smiling face, her long, silky hair, those expressive blue eyes…well, hope soared.

In spite of his resolve to avoid her, he had no other choice than to call her. And with each ring of the phone, his mood lightened even more.

For a moment, he worried that she might not answer, then he heard her sweet voice dance across the line. "Hi, Kieran. What's up?"

"I'm having nanny problems," he blurted out. Realizing his desperation had run away with him, he added, "I'm not asking you to help with that, but do you know of any other people Zach might have used to watch Rosie when Kelly wasn't available? I'm talking about adult women Rosie might actually like."

"He had a few girls he'd call sometimes, but they're all teenagers and not available as full-time sitters. I'm afraid Sandra was always his first choice."

And Sandra wasn't going to be an option these days.

Kieran raked a hand through his hair and blew out a sigh of frustration. "I have a meeting tomorrow that I can't miss or reschedule. And I really dread the thought of taking Rosie with me." Did he dare tell her he knew firsthand why that wasn't going to work?

"I can watch her for you," Dana said.

In spite of his resolve, relief washed over him. Dana had come to his rescue yet again.

"But if you don't mind," she added, "I'd rather you brought her to my house. That way, we can play dress up."

"What's that?" Kieran asked, although he suspected Rosie wouldn't object to anything Dana suggested.

"It's just something we do—a game, actually."

Then Rosie would definitely be on board for that. "You have no idea how much I appreciate that offer."

Nor did she realize how much he was looking forward to seeing her again.

On Saturday morning, Kieran drove to Dana's place in Hyde Park. Dana had told him that she'd renovated one of the homes that had been built right after World War II. But nothing prepared him for what he saw when he pulled up in front of the small, wood-framed house that was painted mustard yellow. The roof and shutters were dark brown, while the porch and window were framed in white, the front door a bright orange.

He doubted it was much bigger than 1200 square feet, but the exterior seemed to suit Dana. And so did the well-manicured yard, with freshly mowed grass and a variety of orange and yellow marigolds lining the walkway.

In fact, he sat in the car a moment, just studying the unique decor and style. He had no idea what the place had looked like when she purchased it, but she'd done an amazing job with the renovation. No wonder she wanted to keep the house for a while before selling it. She ought to enjoy the fruits of her labor.

"Can I get out of my car seat?" Rosie asked. "I can do it myself."

"Sure, princess." Kieran slid out from behind the

wheel, circled the car and opened the rear passenger door for the little girl who was determined to unbuckle herself.

"See?" Rosie said, clearly proud of her efforts. Then she reached for her backpack and hurried up the walkway to the front porch.

Dana, his beautiful lifesaver, opened the door and greeted them with a bright-eyed smile before Rosie could ring the bell.

The child practically jumped with glee, and Kieran's heart reacted the same way. Damn, he hadn't realized how badly he'd missed her.

"Just wait until you see what I have planned for us to do this morning," Dana told the happy little girl.

"Can we go to the park again?" Rosie asked. "Like we did last time I came here?"

"If you want to. But first, we're going to make old-fashioned sugar cookies with sprinkles. Then we're going to play dress up."

Rosie glanced over her shoulder at Kieran, a smile stretched across her face. "You don't have to come back and pick me up until nighttime, Uncle Daddy."

Now, that was the kind of reaction every parent hoped their child would have when dropping them off at day care or with a sitter.

Kieran looked over the child's head at Dana and winked. "Don't worry. I'll be back sooner than that."

"It really doesn't matter to me. We have a full day planned, especially if we pack a lunch and go to the park." Dana placed a gentle hand on Rosie's head, taking a moment to stroke her hair. "Honey, why don't you take your things into the living room?"

Rosie slipped past Dana and hurried into the house, taking her backpack with her. That left the adults alone on the porch, which wasn't nearly as awkward as he'd once thought it would be.

"Before you go," Dana said, "I want to share something with you. A couple of days ago, when Ariana Lamonte came by the history center and researched some old magazines and newspaper articles, I assumed she was interested in your father's move to Austin and the formation of Robinson Tech."

That's what Kieran had thought, too. "What was she looking for?"

"I'm not entirely sure. Apparently, she uncovered an article that suggested your father came to town brokenhearted, and that your mother helped put him on the mend."

"I can see how my mom would have helped him forget the life he once had as Jerome Fortune."

"Maybe, but when I implied something similar, Ariana said she wasn't so sure and suggested there was more to it than that."

Kieran bristled at the thought of a journalist digging into his father's past. Sure, his old man had kept a lot of secrets from the family for years. But what appeared to be an article about the younger Fortunes was sounding more like an exposé of Gerald Robinson aka Jerome Fortune.

Recently, thanks to their dad's numerous affairs, they'd met several half siblings they hadn't realized existed. Kieran had been a little embarrassed by it, but that didn't mean he wasn't curious about the past.

He couldn't very well blame Ariana for her interest in the family, but the fact that there might be some old skeletons for her to uncover didn't sit well with him.

At first when he'd heard about the article she was writing, he'd thought highlighting some of the younger Fortunes might be good publicity for the company as well as for the Fortune Foundation and Peter's Place, a home for wayward teenage boys his brother Graham had established. But now he feared it might have the opposite effect.

He wouldn't mention that to Dana, though. Instead, he shrugged it off, pretending it didn't interest him in the least.

"Nothing about my father would surprise me," he said, glancing at his wristwatch.

"You'd better go," Dana said.

"You're right. I still have to drive across town, and I don't want to be late for that meeting."

Dana glanced over her shoulder and into the living room, where Rosie was already unloading her books and markers. "And don't worry about us. We're going to have fun today."

Kieran didn't doubt that. He took a moment to study the pretty redhead who had proven to be a good friend. "I know I've told you this before, but it's true. I really appreciate you."

And not just for helping him out as a sitter.

Dana's smile set off a glimmer in her eyes. "And like I said, I'm happy to do it."

The morning sun cast a shimmer of gold in her auburn hair. Framed within the doorway of her newly painted house, the colors reminding him of fall, she seemed to fit nicely, leaving her mark on the decor in a special way.

"I love what you've done to this house." And he did, which was odd coming from a man who made it a point to never use the *L* word, especially when he was with a single woman who might get the wrong idea about him.

But this woman was different, and whenever he was around her, he felt a lot of different emotions stirring up inside him.

"Thanks," she said. "When you come back for Rosie, I'll give you a tour of the inside."

"I'd lo...like that." Then he did something completely unexpected—he leaned forward, cupped her jaw and brushed a kiss on her cheek.

A show of affection like that wouldn't have been so bad. But when he caught a whiff of her scent... Was that Coco Chanel? If not, it was a darn good knockoff. It also knocked him off stride. And rather than end the thanks-and-goodbye kiss, his lips lingered on her cheek a beat too long.

Dammit. What was wrong with him?

He needed this woman in the worst way. Maybe even in the *best* way. And he was really going to screw things up if he wasn't careful.

"I'm sorry if I just stepped over the line or dishonored Zach in any way."

"You didn't," she said, her eyes wide, her lips parted.

If she knew what he was thinking, she'd disagree.

"I'll be back in a couple of hours," he said.

"Take all the time you need."

He nodded, then turned to go, knowing that he was going to need a hell of a lot more time to get his racing pulse under control and his mind back on track.

Chapter Eight

Dana stood on the front porch and watched Kieran head to his car, the skin on her cheek still tingling from the soft touch of his lips and the warmth of his breath.

If he'd meant that kiss to be a friendly show of appreciation, then why had he apologized for it? That hadn't made sense, unless he'd had another reason behind it.

She could probably ponder the possibilities until the cows came home, but that'd be a waste of time. She didn't have a lot of experience with men or in reading their intentions, especially wealthy corporate executives. So she wouldn't continue to stand on her stoop, stunned by their latest awkward encounter.

As she turned around so she could go back into

her house, she stole one last peek at Kieran, who was getting into his car.

He glanced over his shoulder at the same time, catching her in the act of gawking at him like a love-struck wallflower at a high school dance.

Unsure of what—if anything—she should do, she lifted her hand and gave him a casual wave, as if she hadn't been affected by either the kiss or the eye contact. Then she passed through the doorway and into the living room, where Rosie was seated on the hardwood floor, coloring.

It had been a month or more since Rosie had last been at Dana's house. That day had started with a trip to the library for the preschool story hour. Then they'd picked up sandwiches at a nearby deli and spent the next couple hours at the park. When they returned home, Dana pulled out some of her vintage clothing and let Rosie dress up like a "big lady," including an application of pink lipstick.

Rosie probably expected more of the same today, but Dana had a better idea, one that was going to be both fun and educational.

As she approached the little girl, Dana said, "I have a surprise for you."

Rosie looked up, her eyes bright, and smiled. "What is it?"

"The other day, when I was shopping at an estate sale, I found an antique chest called a steamer trunk. I bought it so that I could refurbish it. But when I got it home and opened it, I found a treasure inside."

Rosie's eyes grew wide. "Like gold?"

"No, not that kind. A treasure can also mean something special to the person who finds it." When Rosie scrunched her face and tilted her head, Dana reached out her hand and wiggled her fingers. "Come with me."

Rosie pushed aside her coloring book, got to her feet and took Dana's hand. "Where is it?"

"In my guest room. I'll show it to you."

Moments later, as they stood in front of the hundred-year-old trunk that appeared well-traveled, Dana lifted the lid, revealing the old clothing and stage props inside.

A playbill, its pages yellowed and worn, suggested she'd found costumes that had been made for the cast of a 1936 theater performance about Texas pioneers. Along with a few bonnets, skirts, blouses, a man's britches and a red flannel shirt, there was also a child-size calico dress.

At the time she'd discovered the treasure trove, Dana had immediately thought about Rosie. But before she could invite her over for a playdate, she'd gotten the call about Zach's accident, so the plan had never panned out.

Now, with Rosie here, today seemed to be the perfect time to play dress up while having a history lesson and making homemade cookies.

"Instead of going to the library," Dana said, as she began removing a woman's long, blue skirt and the child's calico dress, "let's put on these costumes and have story hour here."

"Those clothes look funny," Rosie said.

"Maybe to those of us living today, but a hundred and fifty years ago, people dressed like this."

"Okay. That'll be fun." Rosie kicked off her pink sneakers and began removing her white T-shirt and denim shorts.

"After we get dressed like pioneers, I'll tell you real life stories about people who lived in Texas a long time ago. And then we'll whip up a batch of sugar cookies from a recipe I found in an old cookbook."

"Will we make enough cookies so Uncle Daddy can have one, too?"

"We certainly will. And we'll also have plenty for you to take home."

Then, when Kieran returned for Rosie…

Dana's thoughts stalled on the handsome man who'd kissed her, then quickly apologized and dashed off to a business meeting. Her cheek was no longer tingling. But that didn't change the fact that Kieran Fortune had kissed her, that his lips and his soft breath had warmed her from the inside out. The affection he'd shown her had touched her in a magical way, transporting her into an unexpected role, like an actress on the stage.

Dana might try to forget what had happened when he left, but that brief kiss and the romantic fantasy it provoked would remain in her memory for a very long time.

The board meeting at the Robinson Tech office had gone into overtime, lasting several more hours than anyone had expected. So by the time Kieran returned for Rosie, it was nearly one o'clock.

After parking at the curb in front of Dana's house, he made his way along the marigold flanked walkway to the front porch. He rang the bell, and moments later, Rosie answered the door wearing a long prairie-style dress, a floppy yellow bonnet and a happy smile.

But what really took him by surprise—and a pleasant one at that—was seeing Dana dressed like a schoolmarm in a long blue skirt and a white, high-collared blouse, her hair swept up in a soft, feminine topknot.

"What's going on?" he asked, unable to quell an erupting chuckle.

"We've been playing pioneer girls." Rosie lifted a small glass jar that held something white and gooey. "And look what we made!"

Kieran didn't have any idea what that stuff was.

When Rosie handed him the jar for a closer inspection, he still didn't have a clue and furrowed his brow.

"It's butter," Dana said.

"Yep." Rosie beamed. "We put milk in this jar, then we put a lid on it."

"Actually, we didn't use milk," Dana corrected. "It was heavy cream."

"Uh-huh," Rosie said, nodding in agreement. "Then I had to shake and shake and shake until my arm got tired. So Dana helped me until it turned into butter. It's not yellow, but it's just like the kind they used to make when my grandma was a little girl and they didn't get to buy it in the store."

"Awesome." Kieran snuck a glance at Dana, who stood before him like a beautiful, red-haired lady from days gone by.

"We not only had a history lesson," Dana said, "but we also had fun while you were gone."

"I can see that." Kieran was growing more and more impressed with Dana's finer qualities each time he saw her.

She gave a little shrug. "I guess there's no secret that I have a quirky side."

"No, you can't hide it from me any longer. But for the record, I think you're the cutest teacher I've ever met."

Her flush deepened, and he glanced away. The last thing he needed to do was to get caught up in his attraction again. But like it or not, he found her adorable, quirks and all.

And there lay the problem. He needed to shake off the romantic musing. So in an effort to do just that, he scanned the inside of her nicely decorated home, which had a retro vibe that suited the house and the neighborhood as well as the owner.

But he didn't just get a visual of her home. The sweet aroma of vanilla filled the living room. "I take it you pioneers also found time to do some baking today."

"We made cookies," Rosie said. "And there's a special one just for you. I put a lot of pink sprinkles on it because that's my favorite color. But you can't eat it until you have lunch. That's what Dana said."

"Sounds fair to me." Kieran gave Dana a wink.

"Can we go to the park now?" Rosie asked. "Dana made sandwiches and apples and stuff. We're going to have a picnic."

Kieran turned to Dana. The invitation to join them should come from her. After all, she'd been entertaining Rosie the entire morning. Maybe she wanted to take a break.

"I made plenty for all of us," she said. "Are you hungry?"

Kieran's brother Ben, the president of Robinson Tech, had brought in breakfast burritos for everyone at the meeting, so he wasn't starving.

"I've never been one to turn down food," he said, "especially if I can share a light meal with two pioneer girls."

Dana blessed him with a pretty smile. "Does that mean you're up for an afternoon at the park?"

In spite of his earlier resolve to avoid Dana, he'd be happy to join in any activity if it included her. "Sure. Why not?"

"Goodie!" Rosie clapped her hands.

When Dana instructed her to go change her clothes, she took off, dashing down the hall, the skirt of her prairie dress sweeping the hardwood floor.

"While she's gone," Dana said, "I have a question for you."

"What's that?"

"Why did you apologize for kissing my cheek when you left this morning?"

Her cheek. Right. It's not as though he'd kissed her on the lips, which he'd been tempted to do.

"That kiss was impulsive, and since I know how much you cared about Zach, I didn't want you to think I was trying to..."

"Take his place?"

"Yeah, I guess that's it." A lot of people might have thought that a computer whiz kid and a cowboy might be unlikely friends, but they'd loved each other like brothers.

"I thought that kiss was sweet. And that it was appreciative of our...friendship."

"I'm glad. I guess I'm the only one stressing about it." Kieran raked a hand through his hair.

She might have just let him off the hook but he was still struggling with what he'd done. He couldn't help thinking that it should be Zach standing in Dana's living room, overwhelmed by his sexual attraction to the pretty redhead. It should be Zach looking forward to taking his sweet daughter to the park for a picnic.

But Zach was gone. And the woman and child he'd left behind were burrowing deep into Kieran's heart. And something about that felt wrong.

"Just for the record," Dana said, "Zach and I weren't as involved as people might think."

Kieran merely nodded. In a way, it was a relief to know they hadn't been talking marriage or engagement. But just because Dana and Zach hadn't been too serious didn't mean they hadn't been sexually involved. And that's what made him so leery about the idea of dating her.

Striking up a romance was sure to lead to more kissing and eventually to making love. And as appealing as that might sound, Kieran didn't feel right about taking his best friend's girl to bed, even if that friend was dead.

Hell, Zach was one of the greatest guys Kieran had ever known—honest, hardworking, dependable and loyal. Yet life had never been especially easy for him, especially financially.

What had he done wrong? Why did he have to die so young, before he'd experienced love and happiness?

On the other hand, Kieran had it all. Not that things had been perfect for him growing up. But unlike Zach, he'd never had to worry about financing his college education, caring for aging parents who weren't in the best of health, trying to turn things around for a struggling ranch or being a single dad.

There seemed to be something wrong about stepping in and taking Zach's place.

And it was too bad Kieran felt that way. Because that was the *only* thing holding him back from admitting his feelings for Dana.

After a short five-minute drive, Dana, Kieran and Rosie pulled up at Westside Park, Austin's newest recreational spot for families.

"I hope I'm not the only kid here," Rosie said.

Dana hoped so, too. Rosie didn't like to play alone, and if there weren't any other children on the playground, she'd want the adults to swing and slide with her. They'd had a lot of fun this morning, but Dana was ready to sit back and enjoy a picnic lunch in the fresh air and sunshine.

"It's Saturday," Kieran said. "I'm sure you'll find plenty of kids to play with."

And he was right. By the time he parked the car, they had a clear view of the grassy play area, with its Western-themed climbing structure and big yellow slide in the shape of a giant sombrero.

"Will you look at that?" Kieran chuckled. "You ladies didn't need to change out of your prairie dresses. You would've fit right in here."

"Maybe so," Dana said, as she unbuckled her seatbelt. "But long skirts aren't very practical or safe for running, jumping and climbing."

After exiting the car, Kieran removed the packed picnic basket from the backseat while Dana unbuckled Rosie. Then they went in search of an empty table near the playground.

They hadn't yet reached the grass when Rosie's breath caught and she slowed to a stop.

"Uh-oh." She pointed toward a small boy who'd just left the parking lot with his mom and was heading toward the playground. "That's the boy from Cowboy Fred's. The one who hit me."

She was right. Dana recognized both the child and his mother.

Kieran placed a hand on Rosie's shoulder, urging her to continue walking. "Let's go say hello."

"No." Rosie dug in her heels. "I don't want to. He was mean to me. He made blood come out of my nose, and it really hurt."

"Yes, I know," Kieran said. "But he told you he was sorry. Remember?"

Rosie looked up at him and frowned. "But what if he does it again?"

Dana cast a glance at "Uncle Daddy," who looked back at her and rolled his eyes. Then he urged the girl onward. "I'm sure he won't. Come on, princess. Let's go say hello."

As they started toward the swing set, each of its plastic seats shaped like a saddled merry-go-round horse, Rosie's steps slowed again. She turned to Kieran and frowned. "How come I have to talk to him?"

"In case you haven't noticed, most of the other kids on the playground are a lot older than you, and he's about your age. You'll probably become good friends—if you give each other a chance."

Dana looked over the girl's head at Kieran. When she caught his eyes, she pointed to her temple and mouthed, "Smart move."

He shot her a dazzling grin, his eyes as bright as the wild blue yonder, then placed the picnic basket on the grass. "I'll be back as soon as we bury the hatchet."

Rosie balked. "What's a hatchet?"

"Never mind," Kieran said. He glanced at Dana and shrugged, not quite able to stifle a grin. "Wish us luck, okay?"

Dana crossed her index and middle fingers to show him she was on his side and that she was hoping for the best.

He nodded, then took Rosie's hand. "Come on, princess. I'll face the dragon with you."

"But he's got a pirate shirt on today," Rosie said, as she reluctantly trudged along with him.

"You're right, but dragons and pirates won't stop a brave princess like you."

Dana followed them on their short trek to greet the mother and child.

"Hi, there," Kieran said to the towheaded boy. "Your name's Michael, right?"

The little guy nodded.

"Do you remember Rosie?" Kieran asked him. "We met you at Cowboy Fred's. And now here we are, ready to have a fun day at the park."

Michael bit down on his bottom lip and shot a careful peek at Rosie, who eyed him back. But neither uttered a word.

"It's nice to see you here." The mom looked down at her son and placed her hand on top of his head. "Isn't it, Michael?" Then she addressed Kieran and Dana. "We just moved to town, so we're still checking out places where we can play."

"I've lived in Austin my entire life," Kieran said, "but this is the first time I've ever come to this park. And that's really a shame, because I would have loved going down that sombrero slide—or riding on those horse swings. Maybe Michael and Rosie can show me how fast those ponies can go."

The boy brightened. "I can go *super* high and fast." Then he looked at Rosie. "You wanna do that, too?"

When she nodded, they both dashed off, with Kieran taking up the rear.

"It's nice to see a family together at the park," Michael's mother said. "Even before our divorce, Michael's dad rarely went on outings with us."

"Actually," Dana said, "We're not a family."

"I'm sorry. I just assumed you were."

It was an easy mistake to make, Dana supposed. She expected Michael's mother to quiz her further, but she didn't, which was a relief. She and Kieran had landed in an odd situation and a difficult one to explain, especially to a stranger.

"My son and I recently moved in with my parents," the woman said. "There aren't any families with young children in their neighborhood, so Michael doesn't have anyone to play with. I tried to enroll him in a preschool that's supposed to be a good one, but there's a pretty long waiting list. So I've tried to take him places where he can meet and play with other kids his age."

"You may not realize this," Dana said, "but there's a story hour at the library on Thursday mornings for preschoolers. You might try going there, too."

"That's a good idea." The woman laughed. "By the way, Mikey isn't the only one who needs to make new friends. My name is Elaine Wagner."

Dana took her hand, gave it a warm shake and introduced herself. "It's nice to meet you."

They both turned to watch the children play. But what really caught Dana's interest was Kieran, who would give one child's horse swing a push, then the next. It was such a fatherly thing for him to do, and knowing what she did about him, that he was a bachelor who didn't have any plans to settle down, it touched her heart.

"Is Rosie's father divorced?" Elaine asked.

There it was—the quiz Dana had been expecting.

Elaine undoubtedly found Kieran attractive—what woman wouldn't? And she probably wanted to learn whether he was available or not. Dana couldn't very well blame her for that. He was one sexy man, especially when he showed his Uncle Daddy side.

But Elaine had been open and forthcoming with Dana, so she figured it wouldn't hurt to answer honestly. "Rosie's father passed away recently, and since I was a family friend, I've been helping her and her guardian adjust to the changes in their lives."

"I'm so sorry," Elaine said. "Divorce isn't easy to explain to a child, but death must be worse."

Dana wanted to agree. As a child, she'd had a difficult time understanding why her parents had died and gone to heaven. Yet in spite of her grief and loneliness, she'd realized that they hadn't wanted to leave her behind. On the other hand, divorces were different.

"I'm sure some splits can get pretty nasty," Dana said, "which could be difficult for everyone involved."

"Ours was tougher on me. Michael's father never had been a big part of his life. He was always too busy for us."

"So he was a workaholic?" Dana asked, connecting the dots.

Elaine shielded her eyes from the sun's glare and looked at the playground, where the kids were swinging. "I assumed that he was because he used to spend so much time at the office. But I came to find out he had a special fondness for the attractive new receptionist."

Ouch. Now it was Dana's turn to sympathize. "I'm sorry to hear that."

"It was a big blow to my ego, that's for sure. But as it turned out, Mikey didn't seem to be too affected by it. It's not as if he'd had a *real* daddy to miss." Elaine continued to study her son, then added, "He does have a good grandpa, so that helps a lot."

About that time, Kieran returned to where the women stood and reached for the picnic basket that Dana had packed.

"We're going to have a picnic," she said to Elaine. "Why don't you and Michael join us? I have plenty of food."

"That's really nice of you to include us," Elaine said. "We ate a late breakfast before we came, so we won't eat much. I also brought some orange slices we can contribute, and I have a blanket in the car we can spread out on the grass."

"Then it looks like we're set." Dana glanced at the playground, which was about ten feet away, to check on the kids. They were just leaving the swing set and running toward the slide, both smiling.

"It looks like Michael and Rosie are well on their way to becoming friends," Dana said.

"I can see that." Elaine handed Dana a small bag,

then pointed toward her car. "If you'll keep an eye on the kids, I'll get that blanket from the trunk."

Minutes later, the two women had taken seats on top of the quilt they'd spread on the grass, the food set out between them. Kieran, who'd stretched out on the grass, drank a glass of lemonade Dana had brought.

While Dana and Elaine chatted, she soon learned that they had a lot in common, including a love of books and an interest in baking. If Kieran was bored with their conversation, he never let on. Instead, he studied a monarch butterfly that fluttered near the picnic basket.

About the time Dana thought they should call the children to come and eat, the boy and girl trotted back to the adults.

"I'm hungry," Rosie said. "Can we have a cookie?"

"After you eat a sandwich. But let's wash our hands first." Dana got to her feet, then walked with the children to the restrooms. Along the way, she listened to the newfound friends chattering away.

"My mommy is a good cooker," Michael said. "And sometimes, when she makes dinner, she lets me help."

"So does *my* mommy," Rosie said.

Dana's heart stalled. The poor little girl had never known her mother, and now she was creating an imaginary one to impress her new friend. She probably wanted to fit in and be like other children her age. Dana certainly knew that feeling. As a girl, she'd wished that she still belonged to a real family, one that didn't include foster parents.

"Me and my mommy made sugar cookies this morning," Rosie said. "I'll share one with you. But only after we eat."

Dana could hardly believe what just went down. Rosie implied that Dana was her mother, but Dana wouldn't correct her now. Not in front of Michael.

Then again, she didn't know how to address the issue at all. She'd read a few parenting articles, but that was a topic that hadn't come up.

"When it was my birthday," Michael said, "and when we lived at the other house that's far away, my mommy made cupcakes for the party. And I got to help put the frosting and little race cars on top."

"It's going to be my birthday," Rosie said. "My grandma said it's going to be in two weeks, and that's not very long to wait. I'm going to have a party, too. You can come, if you want to."

Dana wasn't sure what Sandra had told the child, but it was true. Her birthday was at the end of April—on the twenty-eighth, if she remembered correctly. But she doubted that Sandra had promised her a party. At least, not without talking it over with Kieran first.

That didn't mean Rosie wouldn't have one. Dana would make sure of it—one way or another.

That is, if Kieran wanted her help.

She glanced over her shoulder to where he sat on the grass, only to see him watching her and the children. Or was he more interested in her?

Oh, for goodness' sake. Talk about imagining things. A substitute mommy wasn't as bad as a nonexistent romance. And Kieran couldn't possibly be the least bit interested in her.

He was not only an heir to the Robinson technology dynasty, but he was a Fortune. And just because he'd hung out at the park this afternoon like an honest-to-goodness family man, didn't mean a thing. Nor did it mean that she should waste her time dreaming about things that would never come to be.

Chapter Nine

Kieran couldn't remember the last time he'd been on a picnic, let alone spent a couple hours at a park. And while he could think of a hundred other things he could be doing on a Saturday afternoon, like golfing with buddies or watching college baseball at his favorite sports bar, the day had actually turned out to be pleasant.

Now, as he drove back to Dana's house to drop her off, he wondered how to thank her for all she'd done for him and Rosie today. He'd mentioned his appreciation more than once, but that didn't seem to be enough.

There was something else he wanted to talk to her about, something that he couldn't mention in front of Rosie. Several times this afternoon, the little girl had called him Daddy, leaving off the Uncle. And to make matters even more complicated, he'd also heard her refer to Dana as her mommy.

Dana seemed to let it roll right off her back, which was probably the best approach. But Kieran thought he should address it, although he wasn't sure how.

Maybe he should talk it over with a child psychologist. Rosie might be missing her father—or longing for the kind of family most of the other children her age had. And there was nothing Kieran could do to fix that, no matter how badly he'd like to.

He glanced in the rearview mirror, where Rosie sat in her car seat, her eyes closed. Had she fallen asleep? She'd played hard today, so she had to be worn out.

"You know," Dana said, drawing him from his musing. "We…or rather *you*, should think about the upcoming *B-I-R-T-H-D-A-Y*."

He was going to ask who was having a birthday until he realized there was only one reason for Dana to spell the word.

"Should we plan a *P-A-R-T-Y*?" he asked.

"I think it's a good idea. And if you decide to go that route, I'd be happy to help."

"Thanks. I'll definitely take you up on that offer. I'll give you a call after we get home, when we're free to talk more about it." He took another peek at Rosie in the mirror. Her head was rolled to the side now, her lips slightly parted.

He supposed they could talk more now that Rosie appeared to be sleeping, but it might be best to give it some thought. And yes, that would give him an excuse to call Dana later. And not just to talk about the "Mommy and Daddy" stuff, but anything else that came up.

But when they pulled up into Dana's driveway and parked, he had a second thought and volunteered to carry the picnic basket inside for her.

"I've got it," she said. "It's practically empty now."

"Let me get it for you. I insist." Besides, that would give him the chance to talk with her privately on the porch. He'd still call Dana later, to talk about the party—or whatever.

Before he slid out of the car, he lowered the windows to make sure Rosie was comfortable. Then he removed the picnic basket from the backseat and carried it to the front porch, walking beside her.

"I'm not sure if you heard, but Rosie referred to me as her daddy more than once today. I had a feeling she was going to drop the *uncle* eventually."

"She lost her father recently, so I don't find it surprising that she considers you the next best thing." She slipped the key into the lock and turned to him. "Does that bother you?"

"In some ways. I don't want to take Zach's place in her heart. I want her to remember the man he was and the love he had for her. But that doesn't mean it doesn't please me at the same time. I guess it's complicated."

Dana reached out and stroked his arm, offering both comfort and understanding. "She's only three, Kieran. I know she's bright and will be turning four in a couple few weeks, but the chances of her remembering a whole lot about her father are slim. When was your first memory?"

She was right. He blew out a sigh. Then he set the basket aside, resting it on the small patio table near the door, and studied the woman he'd begun to rely on, the one he admired more than she'd ever know. The one who was not only stroking his arm but touching his heart.

"Did you hear her refer to you as her mommy?" he asked.

"A couple of times. Her grandma always filled that role for her, and right now, Sandra can't be there for her. I'm sure most of her friends at school have mothers, so it seems only natural that she'd try and create a family of her own, even if it's only imaginary."

"Are you okay with that?" he asked.

"This may sound weird to you, but it's actually a little flattering."

"I know what you mean." Kieran liked the fact that Rosie was willing to accept him as the next best thing to Zach.

"I'm sure she'll call me Dana again in time."

"You're probably right."

"The woman who eventually becomes her mommy is going to be a lucky lady," Dana said.

Had Zach lived, Dana might have become that lucky lady. Did she know that? Did she mourn for what might have been? She'd said—or implied—that she didn't. But that's just the kind of thing a loving, warmhearted woman like Dana would say to make things easier on those around her.

Kieran cupped her jaw, and their gazes met and locked. A rush of complicated emotions swirled up in his chest, threatening to wreak havoc on his life like a Texas twister. Yet it didn't scare him, even though it should.

"You're pretty special, Dana."

"So are you."

Unable to help himself, he slid his hand forward, from her jaw to the back of her neck, and drew her mouth to his.

He wouldn't have been surprised if she'd flinched or read him the riot act, but she leaned into him, slipped her arms around his neck and kissed him back—deeply and thoroughly.

It hadn't been all that long ago that he'd had the freedom to date whoever he wanted—and whenever. He'd had a fairly active sex life. But by the way his testosterone was pumping now, you'd think he hadn't had sex since his teen years.

Damn, he couldn't seem to get enough of her sweet vanilla taste, thanks in part to the sugar cookies they'd had for dessert. Nor could he breathe in enough of her classic scent.

As his arms tightened around her and she pressed her body close to his, his blood rushed through his veins, throbbing with intensity. If he wasn't careful, he'd make a scene right here on her front porch. Yet for a man who wasn't into public displays of affection, he didn't particularly care what her neighbors might think. And apparently, neither did she.

"Daaddy!" Rosie called out from the backseat of the car.

Caught with his hand in the proverbial sugar

cookie jar, Kieran tore his lips from Dana's and released her.

"I'm right here," he said, as if answering Rosie's call of Daddy. But he wasn't her father. Zach was.

Rosie rubbed her eyes and scrunched her face. "Were you kissing Mommy?"

Zach might have asked Kieran to step up and be Rosie's father, if the unthinkable happened. But he'd never asked him to take his place with Dana.

"It's not what you think," Kieran told her. "I'll be right there."

As he backed off the porch and stepped onto the lawn, he looked back at Dana and nodded toward his car. "I'd better take her home. I'll…talk to you later."

"Sure." Dana's voice came out so softly that he hardly heard her.

But if truth be told, he didn't want to talk to her about this now or later. Because, for the life of him, he had no excuse for what he'd just done.

Dana had no idea what had just happened.

Okay, she and Kieran had shared a heated kiss. And not just privately, but right outside her front door, where all the neighbors could see.

As far as she was concerned, the kiss had been amazing and so blood stirring it weakened her knees. Yet obviously it hadn't affected Kieran in the same way. But why would it?

Before taking custody of Rosie, the handsome bachelor could be seen every night at restaurants, concerts and galas all over town, a beautiful model or socialite on his arm. And no doubt, he probably woke up the next morning with her, too.

Dana wasn't a virgin, but she wasn't all that experienced, either. So while that kiss had been amazing, at least to her, Kieran clearly hadn't found it remarkable. In fact, he'd been so embarrassed or disappointed that he told Rosie she'd been mistaken, that she hadn't actually witnessed him and Dana in a lip lock.

For that reason, she'd been embarrassed and disappointed by the kiss, too. She'd put her heart and soul into it, but Kieran couldn't have rushed off any faster if his pants were on fire. So she must have done something wrong.

She scanned her yard as well as the sidewalk and street. Fortunately, there wasn't anyone in the vicinity who'd seen what'd just happened. As much as she'd like to have someone to talk to, to offer her advice, she was too new to the neighborhood to have made any friends or confidants. The only person she felt inclined to call was Monica, but she'd never liked sharing her humiliation with anyone, even her bestie.

She blew out an exasperated sigh. How could she have been so stupid as to think that she actually stood a chance with a man like Kieran Fortune Robinson?

There was no excuse, other than the fact that she was falling heart over brain for the guy and had made a real mess of things. The only thing she could do was tell him she was busy the next time he called asking for her help with Rosie.

Of course, watching him hightail it out of here

convinced her that he wouldn't be calling her any-time soon—if ever.

But in twenty minutes, she realized she'd been wrong about that when her cell phone rang and the caller ID told her it was Kieran.

She didn't want to answer, didn't want to talk about what had happened or what it all meant. With each ring, her heart skipped and fluttered until she thought it might stop completely.

Finally, she swallowed hard, cleared her throat and slid her finger across the screen, taking the call before the line disconnected.

"I'm sorry about ducking out so quickly," Kieran said.

She wasn't about to accept that lame apology, al-though she didn't expect more than that from him.

"That kiss took me by surprise," he added, a little chuckle fanning his words.

Apparently, he'd forgotten that he'd been the one to instigate it. So how could he have been taken aback by it? But there was no need to admit what she was really feeling. "Don't worry about it."

She could really go off on him and his quick de-parture, listing all the things he didn't have to worry about, but she let it go at that.

"I need to talk to you," he said. "And not on the phone."

"That's not necessary."

"Sure it is. How about dinner one of these nights? I'll find a sitter."

Like that was going to be an easy task for him to do, especially with Sandra's hands already full.

"I have a lot going on this week," Dana said.

He paused a moment, then pressed on. "How about next week?"

Now it was her turn for silence. "Listen, Kieran. I'm not interested in going out with you—as friends or as a teammate or...whatever. Kissing you was a big mistake and not one I plan on making again. So let's just pretend it didn't happen."

More silence. Then, "You're angry."

No, she was hurt. But since it was her fault for making assumptions, her anger was directed at herself. "Actually, I'm fine. And so are you. No harm, no foul."

"Yeah, well, I think there's more going on than you're admitting. Is it Zach?"

Why did he always bring up Zach? This was about Dana and the insecurities she claimed to have overcome but sometimes still battled, especially at times like this. But there was no way she'd bring that to the forefront of this conversation, so she tackled the one that was easier to admit. "Zach and I were never much more than friends. I can't even remember the last time he kissed me, so what does he have to do with it? Besides, he's gone and out of the picture. But I clearly made a mistake by kissing you, so don't worry. I'll never do it again."

A heavy silence filled the line until she wondered if she'd completely stumped him or if he'd hung up on her. Finally, he responded with a question. "What if I wanted you to do it again?"

She laughed, a short, choppy, insincere burble that mocked the tears filling her eyes. "Let's just forget it happened and get on with our lives. That's what I plan to do."

"What if I don't want you to?"

For a moment, she grasped for the hope he offered, the suggestion that he was actually feeling something for her. And while she'd give anything to have a family of her own, she knew better than to think it might carry the Fortune name. So she'd have to get over this and move on with her life. Because, if she didn't, she'd never stop battling those stupid, waifish insecurities.

"Goodbye, Kieran. I have something pressing to do." And that was true. She had to get off the phone before her voice broke, before she let him know how badly she hurt.

Then she disconnected the line and ended the call. Too bad she couldn't shut out the memory of his kiss as easily.

Kieran glanced at the cell phone in his hand. Dana had hung up on him. For a woman who'd kissed him as though she was staking a claim on him, she'd certainly cut him off just now.

What the hell had happened?

He redialed her number, then waited for her to answer. No one shut Kieran out like that. Her words didn't make a whole lot of sense, other than she'd pretty much indicated that she hadn't been thinking about Zach.

When she answered, instead of hello, she said, "What part of *goodbye* don't you understand?"

Wow. He'd really messed up, and he wasn't sure how to fix it.

"Listen, Dana. We need to talk. You already said no to dinner, but I think it would do us a world of good to clear the air. So maybe we can have a drink, a cup of coffee… Whatever. And I'd prefer to do it sooner, rather than later."

"There isn't anything to talk about."

"Yes, there is. You're angry—and maybe even hurt. And I'm not sure why. If it's because I came on to you so strongly, I'm sorry." Rather than tell her how he was feeling and how afraid he was to end things like this, he added, "I don't want to lose…whatever our friendship has become."

"You don't have to make things into something they're not. I forgive you for dashing off like you did. It's okay if you're not interested."

What was she talking about? Hell, he was incredibly attracted to her and had been fighting every one of his sexual urges.

"Okay, there's clearly been a big misunderstanding. Hell, I felt like a jerk all the way home. And now I'm feeling even worse."

At that, her voice softened. "It's not your fault—it's mine. I never should have read anything into that kiss."

He wasn't sure what she'd thought it all meant. Hell, he wasn't even sure himself. All he knew was that he wanted to take her out on a real date—and it sure as heck wouldn't be to Cowboy Fred's Funhouse and Pizza Emporium or a picnic at a park.

But should he push for that? What if she told him no?

Wow. This was surreal. He'd never worried about a woman turning him down since... Hell, he couldn't remember when. But he'd be damned if he'd accept Dana's refusal sitting down. Not when he suspected there was more going on than met the eye.

Did Dana have feelings for him? He suspected she might, because if she didn't, why would she have kissed him the way she had? And why would she be so angry and upset now?

"Please don't go anywhere. Just give me an hour. I'm coming to talk to you—and without Rosie."

Before she had time to object, he hung up the phone and called his sister Olivia.

When Olivia answered, feminine laughter erupted in the background.

"What's all that noise?" he asked.

"Zoe and Sophie are here, and we're helping Sophie with some wedding planning. May is just around the corner, so we don't have much time."

Sophie was going to marry Mason Montgomery, a computer programmer who also worked at Robinson Tech.

"It's funny you should call," Olivia said. "We were just talking about having Rosie be the flower girl. You don't have any objections, do you?"

"No, I'm sure she'll love that—especially if she can wear a princess gown."

"No problem there. We'll find the perfect dress for her to wear."

"Great. Just send me the bill." Kieran realized his

sisters were busy, but seeing as he had no other options, he told Olivia why he'd called. "I have a problem, and I need a big favor."

"What's that?"

"I need someone to watch Rosie for me this evening, and I hope that someone is you."

"Oh, no," Olivia said, laughing yet clearly serious, too. "I'm not a kid person. You ought to know that. But I'll provide you with a better option. Let me put Zoe on the line."

At this point, Kieran couldn't be choosy. And Olivia was right. Zoe would probably jump at the chance.

Once the phone had been transferred from one sister to the other, he restated his request.

"I'd be happy to watch her," Zoe said. "Where are you going?"

"I need to talk to a friend."

"A friend?" Zoe asked. "Male or female?"

"Does it matter?" he asked.

"Actually, it does. I can watch Rosie for an hour or two, but I have plans to meet some of my high school friends this evening. However, if you have a hot date, I'll adjust my plans."

Her response took him aback. "Why would you reschedule or cancel your plans for me if I'm seeing a woman?"

"Because I feel sorry for you. Instant fatherhood has probably put a real damper on your social life."

"You're right. Life as I once knew it has stalled altogether."

"So who is she?" Zoe asked, connecting dots he hadn't planned on revealing. "Anyone I know?"

"No. And it's really not that serious. It's just…well, I really need to talk to her." It was too soon to let his family think he might be feeling more for Dana than just friendship. Especially when he wasn't sure what to call it himself.

"Can you bring Rosie to Olivia's house?" Zoe asked.

"Of course. I can be there in half an hour. Is this going to interfere with your wedding discussions?"

"No, we'll be wrapping things up before you get here. Sophie will be leaving soon. She and Mason are going out to dinner tonight, and she needs to go home and get ready."

Kieran had planned to ask Sophie a question when he got there. But if she was leaving, he'd better do it now.

"Can you put Sophie on the phone?" he asked. "I'll only keep her a minute."

"Sure."

There was a murmur or two, then the sound of a chair moving across the floor. Finally Sophie got on the line and said, "Hi, Kieran."

"I have a question for you, Soph. Remember when Ariana Lamonte interviewed you for that article she was writing?"

"Yes, why?"

"She went to the history center the other day and seemed interested in some old magazine and newspaper articles about Dad."

"That makes sense. He started Robinson Tech shortly after moving to Austin. I'm sure she's just trying to get a few of her details straight."

Kieran had considered that. "Did anything strike you as odd about her or any of the questions she asked you?"

"No, not at all. Are you worried about something?"

"She's supposed to be writing about the 'new' Fortunes, which didn't bother me because a topic like that could end up being good publicity. But I think she might want to write an exposé about our old man."

"She seemed very sweet and sincere during my interview. I don't think she has any ulterior motives. Besides, with the half siblings who've turned up lately, I can't blame her for being curious about Dad."

"You're probably right. I'd better let you get back to your wedding plans. Tell Zoe and Olivia that Rosie and I are on the way."

After they ended the call, Kieran went into the living room, where he found Rosie playing with a puzzle. He helped her finish putting the pieces together to speed her along. After she chose a few toys and books to put in her backpack, he took her out to the car.

He stayed within the speed limit on the drive to Olivia's, but it wasn't easy. He was determined to get to Dana's house in time to take her to dinner.

Sure, there was always the possibility that Dana would refuse to go out with him, but there was something to be said for Kieran Fortune. He never took no for an answer.

* * *

If Dana had any sense at all, she'd leave the house before Kieran arrived. But she hadn't survived foster care and achieved all that she had today by running from uncomfortable situations, even if she found them downright embarrassing. So she kept herself busy by emptying the picnic basket and putting it away. She'd cleaned up the kitchen after she'd made cookies with Rosie, but she decided to do a more thorough job of it now.

To help keep her mind off Kieran, she turned on the radio to her favorite soft rock station. She loved listening to music from the 1980s and sometimes wished she'd been born thirty years earlier.

She just finished sweeping the floor—or actually, dancing with the broom—when the last chords of a James Taylor hit faded and the next song began.

As Rod Stewart sang the opening lyrics of "Have I Told You Lately," she turned off the radio. There'd be no professions of love today, even if they were only made by a singer. She'd no more than put the broom back in the closet when the doorbell rang.

Her heart pinged around in her chest like a pinball. It had to be Kieran. Was she up for this?

She'd have to be. And on the upside, once they had the talk he insisted upon having and put it behind them, her life would be back on track.

But the minute she opened the door and saw him standing on her porch, all sexy and handsome, she wondered if it was going to be as easy as she'd thought to not only put him out of her mind, but out of her life for good.

He offered her an easy grin. "I came to apologize again for ducking out on you like I did."

She didn't respond. Nor did she return his smile or invite him in. She did, however, scan the yard and look at the backseat of his car. "Where's Rosie?"

"With my sisters, Zoe and Olivia."

Clearly, he no longer needed Dana as a babysitter. That would make it easier to put an end to their friendship.

"I've been struggling with something," he admitted. "I have feelings for you, and I was afraid that it was too soon. Zach hasn't been gone that long, and you probably thought I was coming on too strong."

She placed her hands on her hips. "I told you before that I cared about Zach, but I'm not grieving for him in the way you think I am."

"Yeah, well, after that last kiss, I realized that had to be true." His smile deepened, dimpling his cheeks. But she still didn't return it.

She'd lost her head during that kiss, making a fool of herself, and she didn't need the reminder.

"I have no business getting involved with anyone," Kieran added. "Not when I'm solely responsible for Rosie. She's struggling with the loss of her father and a move from the only home she's ever known. I'm all she really has right now."

"I haven't asked anything of you."

"Yes, I know. And that's the point. You've been

great. And amazing. But if things turn in a romantic direction, it might not be fair to you."

"How so?"

"Rosie has to be my first priority, and the last thing in the world I want to do is hurt you."

"I'm a big girl. I have no intention of letting myself get hurt." Still, even though she'd heard those words coming out in her own voice, she wasn't sure she believed them.

Was she setting herself up for failure?

"I'm attracted to you, Dana. I didn't expect it to happen, but it did."

"You?" A man who could have almost any single woman in Austin? And he found *her* attractive? She slowly shook her head. "That's hard for me to believe."

"Then maybe this will help." He reached out, drew her into his arms and kissed her soundly, thoroughly and with more conviction than she'd ever thought possible.

As his tongue swept into her mouth, mating with hers, she lost all conscious thought. She clung to him, savoring the subtle taste of peppermint and his musky, mountain-fresh scent.

Yet in spite of a growing ache in her most feminine part, she broke the kiss long enough to lay her cheek against his and whisper, "We'd better take this inside. I don't want to provide a show for my neighbors or give them a reason to gossip."

Then she took his hand, drew him into the house and closed the door. Their conversation probably should have continued at that point, but when he opened his arms, she stepped back into his embrace and raised her lips to his.

As the kiss deepened, primal need took over. Her hands explored him, caressed and stroked him, as his did her, until desire threatened to explode. But it wasn't just passion stealing Dana's thoughts and better judgment. Her heart had become fully engaged, too.

That really ought to concern her, and undoubtedly it would once she came back to her senses. If she ever did,

Before she could consider that thought, Kieran's cell phone rang, interrupting the sweet bliss. And Dana was torn between hoping he'd ignore the call and needing a moment to catch her breath.

She opted for breathing and allowing her brain the chance to gather her thoughts. "You'd better answer that."

"Yeah, probably so. But I'd rather not." Still, he reached for his phone and swiped the screen.

Moments later, he glanced at Dana and gave a slight roll of his eyes, then continued the conversation with whoever had called. "No, you're not bothering me. What's wrong?"

He listened a moment. "She's got to be exhausted after a day at the park. And she only had about a five-minute nap. She's probably having a meltdown, but I'll be right there."

After disconnecting the line, he looked at Dana, his lips forming a frown. "I have to go, but I intend to finish this later. What are you doing tomorrow night? Can we have dinner?"

"What about a sitter?"

"I'll find someone."

Dana smiled. "That little meltdown might mean that your sisters aren't going to be an option next time."

"Then I'll call Kelly or one of the other girls. You and I still need to discuss what to do about this."

By *this*, he meant the sexual attraction that had increased to astronomical proportions, at least as far as Dana was concerned.

"Let's take things slowly," she said, wanting to guard her heart.

"Sure. We'll keep things simple and uncomplicated."

She nodded, then watched him leave. Rather than follow him out to the car, she stayed inside. He might want to keep things simple, but for her, simple had left the station a long time ago.

Chapter Ten

As luck would have it, Kieran had no more than picked up Rosie from Olivia's and started the drive to his own house when the tired little girl drifted off to sleep.

He was actually getting used to being a stand-in daddy and even enjoyed it at times. But having to cancel plans, especially those that were romantic in nature, was definitely one of the downsides of parenthood or guardianship. And the plans he'd made while kissing Dana had been both romantic and major.

He'd meant what he'd said about taking things slowly, even though his hormones had argued otherwise just minutes ago. But it seemed that he and Dana were finally on the same page—and on the right track. So at least he could head home with a smile and hope for a brighter future.

He'd just pulled up to his building when his cell phone rang. He glanced at the screen displayed on his dash and saw that it was Sandra calling. He answered quickly, trying to keep the apprehension from his tone.

Thankfully, her response was light and upbeat. "How are things going?" she asked.

Better, now that Rosie had finally dozed off. But having the night end before it had a chance to get off the ground had been disappointing, although he wasn't about to complain to Sandra.

"We're doing just fine," he said. "We spent the afternoon at the park with Dana. Rosie met a new friend, and now she's asleep in the backseat. How are you doing? Is Sam feeling any better?"

"Yes, he is. The meds seem to be working. He's eating better, getting plenty of rest and gaining strength. So the doctor is pleased."

"That's good to hear."

"Anyway," Sandra said, "the reason I called was to talk to you about Rosie's birthday."

"Dana mentioned something to me earlier today, although we didn't discuss it. What did you have in mind?"

"I'd like to host the party here at the ranch—if that's all right with you. It's close to her preschool and the church, so most of her friends live nearby."

"That might be a good idea, but I don't want you to go to any trouble."

"It'll actually be fun for me," Sandra said. "And I promise not to go to any extra work. I can have

Kelly and her friends come that day and chase after the kids. And, of course, you and Dana can take part, too—if you want to."

Kieran laughed. "You strike a hard bargain, Sandra."

"Then you're okay with having it at the Leaning L?"

"As long as you'll let me and Dana do most of the work."

"Oh, good. Some of the parents like to host those parties at places like Cowboy Fred's because it's less work for them. But their food isn't very good. So I'd rather do the cooking. I'll keep it simple and pace myself, so don't worry about it being stressful."

Kieran had eaten enough meals at the Leaning L to know that he'd much rather eat anything Sandra made than Cowboy Fred's crappy pizza.

"I have one other question for you," Sandra said. "I'd like to have Rosie spend the night tomorrow so we can talk about her party and what she'd like. I already talked to Kelly, and she's available for a slumber party. Is that okay with you?"

Kieran didn't have to ponder the decision very long, since that would allow him to take Dana out—if she'd agree to go with him. "I'm sure Rosie would love to spend the night with you. What time do you want me to drop her off?"

"How about four o'clock?"

"Perfect." That gave him time to go home and shower before picking up Dana. "We'll see you tomorrow."

As soon as the call ended, Kieran dialed Don Ramon's, a classy restaurant that not only offered some of his favorite Mexican dishes, like tacos and enchiladas, but also served trendy Southwestern fare and boasted a full tequila bar that was the best this side of the Rio Grande.

When he got them on the line, he requested a table for two on the patio.

"Seven o'clock would be great," he told the woman taking his call.

His plan to take Dana out tomorrow night was coming together nicely.

Sitter? Check.

Dinner reservations? Check.

Beautiful woman to accompany him? Still pending. But he wasn't worried.

Should he order flowers? That might be a nice touch. One way or another, he would make this date extra special—and a night Dana would never forget.

Dana hadn't planned to go out with Kieran this evening, but when he'd shown up at her front door holding a bouquet of long-stem yellow roses and wearing a dashing grin, her resolve to avoid getting romantically involved with him had crumbled.

So now here she was, sitting across a linen-draped pation table with Kieran at Don Ramon's, one of Austin's finest—and probably most expensive—Mexican restaurants.

Kieran lowered his heavy, leather-bound menu. "If you like seafood, the camarones rancheros is good."

"I was thinking about having chili rellenos," she said. "Although there are a couple of chicken dishes that are pretty tempting."

"All the food here is good. You won't be disappointed with anything you choose."

He'd obviously been here many times, and probably with a date. Yet that didn't dull Dana's pleasure at being here with him. The man certainly knew how to treat a lady. He'd made Dana feel special from the moment he'd handed her the fragrant bouquet of roses. And in the car, he'd set the mood with soft jazz playing on Sirius. The royal treatment continued when the valet opened her car door and when Kieran brought her inside.

In the background, near a tree adorned with twinkly little white lights, a mariachi band played an array of Spanish romantic ballads. She didn't understand a word that they sang, but the music cast an amorous ambiance in the room, especially when they moved to their table and gave them a private serenade.

Was she really on an actual date with Kieran Fortune?

She was tempted to pinch herself. Instead, she opted to settle in and enjoy the handsome man's company.

One of the service staff placed a bowl of tortilla chips on their table, along with salsa fresco and guacamole.

"Thanks, Pablo." Kieran reached for one of the

chips and raised it in the air. "They make everything fresh, including the tortillas."

She wasn't surprised. The decor alone—with the white plastered walls and dark wood beams as well as an artistic mural depicting historical life in Old Mexico—was enough to convince her that this wasn't your run-of-the-mill restaurant.

"I'm not sure if you like guacamole or salsa," Kieran said, "but Don Ramon's has the best I've ever tasted."

"It's funny," she said. "I don't like avocados, but I love guacamole. One day, I was having dinner at my friend Monica's house. Her *abuelita*—her grandmother—had prepared a Mexican feast for us and encourage me to taste her special recipe. I did and was surprised at how good it was."

He dipped his chip into the guacamole, then handed it to her. "Try this and tell me if there's any comparison."

She took a bite and had to agree. "This is a little different, but I think it's just as good."

Her thoughts drifted back to the day Abuelita had prepared that amazing dinner, when Dana had felt a part of Monica's entire family. All she'd ever wanted was to be accepted and loved by people who knew her best.

When the waiter had finished pouring glasses of red wine, Kieran lifted his in a toast. "To our first evening out."

Dana clinked her glass against his. If this was their

first evening, then Kieran expected there would be others. She certainly was game, if he was.

After placing their orders, they settled back and enjoyed their wine, which had a hint of cranberry. With a candle softly burning and the mariachis playing, the evening had turned incredibly romantic.

But maybe that was due to the handsome man across the table from her. And for some reason, she had the feeling that the night would only get better with each minute that passed.

She was right.

By the time Kieran was driving her home, her heart rate was soaring and the heat was building. She lifted her long hair off her neck, refusing to give any thought to why she'd worn it down tonight. Still, she couldn't stop one thought from echoing in her mind. When he dropped her off, would he try to kiss her again?

She certainly hoped he would. And if he didn't? Would she be bold enough to take the lead?

When they pulled up at her house, she was reluctant to see the night end. "Would you like to come in for a cup of coffee? Or a glass of wine?"

He tossed her a dazzling, bright-eyed smile. "I'll have whatever you're having."

They got out of the car and walked to the door. Her fingers trembled when she pulled the keys from her purse, and it took longer than she'd expected to slip them into the lock.

Once inside the house, she said, "It'll only take a minute to put on a pot of coffee."

"Do you need any help?"

"No, I've got this." What she didn't have was any idea where this night would go. But she was up for the adventure.

She left him in the living room, then headed into the kitchen. Her hands trembled again as she filled the carafe with water and the basket with ground coffee beans, especially when she heard music playing—something soft and slow.

Kieran must have turned on her television to the music station. She hadn't told him to make himself at home, but she was glad that he had. While the coffee brewed, she returned to the living room, where Kieran stood in the center of the floor.

He reached out a hand to her. "Do you want to dance?"

Her heart scrambled to right itself, as heat and desire warred with her common sense—and her pride. Kieran had acquired a lot of practice over the years and was surely a good dancer. But she'd... Well, it's not like she had two left feet or didn't enjoy dancing. Just ask her broom!

A giggle nearly burst free, but she bit it back. In spite of her momentary nervousness, she stepped forward and into his embrace.

Kieran pulled her close, and she leaned into him, swaying with the music, caught up in his musky scent, the strength of his arms, the magic of his touch.

She realized that he'd only used the music as an excuse for him to hold her, but she didn't care. He was an ace at seduction, but she refused to think about the other women he'd charmed. Not when she wanted to take whatever he had to offer her tonight.

As their bodies pressed together, they stroked and caressed each other. His hand slid up her side, the fabric of her black dress moving with it. When he cupped her breast, kneading it, his thumb skimmed her nipple and sent her senses reeling.

He was way too good at this, which probably ought to concern her, at least a little bit. But she couldn't help her desire for more.

Did she dare mention it?

Did she even need to?

His breath was warm and moist as he trailed kisses along her neck. She leaned her head back, granting him better access. She was clay in his hands, and he was the master artist. Yet he brought her to life in so many ways, making her bolder than she'd ever known she could be.

She'd lost count of the number of songs that played, although it might only have been three, each one more romantic than the last. All the while, they'd kissed and stroked each other until she thought she'd melt in a puddle on the floor.

Why wasn't he pressing her for more?

Because he didn't have to. She drew away, her breathing soft yet ragged, and said, "I invited you in for coffee, and it's probably ready. But I'm tempted to suggest another after-dinner alternative."

"Like I said…" He smiled, his eyes laden with passion. "I'll have whatever you're having."

She nodded, then reached for his hand and led him to her bedroom. "I don't think either of us needs a caffeine boost."

"I don't," he said. Then he took her back into his arms and began kissing her all over again.

She wasn't entirely sure where this was going, but she had a pretty good idea. She might regret this in the morning, but for now, she would enjoy every moment.

Things were turning out just the way Kieran had hoped they would. He'd be lying if he didn't admit he wanted to make love to her, but he didn't know how Dana felt. She certainly surprised him by taking him into her bedroom.

He barely noticed the antique oak bed. All he really saw was Dana. He kissed her again—long and deep. His hands slid along the curve of her back and down the slope of her hips. He pulled her hips forward, against his erection, and she arched forward, revealing her own need, her own arousal. Another surge of heat rushed through him.

Had he ever wanted a woman this badly? Right this moment, he sincerely doubted it. The quiet, dignified librarian was turning out to be even more amazing and breathtaking than he'd thought. If a man wasn't careful, he might be tempted to give up the footloose life of a bachelor and do something new, commit to someone special. Someone like Dana.

When she drew her lips from his, then slowly turned around, she swept her hair to the side like a veil, revealing the zipper for him. He pulled it down, slowly and deliberately. Then he peeled the fabric from her shoulders, taking his time to kiss every inch of the skin he uncovered.

She made a soft sound, almost a whimper, then turned to face him. Her gaze never left his as she let the dress slip to the floor.

He marveled at the sight of her, standing before him in a lacy black bra and a matching pair of skimpy panties. For some reason, he'd expected her to wear conservative underwear, but that was yet another amazing revelation for him. As she'd slowly exposed layer after layer of the real Dana to him, he couldn't wait to see what other surprises awaited him.

Her body, slender and lithe, was sexier and even more perfect than he'd imagined it to be. And tonight, she belonged to him.

Following her lead, he unbuttoned his shirt and tossed the custom-made garment to the side like a cheap suit. Next he unbuckled his belt and undid his slacks.

When he'd removed all but his boxer briefs, she skimmed her nails across his chest, setting off a rush of need throbbing in his veins. Then she unsnapped her bra and freed her breasts, full and round, the tips peaked and ready to be loved.

As he bent and took a nipple in his mouth, she gasped in pleasure. He laved first one breast, and then the other with kisses until they were both fully aroused.

He lifted her in his arms and placed her on top of

the bed. Her red hair splayed upon the white pillow sham, her lovely body awaiting him on top of the white down comforter.

Determined to make sure she wouldn't have a single regret in the morning, he joined her on the bed, where they continued to kiss, to taste and to stroke each other until they were both breathless with need.

"We have all night," she said, as she pulled free of his embrace and removed the remainder of their clothes. "So we can take things slow and easy later. Right now I need to feel you inside of me."

He didn't want to prolong the foreplay any longer, either. And she was right. They had the rest of the night.

About the time he was going to reach for his pants to get the condom he always carried with him, she rolled to the side of the bed, opened the nightstand drawer and pulled out a small, unopened box of condoms.

He wasn't sure if she kept them handy just in case, or whether she'd planned for this night to happen. Either way, he was glad she'd been prepared.

Taking the packet she offered him, he tore it open and rolled on the condom. Then, as he hovered over her, she reached for his erection and guided him right where she wanted him to be.

He entered her slowly at first, but as her body responded to his, he increased the tempo. They moved together in a primal dance, taking and giving until they reached the peak together.

Her breath caught as she climaxed, and her nails

pressed into his shoulders as she let go. He shuddered, releasing with her in a head-spinning, heart-searing sexual explosion that begged to be repeated throughout the night.

He'd gone without sex for a while, which might be why tonight had been so incredibly good...

Oh, hell. Who was he kidding? In his heart of hearts, he knew it was because of Dana. And he feared what might be happening to them. To *him*.

He'd told her that they'd take things slowly, but that's not what had just happened. They'd taken a wild ride to the stars and beyond, and as he lay in a stunning afterglow, he thought that he might never want to leave Dana's arms or the peace and comfort he'd found in her bed.

And that's just the reason he needed to. Making love with her had been anything but casual or simple. It had all the earmarks of love and promises of forever—something that scared a dedicated bachelor like him spitless.

Still, he rolled to the side, taking her with him— as was his custom after lovemaking. But tonight had been different. Dana was different.

For that reason alone, he had to escape before he said something he might regret, made promises he didn't dare make.

But how did a conscientious lover who'd just had the best sex of his life with a woman who'd intrigued him like no other tell her that he had to leave? That he wouldn't be spending the night?

* * *

Wrapped in Kieran's arms, Dana basked in the afterglow of a stunning climax, afraid to move or even blink for fear she'd wake up from this beautiful dream.

She'd just had the most stunning evening of her life, followed by the best sexual experience she'd ever had. And in spite of her reluctance to get involved with a man who lived in a completely different world than hers, she'd fallen hopelessly in love with Kieran Fortune.

She couldn't very well tell him, though. It was too soon, and it might scare him off. So now what? She'd instinctively known what to do just moments before, when they were kissing and caressing, but she was completely stymied now.

Should she invite him to spend the night with her? Or was that a given?

If she'd had more experience with this sort of thing, she'd know exactly how to handle it. But she was such a novice, and Kieran had just raised the learning curve to an unbelievable height.

He pressed a kiss on her brow, his lips lingering as he said, "That was amazing."

She smiled, relieved that she wasn't the only one who'd come to that conclusion. "I thought so, too."

He trailed his fingers along her shoulder and down her arm, sending tiny tingles dancing on her skin. "As much as I hate to leave, I have to go."

No, you don't, she wanted to say. *Stay with me. Forever.* But her self-esteem, which had grown strong after college graduation, had just taken an unexpected hit and now floundered.

"I need to pick up Rosie at the Leaning L bright and early in the morning," he added.

That sounded like a lame excuse. Why couldn't he set the alarm for four or five and then leave from her house? She would gladly wake up with him and send him off with a kiss and a cup of freshly brewed coffee.

She would have suggested that option, but she didn't want to come across as clingy or needy.

"I'd hate to arrive at the ranch wearing the same shirt and pants that I dropped Rosie off in. That would set off suspicion about where I spent the evening—as pleasant as it's been."

That made sense, she supposed. She wasn't ready for the world to know how she was feeling, or what they'd done, either. But one day soon, she hoped to shout it from the proverbial mountain tops.

He pressed a second kiss upon her brow, then climbed out of bed and proceeded to pick up his discarded clothes. For a man who was always stylishly dressed, his shirts neatly pressed, he did look a little mussed.

He cast a smile at her. "You look beautiful lying there. So there's no need to walk me to the door."

No way would she do that. She rolled out of bed, still as naked as the day she was born. "There's coffee in the kitchen, and it's still fresh. I'll pour it in a to-go cup to take with you."

"That'd be great. Thanks." The warm smile he

wore suggested that she hadn't just experienced a bout of hit-and-run sex.

After snagging her robe from the closet, she padded to the kitchen. Then she removed a thermal cup from her cupboard, filled it with coffee and carried it to the living room, where Kieran was preparing to leave.

A small inner voice rose to the surface, threatening to cry out, *Please don't go.* But she stifled it with a smile. "Thank you for dinner. And…everything."

"I'll call you tomorrow." He took her in his arms and gave her a sweet, lingering goodbye kiss. "And I promise to look for a dependable sitter. I'd rather not wait too long before…doing this again."

She practically wilted in his arms. Okay, so he wasn't just giving her a brush-off.

"We said we'd take things slowly," she said, her ego gaining strength once more.

"That's for the best."

She nodded and offered him a send-off smile, suggesting she was in complete agreement. And she was. Taking things one day at a time was the smart thing to do, the right thing.

Still, a wisp of disappointment swirled around her as she watched him open the door and let himself out.

He said he'd call. And he'd implied there'd be other nights like this, so she had no choice but to believe him. She'd cling to that promise, knowing it was the best she'd get from him for now.

Making love with Kieran had been out of this

world, but had it been good enough for an experienced bachelor like him?

Time would tell, she supposed.

Either way, tonight's memory would last her a lifetime.

Chapter Eleven

Kieran had worried that, after their lovemaking, Dana would expect more from him than he was prepared to give. But that hadn't been the case. She'd given him plenty of space in the following days and hadn't asked anything of him.

In fact, each time they'd talked on the phone, he'd been the one to place the call. For that reason alone, he'd found himself more drawn to her than ever. And stranger still, he felt compelled to push for more of her time.

They hadn't seen each other since they'd made love last week, something he hoped to remedy soon.

Today, after leaving Robinson Tech, he stopped by the post office, where he had a PO box, to pick up his mail. Then he picked up Rosie at preschool and headed home.

All the while, Rosie chattered about her upcoming birthday. "All my friends are gonna come on Saturday, even Teddy."

Kieran had never heard that child's name. Maybe it was a new child at school who'd moved up on the waiting list. "Is Teddy a new boy at school?"

Rosie laughed. "Teddy isn't a *boy*. He's a dog. And he's really cute. He comes to the fence when we're on the playground. He's a little dirty, but he's really nice. And when you poke your finger through the hole, he licks it."

Kieran would have to talk to one of the teachers and ask what the school was doing about strays that roamed near the vacant field behind the playground. Slobbery dog kisses on fingers didn't sound very sanitary to him. And what about bites?

"So can Teddy come to my party?" she asked. "We have to pick him up in our car."

"I'm sure Teddy already has plans for that day." Kieran glanced in the rearview mirror and caught Rosie frowning at him.

She slowly shook her head. "No, that's not true. Teddy doesn't have a family. And he's lonely. That's why Miss Peggy called the dog catcher to take him to a special place where he could find a new home."

"Sounds like your teacher had a good plan."

"Yes, but when the man came to get him, Teddy got scared and ran away. So I told Miss Peggy that we could keep him because our house is big, and our family is small. We have room for one more."

"You have a point," Kieran said. "But I'm not allowed to have pets in this building."

"I got a good idea," Rosie said. "There's room for all of us at the ranch. We could all live there, like me and my other daddy did. And then Teddy could be my dog."

"You'll have to talk to your grandparents about that," Kieran said. "I mean about Teddy living there. We already have a home. But you can visit the ranch as often as you want."

"Okay, I'll ask Grandma. But she'll say yes because she likes dogs."

Kieran pulled into the underground parking garage and steered into his assigned space. After he got Rosie out of her car seat, he took her by the hand, walked to the elevator and rode up to their unit on the tenth floor.

"Can Dana come over tonight?" Rosie asked.

That invitation had been at the top of Kieran's to-do list. "We'll have to call and invite her."

"Can I do it?"

"Sure. When we get inside, I'll dial her number for you."

Moments later, Kieran whipped out his cell phone and called Dana. As he listened to each ring, his pulse escalated, reaching a peak when she finally answered.

"Hey," he said. "Rosie and I had an idea, and she'd like to talk to you."

"Sure, put her on."

As soon as he handed over his cell, Rosie started the conversation with the dinner invitation, which he assumed Dana accepted, because the little girl's face broke into a huge grin. Then she immediately launched into a full report of everything that had happened that day at school, starting with apple slices for midmorning snack and a story about a purple whale.

He let her jabber while he sorted through the mail. Power bill, alumni association newsletter and dental appointment reminder. He was just about to set it all on the stack of things that needed his attention when he realized he'd been negligent and had let things pile up.

So he crossed the room to the kitchen desk and went through each item, noting the due dates. At the bottom, he spotted the wedding invitation he'd received a while back. It was addressed to Mr. Kieran Fortune Robinson and Guest.

He set the other things aside and opened it.

Mr. and Mrs. Gerald Robinson
request the honor of your presence
at the marriage of their daughter

Sophie Anne
to
Mason Montgomery

Saturday, the sixth of May
at six o'clock in the evening
The Driskill Hotel ballroom

With the wedding just around the corner, his sisters would want his RSVP as soon as possible. So he pulled out the response card, opened the drawer and pulled out a pen. His right hand hovered a moment over the line where he was to provide the number who'd be attending.

Dana immediately came to mind, since she was the only woman in the world he'd consider taking. But he'd made it a point never to take a date to family events. And while he was sorely tempted to make an exception this time, it was too soon.

Besides, his sisters already had visions of him running off in the moonlight with a special lady. Why fuel their imaginations?

"Daddy!" Rosie called out. "Mommy wants to talk to you!"

Great. That cinched it. All he needed was for Sophie's flower girl to refer to Dana and him as her mom and dad. He'd never hear the end of it. So he gripped the pen tightly and marked a big, solid *1* on the line and then wrote his name. Before he could place the small card into the its envelope, Rosie called out again, "Hurry, Daddy! She wants to know if she should bring dinner. And she also said it was okay if Teddy comes to my party! She said she will bring him if he doesn't have a ride."

Kieran rolled his eyes. He'd have to let Dana know that Sammy wasn't a child before she made him a party favor and put him on the guest list. "I'll be right there, Rosie."

Then he hurried into the living room, pumped that he'd get to see Dana again tonight.

Dana tried to tamp down both her excitement and nervousness while driving to Kieran's house. She was glad that she'd been invited to dinner—and that she'd been told not to bring a thing but herself.

It was especially nice that the invitation had come from both Kieran and Rosie. She'd been a little worried about him leaving her house so quickly after they'd made love, but she'd probably expected too much. He'd mentioned taking things slowly, and... well, now here they were, moving right along.

As much as she looked forward to having some time alone with Kieran after Rosie went to sleep, the focus during the early hours would be on Rosie's birthday party. The little girl wanted a princess theme and, after talking to Sandra on the phone, Dana was determined to make that wish come true.

According to Sandra, Kelly and her friends wanted to decorate the ranch house like a castle. So Dana had gone shopping after work yesterday and picked up party favors, plus tiaras for the girls and crowns for the boys.

Since Dana had volunteered to make the cake, she'd researched various internet sites and found the perfect design, which was similar to one her mother had made her when she was six. To make the three-dimensional "princess," she'd make a cake in a bundt pan, which would form the gown. She'd already purchased a Barbie doll to place in the hole. Then she'd

frost the cake and the doll's bodice with pink frosting and decorate it with edible crystals and sparkles.
Rosie would love it.

Since that cake wouldn't be enough to feed everyone Rosie had invited, including Michael and his
mother, Elaine Wagner, Dana was going to make cupcakes, each one decorated as a flower, that would sur-
round the princess.

Needless to say, Dana was nearly as excited about
the party as Rosie was. She could hardly wait for
Saturday.

Even more exciting was the evening that awaited
her at Kieran's.

After parking her car in a guest spot under his
building, she greeted the doorman, who'd not only
expected her arrival but called her by name. And that
was another sign that she and Kieran were on the right
track. Then she took the elevator to his tenth-floor
apartment and rang the bell.

A happy Rosie met her at the door, which warmed
her heart. But it was the dashing man in the background who nearly took her breath away and sent her
thoughts soaring to dreamland.

Rosie reached for Dana's hand and pulled her inside. "I'm glad you finally got here. We *missed* you."

She glanced over the child's head once more, her
gaze meeting Kieran's. Her eyes asked the question
she couldn't voice. *Did we?*

His wink was the only answer she needed.

"And we have pizza," Rosie added. "It's not the

yucky kind from Cowboy Fred's. We found another place that cooks it better."

"I don't care what we eat," Dana said. "I'm just glad that we all get to have dinner together."

What she didn't mention was that she'd brought a toothbrush and a change of clothes with her—just in case she was also invited to spend the night.

Since she hadn't wanted to appear presumptuous or eager, she'd packed them in a gym bag, which seemed like something she might keep in the trunk of her car for a spur-of-the-moment workout—rather than a planned sleepover.

After all, they'd agreed to take things slow.

When Kieran walked over and took her hand, he looked and smelled so good that she needed a mental reminder. *The operative word is* slow, she repeated to herself. But looking at him, she couldn't help wanting to move things along a little faster.

"Come on into the kitchen," Kieran said. "We should eat while the pizza is still warm. Can I get you a glass of wine?"

"Just half a glass," she said. "I have to drive home."

"You got it," he said, as if a sleepover had never crossed his mind. Then he withdrew a bottle from a small wine cooler near the desk area. "I have a Napa Valley merlot I think you'll like."

She tamped down the minor disappointment. "Sounds good."

Minutes later, they sat at the kitchen table, a glossy black, ultramodern piece with matching chairs, to eat the cheese pizza. It was actually delicious. And so was the vegetarian antipasto salad, which had a tasty vinaigrette dressing.

"Guess what?" Rosie set down her glass, the milk leaving a white mustache on her upper lip. "I get to be the flower girl when Sophie and Mason get married. I'm going to walk in first and drop roses on a rug for the bride to step on. And I get to wear a real princess dress and a flower crown on my head."

"How fun!" Dana told the child. Then she looked at Kieran. "When's the wedding?"

"Saturday, May sixth. It'll be in the ballroom at the Driskill Hotel."

Why wasn't she surprised? Talk about dream wedding locales, at least in Dana's mind. The landmark hotel had been built in 1886 by cattle baron Jesse Driskill and had been providing its guests with luxury accommodations for more than a hundred and thirty years.

"I'll bet the wedding will be beautiful," Dana said. And expensive. The cheapest rooms had to cost at least three hundred dollars a night. But then, a fancy place like that was to be expected for the wedding of a Fortune.

Kieran didn't respond, so she let it go. What she wouldn't give to go as his plus one.

Once they finished the pizza, Kieran told Rosie it was time to put on her pajamas and get ready for bed. But the girl objected. "I want to wear my princess jammies, and they're in the laundry."

"Actually, they're in the dryer. I'll get them for

you." Kieran glanced at Dana. "Don't worry about the mess. I'll be right back."

Dana wasn't about to just sit there, waiting for him to return. So she cleared the table and put the dishes in the sink. She put the leftover pizza slices in plastic bags, then placed them in the fridge. Next, she folded the empty box and took it to the recycle bin, which was located near the kitchen desk.

She couldn't help noticing the elegant invitation spread out on top. In formal script, it was addressed to *Mr. Kieran Fortune Robinson and guest.*

Just imagining herself going to the Driskill Hotel on Kieran's arm shot a combination of excitement and nervousness clean through her.

What would she wear? She might have several dresses hanging in her closet, but none of them would be appropriate for a Fortune wedding. She'd have to go shopping—and not at the usual places she frequented. An event that classy and special would require a trip uptown. Her budget would take a hit, but she'd make it work.

She scanned the invitation. May 6 wasn't that far away. She'd need to schedule a hair appointment, too.

As she put the invitation down, her eyes lit on the matching response card which lay next to a pen. She assumed he was getting ready to mail his RSVP. But her heart clenched and her tummy twisted when she saw a big *1* where she'd hoped she'd see a *2.*

"Thanks for cleaning up," Kieran said, as he returned to the kitchen.

Dana slowly turned around. Aching with disappointment, the words rolled out of her mouth before she could give them a second thought. "You're not taking a guest to your sister's wedding?"

He cleared his throat, as if the question had taken him aback and he needed a moment to form a reply. "I thought about it, but I decided it was better if I didn't. I've never taken a date to family events. For one thing, I know what they'd assume, and I don't want anyone jumping to conclusions."

"That would be terrible, wouldn't it?"

"Not exactly *terrible*," he said. "But I'm not ready to give anyone reason to speculate."

And sadly, Dana had been speculating all evening.

How could she have been so stupid? She'd known full well going into this thing that she couldn't compete with any of the women Kieran usually dated. And she'd never fit into his social circles.

Was she destined to always miss the mark when it came to finding Mr. Right? If so, she'd never be able to create a family for herself.

"You're not upset, are you?"

Upset? No. She was crushed. And angry. But mostly at herself. Yet there was no way she'd let him know any of that. "Actually, I'm busy that day anyway."

As luck would have it, Rosie came trotting back into the kitchen in her pajamas and bunny slippers. "Will you read me a story, Mommy?"

At the sound of that word, her heart clenched. The other times Rosie called her Mommy she warmed to the name, but tonight it chilled her. She wasn't

Rosie's mommy, and she never would be. And what about Kieran? He seemed to be so concerned about his family getting the wrong impression about his relationship with Dana. But what about Rosie?

Dana knelt down, wrapped her arms around the vulnerable little girl and kissed her. "I'd love to, honey. But I have something important I need to do this evening. I only had time for pizza, and now I have to leave."

"When are you coming back?" the child asked.

"One day soon," Dana said, glad she didn't have a nose like Pinocchio's, which would be a foot long now. Then she headed for the living room, where she'd left her purse.

For some crazy reason, she actually expected Kieran to stop her, but he just let her walk out the door as if she'd never belonged there in the first place.

The moment Dana left Kieran's house on Wednesday night and shut the door, guilt slammed into him. And so did a sense of loss. At first, he'd tried to convince himself that letting things cool off between them was for the best.

At one time, he'd enjoyed a single, unencumbered life. If one of the women he dated even hinted that she might want a commitment, he'd almost have an allergic reaction. But after a few days without seeing Dana or even talking to her on the phone, the remorse had really set in. And by Saturday morning, before leaving for Rosie's party at the ranch, he'd had to admit that he'd not only reacted like a jerk, but he'd also been a fool. He was going to have to apologize, and hopefully, she'd forgive him. Something told him she would. Then, once the party was over, he'd invite her over for dinner—and then he'd ask her to spend the night.

But making things right with his lover wasn't the only reason he wanted to get to the ranch early. He'd promised Sandra he'd help. She'd always been a conscientious hostess, and he didn't want her to overdo it trying to please people today.

She was also an excellent housekeeper, and he suspected she hadn't been able to keep up with her usual tasks. So he'd sent a cleaning crew to the ranch yesterday, something he'd insisted on when he'd last talked to Sandra. He knew she'd be uneasy about having her guests see dusty furniture or find her kitchen anything other than spotless. She'd reluctantly agreed and thanked him, saying only that her time was limited these days.

So were her finances, which was why he insisted upon paying for everything. Dana had picked up the tab for the party decorations and the cake, but he planned to reimburse those expenses as soon as he saw her, which would be in a few short minutes.

He and Rosie had almost reached the Leaning L. He'd planned to arrive before the first guest did, but an unexpected business call from a client in New York had thrown him off schedule.

"Is Dana going to be there?" Rosie asked from the backseat.

The child had referred to Dana as Mommy nearly

every day for the past two weeks. Why had that changed?

Had she sensed the issue that had cropped up between them on Wednesday night? He hadn't thought she could be so perceptive, but then again, Rosie continued to surprise him. Either way, he was determined to square things with Dana today and they'd be lovers before dawn. Even the *C* word, *commitment*, didn't sound so bad when it came to her.

"I'm sure Dana is already there. She's making the birthday cake, remember?" Kieran glanced in the rearview mirror and watched Rosie nod in agreement.

He would let Dana know that he'd changed that *1* to a *2* on his RSVP card. He'd have to endure some major taunts at the wedding and long after it was over, but she was worth it.

Moments later, he and Rosie turned into the driveway. He didn't see Dana's car, though. That was odd. She knew how important this party was to Rosie.

He shook off his momentary concern. She'd probably had to stop by a store to pick up something at the last minute.

After parking near the barn, he got out of the car and unbuckled Rosie. "How does it feel to be four years old?"

She beamed and took his hand.

Kelly and several of her teenage friends greeted them before they could walk ten paces toward the house.

"There's Princess Rosie," Kelly said. "Come with us. We're going to get you ready to meet your guests.

We have crowns and tiaras to pass out to everyone when they arrive."

Kieran thought about following them into the house, but since he expected Dana at any moment, he waited in the yard. That would give him the perfect opportunity to apologize in private.

Five minutes later, when the first guests arrived in a minivan, Dana still hadn't shown up. He welcomed the mother and her little girl then pointed them to the porch, where Rosie and the teenagers were waiting to hand out the tiaras and crowns.

By the time a third carload of party guests arrived, he decided he'd better call Dana to check on her. But before he could take out his cell phone, he spotted Elaine and Michael Wagner getting out of a white sedan that had seen better days.

He greeted them with a smile. "I'm glad you could make it."

Elaine, who was helping Michael from his car seat, said, "We wouldn't have missed it for the world. This party is all Mikey's been talking about for days."

By the time she pulled out a gift bag and shut the passenger door, Kieran began to realize Dana might be a no-show.

How could she disappoint Rosie like that? She might be angry at him—and he deserved it. But why take it out on a child?

He headed to the house himself, guilt warring with anger, and entered the kitchen, where Sandra was preparing a pot of coffee.

"Have you heard anything from Dana?" he asked.

"Yes, she woke up with a terrible headache. But what a trooper. She drove out early this morning to bring the cake and cupcakes as well as a gift bag for Rosie."

So she hadn't ditched the party. A headache was a reasonable excuse. Or had she only feigned illness?

He had no idea what to think, let alone do. He wanted to talk to her, but he couldn't very well leave when the party was just getting started.

Before he could quiz Sandra and ask how Dana looked, whether she might need something—or someone—to check in on her, Elaine entered the kitchen. "Sandra, is there anything I can do to help? Dana didn't want you to lift a finger."

So Dana had asked someone to cover for her, following through on her promise to help since she couldn't be here herself. Her kindness and consideration was both amazing and touching.

"Go on out to the living room and enjoy the guests," Kieran told Sandra. "Elaine and I can handle things."

"What would I do without you?" Sandra asked.

Kieran tossed her a grin. "I could ask you the same thing. You've given me some of the best meals I've ever had. And I consider you and Sam part of my family now."

She nodded, unshed tears glistening in her eyes, and walked away, leaving Kieran and Elaine alone.

"Thanks for offering to help us out," Kieran told her.

"I don't mind at all," she said. "In fact, I was flattered when Dana called me on Thursday and asked me to step in for her."

Kieran froze in his tracks. So Dana had known two days ago that she wasn't going to attend the party?

Damn, he'd been more of an ass than he'd thought.

"Is something wrong?" Elaine asked, as she prepared a tray with cream, sugar, a carafe and disposable foam cups.

He shook off his surprise. "No, I was just having a…"

"Senior moment?" Elaine asked. "I know all about those."

Actually, he was going to say that he was having an epiphany.

"Before I married Michael's father," she said, "I lived with my great-grandparents. My grandpa had dementia and his health was failing, so I took care of him at the end."

"That must have been hard on you."

"It was. I hated to see him struggle to remember, but I was glad that I could be with him during his last days. In fact, since I need to find work so I can move out of my parents' house and find a place of our own, I might apply for a job at a local hospice. I don't have a college education or any real experience—other than being a mom and a caretaker."

A thought came to mind, a solution that might work out for all of them. "Have you ever considered being a nanny?"

"No, not really. My parents' home is pretty small, so I can't really watch kids there. And if I went to work at the family's house, I'd have to take Michael with me. Most parents wouldn't want to have an extra child at their place when they're at work."

Actually, Kieran wouldn't mind that. And if Elaine not only looked after Rosie at the ranch while he was at the office, she could also be a caretaker for the Lawsons. They needed someone to look after them, too. They also had a small guesthouse, where Zach had once lived.

This might be the perfect solution for everyone involved.

"Let's have a chat after the party," he said. "I've got a thought simmering that might solve your problem."

He just hoped he'd get another brilliant idea. One that would help him solve the huge predicament he'd created with Dana.

Chapter Twelve

The party was finally over, and the last guest had gone home. Elaine had volunteered to help Kieran clean up, and he'd taken her up on the offer. She'd also agreed to watch Rosie for him later, so she'd followed him to his place.

After he let her and the kids inside, she said, "Take all the time you need. We'll be fine." Elaine gave him a grin. "I can even stay overnight if you need me."

Kieran thanked her, then drove straight to Dana's house. He hadn't called ahead, so he hoped she was home. He'd thought briefly about picking up a bouquet of roses as a peace offering, like he'd done the last time he'd apologized to her, but now that he'd finally realized how he felt about her, he just wanted to get there as fast as possible and tell her.

He rang the bell, shifting his weight from foot to foot as he waited what seemed like forever for her to answer the door. Finally, she stood before him, her hair glossy and flowing over her shoulders and down her back. But the moment she laid eyes on him, she crossed her arms as if to stand her ground.

He wasted no time with small talk.

"I'm sorry," he said. "I was a jerk the other night, and you didn't deserve it. I hurt you when you found out I hadn't planned to take you to Sophie's wedding. That wasn't my intention."

"Forget about it. That's not what upset me. Not really."

Either way, he'd screwed up. "You have every right to be angry with me, and I want to make things right."

"Don't worry about it. I don't want to attend that wedding with you, anyway."

Fixing this wasn't going to be as easy as he'd hoped it would be, and he doubted that flowers would have helped. She was clearly angry. "I didn't come here to invite you to be my date to my sister's wedding."

Her lips parted, and disbelief stretched across her face. "I see. So it's over between us?"

"I hope not."

He offered her a smile, but worry marred her brow, suggesting that she wasn't ready for their relationship to end, either.

Kieran chuckled. "I should have worded that better. In fact, let me start over. My feelings for you were unsettling and hard for me to admit. I didn't want it to happen and I fought it every step of the way."

"I'm not surprised. Your dating habits aren't a big secret."

"It was more than that. I felt as though I was stepping into the life Zach had set up for himself, the life he deserved. And I was wracked by guilt. Then, after a while, I was able to envision my own future—if you were a part of it."

"I told you that Zach and I weren't that close. We never even slept together. It was his family that drew me in. I lost my parents when I was young, and Sandra came close to filling a maternal role for me. That's why I continued to see Zach, even when I knew marriage wasn't in our future. He knew it, too, but he appreciated my help with Rosie—just like you seem to."

"This isn't about Rosie," Kieran said. "It's about *me*. And it's about the feeling that's grown so strong it's going to burst out of me if I don't tell you about it."

She seemed to sway back, as if his words had struck a sensitive chord, but she quickly recovered. "That's hard to believe."

He could see why she might feel that way. "When you walked out the other night, I let you go because I thought it would be best for everyone involved. Rosie was calling you Mommy. And I was having visions of you day and night—and not just in bed, but your smile, your gentle touch. Your laugh." He raked a hand through his hair. "I'd spent so long being a carefree bachelor that I didn't think I could handle a real, committed relationship. And the fact that you had me reconsidering that scared the hell out of me."

She unfolded her arms. "So that's why you didn't stop me from leaving and why you didn't call afterward?"

He nodded. "It took a while for me to wrap my head around the fact that I don't want to be alone any longer. You've brought something into my life that I've never had before—a real sense of love and family."

"Oh, come on, Kieran. Other than my friend Monica, you have one of the biggest families I know."

"Maybe so. But in spite of the number of siblings I have, I've never been all that happy. And I doubt I ever will be. Not without you in my life."

Dana couldn't believe her eyes when Kieran showed up at her door. And now she couldn't believe her ears.

"It may seem a bit sudden," he said, "but I know what's in my heart. I've never felt anything like this, but I know what's going on. I fell in love with you, Dana. And all I want is for the two of us—I mean, the *three* of us—to be together. Not just tonight, but for the rest of our lives."

Dana continued to stand in the doorway, too stunned by his words to move, to even react. To say his revelation had completely blindsided her would be a gross understatement. She had to remind herself to breathe. He *loved* her? That in itself was hard to wrap her mind around, but for the *rest* of their lives? That sounded as if…

"Aren't you going to invite me into the house?" he asked.

His question pulled her out of her reverie and she stepped aside and held open the door for him to enter.

"I hope you'll forgive me for being a little slow on the uptake," he said as he walked into the living room. "It took time for me to figure things out—and to propose a solution."

"I'm listening."

"I know you're not the type for a sexual fling, which is the only kind of relationship I used to have. But not anymore. I only want one woman in my life from now on, and that's you."

This conversation was becoming surreal. Maybe it was time to give herself a pinch.

"Are you sure?" she asked.

He smiled at her. "Absolutely. That's why I didn't want you to be my date at that wedding. I want you to be my bride."

"I don't understand," she said.

"Let's get married on the same day, in the same place and at the same time, as Sophie and Mason."

Actually, she liked the sound of that. But he couldn't be serious. Still, she'd never seen his face so lit up.

When she didn't respond either way, he dropped to one knee, reached into his pocket and pulled out a small velvet box. He flicked open the lid, revealing a sparkling diamond that had to be two carats, if not more.

She gasped, then lifted her hand to her throat and

gazed at him in disbelief. She'd never seen anything like it. For a poor girl who'd grown up without a family of her own, you'd think she'd just been given the Hope Diamond.

"I don't know what to say."

"A *yes* would make me the happiest man in the world. In fact, I'd marry you today, if you'd have me."

He was serious.

And she was...thrilled.

"Then yes," she said. "I'll marry you."

Kieran pulled the ring from the box, dazzling her with the romantic gesture and the sparkle, and she lifted her left hand to let him slide it on her finger.

What a turn of events. Even in her wildest dreams, when she'd lain in bed at night, envisioning Kieran professing his love, she'd never expected it to be like this—so romantic, so sweet. And accompanied by a proposal.

"I love you, too," she said. "And I don't want to wait, either. But I can't see how we can pull off a double wedding."

She'd need to find a dress—and something fancy, especially if they got married at the Driskill Hotel, with his friends and family in attendance.

"Besides," she added, "Sophie and Mason's invitations have already gone out. And they were so perfect, so formal... We'd just be an add-on."

"I already ran this by Sophie, and she thinks we'll make an amazing addition to the ceremony. And as for the invitations, we'll create our own and email them to our guests."

"But...there's another problem," she said, considering the wording Sophie and Mason had used. "I don't have parents to list at the top of our invitation."

Kieran seemed to think about that, but only for a moment. "I have a much better idea."

She tilted her head. "What's that?"

"Picture this." He lifted his hands, his thumb and index fingers creating a box shape. "Miss Rosabelle Lawson requests the honor of your presence at the wedding of her new Mommy and Daddy—Miss Dana Trevino and Mr. Kieran Fortune Robinson."

Tears filled Dana's eyes. "That's perfect. I love it!"

"You're perfect. And I love you." He reached out for her and pulled her into his arms.

Then he said, "All you need to do is tell me where you want to go on our honeymoon."

She stiffened, drawing back so she could catch his gaze. "Getting married with Sophie and Mason at the Driskill Hotel would be a dream come true for me, but we can't go anywhere for very long, especially if we have to leave town."

"Why not?"

"What about Rosie? She wouldn't be happy staying with just anyone for longer than a night. And then there's Sam and Sandra to consider. You and I are all the family they have left. What if something should happen while we're gone? What if they need us?"

"I've got that covered."

She couldn't see how. The guy might be rich, but you couldn't buy affection and peace of mind.

"I hired the perfect nanny," he said. "And she's going to start work tomorrow."

"But you don't work on Sunday."

"I won't need her to watch Rosie at my house. She's going to live at the ranch."

She wasn't following, and her brows knitted in confusion.

Kieran smiled. "I hired a caregiver to look after Sam and Sandra. And she'll also be my nanny. Whenever I need a sitter, I'll take Rosie there. It's the perfect solution. And Sandra and Sam are delighted with the setup."

"Who is this woman? And when did you hire her?"

"It's Elaine Wagner, Mikey's mother. And I hired her today."

"And she agreed to look after Sam and Sandra, too?"

"She was thrilled when I suggested it. And so was Sandra, especially since she'll be seeing more of Rosie."

Dana couldn't stifle the grin that stole across her face. "You are a true problem solver, Mr. Fortune."

He laughed. "Well, there is one little problem…"

"Uh-oh. What's that?"

"I promised Rosie that I would drive over to that empty lot by the school and look for a big, brown, dirty dog named Teddy."

"Seriously? What are you going to do if you find that stray?"

"Take it to the ranch. But don't think badly of me if I admit that I'm hopeful he's already found another home."

She stepped back into the circle of his arms. "Kieran, you are truly amazing. I'm going to love being married to you."

Then she kissed him, thoroughly and deeply. When they finally came up for air, she led him to her bedroom. It was time to celebrate the love they'd just professed.

Dana had never been happier. After spending the night with her new fiancé and making love several times, each one more amazing than the last, she'd kissed Kieran goodbye. Then he went to his place to relieve Elaine and pick up Rosie.

Over an early morning cup of coffee, they'd decided Kieran and Rosie would move in with Dana until they found a new house, something bigger and with a roomy yard. Kieran would be giving up his downtown condo.

In the meantime, she spent the morning cleaning out the guest room, especially the closet, to make room for Rosie's clothes and toys. Her heart soared at the thought of having her new family together under the same roof.

Kieran had called a couple hours ago to let her know that he and Rosie had a few errands to run. That was just as well. Dana wanted to have the room ready when they arrived.

She'd no more than carried the last box out to the garage when her cell phone rang. She thought it might be Kieran, calling her with an update, but it was his sister Sophie instead.

"I just heard the good news," Sophie said. "Kieran told me you agreed to the double wedding, and I wanted to let you know how happy Mason and I are that you'll be sharing our special day."

It was mind-boggling. In less than twenty-four hours, Dana had acquired a fiancé who would soon be her husband, and a daughter. Now she had a sister, the first of many siblings.

Dana smiled. "Kieran and I are looking forward to it."

"If you're free tonight," Sophie said, "I thought we could all get together. Rosie, too, of course. That way, we can talk more about it."

"That works for me. I'll check with Kieran to make sure he doesn't have anything else going on."

"Let me know for sure, but I'll plan for us to have dinner at my place around six."

After ending the call, Dana considered all that needed to be done to prepare for a dream wedding. How would she ever be ready in just over a week?

She pulled a notepad from her desk drawer, as well as a pencil, so she could jot down each upcoming chore and give it a completion date.

The first thing on her to-do list was to call Monica and tell her the good news.

"Oh my gosh," Monica said when Dana got her

on the phone. "You're going to marry one of the *Fortunes*?"

"Actually," Dana said, as she plopped down in her easy chair for a conversation that was sure to go into overtime, "I'm marrying the most handsome, generous and incredible man in the world. He just happens to carry the Fortune name. But believe me, I wouldn't care if he was a Smith or a Jones."

"That's awesome, Dana. I'm so happy for you."

"Good, because I need a favor. I want you to be my maid of honor. Hopefully, you can get the time off from the library so you can help me pull things together."

"One of my assistants is out on maternity leave, so I'm not sure how long I can be gone. But I wouldn't miss your wedding for the world. Besides, I want to help you find something old, something new, something borrowed and something blue."

Dana held the phone with her right hand and rested the left on the armrest, the diamond engagement ring sparkling. She really was going to have to pinch herself for a reality check.

"You know me," Dana said. "I'm big on traditions, so I'll definitely be using that one. It's just too bad that I don't have my mother's wedding gown to wear. That would've given me the perfect 'something old.' But I'll just have to look for a lace handkerchief at an upcoming estate sale."

"Wait," Monica said. "I've got a better idea. My mom wore my *abuelita*'s wedding dress when she got married, and she's been saving it for me. Why don't you wear that?"

"But that's your family tradition."

"Come on, Dana. You're like a sister to me. I'd love to see you walk down the aisle in something that means so much to our family. I'd have to alter it anyway, and you're about my mom's size."

Tears welled in Dana's eyes, then spilled onto her cheeks. "I'd be so honored to wear that dress. I promise to take special care of it."

"I know you will. And now you've got something old *and* borrowed."

"That's true. Maybe I can go to a bridal shop and find a blue garter. That would take care of new and blue."

Monica laughed. "Better yet, how about some sexy blue panties?"

Now it was Dana's turn to laugh. "We'll have to go shopping together and see what we can find." She again looked at her ring, which stood out prominently on her finger. Okay, so it wasn't anywhere near as big as the Hope Diamond. But it reflected a heart *filled* with hope. Not to mention love and everything that was right in the world.

"What about your honeymoon?" Monica asked. "Where are you guys going?"

"At first, I assumed we'd just spend time alone at home. But thanks to Rosie's awesome new nanny, we're going to be able to leave her in good hands. So this morning, over breakfast, we decided on Paris. Can you believe I finally get to visit that city? It's filled with so much history and culture. I'd stay a month, if I could. But since Kieran and I both have work, we're only going for ten days."

"I'm so happy for you. Kieran sounds like a real keeper. I can't wait to meet him. Hey, does he have a single brother or friend who's attracted to petite brunettes?"

"I'll definitely scope out any suitable prospects. I'd love to see you more often."

Monica laughed. "After my last relationship, which turned out to be a dud, I'm holding out for a hero like the ones I've read about in romance novels."

"Maybe a handsome swashbuckler?" Dana asked.

"Or better yet, how about a Scottish laird?"

Down the street, the sound of a familiar diesel engine grew louder. "Listen, Monica. I'll have to call you later. Kieran and Rosie are back from the groomer."

"The *groomer*?" Monica asked. "What'd you do, inherit a pet with your new family?"

"Um, sort of. I haven't met him yet, but from what Kieran told me after finding him in an empty lot this morning, he's a big, goofy dog who looks like he's half wolfhound and part who-knows-what."

"You're adopting a stray that you don't know any-thing about?" Monica asked.

"Kieran said he's pretty friendly. And just for the record, he'll live on the Leaning L. That's where we'll be taking him—after I meet him, of course."

After promising Monica that they'd talk more later, Dana disconnected the line and went to greet her family.

* * *

Kieran had never been a dog person, but a promise was a promise. After picking up Rosie, who'd had the time of her life spending the night with Elaine and Mikey, he'd driven to her school to look for Teddy. And sure enough, they found him.

The big mutt ran right up to Rosie as if she was his long lost littermate. As she hugged him tightly, in spite of his dirty fur, he placed a big sloppy kiss on her face.

It was going to be difficult to say no to this child, which was why he'd placed several calls until he found a groomer that was open on Sundays. After dropping off Teddy for a much-needed bath and clipping, they'd gone to Pet Depot and purchased a collar, leash, food and a bed.

Teddy looked like a brand-new dog when they picked him up, and now he rode in the back of Kieran's Mercedes to Dana's house, panting and thumping his tail against the seat.

After pulling into Dana's driveway and shutting off the ignition, Kieran scanned the well-kept yard and cozy house. For the first time in his life, he felt as though he'd finally come home.

"Can I hold Teddy's leash?" Rosie asked.

The dog had been so rambunctious after being caged at the groomers that he would probably knock her off her feet.

"I'll tell you what," Kieran said. "Let's ask Dana if she wants to take a walk with us. Then, after Teddy gets some of his energy out, you can hold on to him."

"Okay. But don't call her Dana. Her name is going to be Mommy now, remember?"

"You got it, sweetie."

After they all got out of the car, including Teddy who'd nearly jerked Kieran's arm out of the socket as he leaped to the ground, they headed to the front door.

"Mommy" met them with a warm smile before they reached the porch, and Rosie introduced her to Teddy.

"Hey," Kieran said to Dana. "I know you're riding with us to take Teddy to the ranch, but he's going to need to take a little walk first. Would you like to join us for a trek around the neighborhood?"

"I can't think of anything I'd rather do than spend a Sunday afternoon with my family."

Damn. He loved that woman.

"Then let's go," he said.

Dana reached for her key, which she left on a little hook near the door, and locked up the house. Then they headed down the quiet, tree-lined street, birds chirping, the sun shining.

He wasn't sure how long they'd live at her house. That was up to Dana. But it didn't matter. Home would always be wherever she was.

As they turned the corner and headed down another street, Kieran wondered who was happier— Teddy, Rosie, Dana or him. All he knew was that he had enough money to buy anything he'd ever wanted, yet nothing he'd ever wanted had fulfilled him like the woman who'd just slipped her hand into his.

"It's going to be a beautiful day," Dana said.

"It's going to be a beautiful *life*," he corrected.

She squeezed his hand and tossed him a loving smile.

"Can I hold on to Teddy now?" Rosie asked.

The dog had settled into a gentle walk, so Kieran passed the red leash to her, and they continued on their way.

The sun was warm and bright, and a cool spring breeze rustled in the treetops.

"Look," Dana said softly. She pointed to Rosie's shoulder, where a monarch butterfly had landed, its orange-and-black wings fluttering.

He was reminded of the butterfly at the funeral. It was almost as if Zach was letting him know that he'd cast his blessing on this new family.

At least, it seemed that way. And even though it might sound weird, Kieran chose to believe that's exactly what was happening.

He pondered the fragile little butterfly that had once been a caterpillar. Just like its metamorphosis, something inside Kieran had changed, too. At one time, he'd feared fatherhood and marriage. But now, thanks to Dana, he couldn't wait for their upcoming wedding, the tuxedoes and white lace, the promises they'd make—and the little flower girl who'd be a huge part of it all. And for their happy-ever-after to start.

For a guy who'd once been a dedicated bachelor, Kieran had turned over a new leaf. He couldn't imagine his life without Dana and Rosie. In fact, he looked forward to the holidays, something he'd dreaded in the past, and to showering them with gifts of love.

Maybe there'd also be a new baby or two in the future.

He liked that idea. Liked it a lot. Because he couldn't imagine love or family getting much better than this.

* * * * *

*Don't miss the next installment of
the Mills & Boon Cherish continuity*
THE FORTUNES OF TEXAS:
THE SECRET FORTUNES

*When Olivia Fortune Robinson and
Alejandro Mendoza are forced to fake an
engagement, will they be able to tell the difference
between fantasy and reality when their pretend
arrangement becomes an affair of the heart?*

*Look for
FORTUNE'S SURPRISE ENGAGEMENT
by Nancy Robards Thompson*

*On sale May 2017, wherever Mills & Boon
books and ebooks are sold.*

MILLS & BOON®

Cherish™

EXPERIENCE THE ULTIMATE RUSH OF FALLING IN LOVE

A sneak peek at next month's titles...

In stores from 6th April 2017:

- **His Shy Cinderella** – Kate Hardy *and*
  Fortune's Surprise Engagement – Nancy
  Robards Thompson
- **Conveniently Wed to the Greek** – Kandy Shepherd
  and **The Lawman's Convenient Bride** – Christine
  Rimmer

In stores from 4th May 2017:

- **Falling for the Rebel Princess** – Ellie Darkins
  and **The Last Single Garrett** – Brenda Harlen
- **Claimed by the Wealthy Magnate** – Nina Milne
  and **Her Kind of Doctor** – Stella Bagwell

Just can't wait?
Buy our books online before they hit the shops!
www.millsandboon.co.uk

Also available as eBooks.

0417/23

MILLS & BOON®

EXCLUSIVE EXTRACT

When Greek tycoon Alex Mikhalis
discovers Adele Hudson is pregnant
he abandons his plans to get even and
suggests a very intimate solution:
becoming his convenient wife!

Read on for a sneak preview of
CONVENIENTLY WED TO THE GREEK

'What?' The word exploded from her.

'You can't possibly be serious.'

Alex looked down into her face. Even in the slanted light from the taverna she could see the intensity in his black eyes. 'I'm very serious. I think we should get married.'

Dell had never known what it felt to have her head spin. She felt it now. Alex had to take hold of her elbow to steady her. 'I can't believe I'm hearing this,' she said. 'You said you'd never get married. I'm not pregnant to you. In fact you see my pregnancy as a barrier to kissing me, let alone marrying me. Have you been drinking too much ouzo?'

'Not a drop,' he said. 'It's my father's dying wish that I get married. He's been a good father. I haven't been a good son. Fulfilling that wish is important to me. If I have to get married, it makes sense that I marry you.'

'It doesn't make a scrap of sense to me,' she said.

'You don't get married to someone to please someone else, even if it is your father.'

Alex frowned. 'You've misunderstood me. I'm not talking about a real marriage.'

This was getting more and more surreal. 'Not a real marriage? You mean a marriage of convenience?'

'Yes. Like people do to be able to get residence in a country. In this case it would be marriage to make my father happy. He wants the peace of mind of seeing me settled.'

'You feel you owe your father?'

'I owe him so much it could never be calculated or repaid. This isn't about owing my father, it's about loving him. I love my father, Dell.'

But you'll never love me, she cried in her heart. How could he talk about marrying someone—anyone— without a word about love?

Don't miss
CONVENIENTLY WED TO THE GREEK
by Kandy Shepherd

Available May 2017
www.millsandboon.co.uk

Copyright ©2017 Kandy Shepherd

Join Britain's BIGGEST Romance Book Club

- **EXCLUSIVE offers** every month

- **FREE delivery direct** to your door

- **NEVER MISS a title**

- **EARN Bonus Book** points

Call Customer Services
0844 844 1358*

or visit
hillsandboon.co.uk/subscriptions

* This call will cost you 7 pence per minute plus your phone company's price per minute access charge.

SKCB3